The Dreaming

By Jay Wayward

Acknowledgments

To Victoria, for happily listening to all my late-night rants about book ideas.

And

To Teddy, Keats, Salem, Ray, and all the other animal pals who spent time in my lap or on my desk as I wrote this monstrosity.

Special thanks to Pooch and Sara for being the first people to give me feedback on Sif and Buri's adventures.

Cover Design by Diego Sanguino

Sensitivity Edit by Maple Intersectionality Consulting

Developmental and copy edit by Isabella Betita

Proofreading by Hilary Doda

Content Warnings

Graphic Violence

Death

Hallucinations

Drug and Alcohol Use

Depression and Grief

Survivor's Guilt

Imprisonment

Life Changing Injury

Religious Conflict

Nationalism

Depictions of a Child in Dangerous Situations

Implied Torture

Madness

Chapter 1

Young Sif, the Destroyer
Sassinia, borderlands kingdom

Before an army of mercenaries flooded the city in search of her, Keno Sif had been ambling down the street and eating a stolen plum, with nothing on her mind but a night of smoke, wine, and mostly innocent violence. Not even enough violence to earn a night in jail. If it wasn't for her bruised knuckles and the lingering taste of blood, she'd barely remember the brawl at all. It's only on her way back to the inn that the gentle calm of the morning is broken by frantic hoofbeats, and the sound of men shouting orders. Far too much noise over a barfight and some stolen fruit, which means the bounty hunters she came here to lose have already caught up with her.

The rattle of armor and crashing of horses through the capital is a scandal that outshines anything else happening in the small kingdom. Those already awake stand in slack-jawed awe at the military force being allowed to trample through their streets and interrupt the hustle of early morning commerce. Gossip about the army shoots between households like an arrow under the blush of dawn. Those who have been woken up throw open their windows in shock, wondering why Prince Hiyam would allow this.

On the second story of a wood and sandstone inn, Keno Sif crashes into her room and comes face to face with her fellow bandits, Buri the Giant and Ivon of Heron-Muse. She locks the door behind her and flashes a sly grin. The room is dark and cramped, but its location is perfect for keeping watch on the street below.

Ivon is not amused. "By the deities, Keno. This is why I told you to stay here last night. Sassinia is flooded with these bastards. You know I hate prison.

Ugh. The beds are so uncomfortable." Ivon shifts in their seat, as though the mention of it conjures a memory of their last stay behind bars.

"Relax, I made it back. Nobody saw me." Sif wipes the sweat from her brow and takes a seat at the window, not accidentally near a bottle of wine. She peers out the window conspiratorially. Warm wind brushes her sweaty face. Down the street, a group of workers are nearly trampled trying to cross into the nearby market, and a mercenary yells at them to watch where they walk.

"You should've come with me, Uncle," Sif says. "Lot of cute older men. You would've had fun."

Buri smirks but does not respond. He sits in the corner of the room, sewing a tear in a pair of pants. He squints at the needle and thread with his one remaining eye. Although his nickname is an exaggeration, the seat he sits on is too small to be comfortable under his large frame. His tan, almost leathery skin is covered in simple tattoos honoring Aneir, the god of courage.

"Do you think they'll go door to door?" Ivon asks, running a hand nervously through their thick blonde hair. Silver and gold bangles, all stolen, jingle musically on their thin, beautiful wrists. Their clothes would have been considered stylish once, but months of travel have left them in desperate need of cleaning and repair.

"Won't need to," Buri grunts. He stops sewing for long enough to motion downstairs with one massive hand.

"Do you think the innkeeper would turn us in?" Ivon asks. "Our bounties must be pretty high. That last caravan barely even had anything worth stealing, too. . ."

"Who cares?" Sif groans, swishing her cup. Even when cornered by a small army, an easy smile comes to her face. She sits with one muscular, brown arm slung around the back of her chair, and her legs splayed out in front of her. "This is exactly like when Lady Erah-Dune tried to have us executed at Heron-Muse. Actually, that was worse. At least there's no plague in Sassinia. Just a bunch of mercenaries coin-addled enough to get killed over whatever scraps the aristocracy is willing to pay. Foolish thing to die for, if you ask me."

Buri's single eye lands on Sif with something approaching discontent. She puts her hands up in mock surrender. Despite all of her bluster and bravado, she's still reluctant to disappoint her mentor, even if he insists she never could.

"Even a weak enemy can strike a killing blow." Buri is decades older than her, and fond of phrases like that.

"I know, Uncle. I won't do anything reckless. I'm only saying. No need to panic yet," she responds, even though the mercenaries have been on their trail for weeks now and the move to hide in Sassinia was meant to throw them off for good.

Ivon is the one to broach the subject they're all thinking about. "Well, darlings, if you ask me, we have two options. We can hide here, or we can sneak out. Frankly, they're both fucking terrible."

Before they can come to a decision, their conversation is shattered by banging at the door. Buri slowly puts down his needle and thread. The three of them exchange a glance, then Ivon answers, "Uhm. . . yes, hello?"

"Open the door!" The voice shouting is full of stone and steel, ready to draw the latter and put the three of them underneath the former.

"Of course," Ivon calls out, gently lifting a thin dagger. "Give me one moment." Ivon stands up and motions to Sif. The door shakes as the man on the other side continues to bang his fist against it.

"Open it up! We know who you are, and you're all under arrest!"

With precision that can only be the result of experience and practice, Ivon opens the door, and Sif kicks the mercenary straight in the chest. The man's armor clangs loudly as he tumbles backwards down the stairs, sliding to a painful stop at the innkeeper's feet. Another mercenary, a woman in leather armor, charges in through the door and tackles Sif. The floorboards shake with the impact of their fall.

"I got her!" The mercenary leans on Sif with all of her weight. Hot breath pushes through her tightened jaw and bared teeth.

"Good for you!" Sif growls. She swings both fists into the crook of her opponent's arm, bringing their bodies closer together, then headbutts the woman as hard as she can. A spray of blood trickles down into Sif's eye as the mercenary rolls off her, roaring in pain.

Ivon gets to their feet and begins grabbing their things. A lockpick set, a bundle of throwing knives, and a coin pouch with very little coin. "Just once, I'd like to go somewhere with the two of you where we don't have to fight our way out."

Sif sits up, coughing hard. "Hey, we didn't have to fight our way out of Ograna."

Ivon sighs dramatically, then bends over and slits the throat of the woman Sif had thrown off herself. "We fought our way *into it*, though. It's close enough, love."

At the door, the mercenary who fell down the stairs returns to finish his portion of the brawl. Buri stands to his full height, stooping to avoid the ceiling, and grips his axe in one giant hand.

Sif rises to her feet, wiping the blood from her eye. "You don't want any help, Uncle?"

"I do not need it," Buri grunts back. His face tenses imperceptibly as he and the remaining mercenary lock eyes.

The mercenary laughs. "Big words for a heathen sava—"

In one smooth stride, Buri steps forward and, with a swing of his axe, takes off most of the man's arm. The mercenary shrieks and stumbles backwards. With a second blow, Buri crushes in the man's helmet. The mercenary hits the floor, gurgling indecipherably from his ruined mouth. He holds up his remaining hand, begging for mercy. Buri's eye is wide and furious, dreaming of past violence and the violence of the mercenary's death simultaneously.

Then, slowly, he lowers his axe. Sif rolls her eyes but says nothing. She kicks the man's severed arm, still holding its sword, to the corner of the room.

"Oh no," Ivon groans.

"It's fine," Sif says, nudging the armless mercenary with her foot. "He won't get back up."

"No, Keno. The innkeeper is gone."

Downstairs, the innkeeper shouts for more mercenaries. The sound of hoofbeats immediately becomes much louder.

"Fuck. What do we do now?"

A self-satisfied smile spreads across Ivon's face. "You act like I don't always have a plan for getting us out of these situations." They produce a black iron key from a hidden pocket in their shirt. "This, my friend, is the key to the roof. Follow me."

Sif grins in astonishment and quickly follows behind, "Where did you get it?"

"I stole it from the innkeeper, of course."

Down the second story hallway is a short wooden ladder, leading up to a closed hatch. Ivon climbs the rungs quickly, but fumbles the key at the top. Right as it clinks harmlessly on the ground, a dozen pairs of boots—or more—storm into the ground floor of the inn. Something ceramic shatters, and the innkeeper begins shouting about repayment for the damage. Sif snatches the key back up and throws it to Ivon, who catches it deftly in the air.

"Any time now is good, Ivon!"

The lock clicks. "Already done."

As the hatch opens, it reveals a beautiful azure sky and the faint promise of glorious, boundless freedom. Or, if not freedom, at least the promise of not bleeding to death on an unwashed floor in Sassinia. They scramble up through the hatch, just in time for Ivon to close it as the mercenaries reach the second floor. Ivon locks the hatch from the outside.

"Now look," they whisper, gathering the others close. "We don't have long, but we can jump across the next few roofs eastward. Behind the last building —"

Ivon's words fade into the background like the noise of a single leaf falling in the forest. Sif's eyes glaze over and her gaze settles past Ivon's pointed finger, into the desert beyond Sassinia, where a large shard of obsidian juts out of the ground like shrapnel from a great eruption. A piece of a lost kingdom from the old world, from before history and culture were wiped away a dozen or so generations back. Her vision blurs and muscles relax as her focus sinks into the dark, glossy stone. Though she doesn't have the words for it herself, a distant voice whispers to her that the morning of the world has passed and what lies ahead is terrible and uncertain.

"Sif!" Ivon hisses, grabbing her by the shoulder.

"Fuck!" Sif shouts, startled back into reality. She blinks hard, as if fighting back sleep, the pinprick of that distant voice rapidly fading from her memory.

Below them, muffled voices relay the sound of Sif's voice to each other.

"Great, we need to go now." Ivon sighs. "You should know better than to stare at the ruins. The last thing we need now is for that magic to worm its way inside you. Even this far off, a strong spell could find an opening, and. . . oh, perfect. Is that a sandstorm?"

Buri grunts affirmatively. They all know it would be mad to continue east now. But there is no other option. They're low on coin, sleep, and time. This chase has lasted weeks. The city is overrun.

"No choice," Sif says, still shaking off the oddness lodged in her mind.

"No," Ivon agrees glumly. "We'll have to head deeper into the desert, then cut south to throw them off and make for whatever trading town is nearest. Ponda, maybe? Honestly, at this point, I'll go anywhere. Hopefully we can do it all without getting caught up in the storm."

When they turn back to face Sif and Buri, it's with a dashing grin and a gleam in their blue eyes. The hatch leading to the roof trembles, as someone beneath tries to force it open.

"So, what do you think?"

Buri hums agreeably. His thick gray and black beard twitches as he stands up and prepares to leave. After years of traveling with Sif, he knows her opinion before she says it.

"That's mad," Sif says, affirming Buri's guess. "Absolutely insane. Let's do it."

She looks toward the desert, blooming from the center of the continent like the mark of a massive fist's impact. The three of them leap to the next rooftop, racing above the chaos below as dozens upon dozens of mercenaries search the surrounding streets for them. It's almost funny. For generations, ever since the old kingdoms disappeared, regents in countless lands have tried to gather every scrap of property and power for themselves, fighting against a world far more suited to the lack of people than the presence of them. And after all that, they can't even catch a few bandits.

Ivon sighs. "Glad to know we won't be dying today. Probably."

Sif laughs, one hand mounted on her hips. "I'm never fucking dying, and you can count on that."

Chapter 2

Old Sif, the Hermit

Mount Hoda, the northern wilds

In the freezing wilds of Mount Hoda, only one day's walk from the village of Ummun, lives a horrible beast. Parents warn their children about her before they go out to play. Children whisper her myth when the yearning for adventure rises in their hearts. Monarchs wring their hands over her legend as they push their "civilizations" further from their origins, and out across the continent.

"Have you heard of Sif the Destroyer, who murdered King Ottson, and tried to kill Queen Benedicta as well? Who escaped execution at the siege of Heron-Muse? Who broke the heathen saint Teodore out from his icy prison at the edge of the northeastern expanse?"

"Yes," they would always respond, "but she disappeared decades ago, before the Church of Druga civilized most of the continent. There isn't anything to be afraid of now."

In her youth, she was a terror, a thief, and a marauder, cutting a path through borders and trade routes, said to leave burning cities and dead kings in her footsteps. Now, her bones creak and her eyes have lost their sharpness. Her thick, close-cut hair is turning much more gray than black. Her sword is dull. Wrinkles that used to be new now rest comfortably at the edges of her eyes and mouth. She traded her life on the road for a much simpler one raising animals and, very occasionally, doing odd jobs for the nearby villages and temples. It's a matter of pragmatism. Things are better if nobody knows where to seek her bounty, and the people who live here, where she grew up, won't talk.

As the morning sun breaks on her side of the mountain, Keno Sif leaves behind the warmth of her home and begins her hike towards the hidden Temple of Siduri, goddess of dance and debauchery. She latches her cabin door shut in the hopes of keeping out snow and wind, says goodbye to her goats, and sets off to collect an offering to Siduri.

Sif stops along the snowy trail to pick clusters of goddess' pearls from the underside of a frost-covered bush. The hallucinogenic berries, grown only on the Keda Mountain Range, are large and opalescent, blooming only at dawn when their hard shells open in the soft, early sun. The work is slow going, and the cold is becoming agony on her joints. As the sun gradually rises, the berries begin to close up. Sif hurries to gather as many as she can. The pain reminds her of the dexterity she has lost, and the memory of that troubles her more than the ache does.

It's then that she hears an unusual noise over a ridge. The rustling of metal armor on leather, and voices speaking in a southern dialect of the Found Tongue. Southern, to Sif, meaning anywhere south of the grasslands at the foot of Mount Hoda. It's a version of Found Tongue spoken by several monarchies across the continent of Atlas, and worse yet, often spoken by the Church of Druga. Sif frowns to herself and, tying her bag of berries to her belt, stomps through the snow up to the ridgeline.

As she breaks cover from the pine forest, a golden ray of morning sun illuminates her face. She narrows her eyes, looking down on the party, and catches the moment the soldiers notice her.

One by one, they turn their heads and shield their eyes to take her in: a woman with dark skin, muscular for her age and, at the moment, possessed by a sense of suspicion only lightly overshadowed by contempt. A large burn scar flares across her left cheek. She is dressed in furs for warmth and protection, and carries a sword on her back. Her form is outlined by the striking green of pine needles, muted in sight and sound by layers of snow fallen the night before.

The cadre of men appear to be from a kingdom to the south, judging by the armor and weapons they carry, as well as the carts of goods they've likely taken as taxes or spoils from a nearby village. Although it would be sure suicide to raid a northern village with such a small party, only to continue further into the dense forests of Mount Hoda. Very few groups are as unwelcome in the north as monarchists and soldiers.

"Captain Aleksandr," barks a younger man, motioning up towards Sif. The captain, a handsome middle-aged man with wheat-colored hair and a bristling mustache, shades his eyes from the sun now hanging lower over the trees, and catches sight of the older woman. His mustache twitches over lips pressing themselves thin.

"Keep moving; it's just an old woman. Local, probably. We've no time to waste with her."

"Still young enough to take care of you soft hands." She talks like someone who knows the feeling of blood on their teeth. Twenty years ago, she could've killed them all and barely broke a sweat. Nowadays, the fight might be even. If she's lucky. She holds herself like she doesn't know the odds.

The captain smiles with feigned warmth. Sif's stare returns none of it.

Captain Aleksandr calls up to her, plumes of cold air materializing from his mouth as he speaks. "Ah, I hadn't realized you speak the language. We're searching for a missing girl. Have you seen her? She is fourteen, with dark brown hair, brown eyes, and dark skin. Less than five feet in height, with a prominent nose."

"Is she from here?" Despite the distance, Sif's voice seems to carry with little effort.

"No. She's from a country far to the southwest, I'm told, but very important to our master."

"If she's lost here, she's already dead. You should turn around." Many northern cultures pride themselves on their independence. Sif's hometown of

Ummun has always taken care to encourage a kind of strength and independence that is buoyed, but not supplanted by, a close community. The monarchs love a pliable citizenry, though. One that is reliant on the guard and the nobility. Sif can't imagine a child from a kingdom traveling here and surviving.

Aleksandr shakes his head. "It isn't an option. But if you learn anything, there is a reward for cooperation. Enough coin to make life here easy for you."

"Don't have much use for coin," Sif responds bluntly.

"I'm certain we would be able to work something out. Perhaps livestock, or stores of food," he calls back up. His speech is softer and slower; he isn't used to having to shout in this cold air, and it causes his chest to ache.

Sif frowns. What would it take to get these soldiers off the mountain? Maybe she should keep an eye out for this girl, as much as she loathes to do these travelers a favor.

"I'll keep an eye out. You should turn back now, though. Before you're lost too."

Captain Aleksandr thanks Sif for her help, speaking with the sort of politeness that is *nice* but not *kind*. The sort where a person can tell they're being spoken down to. Sif makes a note of where their path will take them. Maybe some of the younger warriors from Ummun will be willing to help her raid their camp tonight, once the embers die down and the cold of the mountain weakens their fortitude. Sif watches their path until the last man is out of sight, then returns to her work.

A few hours down a winding path and through a thick carpet of snow, Sif arrives at a close grouping of evergreen trees, beyond which hides Siduri's temple. The temple stands in the middle of a peaceful clearing. The construction is humble, and the glow of a warm fire inside is inviting after Sif's trek through the frozen woods. The image of comfort and humility is both for its own sake and because Siduri would curse her followers for gaudy displays of wealth or power. Even still, it looks dressed in diamonds under the frost and sun.

Siduri's temple was constructed from stone cut here on Mount Hoda. On its sides are painted and sculpted visions of Siduri, images gifted to disciples under the influence of goddess's pearls. Along the west wall is a row of sculptures. One is of a tall, multi-armed woman holding pipes, flutes, and glasses of wine, the next a heavyset woman lifting a large cask of liquor, and the third a thin, ethereal woman in a flowing dress, dancing with holy rapture. Legend has it that excess stone from the construction of the temple was used to make a set of flutes that would bless the bards playing them with an excess of food, drink, dance, and drugs, but would never provide them money—the holiest life a follower of Siduri could aspire to. Many musicians have left the temple over the years hoping to find out if the myth is true.

Inside, a monk greets Sif with a cheerful smile and nod. He is young, with long, unwashed hair and bright eyes. Loose, plain robes drape over his thin frame, dragging on the floor as he approaches.

"Keno Sif, you always look so healthy." A traditional way to greet an elder; Sif hopes he means it genuinely in her case, but can't quite tell. Sif would prefer it if the kids were blunt, rather than polite. But after a life of listening to almost nobody, Sif is sure trying to order young people around would turn her next cup of beer sour. The pain in her fingers jumps to the forefront of her awareness.

"Basho Ni Vol. How do you like being a monk so far?" Sif asks.

"I like it more than raising goats and fighting," he responds, "I'm doing my best to learn all of the herbs and other plants, and to keep the temple clean. Mother Pak says in time I'll get bored of it and wish I had traveled."

Sif's eyebrows tighten. "Mother Pak doesn't know what she's talking about."

"Um. . ." Basho Ni hesitates.

Sif clears her throat. "Recognize these?"

She opens a pouch on her satchel, revealing the pearls. Basho Ni's eyes widen at their iridescence. "This is my offering for the week. Caught them beginning to grow last month. Is Jinta Vol free to accept them?"

"I'll get them now," Basho Ni responds, then turns and walks with singular focus down a narrow hallway in the back of the temple. Sif removes her boots and places them to the side of the door. The smell of ritual incense lingers in the air. It smells like warmth and spice, and reminds Sif of her sister, who was a priestess years before. It fills her throat and lungs and clears her thoughts on the way out. Across the great, open room disciples of Siduri are cleaning the temple and preparing different substances for consumption. The Fall Festival was two weeks ago, and the stock of offerings to the Dancing Goddess is still more than enough for anyone visiting. Sif can make out the sounds of music and dancing lessons from rooms on the opposite end of the temple. A stone statue of Siduri as the Dancing Lady stands at the far end and two pilgrims sit in front of it, heads gradually nodding further and further towards their chests as alchemy gets the best of them, then jerking back to attention when they feel themselves falling asleep.

Basho Ni comes back, with Jinta Vol shuffling behind them. Jinta is the oldest person in the temple and looks it, with Sif being a very distant second. Jinta is hunched, with a face so wrinkled that it's impossible to tell what they looked like in their youth. Neither the northern berserkers nor followers of the Dancing Lady have a reputation for living long lives. Better to have a passion that burns everything away, than be consigned to the long, dull march of temperance. It's a testament to Jinta's luck, wisdom, and strength that they're still watching the grounds of the temple. They glow with contentedness and pride as they stride across the straw mats with a pine walking stick and smoking pipe. Sif bows ambiguously to Jinta, and they kiss her forehead lightly.

"Jinta," Sif says, forgoing the polite greeting Basho Ni inflicted on her.

"Keno Sif, are you eating well?" Jinta responds, lips turning up only slightly at Sif's brazenness. Controversially, Jinta isn't one to stand on tradition or politeness either.

"Well enough," Sif replies, knowing what Jinta will say next.

"You're still welcome here or in Ummun, if not."

"Yeah, thanks. I prefer the company of goats and chickens."

"That sounds like a nice, quiet life."

"You haven't known many goats."

Jinta and Basho Ni both chuckle. Sif hands over her offering of the goddess's pearls and Jinta accepts them with grace. Jinta leads them to a stone statue of Siduri, where two pilgrims shiver in front of an offering bowl at its feet Their pupils are wide and their gaze flickers. Jinta pours most of the berries from their hands into a clay bowl in front of the statue, eats three themself, and offers the rest to Sif and Basho Ni. Together, the three of them talk in low voices as warm waves of euphoria rise through their bodies. They discuss the weather, the recent births in nearby villages, and the music composed by northern poets and debuted at the fall festival.

The door to the temple opens with a slam, and the men Sif spoke with earlier flood into the temple in chain armor, brandishing weapons. Captain Aleksandr strides confidently into the middle of the room. Without missing a beat, his subordinates begin harassing the disciples and knocking over bowls of ritual incense. They enter with a practiced disdain that reminds Sif of the Church of Druga and, in that moment, she suspects her worst fears about the group have been realized. The hands of Druga, the deity of peace and order, have spearheaded the expansions of modern kingdoms into the wilds, and toppled and burned shrines and temples to heathen deities like Siduri across the continent. Sif draws her sword and bares her teeth, but Jinta motions for her to stop.

"Don't be foolish, Jinta. If they're from the Church, this temple will be rubble in a week."

"We don't know who they are, Keno. Don't be in such a hurry to fight. Just stay here."

Jinta approaches the captain with their hands raised. Captain Aleksandr smirks. Sif grits her teeth. The knights begin to line up disciples. Sif can't hear what Jinta and Aleksandr talk about over the rest of the noise. They only speak for a few seconds before Captain Aleksandr backhands Jinta, his metal glove drawing blood. Sif draws her sword. Basho Ni tries to hold her back, but she pushes him over and storms forward.

One of the lesser knights laughs when he recognizes her. It causes the rest of them to take notice. It must've been an odd sight, having a stocky, older woman with a disfigured face stomping towards a cadre of well-trained knights.

"Put your sword down, old woman. Don't spoil the mood by making us kill you."

"Think of your grandkids, huh?"

"Is she serious?"

The smell of incense has all but died out. Outside, the cold wind howls against Siduri's temple. Aleksandr adjusts his stance, spreading his feet outward slightly. A seasoned fighter can read their opponent's intentions. Sif is out of practice, but she could never miss what is happening here.

Aleksandr holds himself in the shadow of an offensive stance; a mimicry of form without genuine focus. He isn't thinking about defense. He is either trying to show he isn't afraid or hoping he can still deescalate the situation, and he expects to strike Sif down with a single blow. Like she isn't any real danger. It boils Sif's blood to be disregarded so completely.

Sif strides towards Aleksandr as the dim embers of her heart become a fire. She allows herself to be underestimated. To be seen as old and weak. Then, as she approaches striking distance, she dashes forward to close the space between them. The captain is almost too slow. He raises his shield in time to block her attack, but can't adjust his footing quickly enough and stumbles backwards. The confidence on his face twists into shock. He recognizes his mistake and, for a brief moment, there is fear in his eyes. Sif grins wickedly.

"Captain Aleksandr!"

The other knights rally to their captain. Aleksandr regains his footing, eyes blazing and wearing a scowl that promises revenge for the indignity of being knocked off balance. He surges forward, hoping to catch Sif off guard the same way she did to him. She feints as if she will meet him head on, but instead moves to the side and directs him forward faster than he intends. The result should have been Sif throwing Aleksandr to the ground, but he grabs her arm and they tumble together.

She lands next to Aleksandr on the floor, coughing painfully as the breath is wrenched from her lungs. Aleksandr turns on his side to face her, rips the sword from her weakened grasp, then throws it out of her reach. The years of peace have not served Sif well. Her lungs are on fire. Aleksandr straddles her waist and drives his armored fist into her skull. Her vision briefly goes black at the moment of impact. A bolt of fear grips Sif's heart. Aleksandr underestimated her before, but has she overestimated herself? She sets her jaw and meets his gaze, then discards the thought. Nobody will ever be able to say she died afraid.

Sif pushes through the pain enough for her thumbs to find his eyes. She feels the membrane start to give. He knocks her arms to her side and wraps his hands around her throat. With a downward sweep, she slams her arms into the bends of his elbows, bringing Aleksandr in close enough for a headbutt. Hot blood spurts against her chin and neck as the cartilage in his nose breaks against the crown of her head. As he rolls off her, covering his face, she takes his sword, leverages her blow, and rips through the chainmail and into his guts.

It's been decades since her last fight with a southern knight, and their leaders are still sending them out with shoddy armor. Sif says a quick thanks to Siduri for southern blacksmiths while Aleksandr writhes on the floor, bright red blood seeping from his stomach.

She inspects the sword in her hand and catches sight of something that quickens her heartbeat. Carved into the hilt is a set of four interlocking rings, meant to resemble an infinite path made of four parts. The rune of order, designed by the Church of Druga to symbolize "The Virtuous Path." Sif had been right. Paladins of Druga, the deity of peace and order, have found them. Sif isn't looking forward to the kind of peace they'll bring.

The room seems to be moving in slow motion as Sif rises to her feet. Her breath is heavy and loud in the astonished silence. Aleksandr's cries fade into a harsh groan, and then into nothing.

She wipes the blood from her face and snarls, "Who's next?"

Chapter 3

Young Sif, the Destroyer

The Great Desert, outside of Sassinia

After hours of running in sand, Sif can't run any longer. The sandstorm continues to rage endlessly in all directions. A pinprick of despair in Sif's heart widens continuously, despite her effort to summon her courage against it. The security at Sassinia's border was too tight, and the storm too thick to make out the best direction in which to move. Now, it seems like the sky will never clear. Buri and Ivon push along next to her, phasing in and out of sight. The mercenaries hunting them down have the advantage of being fully stocked and on horseback. Meanwhile, the three of them are out of money, time, and options. The only rations they have are a small offering of cured meats from a man whom Buri had flirted with when they entered Sassinia.

In the distance, Sif thinks she can make out the obsidian shard of a lost kingdom, getting neither closer nor farther as they continue their march. But even odds are that it's a trick the storm is playing on her mind.

All around them, horses neigh and humans cry out commands. Their presence is only narrowly masked behind a curtain of sand and the howl of wind. A fight is inevitable, and even if it's one that Sif does not expect to win, she can't stomach the idea of these mercenaries coming home victorious, boasting to their friends and family about having killed her from behind as she hid or fled.

Sif begins to stand and draw her sword when Ivon places a hand on her arm. "We need to stay low and fast, my dear. This isn't the time for a fight."

"It's too late, Ivon. We should be picking them off one by one while we have the chance," she snaps. Then, turning to her mentor, she says, "Uncle, you know I'm right."

Buri shakes his head in disagreement when a horseback rider appears from the haze like a phantom, wreathed in sand and wind, drawing her sword. Chainmail rattles on her muscular frame, and glass bottles of alchemy clink on her belt. Sif adjusts her footing, but is already disadvantaged by having to fight against a mounted rider in deep sand.

"I've found them!" the rider yells. A row of war cries rise up from the storm. A second rider flies into sight, already swinging their weapon. Golden tassels whip back on the horse's saddle. Ivon yells something that Sif cannot make out over the roars of mercenaries celebrating a presumed victory. Desperation has made Ivon's face into a ghost of what it was.

Wave upon wave of mercenaries crash against them. Sif stumbles and leaps clumsily out of danger, blind and exhausted, with barely any time to regain her footing before another attack forces her to do it all again. Outside her field of vision, a horse shrieks as Buri manages to topple it and its rider with a swing of his hammer.

A dim flicker of luck reveals itself when high winds and poor visibility prevent the archers from making their shots at long range. They're forced to creep closer, where Ivon easily picks them off with throwing knives. The surviving archers are afraid to get too close, causing their shots to go wide. Even the horseback riders lose some confidence in swarming Buri. Still, there are countless mercenaries. A battle of attrition can only slow their deaths. Every moment, more enemies arrive to reinforce the few who have fallen. Sif's chest heaves as she struggles for breath. Buri's arms scream with every swing of his hammer. Ivon runs low on knives and cannot retrieve the ones they have lost without throwing themselves into the thick of a fight they're not skilled enough to survive.

What happens next could be called luck, although given its consequences that seems foolish, or even cruel. An over-brave rider rushes Buri, and is toppled from her horse. As she lands, the horse falls on top of her, cracking a string of small alchemical bottles hanging from her belt, and suddenly they both go up in a shrieking explosion and crackle of blinding light.

Sif blinks painfully as her sight slowly returns. The air around them has become unnaturally calm. She can see Buri and Ivon nearby with new clarity, but the woman and her horse are gone. Sif struggles to her feet with a groan, then limps over to where they disappeared. The explosion has uncovered large stone bricks beneath the sand, now blown apart to reveal a sharp drop into blackness. Endless waves of sand wash into the sightless depths.

"Sif!" Ivon screams.

Sif turns just as another mercenary enters striking distance, her weapon raised. No time to react. But before her throat can be cut, the stone beneath the sand gives way. The ground roars and quakes, and all four of them fall into long darkness.

The cacophony is deafening, bellowing even over the sandstorm above. Cold underground air races across Sif's bare, muscular arms. As sand and stone pour down from above and the light begins to die, Sif sees Buri racing towards her. He jumps over her, trying to shield her from the falling debris. Sif reaches for him, grabbing his collar, and thrusts off the ground with her opposing leg, forcing him to switch places with her. Buri looks up at her, speechless as the light dies. As the last of the noise settles, he whispers, "You've outgrown me."

It may or may not be true. What Sif thinks, though, is that Buri is too well-loved to sacrifice himself, that he should allow her to protect him, and that it would be selfish to throw his life away.

What she says is "No, Uncle. I'm just faster than you are."

She pushes herself up and spits a mass of dust, sand, and snot onto the ground.

"Ivon, are you dead?"

"I'm too beautiful to die, my friend. A little dizzy, though. Some of the debris struck me in the head." Their singsong, self-assured voice has taken on a gruff, wavering undertone. Ivon is a great thief and a brave companion, but an average fighter. This week hasn't been good to them.

"Mercenary, you dead?"

"I'm fine," the mercenary snaps. Her voice is dripping with bitterness. Sif doesn't blame her.

A faint gurgling sound, and then Ivon responds, "She's dead."

Sif snorts. "Goddess, you've become ruthless since we last met."

"I'm just short on patience. And besides, I think this is that lost kingdom ruin you were staring at earlier. The magic is dangerous enough without her at our backs. Besides, there could be a lot of treasure here. I don't want to split it four ways."

Sif's eyes widen in the dark. There isn't a child alive on the continent who doesn't dream of discovering ruins of the lost kingdoms, vast civilizations dimmed behind the light of a catastrophe nobody alive can recall or understand. Stories place almost all the most powerful kingdoms in the great sloping desert at the center of Atlas, and if anyone here would know what a lost kingdom ruin looks like, it is Ivon. On the other hand, even a small and well-intentioned spell can cause a person to burst into fire that can't be put out, turn any air that enters their lungs into saltwater, or obliterate their souls so completely that they can never reach the afterlife.

Still, maybe this was a stroke of luck, finally arriving after days of none. While the army above passes by, they can stay safe down below and come back up rich. Hells, maybe the threat of magic will keep the mercenaries away. Now they just need a way back up. Buri echoes that thought before Sif can voice it, and Ivon agrees. Moving with uncommon care, the three of them seek out a light in order to get a better sense of their surroundings.

Up a broad staircase is a set of braziers, and a half-burnt torch capped in char and ash. Ivon lights the brazier with a piece of flint. It catches with a dramatic *fwoosh,* illuminating the high, vaulted ceiling and granite floor, polished to a mirror-like smoothness that has held up since the old world was lost. The flames dance across walls that light hasn't touched in millennia. Carved stone contraptions and rods like a snake's body clutter the walls above them, lined with runes and foreign iconography. Sif's heart swells with wonder at the reflection of strange architecture glittering in the dimness.

"Well, I'm afraid I was right about this place, as I am about most things. Mages lived here. . ." Ivon remarks. "All of this runs on magic."

Sif's blood freezes. "How do you know?"

"Books, Keno," Ivon half-jokes, picking up on the anxiety in her voice. "I know some of these symbols from books."

Sif rolls her eyes. "Funny. Probably going to be less funny when someone burns you at the stake over it."

Ivon laughs at first, but their voice dies awkwardly when nobody else joins in. In truth, any kind of proximity to magic is terrifying. If Sif and Buri are unbothered, it is only because they've encountered so much of it in the past that the horror has diminished somewhat. No one outside of the foolhardy, power-mad, or insane would seek it out. In some circles, there are even whispers that magic is what destroyed the old world and left its ruins scattered across the continent. It'd be rare luck for a magician to come across a kingdom that wouldn't put them to death for their studies. Better to start with the prevention, rather than the cure.

In Ivon's case, though, their knowledge comes from a much more material concern. Not many in the Heron-Muse Thieves' Guild would take work from a magician, which meant Ivon could charge extra for the effort. It's said that the study of magic is a kind of madness, and while similar things have been said about the pursuit of coin, it's been Ivon's opinion that magic has only ever brought trouble and gold only ever solved it. In any case, it doesn't surprise them to learn one of the lost kingdoms might have invested in the arts of the Three Mothers of Demons.

"My doves, this may work out in our favor. I know the exact right fence to move old world magical artifacts."

"Tell me they're somewhere nearby. I don't want to have to hang onto magic for long. Stuff makes my skin crawl," Sif says.

Buri grunts his agreement.

"Oh, no, my fence is back home in Heron-Muse," they reply.

"Ivon, are you fucking kidding me?" Sif asks them, dumbfounded. "We barely made it out with our heads last time."

Ivon winks at her from under their mop of golden hair. "Maybe I am, maybe I'm not."

Before she can respond, the sound of voices from a chamber above resonates through the walls. It sounds like someone giving orders. The three of them exchange glances. Sif grimaces. Her whole body is bruised from the fight above and the fall down.

"How?" Sif wonders aloud.

Buri grunts but doesn't commit to an answer. He strokes his beard slowly. As usual, he is a man of many thoughts and few words.

"Maybe more of the ruins collapsed than we thought," Ivon sighs dramatically.

"They really aren't making this easy," Sif complains. "Lot of trouble over a little bit of banditry."

"Get ready to ambush them." Buri's baritone voice carries the confidence of experience and, even beyond that, trust in his companions. Many of the mercenaries may be conscripted into service, pressured by power or circumstance into danger, and ready to use that same power on anyone in their way. It's a fragile form of strength. Buri, Sif, and Ivon are held together by friendship and memory, so when Sif and Ivon run for the cover of shadows it's because they agree it is the best move, not because of an order. Because they believe trust will win out in the end. Because it'll be bad luck to linger under halls run through with veins of magic.

Within seconds, two soldiers appear at the foot of stairs winding up from the unknown. The reflection of light off their brass armor is dull from years of wear and tear. They both lower their torches and raise their swords. When they speak, their voices are low and trembling. Sif sniffs the air and can smell blood on their swords.

"Someone has been down here. The torches are all lit," says the first soldier, a middle-aged woman with medium-length red hair.

"It might be more old kingdom magic," says the second mercenary, a short, young-ish man. Sif notices his armor is too big for him. It exposes part of his neck and shoulder, the perfect place to slide a blade. He likely bought a used set of armor, since newer mercenaries often don't have funds to purchase the most ideal equipment until a few campaigns in. Sif makes knowing eye contact with Ivon, and the faint scraping of a blade being unsheathed from a leather scabbard reaches her ears.

"All the worse, then," the first mercenary responds. "By Aneir's rings, this place must be infested with a whole host of demons, all birthed by the Three Mothers themselves. Keep your guard up. The sooner we kill the barbarians, the sooner we can escape this pit."

As if on cue, Ivon drops from a wooden beam above, driving a long dagger deep into one soldier's neck. A spray of blood splatters on the back wall. The second soldier turns and swings her sword at Ivon, who blocks it with the body of her dying comrade. The blade clangs off his armor. Sif and Buri leap from their hiding spots, ready to strike her down, but before they can, she drops her sword and raises her hands.

"Wait! I can help you!" she cries out.

"Coward," Buri sneers at her.

The woman notices Buri's tattooed chest, dotted with the symbols of their shared god, Aneir. The patron of warriors and thieves. The father and guide of those who accept danger and reject preying on the defenseless. For a follower of Sword-Eater Aneir to drop their weapon and beg for mercy. . . it is a blasphemy that draws disgust from even mild adherents. If a likely loss makes a person surrender, what good were any brave acts in their past? Now, those acts seem driven less by courage than by the certainty of an easy victory.

"Forgive me, brother. I can't die here, you—"

Sif rolls her eyes. Begging now? It's just sad. "Pick your sword up, mouse. I'll give you a one-on-one fight, so you can croak with some dignity. Maybe Aneir will simply let your spirit die instead of moldering in the Wilted Plains."

Ivon stands, placing themself in front of the mercenary, their hands out towards Sif and Buri. "Now, now. She did say she can help us, and I heard some talk of demons. It's an advantage we could use. Let our new friend grapple with her faith on her own time." They turn to face the mercenary. "How can you help us?"

"I know about how many soldiers are above, and where they are. Spare me and I'll lead you to the surface. It isn't that far, and when I came down here the entrance was barely guarded."

"She's going to stab us in the back the second we're outnumbered," Sif responds matter-of-factly. It's what *she* would do.

Buri wears a frown like he was born with it. "Maybe, but I can't kill her while she is unarmed." He spits on the floor, as though mentioning the mercenary and her blasphemy has put a bad taste in his mouth. If Buri has to kill someone, it won't be like this.

"Ivon, it's you or me," Sif remarks, looking at them for confirmation that this is the plan. She'd prefer to tie up loose ends, but not if it sours the mood.

Ivon shakes their head. "Oh, no. I'm on the soldier's side. I'll take any help we can get. Besides, I don't want Aneir to curse me, either."

"You killed the one who fell down here with us," Sif argues.

"That last one doesn't count, friend, they were as helpless as we were. It was pitch black; anything could have happened."

"I swear I won't betray you," the woman insists. Her voice wavers with desperation.

"See? She swears. What's your name, love?"

"Efa Vir-Thruce."

Buri is infuriated and Sif doesn't believe her, but in the end they relent, on the condition that she lead them from the front. Sif stands close behind Efa, hand casually draped on her own sword hilt, eyes keenly attuned to the woman's movements, ready to push her forward if she doesn't start walking soon.

When Efa looks back into the stairwell she came through, she takes in a deep, deep breath like someone preparing to dive underwater. She peers into the darkness on steady legs, but with trembling hands. Sif wonders what could possibly elicit that reaction.

"Is it true?" Efa asks, turning to Sif. "You're The Destroyer?"

"Yeah." Sif nods, even though the mercenary can't see. "That's what they call me."

"If I don't make it out of here, please make sure I stay dead."

A shiver runs up Sif's spine. "Sure, whatever," she responds, feigning indifference.

The four of them are drawn into the upper levels of the ruins, buoyed by the chance encounter with a land out of myth, drained from a long fight in an unfamiliar land, and disturbed by Efa's request. Moments before she is swallowed by the darkness, Efa produces a hooded lantern and ignites the fuse.

She freezes, then turns to glance at the three behind her. New wrinkles gather at the corners of her wide green eyes.

"Walk," Sif snarls, hiding the fear making a home in her own heart.

Chapter 4

Old Sif, the Hermit
Mount Hoda, the northern wilds

Soft flakes of snow drift down from the sky above the hidden Temple of
Siduri, along a path of quiet solitude. They lay to rest on the limbs of trees,
slopes of the temple rooftop, or in reunion with their siblings on the forest
floor. Mount Hoda strikes a beautiful scene that lends itself to quiet
contemplation and serenity. That peace is why the people who make the north
home have largely chosen to dissuade the monarchies from encroaching on the
land and throwing it into disorder. But every year the kings, queens, and
regents have crept just a little closer, pressed the status quo just a little further.
Now, instead of a meditative brilliance matching the sky above, the temple is
host to a clattering of iron on iron, and blood on stone. A struggle for power
where there should be communion with nature and the divine.

Inside, Sif's murder of the captain has erupted into conflict between
unequipped worshippers of Siduri and a cadre of paladins bristling with
weapons and armor. It's bad luck that the temple is filled with monks and
pilgrims, and not any of the hundreds of local fighters who might still have
youth on their side.

Sif rushes between multiple opponents, gasping for air. She is the only one
of the worshippers trained and armed, and it means that she is, effectively,
fighting alone. She tries against reason to make sure no temple-goer is struck
down. It's futile. The worshippers are doing their best to defend their friends
and their place of worship, but there is only so much a small group of unarmed,
unarmored, and drunk people can do.

The pilgrims meditating at the statue of Siduri disarm one man, attacking
from behind while he fights Sif. They strip his armor away and pummel his

exposed body beneath. His limbs flail without thought, hoping to knock the pilgrims away and regain his feet. Sif leaves them, to confront two more knights closing in on young dancers who are armed with walking sticks and musical instruments. It's an absurd scene and Sif can't help but respect the courage the dancers are showing, to stare down their opponents defiantly, armed with little more than tambourines. The audacity of it tugs at the corner of her wrinkled mouth.

Sif leaps in front of the dancers, panting for breath. She slides her blade underneath a paladin's loose cuirass, feeling the resistance as steel kisses flesh and moves past it. She yanks her weapon out and shoves the downed knight into another. The next few minutes are a blur of violence that Sif's mind only registers unconsciously. The goddess's pearls dull her pain and numb her exhaustion. For each knight that falls, another disciple is free, until, finally, the Church of Druga is outnumbered and surrounded. Sif is drenched in sweat, bruised and bleeding. The darkness that had been creeping in on her periphery recedes.

Basho Ni places a hand on her shoulder, and the weight of his palms lifts her out of the violence, placing her back in her own body. She feels feverish. Her heartbeat pounds in her ears. The disciples gathered around her shake from adrenaline and grief, or else stare numbly at the horror their place of worship has become. People who had been dancers, singers, musicians, travelers, worshippers, lovers. . . now they're just corpses. The scent of blood is heavy in the air.

Basho Ni squeezes Sif's shoulder gently. "Keno Sif, please take a seat. They're defeated."

Sif shakes her head. Her response comes in between deep, wheezing breaths. "Can't let them leave. They're disciples of Druga. I saw the rune of order stitched into their gear. They'll come back and destroy the temple."

Basho Ni blanches. "You're sure? Jinta said—"

"Look," Sif barks, guiding his sight with the point of her finger.

His eyes trail the temple floor to a fallen paladin, along the pool of blood spreading from their chest, and land on a piece of cloth hanging from their spear, embroidered with the four rings of the Virtuous Path. There is no mistaking it.

"What should we do?" Basho Ni pulls his robes tighter against his body, as if trying to find some safety and security in the closeness.

Sif pushes aside the crowd of disciples surrounding the last remaining paladin. He is young, but well beyond his teenage years, with wheat-colored hair and striking blue eyes. His teeth are bright white. He must've come from somewhere that hasn't had to worry about famine and sickness. She lets his gaze meet hers for a moment before she speaks.

"What are your last words?" she asks. Not out of any particular interest in the man or what he might say. Not out of anything approaching respect. But because when the odds are this low for his survival, it seems right to let him have something. He certainly won't be leaving with his life.

"I'd like to know your name." His voice is eerily calm. Almost joyful, even.

"Keno Sif. Waste of a request."

A beatific expression brightens his face. "You're Keno Sif? Sif the Destroyer?"

"Unless there's another Keno Sif around here."

"I knew it. This must be a sign from Druga that we're on the correct path. The Church thinks you're dead. Everyone does. I'm amazed you've evaded justice for so long." His faith borders on frenzy. It must be a sign of madness. Somewhere in the land of law and order, somebody told this man he would be blessed if he died for their cause. And now he welcomes his end, because it may also mean the end of the *barbarian murderer* Keno Sif, a woman he has never met and who has been hidden away for a long time now, who could never do as much damage as his masters do. The sight of it would be disturbing if it wasn't so pathetic.

"Okay," Sif snorts, growing impatient. "Is that it?"

"That is all. May Druga damn you to the void, barbarian. To an eternity with the Three Mothers of Demons."

Sif slits his throat unceremoniously and lets his body drop. The sound of his skull bouncing off the floor makes the pilgrims wince. The disciples are already panicking, whispering fearfully around her. But the last paladin is dead. Surely, that can only mean the temple and the surrounding villages will be safe. Sif hobbles away, hoping to find a place to rest, when Basho Ni begins to stammer something to her.

"Basho Ni, it's okay," she interrupts. "It's over."

"No, it isn't. We have. . . there is something you need to know. I think you should speak to Jinta."

Jinta Vol isn't one for secrets, but they are certainly the kind of person to dole out frustrating tasks. Sif scans the main hall of the temple, but Jinta is nowhere in sight. Sif's joints are crying out for some rest; it's been so long since she was in a real fight, and time hasn't been as kind as it could have been if she'd kept up with her practice. Faint memories of sparring with Buri begin to surface in her mind, but she forces them back under the waves before they can cause her any pain.

"Basho, I need to sit down. Just tell me what it is," Sif grunts.

Basho Ni shakes his head. "I'm sorry, Sif, I can't." He lowers his voice. "It's important that nobody else hears."

Sif storms to Jinta's room in the back of the temple, huffing like a boar. She slides the door back viciously, rattling it against the wall. Jinta is sitting on a bed of wood and straw. Their room is untenably minimalistic. No windows. At least there's a small closet. Sif can't imagine being Jinta's age and sleeping on straw, in a room too small to move around in. Jinta asks her to close the door and, as she does, her foot brushes a doll left on the floor. Sif looks at Jinta, and then back at the doll. It is done up to resemble an aristocrat from one of the central kingdoms, tall, pale-skinned, and dressed in warm, extravagant colors. Sif saw outfits like that when she traveled to the desert, decades before. On a human, the fabric would be cool and smooth. The doll's outfit is coarse, giving it a sense of irony.

"Basho Ni says I need to know something."

Jinta shifts in their seat. A subtle slyness presents itself in their gaze. "Basho Ni is confused."

Sif wrinkles her nose. Her foot brushes the doll, and suddenly she remembers why the knights said they were in the area. She had assumed it was a lie, and they were searching for Siduri's temple, but why would a child's toy be in the temple? With rare exceptions, like for a musical lesson or special cases of sickness, this isn't a place a child would be allowed.

"Do you have a kid here?"

"Well, shit," Jinta swears. They throw their hands up in the air, shattering the sense of deception that hung in the room. "Najah, you might as well come out."

From inside of the closet steps a young girl. She is exactly as Captain Aleksandr described her. Dark brown hair hangs down to her shoulders, and her eyes are an enigmatic pale green. She is thin, with a prominent nose. Though she is covered with scratches and bruises, her clothes are mostly clean. She wears a pale gray and blue tunic, of a type common to northerners who live in the grasslands south of Mount Hoda. As she meets Sif's gaze, her eyes gleam with a mixture of paranoia and defiance, as if to say, *I don't know who you are, but scarier people than you have tried to hurt me, and none of them have succeeded yet.*

"What the fuck is happening?" Sif demands to know. Najah is unyielding. "Jinta, why is a kid here?" Sif asks again.

Jinta rolls their eyes. "Stop being so dramatic, damn it. Najah is here under our protection. That's why I didn't want you to start carving through those paladins. We could've kept her hidden, and never seen them again. It's funny, you really haven't changed much since you left Ummun when *you* were just a girl. Too hot-blooded for your own good."

Sif stares, dumbfounded, nearly raising her voice, before realizing Jinta might be right. "Yeah, maybe I am. Fuck. Look, the Church of Druga wouldn't just let our temple stand. Why do they want her?"

Jinta shrugs. "Couldn't tell you. I was hoping to find out. Then maybe we would have something against them, to protect the temple if it came to that. And it might, now." They put a withered hand on Najah's shoulder. "Unfortunately, Najah has no idea."

Najah nods. When she speaks, her voice is so weak she is practically muttering. "My mom and I have been running from them as long as I can remember."

"Yeah, and where is she?" Sif asks.

Najah furrows her eyebrows. "Dead."

"Don't mind Keno, darling. She won't hurt you; she just has bad manners." Jinta Vol stands up. Their joints pop like strips of bacon in a fire. "Najah can't stay here any longer. It isn't safe for her, or for us. Now that *you* ruined my plan." As always, Jinta seems to delight in being unreadable, which only annoys Sif further.

"Eh? What plan is that? To hide her here forever?" Sif figures Jinta hasn't thought too hard about *any* of this if a little fight could spoil the whole thing.

"Forget it," Jinta responds. Sif rolls her eyes. "Since you mention it, maybe you should take her off Mount Hoda. Away from the temple."

"Take her where?" Sif turns towards Najah. "Got a home in Heron-Muse I don't know about, kid?"

"Getting an attitude with me won't change what needs to be done," Jinta chides gently. They lean in towards Sif and whisper, even though the room is so small Sif doubts the girl can't hear. "If Najah is important, we need to know why, and what to do about it. If she's not, we need to keep her away from here, where her presence might harm the temple. Now that a bunch of paladins have disappeared here, it won't be long until more show up. And, like you said, we can't hide her here forever. Now, you know I can't force you to do anything you don't want to, but you are the only warrior available at the temple. Think of our goddess."

Sif frowns. She should have known. Jinta isn't stupid; they were letting Sif make the argument for the plan they already had in place if any paladins came looking for the kid. Though Sif is sure the original plan was to get someone in better shape. But, barring any younger volunteers, Sif is the only option now. Maybe the old temple keeper had even goaded the paladin into hitting her, knowing Sif would pick a fight. She hopes not, but it wouldn't be the first time Jinta had been whole steps ahead of everyone else.

"Do you disagree, Keno Sif?"

"No. But it can't be me. I'm too old, and too wanted. We need to send word to Ummun. Plenty of young warriors there would love to do the goddess a favor like that."

"Oh, I will. But Najah needs as much of a head start as we can give her, because when the Church of Druga finds us, I'm going to tell them you left with her."

Sif feels her anger building into a shout, but Jinta holds up her hand. "Not to betray you. I know you can handle it out there in the continent, especially when the younger warriors from Ummun catch up. I'm telling them because I want to try and save the temple, and the people who rely on it. The paladins will want something from me. And I have faith that you will be able to do this."

"You know," Sif grumbles, running her gnarled fingers through tangled, gray-black hair, "most people would apologize before asking for such a big favor."

"Yes, I think they would," Jinta responds matter-of-factly.

Sif clicks her tongue against her teeth disapprovingly, then concedes. "Fine, Jinta."

"Thank you, Keno."

"You going to have someone watch over my animals?"

Jinta nods. "Of course."

Sif sighs. ". . .I really like my goats, Jinta. If anything happens to them, I won't be happy."

Jinta nods again, but it's clear they just want Sif to get on with it.

"Where should I take her, anyways?"

"Najah, dear, where did you suggest going? My memory gets worse every day."

"Ravinser," the girl says. Her arms are crossed, and she is chewing on the inside of her lip in between sentences. "Mom wanted to get help from here, and bring everyone to Ravinser."

"For what?" Sif asks.

Najah avoids her eyes, pretending instead to look at something in the corner of the room. "I don't know."

Groaning, Sif lowers herself down to one knee and motions for the child to approach her. "Hey, come here."

Najah's shoulders are high and her face marked with suspicion.

"Don't be afraid."

"I'm not," she scoffs. Sif is inclined to believe her, but damn if it doesn't come as a shock.

"Good for you. Can you tell me where Ravinser is?"

". . . I don't know. My mom and I left a long time ago."

"Great." Sif releases a gruff, frustrated breath she hadn't realized she was holding in. "Know how to read?"

"Of course I do." Clearly, Najah considers that a dumb question, if her tone is any indication. Sif knits her brow, having never entirely mastered reading and not loving how cavalier Najah is about knowing how. The kid is a little bit of a brat. Sif preferred it when she thought she'd be stuck with a scared little girl.

"Just try and keep pace. It'll be a long, dangerous walk, but I won't let anything happen to you."

What happens next is so sudden that Sif barely has time to comprehend it. When she thinks back, though, the moment will feel slow as water carving out a canyon. Najah opens her mouth, likely readying a snappy response, when her eyes flutter erratically, then close. Her knees give out, and she crashes to the floor, unconscious. Sif can't react in time to catch her and Jinta doesn't even try. The old monk lets out a sigh and faces Sif with a sort of bored resignation.

"There's something else you should know."

Etmond of the Valley

A myth recounted by Aseli of the Wood

Long ago, nestled at the mouth of a grass-green valley, was a small town. For as far back as anyone remembered, the town had been blessed. Their land was rich with nutrients, and a warm and predicable rain came down from the mountains often enough that the townspeople thrived on the crops they produced with very little work. Their lives were not carefree, but neither did they spend all day in bone-bruising labor. It was as nice an existence as a person had a right to expect, in a world where so many horrific things could and did happen.

Then, very gradually, something horrific did happen. It wasn't a single event, but an accumulation of small, unfortunate ones. Too long without rain, then not enough rain to satisfy the crops. Hunger weakened the livestock, which invited disease. The next winter wasn't the worst they'd had, but it was made worse by a combination of bad luck and inexperience. Nobody in living memory had dealt with so much hardship at once. Before long, starvation and sickness began to take the town. It was a slow, miserable death.

While most of the townsfolk argued over potential solutions, Etmond, a young man who had inherited a farm from his late aunt, prayed. He prayed to the spirit of the mountain for help. He prayed to Druga for safety. He prayed to the Lunar Goddess for protection from death. But even in the old days, the deities were fickle. Still, Etmond was certain that if he prayed hard enough, and with enough devotion, one of them would save his home.

Josephine, a blacksmith's daughter, and one of the only villagers brave enough to offer to travel for work and money to bring home, came back one day with a pack of food, some coin, and a tale about a strange priest she had met. The man was a priest of a goddess named Siduri. Josephine passed what food she had to her neighbors, and told them about the nights spent dancing and drinking with the priest, and with whatever other strangers stumbled across the revelry. Etmond's eyes shone at the mention of the endless wine, food, and alchemy worshippers shared amongst each other. When the story was over, he resolved to make his plea to the Dancing Goddess.

In his home, he set up a small shrine of candles, perfume, and a glass of the finest wine available. The expense of it and the time it took elicited some disdain from his neighbors, who felt he was wasting time and coin that nobody had to spare. Josephine alone had faith in the plan, and walked him through what she remembered from the priest she had met.

The first night the shrine was complete, he waited until midnight, closed his eyes, and made a heartfelt plea to Siduri to save him and his home from starvation. He breathed in the perfume, drank the wine, rang the brass chimes, shuffled in an awkward but soul-true dance, and sang his prayer. His head filled with a strange and dangerous jubilation, one that could be attributed to wine and the euphoria of the dance and ritual.

He got his answer quicker than he anticipated, as his plea turned imperceptibly from following a list of requirements to following the rhythm of his heart, the pulsing of hot blood that searched for exhilaration and bliss.

When his eyes opened, he caught sight of a strange light shining from the forest outside of his window. The light drew him out of his home, away from his village, and past the treeline, deep into the pine-scented wood, where he met Siduri. She stood beneath the boughs, a doe formed from silver moonlight.

"Etmond of the Valley," she said. Her voice was smooth and beautiful. It was the taste of sweet grapes and the sound of tuneful music. Yet, in his head, it was as wide as the sea and echoed like a shout of overwhelming joy.

He fell to his knees. "Is it you? Siduri?"

He felt the doe smile at him with her eyes. "It is. Please, stand up. I heard you calling to me. I'm happy to hear Josephine met my priest, and happy their words found you. Tell me, what would you like? I'd like to hear it again in your own words."

Etmond's voice shook as he spoke. The shame and worry of the past had built up in his head, and now it flooded out of him. "My lady, all I want is enough food and water to feed my village, and help us survive until our luck turns back around. I couldn't ask for more."

"That is very reasonable, Etmond. Of course I will help you."

"I'll do anything to repay you, I swear."

"I won't ask for repayment, although I do have one condition."

"Anything, my lady."

"I will give you three days and nights of endless food, drink, and alchemy. Your whole village will share in it, and dance and sing. In that way, I will know your people, and your people will know me."

Etmond of the Valley nodded. Silent tears of relief ran down his face. "In your name, my lady."

Siduri shook her silver head. "In your own names, Etmond. I will gift you three days and nights worth of indulgence. *But*, nobody in town will be permitted to hoard this wealth. If anyone abuses my gift, they will have betrayed our pact."

Etmond nodded again. "You have my word. I will let everyone know, and I will do my best to make them keep to our deal."

"Then it starts tomorrow."

Etmond felt his chin lifted by graceful fingers, and warm lips pressed against his forehead, as he awoke in his bed.

Etmond told his neighbors of his meeting, and the condition of his deal with Siduri. They responded with polite disregard. None of the other deities had seen fit to notice them. Why would this new goddess be different?

But that night, as they slept, food appeared in the cellar and kitchen of every home. The smells of braised ham, warm pies, and a myriad of other dishes filled the air when they awoke. There was fresh water and dark beer, cool, smooth liquor and sweet fruit. There were foreign spices that tasted like nothing they had felt before, with so much beauty it brought a tear to the eye, and herbs that summoned a comfortable nostalgia, soothing the mind and spirit. The town was known for its temperance, but the people who lived there danced with wild fervor under the influence of wax moth, traveler's leaf, and other forms of alchemy.

They went on like that deep into the night. In the morning, despite having eaten, drank, danced, and drugged to nauseating excess, they all agreed it was the best they'd felt in a long time. Etmond saw all of this and felt pride well up inside himself for his part in it. In his heart, he thanked the silver doe from his dreams.

The second night was very similar to the first. But, as the warm breath of dawn awoke on the horizon, a small fear tugged at Etmond's heart. He wondered what would happen when the three days Siduri had given them were over. Would the village survive? Should he have asked for more time? Now that he had a stomach full of food, the idea of going back to how things had been filled him with dread. He found himself a little less joyful and a little more distracted while his friends and neighbors ate and danced. It was the next morning, as the sun rose, that he decided to save a little bit.

It was a small amount at first. But when nothing bad happened, he reasoned that either Siduri had wanted him to do this after all, or that she, like the rest of the deities, had adopted a habit of disregard and negligence. While the rest of the village sang and ate, he hid food and wine in his house for later. When times were hard, his neighbors would naturally thank him yet again for his prudence.

The next night, while the town adjusted back to their normal lives and basked in the afterglow of their good fortune, Etmond locked himself inside his home and ate alone. He told himself that if things started to get bad again, he would share with his neighbors, but that it was too much risk with too little reward to do it now. For now, it would just be for himself.

The second night after things returned to normal, Etmond did the same. He locked his door, closed his windows and ate his dinner in silence by the dim candlelight. He said to himself that nobody else had done such good for the village. By virtue of that, he deserved to have his fill, even if others had to ration. It seemed fair that he would get some kind of reward. In fact, he spent so much of his time rationalizing keeping the food for himself, that he hardly enjoyed the meal. If anyone had mentioned to him that he was breaking his deal with Siduri, he might have been surprised to remember it.

The third night, he locked his doors, closed his windows, and sat down to eat. At the exact moment he took his first bite, a terrible wind blew out the candle in his room. The food turned to ash in his mouth. A fire roared to life in front of him, scorching his face and causing him to shrink back in pain. When he opened his eyes, he was prone before a flickering campfire in the same woods where he had met Siduri.

From just beyond the reach of the firelight, hundreds of pale eyes leered at him in fury and judgement.

"Betrayer!"

"Thief!"

"Hoarder!"

Siduri's voice roared from the dark night on a bitter gust of wind. With each accusation, Etmond felt madness building in his head. Panic, nausea, and disorientation tore through his body and mind.

"Miser!"

"Churl!"

"Deceiver!"

"You swore you would not hoard any food, Etmond. And for every day I blessed your town, you betrayed me! You were given a gift to share with all, but you hid selfishly in your hovel, thinking only of your own desires."

He begged for forgiveness, but the words came out in broken pieces. A feeling of impending doom bore down on him, twinned with hallucinations beyond even his most hateful nightmares. He tried to shut his eyes, to claw at his face, but his arms had lost strength. Overcome with despair, he fled into the night, wracked by pain and gibbering his lament.

The next day, the townsfolk found Etmond outside of his home, covered in blood, tears, and vomit. He rolled his head listlessly, and his words came out as nonsense. Though there was very little to be done for him, the townspeople kept him fed and cared for, remembering the three days and nights they had been gifted.

A week after Siduri's blessing, the crops began to grow like they had before. The villagers smiled, and vowed to share this new stroke of luck, to keep them together in the good times and get through the hard times, just as those three days and nights had before.

Chapter 5

Young Sif, the Destroyer
The ruins of a lost kingdom

"Stop," Efa whispers. Terror weighs heavily in her husky voice. She puts her hand back to halt Sif's momentum, but Sif knocks it away. From an unseen corner of the ruins echoes a sound like shuffling armor. Slow, scraping, and metallic. Sif cocks an eyebrow. It's not quite the sound of approaching mercenaries. If it were, maybe Efa wouldn't have tried to slow their progress.

"What is that?" Sif hisses.

Efa murmurs inaudibly, and Sif draws her sword. Not to hurt her—yet. To prepare for an ambush, or to defend herself against whatever magic has affected Efa so profoundly. She feels a chill rush over her skin. The crumbling walls around her feel much closer than before. If she actually has to swing a sword in here, it will be difficult.

Efa turns and looks down at Sif's hands, which grip her blade tightly. "You might as well put that away."

"Eh? For what? Don't want me to hurt your friends?"

Efa shakes her head and peers back in the direction of the strange sounds. Wafting in from the shadowed halls ahead, Sif smells the faintest trace of blood.

"Not even you can hurt them now. I wish you could. They're already dead. The Lunar Goddess of Death rejected them. We were scouting the ruins for you when dead men in red uniforms ambushed us, and killed them. The tunnel started to collapse and trapped them under the rubble. I don't know where the red-uniformed men are now."

Sif swallows hard and listens with her. She had fought moon-cursed dead in Heron-Muse, and has hoped never to encounter them again. It's not a sight that's easy to drink, smoke, or live away the memory of. Souls abandoned by the Lunar Goddess and tethered to out-of-synch flesh. She tries to recall if any kingdoms use red uniforms for their soldiers, but draws a blank.

"You could've mentioned that before," Sif says.

Efa grits her teeth. "I tried to. You were more interested in killing me."

Sif doesn't respond.

"I don't think they're getting any closer," Efa muses after a beat.

"Not any further either," Sif remarks. Buri grunts in agreement.

"That's good," Efa responds. "It means they're still pinned under the debris, where I left them."

Ivon's breath picks up in the back of the line. Not that Sif blames them.

"Let's go now, then," Ivon adds. "Before anything else happens."

Efa nods and leads them onward, beneath pillars poised to collapse and a ceiling ready to crumble, through cracks in walls, and up stairs with steps like splintered bones. All the while, the sound of shuffling becomes closer and closer. It reaches its peak around the same corner where the first hint of sun streams in from above. She knows where to look because Efa avoids it. There, beneath hundreds of pounds of fallen stone, are two men in brass mercenary's armor, half-crushed but still writhing in eternal agony. Their nails have peeled back from the effort of trying to claw their way out from under the rubble. The mercenaries must've run across the ruins right after Sif did. The stone underneath them is still slick with fresh blood. Their mouths are muttering something, but she can't hear what. Sif doesn't notice she's staring until Buri touches her shoulder. Ivon and Efa are waiting for them further down the corridor.

"Nothing you can do, Keno," Buri murmurs.

"I know, Uncle."

The two of them turn to follow Ivon and Efa into the sunlight, but Sif's focus remains on the scuffling of the moon-cursed dead behind her, tethered to their spot by their own bodies, lusting after lives they've already lost. No surprise Efa didn't want this. Past the rim of broken stone, Efa leads them into the aftermath of the sandstorm. The wide blue sky above them seems impossible. Most of the mercenaries have moved on, maybe scattered in the storm, or lost in the ruins. A small cadre rides in the distance, maybe ten riders total. Sif and Buri kill five mercenaries guarding the horses nearby. As they saddle up, Efa steps to Buri and speaks.

"Giant," she blurts out. "I challenge you to a duel."

Buri turns from his horse to face her. "Very well."

"Where will you go next?" she asks. "Let me go with you and, once we arrive, you and I can settle this. I appreciate you sparing me from. . . *that*. But I can't let Aneir see me as a coward."

Sif rolls her eyes. What is it about fighters from the cities always wanting to die with honor? Seems like a waste. What happened in the ruins already happened. Better to focus on living. Buri doesn't agree. Honor doesn't keep him awake at night, but another sort of code does. A warrior who only kills the weak can't claim to be brave, strong, or skilled. At the time, Efa's surrender had seemed like a sign of weakness. Maybe it was, but Sif finds it hard to blame her.

Buri nods at Efa with a begrudging respect. Many of the deities give humanity no gifts. Aneir has at least given each soul a heart strong enough to face fear and not devolve into petty brutality and wanton slaughter, if that is what the heart's owner desires.

"You northerners are an odd bunch," Ivon comments to Sif.

"The woman is one of yours. She speaks in a southern tongue."

"Southern tongue, but northern god."

"Wouldn't that make you a northerner as well?" Sif asks, knowing Ivon isn't nearly as particular as Buri when it comes to the god of courage.

"Huh, maybe I am," they joke.

Sif rolls her eyes. "Get on your horse, Ivon."

Ivon scoffs dramatically and leaps onto their horse with fluidity and grace that only a brilliant thief could possess. Sif notices Buri does not tie Efa's horse to his own. If she's smart, she'll use that as an opportunity to escape. The four of them ride out, leaving the pit of sand, stone, and deep magic behind them. Sif remembers the promise of money she thought it held at first. It wouldn't have been worth it.

That night, she eats the last of the goddess's pearls she'd preserved and falls into an uneasy sleep. She has only the one dream, but has it over and over, and will continue to have it for some time. The moon-cursed dead chant a hollow song to her from their place under the blood-slick rock. Her feet carry her forward of their own will, until the hoarse, mournful dirge becomes clear. Somehow, her heart knows these are the words they spoke to her in the ruins, which she could not make out at the time.

Agartha is a city in a hole in the sea
At the end of the world
In the pitch of a dream
The prison of hope
The gnashing of teeth
Agartha is a city in a hole in the sea.

Chapter 6

Old Sif, the Hermit

The hidden Temple of Siduri, Mount Hoda

"Druga must hate this girl," Sif remarks, gazing down at Najah's sleeping form.

"Oh, who knows? Since when have the deities cared much about what happens down here?" Jinta responds. Bold words, considering their position in the temple. "Maybe Najah's mother had a falling out with someone, and they cursed the girl in revenge. Mages are capable of all sorts of petty injustices." Jinta's voice softens. "Even hurting a defenseless child."

Despite Jinta's show of concern, Sif gets the impression that they just want her and Najah out of the temple. Najah hasn't even woken up when Jinta wraps her in a fur cloak, shoves her into Sif's arms, and pushes the two towards the mouth of the temple, past mourners in fresh, blinding grief. Only a handful are aware enough to register surprise at the presence of a young, southern-appearing girl.

"Too much coincidence," Sif says in response to Jinta's theory. "There's no reason a regular girl should be dealing with all of this at once."

"Well, of course not, but I doubt Najah is a regular girl," Jinta responds.

The way Jinta explains the curse, it sounded simple. Every once in a while, for no apparent reason, Najah will fall asleep. There seem to be no rules governing when it happens, or for how long she stays asleep, but once it does there is nothing that can be done to wake her. In the month since Najah arrived at Siduri's Temple, she's been affected by her curse three times, and Jinta hadn't able to rouse her during any event. Today is the fourth time. As Jinta speaks, Sif looks down at Najah, whose body twitches, eyes rolling behind their lids.

"She has nightmares, I think," Jinta explains. "She mumbles a lot of the same things about gold, and an old well, and Druga."

Sif waves her hand. "Didn't ask."

On top of that, Jinta confesses that she doesn't believe Najah is being honest about her affliction. During her stay, the young girl has been closed off and evasive. Maybe on its own, they would have taken her attitude as the product of trauma and mistrust. But on a few occasions, Jinta caught her speaking to herself when she thought she was alone. Too many odd occurrences surround the strange child. It makes more and more sense that Jinta would be in a hurry to rid the temple of the young girl. Sif had only just stumbled into the mess today and she already yearns to be rid of it. If Jinta can come through for her, then all Sif needs to do is take the girl to an old outpost from the war and wait for younger, stronger, and more willing reinforcements.

-

Najah wakes up halfway to Sif's cabin, cradled awkwardly in the older woman's arms, and begins to swing her limbs with wild, frantic abandon. Sif catches a fist to the mouth and drops Najah in the snow at her feet.

"What are you doing?" Najah yells, scrambling to her feet and raising her thin fists.

Sif scowls. "Helping you escape, brat! You yanked on my earring."

Najah hesitates. "Escape?"

"From the Church of Druga, kid. Or did you want to keep sleeping on that floor until more paladins rode up?"

Najah glares at Sif, chest heaving, clouds of breath materializing from her lips. Slowly, she puts her fists down. "No. Sorry," Najah admits. She offers up a clumsy explanation, "I don't know you. For a second, I thought. . . I don't know."

"It's fine," Sif grumbles, fingers tightening the clasp on her earring. Then, after a beat passes, "If anyone tries to carry you off, don't just swing your arms around. Aim for a weak point. Eyes, throat, groin. Steal their weapon if you can."

Najah clears her throat, then reaches down to pick something up out of the snow. It's a necklace made of rough twine, with a wooden pendant of a crudely carved fox. "Right. Thanks, I guess."

Looking at the graceless young girl in front of her, memories of her childhood with Buri flash in the periphery of Sif's mind. When she was young, she had been a brat too. Sif almost smiles when the memory turns sour. She shoves it back into the darkness, replacing the hint of fondness on her lips with stern disregard. "Hurry up, since you're awake. I don't want this to take longer than it has to."

-

The rest of the hike up the mountain is just as awkward. Both women feel mismatched with the other. Najah complains often about the cold, and Sif is plainly uninterested in providing any solace. When Najah inquires, too casually, if the plan is still for a separate group to join them, her tone does very little to conceal how uncomfortable Sif makes her. Sif assures her they won't be traveling together long.

At Sif's cabin, Najah is immediately drawn to the goats in the pen on the side of the house. Despite complaining about the cold, she forgoes shelter to call the goats—named Ivon, Buri, and Sunnhilde—over to her.

"You're gonna get bit," Sif warns, although she is not overly concerned. She isn't in the habit of trying to influence other people, and if Najah wants to try her luck, Sif figures it's her right. The goats shuffle over to Najah and allow her to stroke their heads. Sif murmurs to herself in surprise.

The inside of her cabin is an absurd mess of tools, weapons, and other paraphernalia. It's warmer than outside, but not as warm as any traveler would want. Every inch is neglected in a way that borders on defeating the purpose of her half-hearted attempt at organization; an outsider would have trouble discerning whether a second person lives with Sif, or if her home is just in that much disarray. A faded wanted poster hangs from the wall, maybe the only item still in good condition. There are bottles of pickled vegetables inhabiting most flat surfaces, paired with partially processed hallucinogens and an assortment of small arms—an axe for cutting wood, a dagger from Feigrvoller.

An old memory of Buri's hometown rushes through her as she lays eyes on the dagger. A dozen people stuffed into a small cabin, the air thick with the earthy scent of countless flowers and herbs hanging from the roof. Psalms to Aneir the Sword-Eater. A long fire stretching into the grave-cold night air. Najah's laughter yanks her out of remembrance. Outside of Sif's window, the oldest goat is licking Najah's hands. The young girl talks to the three goats as if they're people, but her voice is muffled by the distance between them. Najah must see Sif watching from the corner of her eyes, because she stops everything and walks inside with a causal gait, stealing a clumsy glance at Sif through the window on her way.

Inside, she takes a seat near the entrance, wrapping her arms around herself for warmth.

"Who is that?"

Sif follows her gesture to the wanted poster. Part of it is torn away, but what remains depicts Sif, Buri, and Sunnhilde, all still young and alive. Maybe a little more menacing than is realistic, although Sif supposes that's a matter of perspective.

"My uncle, Buri, and my wife, Sunnhilde."

"Your uncle doesn't look anything like you," Najah's skepticism is evident. "Besides, I heard barbarians don't have wives and uncles."

"You're fucking talkative all of a sudden." Sif lifts a burlap pack with a grunt and begins shoving in supplies. "Since you're so curious, we aren't related. So what? Buri is my uncle and Sunna is my wife."

"Well, sorry for asking," Najah responds, clearly not sorry at all. "Where are they now?"

"Not here," Sif deflects. "Let's talk about Ravinser. Got a map?" Najah just shakes her head. "Any idea where this place is?"

"Far to the south. I haven't been there since I was a little kid, so. . ."

Sif begins stuffing a second pack with supplies for her new ward. "Well, you picked a weird way to get there, heading north."

Najah tenses. "My mother was bringing us here when she was killed. She thought the northerners would help us. Ravinser is just where she said I should go if she. . . died. But I was already almost here. I thought things would be different."

Sif doesn't respond, and Najah pretends not to notice her freeze for a moment. She can't help but wonder what Najah's mother expected. Maybe she heard this was a place full of people who hated the Church of Druga, and who had resisted the expansion of empires into the surrounding lands since before the war even started. Sif feels a small amount of guilt for not living up to whatever vision Najah had in mind, even as she thinks that her assumptions are irrational.

It is a harsh world, and it is only getting worse.

From amongst the incomprehensible mess in her home, Sif produces a long, thin dagger with a wood and leather hilt. Nearly a small sword. It comes to an extreme point, and glints in the light like new.

"You know how to fight?"

Najah regards the dagger with wonder, revulsion, and uncertainty, filled with the sensation of wanting to touch something she knows will hurt. Holding it could be a tipping point she never recovers from.

"I. . . don't think I'm allowed to use that. My mother is a. . . *was* a pacifist. Mostly."

Sif makes a disgruntled noise. "The only one here who could stop you is me, and I won't do it."

"It'll just cause trouble," Najah suggests. At the same time, she walks over to touch the dagger's hilt. Maybe the suggestion was meant more for herself than for Sif.

"Look, you can do anything you want to, if you're willing to deal with the consequences. The consequence of carrying a weapon is injuring yourself, or losing a fight you should have run from. Don't hurt yourself, or lose, and you'll be fine."

Najah doesn't respond. Sif can't tell if the girl is considering her options, or if she's afraid to speak her mind against the adult arguing with her.

"You can take it or not. But you should pick the option you want, not the option you think you have to."

"I guess I'll hold it for now. Is it real?" Najah asks, gently taking the weapon from Sif. Her hand dips with its weight, a result of the unexpected heft.

"Yeah, so don't play with it," the older woman grumbles.

As they leave, Sif hangs a bundle of dried lavender on the front of the door, shutting the twine that binds it together in the top of the door frame. Her fingers trace the dull purple idly before she sighs and pulls away. "Alright, let's go."

"What was that?" Najah asks.

"In case someone swings by," Sif mutters. "So they know I'll be back soon."

-

It is two days of grueling hiking before they reach the foot of Mount Hoda. At night, Najah complains more than ever about the cold. Sif doesn't allow a fire, but reluctantly lets the girl borrow her cloak. The last morning of their trek, the smell of snow and cold air gives way to the smell of frost on grass and warm sun as they reach the foot of Mount Hoda. Despite herself, Sif feels invigorated. It's been a long time since she journeyed off the mountain. Something about seeing home rising behind her feels like setting out for the first time. Except this time, with an odd, bratty child and an overwhelming amount of joint pain.

A wooden gate rests at the foot of the main path. On both sides are offering bowls to two saints, complete with small stone statues of each one. Saint Daado is thin and dignified, with round features and a halo of tightly coiled hair. Her inscription calls her Saint Daado, patron of travelers, diviner of the litany of guidance. Buri is taller as a statue than he was in real life, and more muscular. In life his face was angular and slightly sunken and, though he was very tall, people always seem to expect an actual giant out of myth rather than a man. The statue's single eye is disappointingly lifeless. Sif lingers on his inscription.

Buri, the giant of Feigrvoller, imbiber of the six poisons, protector of the narrow pass.

He would think the whole thing was embarrassing. She puts a coin in each bowl and silently bids farewell to Mount Hoda.

On their side of the horizon rests a small farming community that glistens in the afternoon sun. If memory serves Sif well, it will be the perfect spot to gather themselves before the grueling journey southward, through the territory of the Church of Druga and the monarchists whose armies stalk behind them and wait ahead. Sif hopes the young girl is prepared. Though if that's not the case, it will be someone else's problem soon.

Chapter 7

Ivon of Heron-Muse
The Great Desert

Ivon, Sif, Buri, and Efa set off for the market-city of Ponda, the nearest city that they don't believe they have a bounty in and might offer work. After hours of riding, a curtain of stars gradually pulls down over the sky and they make camp. Ivon offers to take first watch. The image of the moon-cursed dead still lingers in the periphery of their mind anyways, keeping sleep at a distance.

"We should start a small fire," Ivon suggests, as the others prepare to lay down.

Efa shakes her head. "It'll draw unwanted attention."

Sif scoffs, violently shaking out her bedroll nearby. "Come on. You really think we haven't lost those mercenaries?"

"They're smarter than you think," Efa responds. "But no. A fire will attract spirits lost in the desert."

"Eh? If all it took was some light, they'd have found a way out by now," Sif argues.

Efa lays her head down and turns her back to Sif and the others. "Do what you will, but remember, I warned you."

"Great, I was going to. And you should be thanking me; I can cook a great stew once the fire is going."

Efa doesn't respond.

"Ivon, sure you want to be first up?" Sif asks.

"Of course. I don't want you waking me up halfway through the night," they reason to their comrades. And to the mercenary temporarily stuck with them, until Buri kills her in Ponda. Or hey, Ivon figures, maybe she'll win.

Although Sif would kill Efa if that happens. The thought of it all makes Ivon feel exhausted.

Part of them misses the days of pulling off petty heists in Heron-Muse. It wasn't the easiest place to live, but districts in the city changed ownership so often that it wasn't hard to live as a thief. Not as hard as it's been to live as a thief who is also on the run from a small army, in a foreign land.

After a light meal, as the rest of the party falls into an uneasy sleep, Ivon indulges their nostalgia under the pale starlight. Room and board in a small wooden hovel near the Cold Lantern shrine, where people were too nervous of offending the monks to make much of a scene. Gambling in the Rukeyy district. A rotating cast of lovers from all and no genders, but that memory is soured by the memory of why those lovers left. Mostly jail, or fear of jail or death, or a general aversion to Ivon's personality. There's no accounting for taste. They absent-mindedly stroke their blond mustache, grown uncharacteristically ragged over the past few days.

Ivon sighs and turns to look at their sleeping companions. When they turn back, a figure is sitting across from them. A man in a black cloak, but with Heron-Muse mage's colors beneath.

Ivon swallows hard. It's a sight they've feared for a long time now.

"You remember me?" the mage asks. Their voice is like a dagger hidden in silk clothing. Elegant, but with an edge.

"No," Ivon whispers.

The man chuckles. "Yes, you do." As he steps closer, the pale skin of his face becomes barely visible in the soft firelight. His cloak is accented with golden thread, and the tufts of desert grass turn an ashy gray under his boots before they die.

Expectation burns in the man's eyes. The pressure to provide a better answer builds in tandem with Ivon's fear. Provide a better answer. In truth,

Ivon does not remember this man specifically, but is certain of where he's from and why he's here.

"You're with the Heron-Muse Mages' Guild," Ivon admits, voice wavering. When Ivon left Heron-Muse with Sif and Buri, they had taken a job from the mages. Not really of their own volition. They hadn't completed the job, and left their Mages' Guild liaison for dead. There had been special circumstances, but Ivon had decided it would be best to leave town. They had hoped, and even convinced themself, that the Mages' Guild would cut their losses rather than track the three of them down.

"Correct!" the mage confirms with a wide smile. "So, it's clear that you owe us. A lot of us, what is left of us, think you should just be killed. Killed, or worse."

Ivon has an idea of what worse is, and it makes their skin crawl. A slow death is better than what some mages do to themselves by accident. Ivon can imagine very well what they might do on purpose, out of cruelty.

Ivon reaches for a knife in their boot and inhales to warn their friends.

A spark of eerie green magic, and their body is frozen. Hundreds of invisible, clammy, freezing hands hold them in place, keeping a tight grip on their mouth and throat.

"Ah-ah," the mage chides. "You didn't let me finish. We decided, narrowly, to give you a chance. What did you take from the ruins?"

Ivon feels a cold sweat run across their skin. The Mages' Guild must have been watching them for some time now.

"Nothing."

The mage frowns. Ivon feels the invisible hands search and squeeze and prod along their body.

"Are you stupid?" the mage asks, once he confirms that Ivon is telling the truth.

"How dare you?!" they bite back, voice muffled behind corpse-like fingers. Ivon could explain the moon-cursed dead, and the strange emptiness of the ruins, and their hurry to leave before they were found by mercenaries. But what would it help? The Mages' Guild isn't known for its understanding.

"Don't waste your energy. You're going in the direction of Ponda now. Is that your destination? Nod your head."

Despite their reluctance, and despite the humiliation of being powerless, Ivon nods.

"There is an inn I want you to stay at, and inquire about a job while you're there. You'll do the job, and bring Keno Sif and The Giant with you. They owe us too, really. But you know how barbarians are. Can't trust a one of them to do an honest day's work."

Ivon glares at the mage silently. They feel the hand gripping their mouth relax. The mage nods, giving them permission to speak.

"And say that I don't want to? I didn't kill your liaison, you know. They just couldn't handle the job. That's hardly my fault."

"Who said anything about fault? This is about debt. Something you'd understand more than those savages."

"I can get money."

If the mage has any feeling about that, he doesn't show it. "You're misunderstanding. You will do the job. You know what we can do to a person, Ivon. What can happen to your body, mind, and soul. You will do the job, or all three of you will pay. And you'll keep this conversation between us. At your destination will be any number of valuable magical trinkets. Just pocket a few, and come back home safe."

The mage pats Ivon on the head, the gesture a sick mirror of paternalism. Ivon shuts their eyes in disgust. When they open them again, the mage is gone. Only the howling, dark desert remains, stretching out vastly under unknowable stars.

As soon as Ivon can move, they scramble to kick out the fire. Sand and embers splash across the campsite, waking the rest of the group.

Sif sits up groggily. As she does, her sword's edge glints in the moonlight. "What is it?!"

Ivon falls to their knees, panting and sweating.

"Ivon!" Sif spits out. "Why did you kick out the fire?!"

All three of Ivon's companions are frantically searching the dark for danger that isn't here any longer, but will haunt their every step for a long time to come. Ivon wants to confess everything, but has no way of knowing if they are still being watched. In fact, they find it hard to believe they'll ever be alone again.

"It's nothing," Ivon says, mustering a smile. "I figured maybe Efa was right about the spirits. Go back to sleep."

Chapter 8

Old Sif, the Hermit
The foot of Mount Hoda

Sif and Najah walk from the plains at the mountain's foot and into town. It isn't more than a few minutes before the villagers notice Sif and Najah in their streets. Najah, who is only alive because of her ability to remain unseen and uncaught, is clenching every muscle in her body. Sif can tell the girl is waiting for the boot to drop. For the moment when she's forced to sprint through town, across fields of crops, and back to the relative safety of the wilderness. Animals might try and kill a person, but they don't torture or imprison them.

Amusement plays at the edges of Sif's features. "Calm down, kid. You're just upsetting yourself."

"They're talking about us."

"So what?" Sif asks. "It's gossip. I've heard shit about some of these farmers you wouldn't believe."

"It's not good to be out in the open," Najah mumbles. Still, she relaxes a little. She feels very aware of the dagger on her belt, and then very guilty about that awareness. Najah tries to break that line of thought with more conversation, "I guess you've been here before?"

"Eh. . . yeah, I've been to Hontori. But they probably don't remember me. People from my village fought beside people from here during the war. Hontori is northern enough that they needed us, but not so northern they wanted a bunch of Ummun *barbarians* hanging around too long." The way Sif says barbarian makes it seem like a joke, but not one Najah is supposed to laugh at.

Najah mulls that over. ". . .Are they going to be, I don't know, nice?"

"Hold on, kid." Abruptly, Sif sits down on the porch of a wide, wooden tavern, her round face grimacing as she does. One hand is on her knee and the other on the raised porch to steady herself.

Najah watches the older woman with waning patience, fingers drumming against the side of her leg anxiously. "Sif, what are we doing here?"

"You need to be a little less serious, Naj."

Even as Sif speaks, Najah feels her frustration growing. After all, Sif was the one who suggested they not start a fire on the mountain. The old woman is impossibly single-minded. And the more she mulls it over, the less tolerable it seems. When she speaks up, the words explode out of her chest.

"I'm not your fucking. . . *pack*, okay!?"

Sif furrows her eyebrows, "Pack? What?"

"I'm a person! You can't just drag me around and not tell me anything!"

Sif is speechless. Had she withheld important information, or been insensitive? Maybe the girl is just sensitive? Sif wonders what Buri would do, and finds herself a little ashamed at the thought that Buri would not have been in this situation. He would have known exactly what to say and how to act.

A man and a woman walking by look at Sif and Najah pityingly. They consider stepping forward to intervene, then notice Sif's Ummun clothing and hurry off instead. Roused by the noise, a young blonde woman steps out of the tavern.

"Is everything okay out here?"

Najah bites her tongue, but does indulge in a flurry of unkind thoughts.

"You work here?" Sif asks the blonde woman. She nods. "Get me a drink, please. And I need to know if that field of yellow-stars is still to the south."

Najah notices people in the tavern eyeing them. She suppresses the urge to hide.

"I don't know what field you're talking about, but I can ask."

"Shit," Sif swears. Then, "Yeah, that'll work."

The woman leaves Sif and Najah alone on the porch. The door inside swings back and forth, creaking. Sif turns back to Najah. The young girl locks eyes with her, swelling with determination to not back down. Sif looks at her appraisingly. Najah opens her mouth, but it's Sif who speaks first.

"Yeah, I guess you're right. Sorry. It's been a while since I've had to do this." Sif waves her hand in the air, a vague reference to their general situation.

Sif's apology takes Najah by surprise. She wants to put her response together flawlessly, to seize the opportunity. Instead, what comes out is a question that sounds much more bitter than Najah intends. "Since you've had to watch a kid?"

Sif snorts. "I guess so. I meant since I've been travelling with someone I don't know well. But yeah, been a while since I had to watch a kid, too."

"Why are we here?" There is a confidence and an insistence in Najah's voice now. Steel being formed.

Sif sighs. "I'm not as strong as I was. I'm sure the warriors from Ummun will catch up to us in a day or two, but I can't. . . I'll be in a lot of pain soon." The lie of it is that Sif is already in too much pain. Her expression is bleak at first, but a sudden, fragile grin quickly rises in its place. "We can't all be young and strong, running from the law. I have to make it to our meeting spot in one piece."

Najah hadn't realized the toll this was taking on her companion. Since her mother died, she's just been passed between temporary caretakers, people who didn't care about her at all, but wanted to keep her away from Druga's paladins. She doesn't believe Sif cares about her, but maybe the old woman isn't as cruel as she had assumed. And it is nice to hear a compliment. Even if it is a strange one, like respecting Najah for her ability to remain alive and out of prison.

The bartender brings Sif a wooden mug of brown ale. Its foamy surface dimly reflects the mid-day sunlight. In time, the patrons of the tavern return to their own business. Sif sips her drink as the bartender explains that the flower fields were burned in the war to keep painkillers out of the hands of northern barbarians. Najah remembers a story she'd once heard, that certain plants imbued northern warriors with a blinding rage that increased their strength and dulled their pain.

The bartender and Sif talk for a while and, as luck has it, a new field is growing to the west. It is smaller, but Sif would be allowed to take a pouch in remembrance of her people's help during the assault on Hontori.

In the fields, a middle-aged man with graying hair and a thick beard stops them. He had been tending to the flowers and takes an interest in Sif and Najah as they approached. The way he eyes Sif, Najah knows he recognizes by her clothes that she is from the mountain. He helps them find the best part of the field to pick flowers, but his presence makes Sif tense up.

"Mind if I ask where you're headed?"

Sif meets his gaze, "Meeting a friend in a small village to the east."

"Awwagara?" he asks. Najah frowns at his insistence, even as she reminds herself that he might just be friendly. Sif said the people of Hontori have good history with the northern peoples. Still, Sif freezes before she responds. Long enough that the lie is evident.

"No."

Before they leave, the man wipes sweat from his forehead and says, "Might be a funny question, but are you Keno Sif?"

Najah feels Sif glance at her from the corner of her eyes. "No," Sif lies again, "I'm Kanae Vol."

"A priestess?" the man asks, recognizing the surname. "Well, good travels to you and your child. Traders have been arriving with troubling news. We've heard word of angry spirits, and demons preying on travelers."

"We'll be careful," she responds with indifference.

The man nods. "Very well. May Siduri bless your journey."

That would have been that, except in the southern kingdoms, where Najah was born, the blessing of Siduri isn't something a person is brought up to want.

And when the man names the Dancing Goddess, his eyes meet Najah's, and the young girl thinks she sees him read her heart. Or maybe it is nothing.

Chapter 9

Old Sif, the Hermit
The path from Hontori

"I need to rest," Najah admits.

Sif stifles the urge to argue. Truth be told, she had been hoping to make much better time today. She had expected to meet the younger warriors within a day or two of leaving Hontori, but she's still ferrying Najah along by herself. The longer Sif is gone from home, the more irritable she becomes. Najah seems demoralized by Sif's impatience, but it's a hard thing to shake. Sif can't stop thinking about the lavender hanging from her door. It's not good to be gone long.

On all sides of them, tall, tall trees reach up to the sun and sway in the wind. The weather is mild and the leaves protect them from the sun. In the treetops, birds sing and chase each other through the branches. If they were on a road it would be a nice day to travel, but between their clashing personalities and the underbrush slowing their progress, both of them could use a moment of respite.

"There is a clearing ahead we can stop in. After that, it won't be long until the outpost where we'll meet the others," Sif says.

Najah grumbles miserably but doesn't argue.

The clearing is bordered by a band of oak trees and in the center is an old campsite. A trio of arrows are lodged in the oak farthest from them. Najah notices it and points it out to Sif.

"Don't worry about it," Sif assures her. "The woods aren't that dangerous. Probably some half-drunk travelers fooling around."

"Then I want to light a campfire," Najah insists. When Sif starts to argue, the young girl interrupts her. "You said it's safe. Live a little."

Sif can't help but chuckle. It's hard not to respect Najah's audacity. "Fine, but if we get attacked by bandits or spirits, you're on your own."

"I'll be fine," the young girl responds. "You're too old to outrun me."

Sif bursts into a full belly laugh. Najah even smiles a little bit. Within minutes, Sif has a fire going, but Najah is too fast asleep to appreciate it.

"*Mom. . .*" Najah murmurs in her sleep. Quiet and painful, the sound of a heart breaking.

Sif sits with her back against an old, crooked tree and watches the young girl. She seems to be having a nightmare already, just like when they first met. In the far distance, through the trees, is the crown of Mount Hoda, silvery under the pale moon.

Though Sif is tired, she's filled with too much energy to sleep. As Najah dozes, Sif wonders if this was how Buri felt when they first met. Preoccupied with leaving, annoyed at the task in front of him. Fearful that he wasn't strong or good enough. It doesn't seem like him. From the moment they met, Buri was a perfect mentor. Sif's skill-fathers taught her how to fight and survive, but Buri helped her learn more. Something important, but intangible. Hard to describe.

The grief building in her heart tells Sif that Buri never thought of her as a burden, even though she couldn't have been much older than Najah when they met. The only real difference between them is that Najah looks like she's been kicked all across the continent and still doesn't want to hold a weapon. Sif's mind wanders from Najah and Buri to Sunnhilde, then to Ivon, and before she knows it, she's asleep.

-

She wakes up to the sound of Najah shouting her name. Sif springs to her feet and draws her sword. The steel flashes under the dawn sky. A cloud of dust rolls across the campsite from Sif's sudden movement. Her mind is still bewildered by sleep.

"I'm hungry," Najah says, holding the dagger in her left hand.

"What?" Sif asks.

"I'm hungry."

"Did you yell my name?"

"Yeah, you wouldn't wake up when I said it at first, I thought you were dead."

Sif sheathes her sword. "Goddess' song, I'm not fucking dead. How old do you think I am?!"

"Old," Najah responds, bluntly.

"Get some dried meat out of my pack, you little brat." Najah sticks her tongue out, but does take the offering. She pulls it apart with a suspicious look on her face but, after a cautious bite, devours it ravenously. Sif slumps back down in her seat under the old oak, closes her eyes, and feels her heartbeat ease back to a normal pace. In the sky above she can just make out the sound of pygmy woodpeckers chirping. She cracks an eye to the sight of Najah with a mouth full of food, handling the dagger as if she is trying to get a sense of the weight. Sif wants to tell her to be careful, but doesn't. The touch of the wind and song of the sun-drenched forest are almost enough to lull her back to sleep, when a twig snaps from somewhere behind the campsite.

Sif stands and puts a hand on her sword. Across the clearing is a pale woman with dark hair, dressed in plate armor. She is watching Najah with an amused smile. Najah finally catches sight of the woman, drops her dagger and steps back towards Sif, then stumbles forward to clumsily retrieve it.

"I won't hurt you," the woman says.

"You *can't* hurt me," Najah growls. A lot of bravado for a girl afraid to fight.

The woman laughs coolly. "Okay, killer."

Clumsy as a newborn, Najah raises her dagger at the stranger. Her other hand clasps her fox necklace as if to protect it, or else with the thought that it might protect her.

"Get back," Sif growls, pushing Najah behind her.

"Woah, woah." The woman holds her hands up, but she isn't afraid. The grin on her face is cocky and self-assured. "Put your sword away, friend. I'm here to help you. I'm Kisha of Ummun. I just killed a half dozen paladins tracking you two down the mountain. Didn't expect to see you before I arrived at the outpost." Kisha holds her leg out, showing off the splatter of blood on her boot. "I heard you need help." She turns her attention to Sif. "Obviously, I had to meet you. You're a hero."

A hero, Sif thinks bitterly. People will believe any stupid thing they hear.

"Here," Kisha says, turning around to show off her gear. "You can check my armor. It's made in Ummun. Got a letter from Jinta, too."

As Kisha turns, Sif scans her armor. The design, the materials, the age—it's definitely local. Satisfied for the moment, Sif gets close enough to snatch the letter from Kisha's outstretched hand and passes it to Najah, who almost refuses to take it until she remembers Sif's difficulty with letters.

Najah scans the crumpled letter and then nods to Sif. "It says it's from Jinta Vol, and that we're meeting at an outpost."

"Does it mention Kisha by name?" Sif asks.

"Well, no. But it doesn't mention anyone else, either."

"There were a lot of us," Kisha explains.

"I don't remember seeing you around Ummun," Sif comments. Most of the edge is gone from her voice.

Kisha shrugs. "I travel. Home is a little boring."

Sif nods. It's not like she wasn't the same in her youth. The second she became a fighter-in-training and earned her last name, all the adults started telling grand tales of adventure and battle. It was hard not to look around at her snowy little village and feel like a bird in a cage. "Yeah, that's fair. You said there are more with you?"

Kisha runs her fingers along her jawline. "About that. A bunch of other people came with me, but the paladins put them down."

"All of them?" Sif is incredulous.

"Yeah. The Church has some woman fighting with them. She's a force of nature."

"She dead now?"

Kisha shakes her head no. "It wasn't even close, Auntie. It was a slaughter. I was barely able to escape while she was distracted and make it here to warn you."

Sif suddenly realizes she is still holding Najah back. She lets her arm fall to her side, and beside her Najah's eyebrows furrow skeptically.

"It's fine," Sif assures her.

"Right, but. . . does this mean you're leaving already?"

"Already?" Sif laughs. They'd both been waiting to be free of each other. But then Najah's eyes harden. The staggering disappointment on the young girl's face makes Sif admit something she has been denying to herself. There would be no going home yet. Her chest tightens with this new understanding. She can't just pass Najah off to another stranger, the way Jinta did. Even if she could, apparently the Church of Druga has some young, powerful cultist who can cut down a whole group of Ummun warriors. Sif can't go to whatever meager afterlife the deities might afford her and let her story be one of an old woman who greedily hoarded her last years at the expense of a young child's safety. She has to see Najah as far along as she can. Even if it means going all the way to their destination in Ravinser.

"You okay, Auntie?" Kisha asks. "You look upset. Did you know some of the others coming down?"

Sif shakes out of her reverie. "No, probably not."

"Do you need anything for the road back, then?" Kisha asks.

"No," Sif grunts. "I'm not turning around. We should head out now."

Najah's eyes soften, but not much.

They gather their things and begin the march again, quick as an arrow. Sif hadn't expected the Church of Druga to be this prepared, or quick. After all this time, the monarchs are finally getting their foothold in the last peaceful, free land in Atlas, and it is all because of this girl. Sif looks down on Najah, and an uncomfortable tension builds in her chest. A battle between care and blame. Najah meets her glance and nods, facing forward with a determined gleam in her eye, her hand on her dagger.

"Careful, little one," Kisha jokes.

Sif doesn't have the stomach for it.

Chapter 10

Young Sif, the Destroyer
Ponda, the market-city

In the middle distance gleams the market-city of Ponda. As they approach, sparse tufts of grass become more frequent under the hooves of the horses. The distant clatter and music and rustle of trade rises in volume. Ivon steals a glance at Efa, trying to see if she is afraid. Her otherwise stoic face is betrayed by a minimal crease in her brow, something only a person like Ivon, who is disposed towards reading others, would notice. If Sif and Buri have any particular feeling, they don't show it.

Outside of Ponda, Buri and Efa prepare for their duel. Sif loans Efa her sword, who takes it as a kindness, although Sif only does it because she thinks Buri can't lose.

Ivon finds the offer distasteful and suggests they stop in town first.

"Some things are worth taking the extra effort, love," they complain.

"Ivon," Sif mutters by their side. "When Buri kills her, we'll take her coin. Do you want whatever weapon she buys, or the money?"

They don't buy Sif's reasoning. "Could you really live with yourself if she kills him with your sword?"

Sif leans back from Ivon. Her face twists as if they had told a joke that offended her. "He won't lose. If he's brave enough to fight, you should be brave enough to believe in him."

Ivon grimaces. "I suppose."

Soon, the late noon sun hangs over Ponda, lighting up the stalls of fine, fluttering cloth and clutter of adobe and wood buildings that jut out from the land in beautiful, impractical disorder. A wash of golden light cradles the city. A small crowd of people in fashionable headscarves catch sight of their impending duel at the border and watch from a distance. Sif can smell the faint, heady scent of qahwa on the breeze.

Slowly, Buri and Efa approach each other. Ivon's heart hammers in their chest. What is the point of all this?

"Are you ready?" Buri's voice is deep as a mountain, and he holds his hammer as if he had been born with it. Efa shifts in her armor uncomfortably.

"I'm ready, giant."

They each offer a prayer to Aneir, then take a few steps back from each other. Efa's nerves betray her in the way her hand shakes, despite the steel in her eyes. Buri is placid and immovable. Serene. It's Sif who feels a strange, abrupt discomfort whisper in her heart.

Buri's lips move. He says something to Efa that neither Sif nor Ivon can make out. Efa pauses, then nods and adjusts the grip on her sword. After a beat, the two rush each other. She dodges his first attack, ducking under his hammer and moving to gut him. He parries her follow up and, quicker than the eye, crushes her chest. The onlookers gasp. Her ribs splinter audibly. The momentum carries her backwards, and she lands awkwardly in the sand. She is trying to take a breath, but cannot. Instead, she makes a loud, rasping, brutally painful gurgle.

"Fuck," Ivon swears. They turn away.

Buri approaches Efa. She holds her sword close to her chest as he leans down to her and pulls a knife from his boot, then swiftly ends her life. The sand under her body is already a deep red. Buri mutters something to her. Sorrow floods his features as he stands up. Then, with a deep breath, alone under the sun, he returns to himself.

Sif shakes her head. "She should've snuck away last night."

Ivon turns to face Sif. "Probably so, but you know how some of these warrior types are. They're not like us."

"Like us?"

Ivon sighs. "You know. They have. . ."

Ivon looks back at Efa, and in that moment they feel a stronger sense of connection to the woman than they ever did while she was alive. There is something in her that they now see in themself. Efa fought Buri for the same reason Ivon wants to tell their companions about the mage. But Efa, it seems, is stronger than they are. It doesn't bode well that it got her killed.

When Ivon meets Sif's gaze again, their eyes hold pools of despair.

"She can't run, Keno. It's not enough to live. She also has to live with herself."

-

In town, Ivon reveals that they know of a perfect spot to hole up, an out-of-the-way inn called Beqe's. Sif, who wants the freedom to stretch her legs a while, pushes against the idea, but Ivon's insistence—and assurance that they can get the group a good job there—wins her over, although just barely. In the true heart of Ponda is a monumental center of commerce. Ponda is near enough to all of the central kingdoms of the desert that it is the natural rest point for any traders on the way to Hvek, Phosita, or beyond. The streets pulse with life and display a dizzying array of color and texture. Sif, Buri, and Ivon abandon the mercenary joy of the town proper for its dim and cramped back alleys. As they do, Sif makes a mental note to come back to one of the stalls of food or houses of brilliantly dressed sex workers before they leave town. Her eyes linger on the sight of pretty men in ornate jewelry walking in and out of the brothel.

Beqe's is only a short walk from the market, but it feels worlds away. The wind picks up a chill. The lively nature of the main roads is replaced by a distant coughing. The homes are in clear disrepair when compared to the shops. Sif doesn't remember Ponda being like this.

"What happened to this place?" she wonders aloud.

"Nothing," Buri responds. "This is the market city. Their leaders care more for the markets than for their people, so the people suffer."

"I. . . guess I don't remember it," Sif admits.

Buri looks down at her with a shine in his eye and a slight smile, and reminds her. "You were busy chasing after that poet. The genderless one with curling black hair."

"Chasing? You make it sound like they weren't interested. First of all, Uncle, nob—"

"We're here," Ivon cuts off Sif, gesturing to Beqe's. The two-story building has only a very small sign above the door denoting what it is, and cracks in the walls that ensure anyone entering meets a minimum standard of courage.

The first floor is dark, filled with smoke and stained with years of piss and beer and gruel. Perfect if you don't want to run into a lot of people. Or, Ivon thinks bitterly, if you're planning to throw your truest friends into danger.

If the three of them are lucky, the mercenaries might have scattered after what happened at the desert ruins. Cut their losses and let the wind blow them to whatever corner of the continent in which they find comfort. If they're unlucky, then a company of moon-cursed profit-fighters will have been following them to Ponda.

Sif pats Ivon on the back. "You look tense. Let's have a drink."

Before anyone can argue, Sif is at the bar, paying with coin from Efa's pouch. Sif says a thanks to the dead woman's spirit and, uncharacteristically, mutters a prayer to Aneir for her soul. A very quick prayer.

In the corner of the first floor, where the dim light from the window doesn't reach, Ivon and Buri sit quietly for a moment.

"What?" Ivon asks, noticing they've caught Buri's attention. His single eye is trained in the distance, like he can see through them.

"You're upset," he remarks. His voice is even and still. He is neither making an accusation nor asking a question. He is stating a fact, and offering Ivon the chance to do what they want with the knowledge that Buri has noticed. Ivon takes a moment and considers how best to respond. Buri has always been more perceptive than he appears. But the words don't come out in time.

"You don't have to say anything." Buri grunts.

"I want to," Ivon starts, "but it's difficult—"

Sif slides into a chair beside them and slams three mugs of a golden-brown drink on the table. "What's difficult?" she asks. A broad, roguish smile hangs easily from her round face.

Ivon sighs and takes a mug. "Nothing. What are you so happy about?"

"Look around, blue eyes. We've escaped with our lives again, and the whole world is ahead of us."

"Not without some coin, love. I've got barely a single hauwling in my pocket. We were supposed to come out of those ruins with enough treasure to live comfortably for a while. We might not even have enough now to make it out of the central desert kingdoms and back to the riverlands."

From behind the bar, a woman calls out to them. She is thin and short, with close-shaved dark hair and a spatter of freckles across her nose. Her gaze, when it locks with Ivon's, is leaden with terrible meaning, and in that moment Ivon knows they are too far in to back out.

The bartender walks around her perch and heads towards them. "Hoping for work?"

Ivon nods, slowly. "You read my mind, dear."

"What do you got?" Sif asks.

The bartender crosses her arms and sighs. "Man named Henri owes me money. A lot of it."

"How much is a lot?" Ivon presses.

"Ten lidas and some change. I need someone to encourage him to pay up."

Sif and Buri trade a knowing look. With a few lidas, they could pick a direction and hole up there for weeks.

Sif sighs and turns to face the bartender. "How bad do you want me to hurt him?"

Buri grunts disapprovingly. He doesn't like the idea of fighting somebody potentially unarmed and in debt. Leaving aside the deities, it'd just be sad.

The bartender lights a pipe. The orange glow casts long shadows on her face above, cold eyes sparkling in the dark. "Bad. But don't kill him. Need the money first, yeah?"

"You want me to kill him after?"

She pauses to mull it over. "Probably not worth the trouble."

Across the table from Sif, Ivon is effortlessly wearing the guise of someone ready but not overly eager to accept. Still, they wonder if the job could be this simple. Did the Mages' Guild only want this man hurt? Surely the bartender is their contact.

Buri fixes his single green eye on the woman. "Is he armed?"

"Sure. Fancies himself a swordsman. He's just a drunk and a gambler."

"Deal, then." Sif stands, spits in her palm, and sticks her hand out. Surprisingly, the woman follows her lead and they shake.

The bartender directs Sif to the western district of Ponda, where she thinks Henri is staying. Despite Ivon's protest, Sif and Buri strike out on their own. They reason that after all of this travel, it will be better if Ivon sleeps now and keeps watch later when they return. Ivon is uncharacteristically reluctant to agree, but is forced to concede when Buri assures them it will be a simple, short job. Even if Buri's warm voice and kind words twist like a knife in the gut.

-

Sif and Buri walk quietly through the bruised sky night into the western district. Sif hasn't been there in at least a half-dozen years, but the memory of rotten wood and mud is fresh in her mind. If the eastern district has lost much of the liveliness of the markets, the western district has lost it all. It's the place where civilization eats itself to sustain growth elsewhere. Laborers are up late gambling. Elders are sitting drunk around a fire, sharing stories. Petty thieves huddle in alleyways, waiting for an opportunity that would be worth risking their lives for. The sudden cold pricks the hairs on Sif's arms.

"Uncle, what do you want to do after this?"

"Already doing it," he intones.

"Ugh." Sif fakes throwing up but has to hide her smile to do it. "Well, I'd like to find somewhere to lay low for a few months. Maybe near the Deer Paths, or on the west coast. Never been to some of the port towns there."

"Smells like fish," he says. Sif can just make out a twitch of disgust on his face, hidden by his bushy beard and eyepatch.

"Right, but it's hard work and that means lots of strong women. And men, in your case."

"Getting tired of boys chasing you around?"

"Goddess no, but I like the artists. Give me a man with a lute. Strong men are too full of themselves."

Buri chuckles to himself. "That is true, sometimes."

"Not saying you are."

"*You* are," Buri says with a glint in his emerald green eye.

Sif bursts out laughing. "You old bastard!"

Buri pushes her playfully, hard enough to surprise her but not enough to knock her over. She pretends to draw a dagger out of her boot and challenges him to a fight, at which he chuckles and declines. The two walk the rest of the way in silent good cheer, basking in the familiar warmth of old friendship, unaware of the horror awaiting them.

Chapter II

Najah

The northern woods

Wooden charms hang from the high, yawning branches of oak trees. They twist in the wind, spinning on threads of twine, each carved with prayers beseeching deities for protection and spirits for leniency. Below them all, Najah hops over rolling roots and slick patches of moss. Some time ago, she had walked ahead as Sif and Kisha fell behind to discuss their plan to reach Ravinser. In the silence, Najah communes with the tree frogs, the buzzing insects, and the harrowed, ever-running rabbits.

A twig snaps behind her. "Hey you." Najah turns to see Kisha grinning at her, cutting pieces from an apple with a long, wooden-handled knife.

"Hey," Najah says.

"Want a slice?" Kisha asks, holding out the apple.

Najah looks Kisha up and down. She has a strong form, a spirit that is strangely at ease with the horror of surviving an attack. Maybe Kisha is like her. Someone who survives. Maybe someone who survives even better than she has, since Kisha still feels like smiling.

"You in there?" Kisha jokes, waving a hand in the air.

"Yeah, sorry. No, I'm not hungry right now."

Kisha examines Najah's face. Her grin droops and brows draw together in concern. "You okay?"

Overhead, the clouds have turned gray, and droplets of water begin to patter softly on the leaves and dirt. The smell of fresh rain and old forest. Above, a bird returns to its nest. Najah's heart is torn between the distraction of the forest's song and the necessity of unburdening herself.

"I miss my mom," Najah admits, turning her head so Kisha can't see her blinking back tears. She touches her mother's necklace reflexively, feeling the smooth wood of the fox pendant with her thumb. The twine is rough on her neck, but she hasn't taken it off intentionally since the first time she put it on.

Kisha only nods and continues slicing and eating pieces of apple. Najah doesn't know what she's waiting for, only that she wants the hole in her heart to disappear. Running all her young life is bad enough, but the anger and sadness makes it worse. Najah would give anything to have a home or a family, but she doesn't even have anything to give. Still, Kisha only silently muses over her apple.

"Why did you decide to come with us?" Najah asks. The child in her secretly prays to find a friend in Kisha, even as the survivor in her works to kill that hope.

"I came for you, kid," Kisha responds, very matter-of-factly.

"Why, though?"

Kisha tosses the apple over her shoulder. "Hells, you have a lot of questions, huh?"

"So what?" Najah does her best to make a brave face for the second strange warrior who has come into her life. Making a brave face is easier than feeling it, though.

Kisha chuckles, like she can see right through Najah. There is a warmth to her laugh, though. Not a kindness, but like maybe Kisha is impressed. *Almost* how Sif sounds when Najah makes the old woman laugh.

"I did it because I want to," Kisha says. "There'll be a lot of fighting to do, and I like to win. Lot of winning means a lot of coin. Besides, you need me."

"ou're here for the money," Najah accuses, even though she doesn't

that is what Kisha meant.

en tosses Najah the last apple slice. "It's how I afford this

ne on, Sif is finding us a place to wait out the rain."

Najah follows behind, expecting a short, quiet walk, but Kisha begins talking again almost immediately.

"I'm with you because when I was a little girl, I heard stories about Keno Sif. And when I was a little older, I met her when she came to my town for a few days. I've always been good at killing. When you're good at something, you hear a lot about people who are better. Get it?"

"Yeah."

"Good. So, when I was your age, I wanted to be like Sif. Strong. I got word Keno Sif is alive, and now that I'm older, I wanted to see what the big deal was. You should've seen how afraid the civilized lands were of her back in the day. To some of us, she was a legend."

"So, you didn't come for me." Najah tries to hide the bitterness in her heart. She wants to sound self-assured, like the woman walking with her does, like she is impossible to wound.

"It can be both," Kisha insists with a smile. And despite her question not being entirely answered, Kisha's smile is so charming that Najah thinks maybe that is good enough. Maybe this isn't everything she wants, but it can be good enough.

The forest floor turns to mud as the rain picks up. Lightning burns in the distant sky. In the mud, Najah can make out the tracks they're following Sif by. The patter of droplets on the leaves above them becomes louder.

"Why is Sif here?" she asks Kisha. It's something Najah had been wondering. Maybe she doesn't mind having the old woman around, but when Najah asked if she was leaving already, Sif had laughed at her. The wound is still fresh. For a moment before then, it had felt like they were friends. It shouldn't be a surprise, she thinks. From what Sif said when they met, the whole trip is an unwanted burden.

"Sif is a killer," Kisha responds, matter-of-factly. "She's left an ocean of blood in her path, and Jinta Vol is hoping Sif will be so busy killing that she'll also manage to keep you safe."

Najah freezes. That wasn't what she had asked at all, but the shock of Kisha's answer left her almost speechless. "I don't believe you."

"It's true. They call her the Destroyer because she killed the King of Phosita. Legend is, she killed most of the army, too. I hear a bunch of people went missing. That country is still fucked. She went after the Queen of Hvek as well."

Najah doesn't know what to say, or to think. Why had her mother, who remained a staunch pacifist to her last breath, want help from these northerners? It couldn't possibly be that she meant to deliver her daughter into the hands of remorseless murderers.

"Ah, I'm sorry," Kisha adds sheepishly. "I didn't mean to scare you. I'm a killer, too. So are all the paladins after us. Everyone in the world is a killer. Better to be on the side with the best ones."

In the distance, Najah can see Sif starting a small fire under a rocky outcropping. It is difficult to account for the old woman who told her how to fight off a kidnapper being the same person as Sif the Destroyer, who picked fights with the rulers of Phosita and Hvek. The tension in Najah's stomach sends a small ripple of nausea up through her. Her mind is overtaken by a terrible curiosity, and even if Sif is not who Kisha says, Najah can't help but wonder what things Sif has done to earn her reputation.

"Is it really safe?" Najah asks.

Kisha meets Najah's eyes, smiling devilishly. "Nothing in this world is safe. But that's the fun of it. Stick close to me. I'll protect you."

Chapter 12

Old Sif, the Hermit
The northern woods

Over the last several days Sif, Najah, and Kisha fall into a comfortable acquaintance. For the most part, Kisha and Najah walk together. Kisha is much better with children than Sif. Or must be, because Sif can't help but notice that there is new and noticeable gulf between her and the two of them. It makes sense. Kisha is still young and strong. She has a weightless cheer that is undampened by difficult travel, and a boundless confidence that, although it borders on aggravating to Sif, must be reassuring to a child. Sif figures it all suits her fine. She didn't come along to make friends, she did it to help the temple.

"So, what's the plan anyways, Auntie?" Kisha asks one afternoon as they crash through the deep forest. "We're heading for Fal River?"

"Yup," Sif grunts.

Kisha nods agreeably. "So is the plan to take a boat to the ocean and head south?"

"Uh-huh."

"Good call. Easy way to get to where Ravinser used to be."

Sif freezes. "Used to be?"

Kisha passes her, but slows to a halt as she realizes Sif has stopped. Najah keeps walking, as if she is trying to put some distance between them. Kisha meets Sif's stony gaze. "Yeah, Ravinser burned down years ago. I thought you knew."

"Shit," Sif swears. "You know where it is, though? You've seen the ruins?"

"Yeah, yeah. I happened to travel through a few years ago. It was a logging town, or something. Got burned to a crisp. Najah really didn't tell you? I thought the whole point was to get her there."

In the distance Najah leaps off a log after a fat, brown toad. "No, she didn't say anything."

The tension in the air is palpable. Eventually, Kisha lowers her voice and says, "Not really normal right? She has to know. Between you and me, this whole job is fucking odd. Too many unknowns to account for."

In the distance, Najah jumps over a fallen tree covered in thick, green moss. Motes of pollen dance in the golden beams of sunlight warming the forest floor.

"She's young," Sif responds, brushing off Kisha's odd line of thought. "She could have forgotten. Or maybe it happened after her family left."

Kisha is unconvinced. "Thing is, we talked about Ravinser the other day. I don't remember everything we said, but I got the feeling she did know."

"She said she knew?" Sif asks, despite herself.

"Eh. . ." Kisha hesitates. "We sort of talked *around* it, if you know what I mean. Maybe I misunderstood."

Sif releases a heavy sigh. "Alright. For now, we make our way to Fal River. Upstream in the west is a walled port city, Ambre. We can rest there, find a decent map, and figure out what to do next."

Very suddenly, the sense of being out of place overcomes her. She looks back and forth between Kisha and Najah, then looks again. A trio of birds rustle in the tree branches above them. Rays of afternoon light dapple the forest floor below her. Suddenly, Sif has the feeling that she's been moving without knowing why for some time. It's something she has never felt before and, justified or not, she finds herself mistrusting both Najah and Kisha.

In the distance, Najah yells that she can hear water. They must be nearing the riverlands.

"Don't go too far," Kisha calls out, in a sing-song voice.

From just out of sight, Najah shrieks, "Help!"

The forest erupts into a blur of green as Sif and Kisha take off. Branches scratch Sif's arms and face. Animals scatter on their approach. Najah continues to yell, but Sif can't tell what. By the time Najah is in sight, Kisha has already met her and cut down a man with an axe and bow. Sif only catches the arc of blood before his body hits the ground. Najah is scrambling up from the dirt. Her dagger gleams among a patch of weeds, where the young girl had tried and failed to draw it.

"What happened?!" Sif barks.

"H-he just appeared out of nowhere, a-and I didn't know where you were —"

"It's okay, you're safe," Kisha says, soothingly. "He was just a scout."

"These are hunter's clothes," Sif says, bending to examine the man's garments. A woodcutter's axe, a bow that appears handmade, and clothing made from cotton and leather.

"He's a scout. He recognized me," Kisha affirms.

Sif looks to Najah, who nods. Her eyes are still wide, body shaking.

"H-he did. He said her name."

"Word must have gotten out about the fight before we ran into each other," Kisha admits with a grimace.

The forest doesn't feel so peaceful anymore. All of the things Sif had been noticing, the rustle of leaves, the sounds of life, take on a sinister new meaning.

"We need to keep moving, now. Faster. Even if the Church isn't behind us, they'll eventually notice when a scout doesn't return. Once we make it to the river, we can hop a boat."

What Sif doesn't say is that it is still several days to the river, at best. That if the Church of Druga has scouts here, they probably already know the river is their destination, and have sent soldiers ahead. The Church of Druga may not have a kingdom of their own, but they have friends in the most powerful monarchies on the continent. At this point, the three of them might as well be walking in the dark.

They walk on anyways. Najah first, probably eager to escape the sight of the dead scout.

"Hey, kid!" Sif shouts. Najah turns to face her, a mixture of fear and bewilderment and anger on the young girl's face.

Sif bends down, scooping something up from the forest floor, and presents it to Najah, hilt first. It's her dagger, almost lost but still shining like silver in the daylight.

"You forgot this."

"Good eye," Kisha remarks, ivory teeth barely peeking out behind a subtle grin.

Chapter 13

Old Sif, the Hermit
The banks of Fal River

Three days later, early in the morning as the first blush of sunlight yawns above the horizon, the three of them approach the edge of the forest. Kisha and Najah, walking ahead of Sif once more, name the animals they see in the bushes and trees. Moon beetles, red fox, and a rat snake; powder-blue woodpeckers, golden-ringed dragonflies, and any number of nimble, chittering squirrels. The energy that filled Sif earlier in their journey has depleted now and taken something more from her on its exit. Her boots feel full of rocks when she lifts them over the brush or hops over a stream. On reflection, she hasn't slept much. Her mind continues to return to Buri, to his last words, as if there's something his memory has to impart to her, but her mind is so numb that no such revelation appears. The forest waves back and forth around her in a dreamlike glow as the afternoon lulls on. The only thing that brings her back from her trance is the sound of Kisha and Najah yelling for her.

"Hey, Sif! There's a small tavern up ahead. We should see if they'll give us directions."

She shakes the clouds from her mind and jogs ahead to catch up with them. The tavern breaks into view just past the treeline. The sight of mostly open sky is a relief. It means the chances of an ambush have fallen. Besides that, the tavern is situated on the banks of Fal River. The rush of water can be seen and heard just past it to the south, and a dirt road going east to west leads off the building. Old, tall, and made of sturdy wood, it boasts a modest sign above the door that reads, "Lopes and Sons."

The door lets out onto bright planks of creaking wood, cleanly swept and polished. Dozens of small tables rest under the haze of daylight that breaks through one of a half-dozen windows placed evenly around the building, most decorated with the names and images of several deities known in this part of the world: Druga, Een, Shen, Asthia, and Nnedsu. The Lunar Goddess of Death is depicted as the full moon, and known by her title rather than her name, as knowledge of either is forbidden to the living. Sif can't help but notice the exclusion of Siduri and Aneir. Just on the other side of the door is a small statuette of Daado, the patron saint of travelers, practically identical to the one at the foot of Mount Hoda. Too far south for Saint Buri of Feigrvoller, Sif supposes.

"Beware, ladies. We're in the presence of holy people," Kisha jokes. Until that moment Sif hasn't given much thought to which deity, if any, Kisha tends toward. From Kisha's joke, it seems like none. It's unusual but not unheard of. There is a path for almost everyone who wants one. For Sif, Siduri was the obvious choice because she offered excitement with very few rules.

Exhausted beyond her means, Najah picks a table to lay her head down on. Kisha and Sif walk up to the counter, but the proprietor is out of sight. The only people in the building, as far as they can tell, are three men drinking in a corner, covered in dirt and wearing grass-stained tunics.

"Hello!" Kisha cries out. "Anyone here?"

From the back, three people appear. A middle-aged woman and slightly younger man carry an empty basket out the back door, while an old man splits from them and trudges over on a wooden cane. He's tall and lanky, with a mop of thick, gray hair, and a face marked by stubble. He doesn't have the physique of a fighter but he looks to be blind in one eye. The price of a long life on the continent; between herself, Buri, Ivon, and Sunnhilde, only one of them had escaped some kind of disfigurement. Or worse.

The old man utters his greeting in a hoarse, raspy voice. "Good afternoon. What can I do for you? Need a room?"

"Just some directions, old man. And, uh," Kisha motions at Sif with her thumb, "a drink for me and my friend." She turns to Sif. "On me, Auntie."

"You sure?" Sif snorts. She remembers what traveling was like at that age, hardly a coin to spare sometimes, even for a warm bed and decent food. It probably didn't help Sif that Siduri frowned at holding onto coin for too long. To her surprise, Kisha pats a pouch at her side that jingles with an abundance of coin.

"You've been carrying a fortune with you since Ummun?"

"I make money everywhere I go," she responds coolly. "No shortage of people who need muscle."

"Some things never change," Sif replies. Her whole body sings with relief as she takes a seat at the bar.

Kisha offers a single, breathy *ha*. Half a laugh, less like Sif had said something funny, and more like she had touched on something Kisha had in mind. "You might be surprised."

Before she sits down, Kisha turns to Najah and calls her name. Nothing.

"Hey, kid! You awake?"

Sif tenses at first, thinking maybe something is wrong before she remembers the curse. Guess that is still something wrong, but at least she's already sitting down this time. Like always, Najah seems to be having a nightmare. The sight of it makes Sif uneasy. The old man sets their drinks down and opens his mouth to speak, but Kisha waves him off to get a private moment with Sif.

"We should talk, Auntie."

"*Sif* is fine," the older woman responds, taking a long sip of her drink.

"Oh? That's fine. I'll just speak my mind, then. What do you think the Church of Druga wants with Najah?"

"Eh? No clue. Jinta wants me to find out. I figure we'll have plenty of time to think it over in between here and Ravinser."

"The town that doesn't exist," Kisha adds.

Sif eyes Kisha impatiently. "Just say what you want to say."

"We're taking a kid we don't know to a place that doesn't exist, for reasons we aren't sure of. For what? To save her from a fate that we don't know anything about, either."

"So, you want to stop traveling and what? Investigate?"

"No," Kisha shakes her head. "I think we need to hand her over, in exchange for the safety of Feigrvoller and a fat pouch of lidas. The Church has ties in almost every kingdom. You're a lot older than you used to be, and I'm only one person. Besides, even if they're going to hurt her, which we don't know, it's just as likely that our little adventure here is going to antagonize the paladins into burning Siduri's temple back in Feigrvoller before we can find any answers."

Sif drains the rest of her cup and pauses to stare off in the distance.

"You just going to stay quiet?" Kisha asks.

". . .you keep saying Feigrvoller," Sif responds.

"So?" Kisha asks, like Sif is dumb for pointing it out.

Sif turns to face Kisha. "Tell me your name."

Kisha narrows her eyes. "You already know it. Kisha."

"Not Kisha Sif?"

Kisha erupts into laughter. "Alright, alright. Fuck."

Sif curses herself for not realizing it earlier. Kisha isn't from Ummun. A warrior from Ummun would introduce themselves with a surname, and that surname would probably be Sif. Now Kisha is talking about Feigrvoller, when she should be talking about Ummun. Sif thinks back to when they met at the camp. The arrows in the tree. Kisha was somehow the only person to survive her battle, but the only blood on her was on her boots.

"You killed the warriors from Ummun, right? When you said the paladins had a strong woman with them, you meant yourself."

"You got me, Auntie. I couldn't resist that little joke. I would've cut you both down when we first met, but I recognized you. We met once before, you know? I'm from Feigrvoller, just like Buri. I was at his funeral."

Sif's heart seizes. A heavy weight regains its footing in her chest.

"Nothing I just said about this little journey was a lie. The kid doesn't even like you. Let's just hand her over while she's asleep. She'll wake up in custody. You won't even have to see her face. We can split the bounty and have some *real* fun." Kisha pats her sword scabbard and grins.

Sif curls her upper lip. "You're an embarrassment to Feigrvoller. Buri would be ashamed of you. It'd be better to die than to make your money killing for them."

Kisha shoots up, knocking her chair over. It slams into the ground and tumbles along, rolling to a stop in front of the single occupied table. Najah doesn't even flinch at the sound.

"What do you know, eh?! Old woman too scared to come down off her mountain. You were *powerful*. You could have had money, titles, lovers, thrones, anything! But you just let yourself get old and pathetic. Coward!"

Sif stands up and puts a hand on her sword. "A waste of words, coming from someone willing to give a child to torturers if it'll avoid a difficult fight."

Kisha's face is bright red. Rage courses through every muscle in her body. This is not how she pictured this conversation going. Maybe that is why, when the old man approaches and asks them to take their quarrel outside, she draws her sword and separates the man's head from his body. The other patrons leap from their seats and sprint for the door, knocking over chairs and tables.

The movement jostles Najah, who slips from her seat and crashes onto the floor with a sickening thump. Sif turns to help her, but Kisha kicks the old woman hard in her ribs, sending her to the ground.

"Whatever, you old hag. I didn't want to have to kill you, but if you don't want to move on with the rest of the world, fine."

Kisha thrusts her sword downwards, hoping to pierce Sif's leather armor. She narrowly knocks the blade aside with her own and catches Kisha's arm on the backstroke. The attack clangs off of the vambrace protecting Kisha's forearm.

Kisha stomps on Sif's chest, knocking the air from her lungs, then raises her sword high for a killing blow. Still struggling for air, Sif strains forward and wraps her arms around Kisha's leg, then thrusts her whole body backwards. They roll to the ground, all swinging limbs and bared teeth. Kisha's face crunches against the boards, breaking her nose. The two jump up to face each other on even ground.

"Okay, okay." Kisha spits. Blood streams down her face from nose to neck. "Maybe you still have a little fire left in you. I saw you struggling through the forest, though. You can't beat me. I'm not like those assholes you killed at the temple."

Sif grinds her teeth. "How did you know about that?"

"Same way I found you so fast, fool. The mountains are swarming with people working for the Church of Druga. You *really* don't know how important the kid is to those freaks. She must be some priest's illegitimate daughter."

Sif hurls a mug from the bar at Kisha's skull, interrupting her monologue. The old woman races forward, thrusting her sword at a gap in Kisha's armor, but Kisha is too fast. The younger woman steps forward, letting her plate take the blow. Sif's sword bounces away with a pathetic *clink* as its wielder stumbles into Kisha's fist. Blood rolls down her eyes, darkening her vision. She swings her sword haphazardly, hoping to hit Kisha, or at least keep her awa͟   enough to recover. Her blade cuts through the air uselessly.

͟u! You're already winded! Are you serious right now? This is

͟an't believe you're the woman who killed King Ottson."

replaced with calm self-assurance.

Sif doubles over, taking heavy breaths, trying to keep an eye on Kisha through the blood running down her face.

"Killing him wasn't the hard part," she rasps. "The hard part was getting close enough."

"I'll keep it in mind," Kisha sneers. "Say hey to The Giant for me."

Kisha knows her opponent is weakened. She risked a lot to travel with Sif and try to convince her to change sides, but at least now she'll get to say she killed a legend. She thrusts forward for the fatal blow.

Sif grins unexpectedly and meets her lunge, expertly deflecting the attack downwards, and opening Kisha up for an attack. Kisha roars.

It was clear Sif couldn't win in a head-to-head fight, so instead she used Kisha's arrogance against her.

Killing him wasn't the hard part. The hard part was getting close enough.

Kisha grinds her teeth. The old woman had bragged about the plan right to her face. Sif's sword slices through the air, glancing off an embellishment at the top of Kisha's breastplate rather than slicing through her neck. Sif lets the momentum carry her past Kisha, turns her sword, and strikes the younger woman's right leg. This time, the blade connects with flesh. Kisha drops to one knee, unable to support the weight of her armor on the injured leg.

"That was a cheap trick, you old hag."

Sif snorts loudly, then spits a mixture of blood and snot. "You're just mad you lost. I've known hundreds of people like you, Kisha. Got any last words?"

"You haven't met anyone like me, and I haven't lost yet." Kisha picks the pewter mug up from the floor and flings it at Sif. It hits her above the eye hard enough to make her flinch.

Sif steps back, thinking Kisha is going to use the same trick Sif had used a moment before. She is only partly right. Kisha pulls a dagger from her belt and lets it fly. Bewildering agony erupts from Sif's chest, and she collapses to the floor.

From outside come the sounds of wagon wheels and horses. As her vision flickers and mind swims, Sif thinks to herself that one of the men who ran must have led a caravan here. A loud, masculine voice pleads with someone for help.

Sif's face twists with exertion. She prepares to pull the dagger out of her chest and defend herself. The floorboards are cold and smooth on her cheek. The metallic scent of freshly spilled blood lingers in the air. Kisha unstraps her breastplate, losing enough weight to walk, and begins to limp towards Najah. Sif steels herself for the pain, then leaps up from the floor towards Najah, dragging herself the rest of the way when she lands. Sif rips the dagger out of herself and holds it towards Kisha. Blood splatters on the floor. Sif's hands shake from the wave of wooziness threatening to sink her. Kisha's eyes dart to the windows, where a gang of newcomers rushes towards the inn.

"I'll get you next time, Auntie. You got lucky. See you in Ravinser."

Kisha moves towards the back door just when the middle-aged woman and young man come back in. Kisha pushes them away and the woman tumbles into the mud outside, but the young man digs his fingers into the doorframe, trying to resist. He lets out a heartbreaking wail at the sight of the old man's corpse, and swings his fist at Kisha. Kisha guts him with the same ceremony she might use to brush away a fly. The back door closes behind her. Behind it, the woman starts to cry for help, then falls silent.

Sif lifts her voice in an ursine bellow, daring Kisha to come back and fight. She rages like that until the travelers outside come in the tavern and find her passed out on the floor, still shielding Najah with her body.

Chapter 14

Young Sif, the Destroyer
Ponda, the market-city

Keno Sif and Buri the Giant wait in an alleyway across the street from where Henri the maybe-swordsman is supposed to be hiding. It's a small building that could be a home, except for all the noise inside. Jeering and arguing and the twang of an out-of-tune instrument clatter dimly into the road with the bleary yellow candlelight. The dirt road in front of the building has been churned into thick mud, covered in boot prints from the comings and goings of people. The western district of Ponda is on the lower end of a hill, and everything up east drains down west and then just. . . sits. Some areas don't dry at all, and stay covered in slick muck and mosquitos.

A flash of memory lights up Sif's mind, and she recalls coming to Ponda as a young girl. Even accompanied by Buri and a caravan of actors and musicians, shopkeepers would scowl at her and try to shoo her away, worried that she would try to steal from them or make their well-off customers feel uncomfortable. More than one complained that she shouldn't have left the western district. She guesses this was where they meant. As a kid she was already used to people treating her oddly for being a northern *barbarian*, but it was always worse in the bigger towns with lavish markets. People thought she was stupid because she didn't understand how the market worked at first, but she'd figured if anyone was stupid it had to be the people who decided to put the extra hurdle of money in between them and the things they needed. Even being brave and strong for a kid, she would've starved within months if she hadn't run across a temple to Siduri, and eventually Buri.

Sif groans. The boredom is too much. Her mind keeps wandering to unpleasant memories.

Buri raises an eyebrow.

"I shouldn't have agreed to this so quick," Sif grumbles. "Why do I listen to Ivon? Maybe we just knock this guy out and empty his pockets?"

"He won't have money," Buri responds in his deep, growl of a voice. A fair point.

"Definitely not any lidas. Fuck this." Sif stomps towards the building, ready to crack skulls, but right as she is reaching the point of no return, Henri staggers out in front of them and down the street, unseen to anyone but Sif, Buri, and the frozen stars above. His clothes were clearly fine once, but are now stained and show signs of wear. His hair is curly and unkempt. His red eyes and unshaven face give him the air of someone who took a night of carousing and stretched it out into weeks or months. As the door swings shut, Sif catches a glimpse of gamblers playing cards around a table. It explains a lot.

"This is our chance," Sif says, but Buri puts a hand on her shoulder.

"We should see where he is going. It will be easier if we know where he lives."

"He might be heading to meet more people, Uncle." It could be true, but it doesn't take someone who knows her as well as Buri does to realize she just wants to be done with the job.

"We have time," Buri assures her. She groans, but has to agree. Unless he's walking into a crowded guard tower, how much danger could more people possibly pose? A few drunks, gamblers, or cutthroats won't stop them.

"Fine," she grumbles. "Let's keep our distance for now."

The walk is longer than expected, just darkened road after darkened road. Dead flowers hang potted on a windowsill. Mangy dogs snap at each other over scraps. Sif tosses a couple coins to a young boy begging at the mouth of an alley, which makes Buri smile. At some point Henri stops and washes his face in a fountain, staring morosely at his reflection in the rippling water for a long minute afterward. The statue in the middle is of a merchant-soldier, clearly neglected in this century and given over to moss and time. Washing his face doesn't help; Henri looks like he's been living double the life in a normal amount of time. He resumes his stroll just as haggard as before, only with the addition of being damp.

Eventually Henri enters a mud-and-wood home and Sif begins preparing herself for the fight, scanning the area for details that might alert her to potential hazards. Candles are still lit inside, orange light visible through shuttered windows. There is definitely someone other than Henri inside, but it's hard to say how many more. Sif squints her eyes and leans forward, trying to pick up on movement or noise. It's no use. A few homes over a group of locals are loudly, drunkenly, shouting at one another.

If they give Henri a few minutes to get settled and start to doze off, it might be a quick fight. With any luck, their sudden entrance will surprise anyone else in the home. As the night lingers on, the streets become entirely deserted. Sif is about to voice her thoughts when Henri exits the building, trailed by someone carrying a hatchet. This new person has an eyepatch, greasy blond hair, and the physique of a dockworker. Despite her desire to close the knot on this job quickly, Sif finds herself curious about what the two might be up to. It's become clear that Henri is doing more than taking a long walk home. Cold silence carries the sound of Henri's friend chiding him for being drunk, and the joyful whispers of a possible windfall that's set to make the both of them wealthy within a few months. In time, the two arrive in front of a guard tower.

"Just our luck. . ." Sif grumbles. Of course Henri would go to a guard tower after she had joked about it earlier. But as they get closer, it doesn't seem like the tower is occupied. At least not by a regiment of city guards. The blue and cream-colored banner hanging from the top floor is poorly maintained and only a faint trace of candlelight escapes from inside, on the first floor. An acrid scent lingers around the perimeter that makes Sif's eyes water. Buri, on the other hand, seems barely affected.

"What is your deal? Having the one eye helping that much?"

Buri pulls his mustache. "Filters the scent."

"Ha ha," she responds, deadpan.

They creep up to the side of the tower and peek in through an open window. If there ever were guards here, they haven't been around in a long time. Somebody has set up rows of ground herbs and discolored liquids in a variety of glass containers. Maps are scattered across the walls and tables, while stacks of leatherbound books crowd the floorspace.

Buri grunts unhappily. "Alchemist's workshop."

At best that means poisoner; at worst, it means a mage.

"Let's do this before anyone else shows up," Sif suggests.

Buri nods. They circle around to the front door and, on a silent count, kick it open. Wood near the lock splinters. Henri and his companion jump back in surprise, bleary eyes wide with fresh shock. Sif and Buri rush forward, but before Sif can start to shake him down, Henri draws his weapon. The foil gleams dully in the faint candlelight and Sif laughs despite herself. The man carries a sword for fencing? To her mind, it's a weapon more suited to sport than real combat. Henri's face turns from a ruddy, tanned white to maroon, and he lunges at her. Henri's companion tries to back him up, but is intercepted by Buri. Henri's messy lunges don't take much effort to swat aside, and Sif does her best not to kill the fool.

"Put your damn sword down, Henri, and listen to me before I fuck your life up."

While Sif doesn't register it at the time, she will recount the sound that comes next as deafening. A glass container scrapes against a wooden table as Henri's friend picks it up and hurls it across the room. The vial shatters against Sif's cheek, and whatever abhorrent mixture is inside of it catches fire when exposed to the air. Agonizing, searing pain explodes across her face as it is consumed by a sickly green flame. The light, so close to her eyes, is blinding. She howls out, her voice heavy with rage, pain, and fear. She swats pointlessly at the flame. Embedded glass knifes her palm, and inextinguishable fire scalds her fingers. Tears running down her face evaporate before they can fall. It is over in moments, but the agony drags on. Like marching across the desert on foot, under an ever-burning sky.

Sif writhes on the floor, clutching her face. Through her blurring vision, she sees the rest of the fight, but can't make out the details. From the doorway, a dark figure leans down towards her with a glass vial. Sif can't do anything but drink as the figure coaxes a bitter liquid past her lips. Like a flash, the pain is extinguished. Sif looks up at her rescuer. She has a round face, framed by delicate curls of red hair. Golden rings adorn her right ear and nostril. She wears layers of hemp and cotton traveler's clothes in varieties of earth tones, and, notably, a very fashionable forest green. Her hands are adorned with intricate rings. A small scar runs along her forehead, only narrowly visible from Sif's point of view on the floor. She smiles fondly at Sif, as if they had met before.

"Well, well. You two killed my bodyguards."

Knowing nothing other than Sif's recent pain and the danger of proximity, Buri leaps at the woman.

"Sleep," she suggests. In a fraction of a second, Buri crumbles to the floor like a puppet with cut strings. Sif, still hobbled by the shock and pain that flooded her body, throws a clumsy haymaker at the red-haired woman's knees. The woman easily dodges it with a nimble step backwards.

"Witch!" Sif growls. Hate thickens every letter of the accusation. She rolls sloppily to her feet, grabbing her sword off the ground in one smooth motion.

"Go to sleep," the witch commands.

Despite herself, Sif obeys.

Agartha is a city in a hole in the sea
At the end of the world
In the pitch of a dream
The prison of hope
The gnashing of teeth
Agartha is a city in a hole in the sea.

-

"You awake yet?"

When she comes to, Sif tries to gather her thoughts. She feels disordered and exhausted. Her skin is drenched in clammy sweat, and a headache is crashing around the inside of her skull. Beside her, Buri is tied to a chair and the sight of her friend makes her struggle against her own restraints. A thick coil of rope wraps around her arms, chest, and legs. They're in a small stone room lit by torches. There are no windows that she can see. No weapons or implements of torture, which is a small relief. This isn't the first time she's woken up a captive. As she comes back to herself, the pain in her cheek renews itself. Sif is suddenly and acutely aware of a bandage on her face. A cold ointment underneath sits uncomfortably against her skin.

"I need to see myself," she mumbles. The man who woke her takes a step forward, as if inspecting her. Sif struggles to lift her head enough to look him in the eye. He's old, with steady hands and dark, wrinkled skin. He is going bald on the crown of his head, and his face holds a paternal sort of countenance that suggests a patient and intelligent mind. Not the face, Sif hopes, of a jailor.

"I can help you with that," he confirms. "But we should talk first. My name is Ejigu. You're Keno Sif, is that correct?"

Sif nods. "Yeah." Her throat is parched and the word comes out as a croak.

"I was told you follow Siduri. Is that true?"

Sif nods again. "Yeah."

"Then you're in the right place. I am a priest of the Dancing Goddess. I have something I'd like to give you. If you take it, it will wake you up. Are you comfortable with that?"

Though still groggy, Sif nods for the third time.

Ejigu holds a small wooden board up to her with powdered mushrooms laid out on it. Sif recognizes the powder as eidolen goldcaps—mushrooms that grow in the north, although not anywhere near her home in Ummun. She snorts the powder and a rush of energy floods through her body in less than a dozen heartbeats. The goldcaps make her furiously blink back tears, and the pain in her cheek becomes more acute, but she feels like she could fight two dozen brawlers and then go out dancing. The sudden, overwhelming clarity allows her to focus on her surroundings with renewed attention. Small, stone statues of a woman dancing and smoking a pipe are set into rough cutouts in the walls. Ejigu's robes are a southern variation of the monks' robes she has seen up north. Somehow, she and Buri have ended up in a temple of Siduri.

Sif nods her head in Buri's direction. "Is he alive?"

The man nods. "Yes, he is perfectly fine. A good friend of mine brought you here to heal, but she was worried you might attack me if you woke up unrestrained."

Sif takes a moment to think about that. It was a fair assumption. Nothing unites the continent of Atlas as much as the hatred and mistrust of magicians. If the witch was here, Sif surely would try to kill her.

"So, what now?" she asks. "I won't hurt you. Not unless you're thinking to keep me tied up."

"I appreciate your understanding, sister. Now I'm going to make you an offer, and then let you go."

"Yeah?" Sif asks. "And if I say no to your offer?"

The man takes her words with patience. "I'm not going to hurt you, or make you do anything against your will. As I explained, the ropes are for my own safety. Will you listen to my offer?"

Sif looks back at Buri. Through her watery eyes she can see his chest rise and fall.

"Yeah, I'll listen. Ropes off first."

The old monk walks behind her, his cane tapping against the floorboards. Sif feels the ropes around her wrist loosen. She rubs the spot where ropes have left her skin a little raw and, cautiously, brushes the side of her face where she had been burned. It stings a little, but whatever is under the bandage helps.

"Alright, Ejigu. What do you want?"

"The woman you fought, and who brought you here, is named Sunnhilde. She is a worshipper of our lady Siduri, and one of the most brilliant people alive. Everything she says and does, I put my faith in. She has never yet let me down. Whatever happened—"

"I get it," Sif snaps, still irritable from the direction of her night and even more so because of Ejigu's sympathy with the witch. "Cut to it."

"Sunnhilde is going on a long voyage across the sea. It will be very dangerous, but very lucrative. The two people you killed were her bodyguards."

Sif laughs, then winces as the movement causes a fresh stab of pain along the side of her face. "And she's offering us the job?"

Ejigu smiles. "Exactly. Sunnhilde is a good woman. She isn't holding a grudge against you. When she dropped you off, she was worried for your health and hopeful about your response."

"She can be as good as she wants, I wasn't born yesterday. I won't put our souls in the hands of a witch."

"A witch?" Ejigu seems amused by the statement.

"She put me to sleep with a wave of her hand."

Ejigu chuckles. "No. I told you, she is a very smart woman. And an alchemist. Among other things. She doesn't serve the Three Mothers of Demons."

"Fine." Sif doesn't buy it, but finds herself drawn in nonetheless. "Let's say she doesn't. We'd still need to talk payment. What is she offering?"

"It is a journey to find treasure. Your payment depends on what you find."

"Oh yeah? Where is all this treasure, then?"

"A lost city in the sea. I believe Sunnhilde called it Agartha."

Chapter 15

Old Sif, the Hermit
Fal River

The dock is only a few days ride west. Sif was lucky to be wearing thick leather when she fought Kisha and her wounds are minimal, although they don't heal as quickly as expected. The owners of the wagon, the people who had saved her and Najah, were headed west already and offered to let the two of them ride along. The wagon is cramped, most of the space taken up by barrels of fruit, but it is at least out of the sun, allowing Sif to sleep in peace as she recovers.

They arrive just in time for the ship setting off to Ambre, but when Najah tries to run aboard, Sif stops her.

"Kisha knows we were planning to go to Ambre. We're heading east instead."

Najah's brow furrows at the news. There is fresh sadness in Najah's eyes at the mention of Kisha's name. At knowing yet another person she had begun to trust couldn't be counted on. It's a cruel world.

"That's closer to the church, though. . ." Najah trails off. "We'll be right above the central kingdoms. It's not safe."

Sif nods. "Yeah, I don't like it either. If they're sending as many paladins after you as Kisha said, we'll want to go in the opposite direction. We'll skirt the edge of the desert, out of the borders of the central kingdoms, but far away from Ambre and the western coast."

"It's a bad idea," Najah asserts. Her voice is deadly serious. The sight of the young girl making such a serious expression almost makes Sif laugh. Then she remembers the hurt that expression must come from, deadening any mirth that had taken root.

"If we run into trouble, I'll hold it off. You just run."

Matter-of-factly, as if any other suggestion would be absurd, Najah responds, "I was going to."

Sif's laughter comes out as a snort.

-

The riverboat they take east is called *Lyr's Grace*. They hole up in a small room beneath the deck where Sif can continue to sleep off her wound. Najah suspects Sif isn't healing at all now, but can't get the old woman to admit anything. What time Sif doesn't spend sleeping, she spends gambling, despite being cursed with a preternatural lack of luck or skill regarding games of chance. Najah spends most of her time alone, either sitting silently in their room or watching the land pass by from the deck. The river route takes them by farmers herding sheep, a procession of women in animal masks, small statuettes of Saint Daado and, one harrowing sundown, a village burning to the ground. At the sight of the flames, Najah remembers the warning they received from the farmer, that angry spirits and demons have been attacking travelers. She also thinks about Kisha, who told her Sif is a killer.

One evening, while Najah is enjoying the passing of clouds above, Sif stumbles out from below deck, hair and clothes disheveled, and leans against the deck railing beside her. Cool air races across wide-open country, under the purple-blue sky, and dances across Sif's clammy skin like sparks. The boards in the deck creak, and nearby two men are trying to flirt quietly with each other, but their cheery laughter doesn't leave much hidden from anyone on deck.

Sif means to start the conversation, but Najah beats her to it.

"Are you a killer?"

Sif's gaze flickers over at Najah from the corners of her eyes. "Yes."

"At first, I thought you were just a mean old woman. Then I thought maybe you were nice." Najah balls up her fists, voice wavering more noticeably as she continues. "Then Kisha made me feel like I shouldn't trust you. Now I know I shouldn't have trusted Kisha, but that doesn't mean she was wrong about you, either. I noticed that when adults lie, they like to leave in part of the truth. It makes it more real."

Sif makes a thoughtful noise and says, "Okay. So why are you worried I'm a killer?"

"It's wrong. The people after me are killers, too. Why should I think you're any different? Kisha wasn't."

"You're worried I might hurt you."

It's a statement, but Najah still answers, "Yes. My mother said people use violence to get power, and that all either does is hurt people."

Sif turns to face her, looking Najah in the eyes for the first time in days.

"Let me tell you what I think. There is nobody in this world who's not a killer. The fish this boat catches are all killed when they're brought aboard. People at our destination will pay the fishers to catch more. When we go into town, there will be people who sell the carcasses, and people who count on those sales to collect taxes. There will be people killed for stealing fish, or not being able to pay the food tax. Any city you can reach has been the site of a struggle for land or authority that ended in blood. There aren't enough graves for all the murders in this world. Not unless you pick and choose which murders count as real."

Najah grimaces at her words. Sif softens her tone in response, flashing a weary smile. "The difference between me and most other killers is that I don't shy away from what I've done, and I don't ask others to kill for me. The least anyone can try to do is live in a way that is honest with themselves, that doesn't do harm they aren't willing to accept their part in."

Najah doesn't have a response. Who would? Kisha said everyone is a killer, so all a person can do is try and be on the strongest side. Now Sif is saying something similar. Everyone is a killer, so all a person can do is be true to their part in it and take what responsibility is theirs. All Najah wants is to be free from killers, and to be safe, and to have her mother back.

When Najah doesn't respond, Sif says, "Hurting children isn't something I want to have to hold myself responsible for. But Druga's paladins will. Decide which killers suit you best."

Najah turns Sif's words around in her head. "I don't care for that explanation."

"Me either, but it's still true."

The two stand next to each other as the cool river air becomes cold under the setting sun.

"Why did Kisha. . ." Najah struggles to get the words out and hold in her tears at the same time. In that moment, Sif recognizes a piece of her younger self in Najah. Not the piece that fought and thieved across Atlas, but the piece that had been dealt a horrible loss and didn't know how to get all of the grief out. The part of her that wanted to hide away from the world that she used to find exhilarating. Najah's courage suddenly astounds the old woman. She puts her hand on Najah's shoulder and squeezes it lightly.

"Sorry, Naj."

-

That night, Sif dreams of Buri's funeral. It was in his home village, Feigrvoller. It was unseasonably warm and despite not being back for years, his home was packed with people paying their respects. The rafters of his cabin were adorned with musty, dried flowers. Buri had no children or siblings, and his parents had passed decades before. It was only Sif, surrounded by her grief and people whom she didn't know but who seemed to think they knew her. A boat lost in a lightless storm.

And somewhere in that memory was Kisha. A young northern girl who would grow up on Sif's legend. Who would confuse power and strength so completely that she would use her memory of Sif as an excuse to murder in the name of imperial conquest.

In the dream, Sif knew but didn't know her. Kisha circled the funeral like a wolf. Sif only caught glimpses of her sly smile and cunning eyes in the incidental parting of bodies moving in and out of her dead friend's home. Hidden among the flowers hanging from the rafters was the moon, sharpening into the glint of Kisha's knife, and when Kisha drives it into Sif's gut, the three of them are transformed. Sif holds the blade, Buri dies again, and Kisha is gone.

-

In the straining dawn, through a haze of exhaustion, Sif watches as a formation of paladins from the Church of Druga marches through the sea of grass along the riverbanks, heading in the opposite direction of *Lyr's Grace*, thank the goddess. A half-dozen towering banners emblazoned with the symbol of the Virtuous Path flap in the cool wind. The sun is a sullen and smoldering coal on the horizon.

From beneath the deck, Najah patters over to Sif, unaware of the paladins nearby. "Hey, Sif! Cécile is teaching me how to play cards! Bet I can beat y—"

The joy in her eyes dims at the sight of the army passing by. One of the cards slips from Najah's hands, sliding between the boards beneath them. Sif nudges Najah behind her, out of view.

". . .they're looking for you, too." Najah reminds her.

Sif blinks hard, trying to shake the night's dream from her mind. As if by focusing hard enough, she can push it back inside her and replace it with the energy of someone younger, with a better night's sleep.

"Eh, you're right. Let's go back down. I'll show you how to cheat at cards. Then we'll see what Cécile has to say."

-

Two days later, *Lyr's Grace* arrives at a small port in front of a city called Béma. Sif's discomfort and sleeplessness have escalated to include a mild fever, persistent cough, and difficulty focusing. Béma is bigger than either of them expects. It is a sprawling organism of flat stone streets, tall, thick, sandstone buildings, and thousands of bustling workers. Banners claiming allegiance to the central desert kingdom of Hvek or the riverlands country of Ograna hang from occasional balconies, despite both kingdoms being a relatively far trek. When Najah points out that Ograna is one of the few countries that still resist the Church of Druga, Sif realizes the young girl has traveled through Atlas *much* more recently than she. Of course Najah would have an idea of the continent's politics, especially where it concerns places she might be safe.

As it turns out, that line of thought quickly bears fruit. Sif and Najah approach a dockworker to ask where they can find a mapmaker. He wipes his brow and gives them clear directions down the street, but follows up that good deed by delivering the worst news they could hope to hear.

"You won't get far for now, though. The city is shut down, but you're free to move around inside. Word's that the fuckin' Druga cultists pressured Lord Tahan into closing the borders. Bunch bastards oughta mind their business. Stay in their own homes worshipping their asshole deity."

"They say why?" Sif asks, hoping that she doesn't already know the answer. Najah shifts uncomfortably to her right.

"Feh. They don't tell us anything they don't have to. Good luck to you both though, ladies. I'm sure things will open up soon. Sometimes Druga gets their say for just a few days, sometimes a few months, but they forget us soon enough."

"A few months?!" Najah yells. She throws her arms out in disbelief and anger. The dockworker nods grimly. At least someone other than Sif sympathizes with her. With what little of her trouble he understands, anyway.

-

Down the pier, away from the crowds, Sif looks down at Najah and, in a low voice, asks, "Anyone ever teach you how to steal?"

"No. Are you going to?" Surprisingly, Najah doesn't sound like she finds the idea disagreeable. Perhaps their earlier conversation had an effect.

"Sure, but I haven't picked a pocket since I was a kid, and I don't have the energy for a proper robbery right now. Want to help?"

"Sure, uh, h-how?" Najah runs her fingers along the hilt of her dagger nervously. Testing again how it feels against her fingertips. Flexing the memory of when she pulled it on the scout in the forest, before Kisha betrayed her.

Sif senses Najah's anxiety. "Don't worry, you don't have to hurt anyone. Not like that. Follow me."

Sif walks with Najah down the street, pausing once in a while to take an extended look at her surroundings. Najah begins to worry the older woman is playing some kind of game, until eventually Sif stops in front of a narrow alleyway.

"I'm going to stand around the corner, there. Wait a bit, circle the block, then come back here and try and get someone with some coin to follow you back there."

"You're going to. . . hit them as they walk around the corner?"

"Yeah. That okay?" Sif is gruff, but not disingenuous. It's a far cry from their first real argument, when Najah accused Sif of treating her like her feelings don't matter.

"What if I say no?" Najah asks.

"I'm not going to force you, but I can't do it without you. I, uh. . . my wound is infected. With some money, we can get medicine and a room to hide out in until I recover enough to get us past the border."

Najah nods. "Alright, Sif. Let's do it."

Sif pats Najah on her back. "Let's do it."

The Blacksmith's Apprentice

A myth recounted by Aseli of the Wood

In the southeast of Atlas, before it was ever called that, on a grassy plain under rainy skies, was a town called Coria. Coria was once a farming village, but eventually a wealthy family was awarded governance over it for their role in the conquest of the region. The Brals Family settled outside the village itself. A castle was built for their permanent residence and, gradually, the town reached towards it and began to envelop it. As a result, the castle was surrounded by the homes of peasants who could see it and touch its walls, but never rise to meet it.

Some viewed this as a blessing. The Brals Family spent most of their time in Coria. This led to an increase in the demand for fine goods, which meant more merchants, more skilled artisans, and more business. Before long, everyone was busier than ever, and the few who got a jump on the economic change, through either luck or guile, fared even better. As wealth moved up, much of the work naturally moved down. People who had once poured their lives into their crafts now outsourced them to someone else and collected the profits themselves. With this adjusting of the scales there were some who had lots of money with no need to work, and some who had lots of work with a great need for money. In time, it wasn't unusual for people to have neither work nor money, as the last person these new merchants would trust with their shops was somebody who didn't have those two things already.

In Coria lived a warrior who didn't yet know that's what she was. There was a time when she had simply been a child, grieving a loss that came from living in the shadow of Castle Brals. She had lost someone important to her, and once the body was buried, she became forced to set her mind on how to live. She had no more family, and the orphanage was full, so she looked for work. Work was hopelessly sparse, and she would have considered thievery, only nobody outside of the castle wall had anything worth stealing, nor any money to buy stolen goods.

Not finding an answer on how to live, she set her mind on how to die instead. Since two people had been responsible for her loss, the Warrior decided those two people would be the ones to pay the price:

Basten Brals, next in line to take Lordship over Coria, and the golden child of the Brals. Rumored to have a love of both coin and risk.

Sophia Earll, a woman who had made her fortune in the processing of a plant called Adder Eye. She had been born into a merchant family of moderate importance and no noble leanings, but had somehow considerably increased her wealth and standing.

Of course, how could a young child kill two of Coria's most prominent citizens? Chances were she would be caught and imprisoned or killed before she could do anything as mild as maiming even one of them. She didn't assume she would be alive after the grim work, but at least she'd die with weightless shoulders. But with nowhere to go but forward, she sat her sights on a sword. With a sword she could get work, gain skill, buy better weapons and armor, and one day, get her revenge.

She had a list of blacksmiths to bargain with or steal from. Most of them knew her, though. If she suddenly took an interest in their work, only for something as valuable as a sword to disappear, she would be finished. She could try to get a job, but being orphaned, untrained, and homeless made her an unattractive apprentice. She prayed to the Lunar Goddess of Death for revenge, to Aneir the Swordeater for courage, and to Brilliant Een for knowledge. Progress was slow, if she was truly making any at all. The whole situation had begun to tax her, until the day a new shop opened up.

The small shop and forge appeared overnight, looking for all the world as if it had been there for months. The Warrior did a double-take when she first noticed it. Maybe her grief and her single-minded focus had blinded her to the shop being set up. Coria was growing more every day. Stranger things have happened.

Manning the forge was a large, well-fed man with a balding pate, brown skin, and an unkempt black beard. The Warrior stood on the tips of her toes to peek in the window and, as if he had expected her, the Blacksmith smiled at her with paternal delight. She ducked out of sight reflexively. When she took another look, the Blacksmith waved her in.

"Can I get your name, young lady?"

The Warrior gave her name. A short, flowing word that suggested movement.

"Can I ask what brings you to my shop? Are you beginning your swordsmanship training, or hoping to purchase a new weapon?"

The Warrior looked at the Blacksmith suspiciously before responding, "I'm beginning my training."

"Indeed?" The Blacksmith asked. "Well, how do you like your teacher? I'm new to the area, and would be interested in meeting some of the local teachers."

"I don't have one yet. I'll teach myself," the Warrior insisted, hoping the Blacksmith didn't think that sounded as foolish as most people probably would.

"That's admirable, I taught myself as well. It can be difficult, though. And unsafe. Are you sure you don't want to find a teacher? You would be less likely to hurt yourself."

The Warrior grew red in the face and responded, "No. I need to learn to fight now, and I can't afford a teacher."

"In time, perhaps you could save enough money."

"I don't want money and I don't have time. I'm behind schedule as it is."

The Blacksmith took a moment to mull this over. "Well, I'm too busy in the forge for proper lessons, but maybe I can help you. I will loan you a sword and send you on an errand. If you complete the errand, you can keep the sword and I will continue to train you. Would you like that?"

The Warrior was tempted to accept without thinking, but a life of cruelty and hardship made her reconsider. Nobody in Coria cared about anyone other than themselves.

"What do you get out of this?"

"I've had apprentices before, in smithing and war. The joy of seeing a worthy person blossom to their potential is enough for me."

". . .do you swear?"

The Blacksmith put a hand to his heart. "I do, on my life."

"Then I accept, sir."

The Blacksmith pulled from under the counter a short sword that could only be described as a work of art. The blade was the perfect weight and length for a young apprentice. The handle was ornate, yet utilitarian. The Warrior's heart skipped a beat when she saw it. She wasn't sure if she should take it, but the Blacksmith's amiable face convinced her.

"Here is what you should do, if you want to keep this sword and become my apprentice. The captain of the guard, Bas Visser, carries a ring on him. It is silver, with a depiction of a goat's head. Take it from him and then come back here."

"Take it from him how?" the Warrior asked.

"Any way you like. I'm interested to see how you accomplish the task."

That night, the Warrior slept on top of a pile of flattened, molding hay, and thought. The way the Blacksmith spoke, she was sure that this was a test. The Blacksmith could make his own ring if he wanted. The sword he gave to her must be worth more than an old silver ring. He had also said he was interested in seeing how she would accomplish her goal. So, the question wasn't whether she could get it, but how she would choose to get it. It was a test of both ability and character.

The Warrior considered poison, but decided against it for two reasons. Firstly, she had no training as an alchemist or herbalist and couldn't reliably create a poison, assuming she could even get the materials. Secondly, the Captain wasn't on her list. She barely knew anything about him, and didn't want to kill a man in such a pathetic way just for personal gain. It would make her feel like Basten and Sophia, murderers who couldn't even get their hands dirty.

That left two options. She could pick his pocket, or fight him for it. She wasn't sure if either was right, or both, or neither. But she decided on picking the ring off of him, if for no other reason than challenging a grown, heavily armed man to a fight was a battle she would lose before it began. Surely if the

Blacksmith wanted Bas Visser dead, he wouldn't have tried to accomplish it by asking a child to rob him. It stood to reason that taking a less violent route would be acceptable, even given the ultimate goal of her training.

The next day, she found Captain Bas Visser and tailed him for the day. The Warrior noticed that he wore the ring on a chain around his neck. It was an ugly piece of jewelry, but he wore it publicly as a point of pride. The Warrior wondered why that was, and what the Blacksmith had to do with it.

That night, she settled on her plan. The following day, she loaned her sword to a jeweler in exchange for a pair of shears. She stalked the Captain through the streets of Coria. When he had become tired after a day's work, and when the crowd was thick with people returning home, she passed him by and snipped the chain from his neck while he was distracted. The Warrior was no master thief, but had been stealing to survive and her sleight of hand was enough for the task. The theft would have been a success, but the Warrior was so focused on her goal, the ring, that she dropped her guard. The chain slipped out from the ring, away from her grasp. As it landed beside the two of them, Captain Visser's face turned red and bloated.

The guards chased the Warrior up and down Coria all through the frenzied night. Hours into the chase, the Warrior began to worry that Captain Visser's pride was going to win out over her own. It was near midnight when word rang out that a fight between two noble houses, in town at Lord Brals' request, had erupted, and the fight was spilling out into the streets, damaging nearby businesses and waking sleeping workers. Captain Visser reluctantly diverted his guards across town to reestablish peace before somebody was killed and an arrest had to be made. It was exactly the stroke of luck the Warrior needed, as if the deities themselves were on her side.

Once the coast was clear, the Warrior snuck into the Blacksmith's shop, but found that it had been completely emptied out. There was not even a trace of soot on the brick floor. Her first thought was that the Blacksmith had to leave unexpectedly, maybe going home due to a family emergency, or pressured out of town by guards who had noticed him with the Warrior. Bereft, she ran to the city gates hoping to stop him before he left, but all she saw there were the wide, empty grasslands reaching out to the horizon, and a woman loading weapons and armor onto a covered wagon.

The Warrior felt tears well up in her eyes as she approached the woman, hoping against hope that she might have seen the Blacksmith leave.

"My lady, have you seen a blacksmith nearby?"

"Little warrior, you don't recognize me?"

The woman in front of her was very tall, with strong limbs, dark hair, and bronze skin. She bore no real resemblance to the Blacksmith, except that her face was warm and strangely paternal.

"Is. . . it you?"

"It is, my apprentice. I only came to Coria because of you and that ring. And now both are here. Consider the ring a gift to you. Another apprentice of mine used to wear it, until Captain Visser killed him in his sleep."

The Warrior held the ring up in the light. It was a plain, dull silver. The goat's head was passable, but not a masterwork. Through it, though, she recalled a story her father had once mentioned, about a god from the north named Aneir. A god who reveled in danger and punished those who preyed on the weak or defenseless. Who sometimes took the form of a man, sometimes a woman, and sometimes an old black goat. When the Warrior looked up at Aneir, the god smiled back knowingly.

That was how the Warrior, a girl from the city of Coria, became an apprentice to Aneir the Swordeater.

Chapter 16

Young Sif, the Destroyer
Ponda, the market-city

In the time it takes Sif and Buri to wake up, leave the temple, and walk back to Ivon, Sif feels as if she is stumbling through a dream.

Agartha.

Had she heard the name before and not registered it, so that it seemed more important in the context of her nightmares? It could be a simple coincidence. Unusual things happen all the time.

Sif doesn't find the explanation convincing. The thought occurs to her that something more might be at work, and it inflicts her sense of calm with creeping paranoia. As she floats numbly out into the street, she can feel Buri's eyes on her, his concern growing. He makes an out of character attempt to spark a conversation, but Sif brushes it off. Buri is silently surprised their defeat has had such an impact on her.

The thing that stands out now, though, is that the monk talked to her about the offer and not Buri. But Buri is the one who killed the bodyguards, and the witch would have known that. If the truth is that she only wants a stronger replacement for her hired swords, Sif would barely enter into the equation. Absent-mindedly, Sif runs her fingers along her bandaged cheek. She never got a look at her wound.

Sif keeps returning to the thought that she has been bewitched, somehow. And, while she hates to admit it, part of her lingers on the memory of the witch's face. Or, if she believes Ejigu—which she does not—the alchemist's face. Magicians are capable of astounding evil, and it might not be too much for the witch to have planted the memory of dreams she never had, or to have found her days ago and planted the seeds of her recent nightmares. For all Sif knows, Sunnhilde could have bewitched Ejigu as well, got this poor old man wrapped up in her plan.

Still, part of her feels she should trust the monk. They follow the same goddess, after all, and even though the deities mostly keep to their own, maybe being devout would move Siduri to protect him.

When Sif shares her rambling thoughts with Buri, he listens quietly and responds, "If you begin from the assumption that your mind is untrustworthy, or that Ejigu's is, there is no end to it. Maybe I am bewitched. Maybe Ivon. Maybe none of this is real, and you're sitting in a cell somewhere."

Sif recoils. "Damn, Uncle!"

"I only mean that we should start from a place of trust until we know there is deception. Otherwise, paranoia will undo us."

"Could've just said that. . ." Sif grumbles. Still, talking it out does clarify things.

-

All of these thoughts come to a head the morning after, when dazzling light burns down from the cloudless sky and pries Sif's eyes away from her troubled sleep. She walks down to the street and finds a vendor selling a dark-roasted Syrisian coffee. Sif practically gags at the bitterness. It's the kind of thing Buri would like, and that man can't season food properly to save his life. She tries to drink the rest of it but gives up, and instead brings the mug upstairs to offer her uncle. Siduri would roll her eyes at Sif grimacing through the drink when it could bring someone else happiness.

When she arrives back in their room above Beqe's, Ivon and Buri are up and discussing what to do about the job last night. With Henri dead, they have no way to get the innkeeper her money, short of finding out where the man lived and hoping he stashed something of value there. Sif slides Buri the mug of coffee and says, "We've got a bigger problem."

"Hmmm," Buri agrees, taking a long sip out of the mug in front of him.

"Did Buri tell you what happened?" Sif asks Ivon.

They lean back in their chair and brush a strand of blond hair from their sapphire eyes. "No, he told me we should wait for you. Honestly it was very annoying; you're both lucky I love you so much."

"We got a job offer. Something a lot more profitable, that will take us away from any mercenaries for a long while."

Ivon perks up, but under their excitement is something. A nervousness. A strain. Maybe, Sif thinks, Ivon hasn't slept well either.

"A woman offered me and Buri work as her bodyguards on a journey to find a city called Agartha."

"Oh, Sif. I don't like that," Ivon responds. "Agartha is one of the lost kingdoms. The stories about it are not pretty. I heard a bit about it when I was doing jobs for the Mages' Guild in Heron-Muse."

Sif sighs. "Well, let's hear it. . ."

"It was a city at the end of the world, where the barrier between our world and the home of the Three Mothers of Demons is weakened. Naturally, that makes any magic practiced there potent. It's one of the lost kingdoms we actually know a little about, and none of it is good."

"Shit. So maybe this woman really is a witch," she says to Buri.

Ivon stammers for a moment, a rare instance where their tongue can't find the words their mind needs. They settle on, "Well, who knows? Agartha was said to be very prosperous for a time, before whatever destroyed it. There may be treasure."

Sif nods. "Yeah, that's what I was told. If there is, we'd be paid a cut of it."

Ivon forces a smile. Their conscience screams at them to confess their conversation with the Mages' Guild. Their sense of survival begs them to keep up the charade. Ivon thinks of the moon-cursed dead. It's not the worst thing a spell could do, by far.

"That's no slight offer. If we're lucky it will be a large cut, with not much more than a long sea voyage to contend with."

"We should learn more about this woman, first." There is an edge to Buri's suggestion, his voice underlined with a tone that suggests murder, but also fear. Now that he knows what Agartha is, he doesn't believe she is an alchemist.

"The thing is, the woman gave you a choice. She could've killed you or controlled your mind, but she didn't," Ivon responds. "It wouldn't hurt to hear her out. It would also give us the opportunity to gauge how dangerous she may be."

Buri's beard bristles with the motion of his disapproval, but Sif rolls Ivon's argument over in her head. On one hand is the inherent danger in magic, the potential she is somehow being manipulated, and, of course, death. Truly, if Sunnhilde is a witch, death is one of the better outcomes.

On the other hand, there's adventure, coin, answers about her dreams. . . despite herself, and to her surprise, Sif's memory lingers on the memory of Sunnhilde's eyes and lips and cheeks. She clears her throat loudly.

"Uncle, if things go bad, we can always fight our way out of the meeting. Or run."

Buri's mouth twitches behind his beard. He weighs the opinions of his friends, his own intuition, his choice to follow Aneir, his fear of the Three Mothers of Demons and their magic. If they have to run, will Aneir curse him for abandoning the fight? The worst thing that could happen in a normal fight is death. But a spell gone awry could chain one's soul to the Three Mothers of Demons, or obliterate it completely. Or leave a person like the mercenaries in the old kingdom ruins.

Ivon, sensing Buri's hesitation, begins to speak up. "My dear, have I told you the story of the two footmen?"

Buri holds a hand out, cutting Ivon off. Setting aside his own concerns, Buri nods in agreement. He trusts Sif and Ivon's choice but, more than that, he doesn't believe he can stop Sif if she chooses to go. And if their worst suspicions about the trip are true, he can't let her face it alone.

Ivon groans dramatically, leans back in their seat and blows an errant strand of hair from their face. "Well, I guess if you two go, you'll need someone with social graces to speak for you."

"You were the one suggesting we give her a chance," Sif responds.

Ivon feigns offense. "I just want to make sure you're both thinking this through."

"You remembered there is treasure," Buri states matter-of-factly, but missing the real reason.

"It can be both, dear," Ivon jokes, happy in the moment to pretend.

-

Following a light breakfast, Sif produces a knife from her boot and shaves wax from the tips of the candles in their room. They leave the innkeeper with a lie about heading out to find Henri, then make for the guard tower Sunnhilde has set up in. Outside, they prepare to stuff the wax in their ears, the theory being that if their potential employer is a witch, she won't be able to affect them if they can't hear her. As they stand outside, splitting the wax between them, a voice calls out to them.

"You do know that isn't how magic works?" Sunnhilde asks. She doesn't bother to hide the amusement on her face.

"So you say," Sif retorts. Part of her feels foolish to have been caught, but beside her Buri and Ivon tense visibly.

"Maybe, but if I was going to do something, wouldn't I have done it by now? Really, I've had so many chances. Ejigu told me you might think I'm a witch."

Sif tosses the candle wax on the ground and tries to hide her embarrassment.

"You can come up if you want," Sunnhilde sings as she turns away from the window. Sif thinks her voice sounds like clear water, then tries to unthink it quickly.

Upstairs in the tower, Sunnhilde inspects the group. "So, I know *you're* Sif, and *you're* Buri, but who are you?"

Ivon bows with a flourish of their right hand, an imitation of how one might bow to nobility despite the fact that no sane noble would ever entertain an audience with Ivon.

"I'm Ivon of Heron-Muse, master thief."

Sunnhilde seems to approve. "Very interesting; I should have guessed you would be with these two. I've heard some interesting stories about the three of you. I'm sure you'll be useful. Were you really around for the destruction of Heron-Muse?"

Ivon beams, happy for a chance to recount their own adventures and more than a little pleased to learn they have a reputation. "I was, in fact. We were almost executed by Lady Erah-Dune that e—"

Sif elbows Ivon hard in the ribs.

"Ah! Aneir's horns, Keno! I'm not a pile of ugly muscle like some people in this room; you can't just throw your elbow around."

Sif cuts them off. "We haven't agreed to anything yet, Sunnhilde. What would the job be?"

Ivon pales. "Sunnhilde? Not Sunnhilde of the River, surely?"

"That is me. Not a title I chose."

Ivon immediately finds a chair to sit down in. Sif cocks an eyebrow curiously.

"Go on, Sunnhilde," Ivon murmurs. "You were telling us about this job."

"I am travelling with Queen Benedicta Yden of Hvek to find the city of Agartha. It is a long voyage by sea, and my queen wants to use my skills to find what magic weaponry we can and bring it back."

Sif and Buri exchange bloody glances, and Sunnhilde immediately notices.

"*But*, what her royal majesty doesn't know is that I don't intend to help her. When we get to Agartha, we'll gather as much harmless treasure as we can and then execute the royals. Obviously, that is why I need you two, Keno Sif the Destroyer and Buri the Giant. You killed King Ottson. Murdering royalty should be nothing new to you."

For Keno Sif, this changes everything. A blow against magic and royalty all at once, and treasure to bring back. She pictures enough gold that she has to blow it on the most obscene, frivolous things to avoid Siduri cursing her for hoarding it. She is rapidly warming up to the idea, and when she looks back to Sunnhilde, the other woman's smile makes Sif's heart skip a beat.

"Killing royalty is a lot of risk," Ivon comments, having regained some of their color.

Buri stares meaningfully at the young, vainly dressed thief. With that kind of attitude, Aneir might roll their ankle the next time they try to break into a home.

"Oh, fine. I was just saying," Ivon concedes without further argument, realizing the damage their off-handed comment could have done to their goal of paying back the Heron-Muse Mages' Guild. And, more importantly, to everyone escaping with their lives and souls.

"Then we're set?" Sunnhilde asks, hopefully.

Sif's companions nod reluctantly, but Sif is already wearing a roguish smirk, imagining the new lands she'll see and dangers she'll overcome. "We'll do it. Who are we killing, and when do we leave?"

Chapter 17

Old Sif, the Hermit
Béma, on the banks of Fal River

"Over here!" Najah is halfway down the alley, calling out towards the street at a distant figure. Sif crouches around the corner, wincing from the pain in her joints, and listens for incoming footsteps. They make eye contact as soon as Najah turns the corner, followed by a middle-aged man in fashionable clothing. He doesn't have time to notice Sif before she knocks him unconscious with a haymaker. He crashes into the wall, then slides over onto the ground.

"Is he dead?!" Najah's voice pitches up in alarm.

"No, of course not." Then, after a beat, Sif checks his pulse.

"I saw that," Najah grumbles.

"I was just making sure. Check his pockets."

The pair find ten hauwlings and a single blessed lida. They split it evenly and Sif pretends not to smile as Najah clinks the coins together in her hands, eyes wide with awe.

"This is the most money I've seen in my life!" she exclaims.

"Yeah, we did pretty good. Now's where we leave before the guards show up, though."

They find a doctor only three blocks away; in the time it takes them to cover that distance, Najah notices how much worse Sif has gotten. Her skin is waxen, her breathing heavy. The doctor asks how Sif was hurt and, with a laugh that turns into a cough, Sif concocts an elaborate story about a robbery. The doctor prescribes a mild ointment and tells Sif to drink water and get as much sleep as possible.

Further in town, where the plain beauty of the architecture turns cramped and leaning, they find a room to rent. Najah doesn't understand why they have to go somewhere like this when they have so much money.

"When you're in trouble, money never goes as far as you'd think," Sif responds.

The room is on the top floor of an old, rattling inn that leans like it might collapse any week now. Moss grows around the windowpanes, and the inside smells like mold. The boards creak and are too far apart to keep the wind out. Sif collapses onto the bed with a loud groan.

"Are you going to be okay?" Najah asks.

"Yeah, I just need to rest. I'm not as young as I used to be."

"My mom died because of an infection," Najah responds.

Her tone is so even that for a moment Sif doesn't realize what was said. She leans up with a wince, propping herself up on her elbow. "Do you want to talk about it?"

Najah turns her head to avoid making eye contact. "No."

Enough time for a breath passes.

"One of the paladins caught us hiding under a wagon, and cut her. We had to walk through a river to escape and I guess maybe the water was bad. So she got a fever and couldn't walk as fast. We wanted to find a doctor, then one morning I woke up and when I went to start a fire, she was already dead. I couldn't even bury her because the ground was frozen. This necklace is all I have of her." Najah motions to the wooden fox pendant hanging from her neck by old twine.

"When was that?" Sif asks. The moment is uncertain, like thin ice. She isn't sure how to encourage Najah without making her feel pressured to reveal something she'd rather keep hidden.

Najah shrugs sadly, taking a seat next to Sif on the bed. "I don't know. It feels like everything is happening really fast and really slow all at once. After mom died, a man let me hide in his kitchen, but the paladins killed him. Then I was on my own until a farmer took me in, but she kicked me out when soldiers started asking around. I snuck in the back of a wagon to get further north, but I left that same night because the owners said a prayer to Druga and I thought they'd turn me in. Then a man helped me get to Jinta, and I was only there a little bit before I left with you. Then Kisha left, and I guess now you might die, and I'll get passed on to someone else or the paladins will kill me, too."

Sif is speechless, not just because of the tragedy but the resigned hopelessness in Najah's story. Sif left Ummun around Najah's age because she couldn't seem to stop causing trouble and couldn't devote herself to stable work. It was easier to leave, and it had seemed like it would be more fun than the endlessly dull lessons on fighting stances she'd already known, then eventually getting stuck doing guard duty unless some war broke out. Najah had been forced from her home, cursed, burdened with the knowledge of death. The hopelessness must be overwhelming. Sif wonders how a person could feel like that and keep going.

Sif had been hoping for a quick resolution to their journey together, keeping Najah at a distance to make things easier. Maybe it is time to let that go, like Buri might have done for her after *she* left home and met him. Wherever she came from, Najah is just a scared, lonely, angry kid. One who has somehow found the ability to summon more courage and strength than she should have ever had to.

Even with her intentions set, the words don't come easily. Sif's mouth hangs open uselessly, her silence the punctuation to Najah's fear.

"Naj. . ." Sif reaches out to touch Najah's shoulder, but then pulls back. "I'm not going to die. I promise. It takes longer to recover the older you get. I'll be around, and you'll probably get sick of me before then. Be. . . brave. For a little bit."

The bedframe groans as Najah lays back, and when she doesn't respond Sif realizes she's fallen asleep. Whether it's from the journey or her curse is uncertain.

Sif lays on her back and stares at the ceiling, feeling the cool ointment against the wound Kisha left her. She feels the heaviness of her breath, the heat on her skin, the pain in her chest and bones, and hopes she didn't lie to Najah.

The Woman from Coria

A myth recounted by Aseli of the Wood

Aneir was a strange but kind teacher to the Warrior. He showed her forms and helped her to know the basics of combat. He talked at length about philosophy and history. Surprisingly, and frustratingly, after their first month together passed, she rarely saw him at all. He preferred to give her opportunities to learn through experience. He eschewed sparring sessions entirely, although the Warrior did not harbor any illusions about winning against the god of courage.

Once she had grown a few years, he encouraged her to seek her own adventures, promising he would continue to train her as long as she brought him back interesting stories. His reasons were obscure, and when the Warrior asked, Aneir found ways of deflecting the question. She eventually assumed that this new method of teaching was something akin to her first test.

Like most of what Aneir said, there was a gulf between what words left his lips and what he meant. In time, the Warrior quickly learned that her stories weren't to entertain him, but so he could help to guide her. He would ask her why she did one thing and not another, what she felt about different decisions and whether she would change them, looking back. He encouraged her when she said something wise, and gently redirected her when she said something foolish.

One day she spoke about a sword fight with a series of duelists. She had thought it would be amusing to fight them all at once, in part because they were all aggrieved at her insulting their swordsmanship. The three hadn't realized the plan until they all arrived at once, and then they were incensed at the insult implied by the match-up. What warrior wouldn't be aggrieved at the suggestion they had less than one-third the skill needed to defeat their opponent? Nonetheless, the Warrior hadn't backed down, and the fight hadn't lasted long.

The Warrior was close to finishing her story. ". . .but the last man dropped his sword, and I let him run. It seems odd. He agreed to a duel to the death, then ran once he thought he would lose. I doubt he would have given me the same chance."

Aneir was suddenly very serious. "Do you think you should have struck him from behind, then? Forced him to keep to the terms?"

The Warrior shook her head. "No, no. The point of the duel wasn't to kill him, it was to prove my skill. Besides, it wouldn't take much skill or bravery to kill someone weak and unarmed."

Aneir relaxed. "I was almost worried you'd forgotten why you came to me."

"For revenge," the Warrior said, not exactly understanding the connection.

"Is it revenge?" Aneir asked, leading her somewhere she couldn't yet see.

"Of course?" she asked.

Aneir crossed his legs and leaned forward. As he clasped his tattooed hands, the silver rings on each finger clinked delicately. "And the people you want revenge against, are they powerful?"

"Of course."

"Are they strong or weak?"

The question confused the Warrior for a moment. After a moment, they thought they grasped the meaning. "Both, I suppose. Power affords them the strength to carry out violence, but the violence is only to maintain their power, and they rely on others to inflict it. The cycle prevents them from gaining courage, or strength of body and will. It's a trap they spring on themselves."

Aneir stroked his beard. "I think you know more than you let on, my pupil."

"Enlighten me," she responded.

"Simply moving is not the same as living. To fully embrace life requires a purpose. A strong hammer breaks stone. A strong axe splits wood. A strong sword pierces armor. What use is someone who can only use a strong sword against naked flesh? They're the worst kind of coward, because they attack knowing there is no chance they'll be hurt, but they fear it anyways."

The Warrior mulled it over. "Ah. Anyone can feel strong by hurting someone weak. True strength also requires knowing oneself and having clarity of purpose."

"Close, close. So, why did you come to me, then? You seem strong, and you have purpose. If you wanted revenge, you could have it."

"You. . ." the Warrior hesitated. "You told me I'm not permitted, yet."

"If all you needed from me was the skill to kill, you could kill them now. What would it matter if I disapprove?"

Aneir spoke as if he wasn't a god, even one that wasn't particularly prone to doling out petty punishments. For the sake of resolving the question, the Warrior also pretended.

The Warrior shook her head. "I'm. . . sorry. I think I see what you mean, but I can't quite grasp it."

"No need to be sorry. I am asking a lot. Let me ask you one more question. If you could go back and get your revenge sooner, by gaining power the same way your enemies did and hiring killers, would you?"

The Warrior was shocked and offended. "My rise to power would require deaths, I assume? Like those of my fathers? People who never knew they were in a fight, much less agreed to be in one?"

"Naturally," Aneir responded.

"Never," she responded through clenched teeth. "I would rather die myself."

"Hmmm. If I were mortal, I would feel the same. I'm glad we found each other. You've become wise."

The Warrior smiled at her teacher's praise, even though the line of questioning continued to weigh on her mind. Sometimes, a conversation with Aneir was more exhausting than she would have thought possible. "I think the nobility does you a disservice, calling you a god of war."

Aneir smiled, and she saw the wrinkles in the corner of his eyes as he did.

"Yes, so do I. Still, the time to fight is approaching. I say we take a trip to Coria." Within a few weeks, the Warrior was back in her hometown. It wasn't long until word got out that Sophia Earll had been murdered; it was all anyone could talk about in noble circles. Sophia had been on a night walk with her retinue of guards, and each one had been cut down. Popular gossip had it that Sophia had been found with a sword in her hand. It was an odd detail, because she hadn't been inclined at all towards sword fighting. More than that, she had amassed the strongest guard in the city by buying children from their families and having them trained from a young age.

The noble and mercantile classes were outraged. They hired more protection and instituted a curfew for the good of the city, though only enforced it in the part of the city where nobody with any coin would frequent. The aristocrats were free to come and go as they pleased, although many of them preferred to stay behind their walls.

The first night of the curfew, the Warrior climbed the same castle wall that had separated her from her revenge as a child. Years of Aneir's guidance had made her strong and agile. The full moon bathed the night in a silver light and, knowing the Lunar Goddess of Death ferried the dead into the afterlife, the Warrior decided it was a good omen. A serving boy with a broken arm let the

Warrior in through a window, happy to assist anyone who would avenge him against the man who had beaten him over a dropped plate.

The benefit of Aneir's instruction meant that the Warrior was more than capable of facing danger headlong, but it also meant that she wasn't used to skulking. It wasn't long before the castle guard found her and an alarm was raised. Dozens of guards in dull iron rushed from doors across the grounds, armed and trained to die for their lord. But Basten Brals, the Warrior's target, was not their lord. The bulk of the guard ran to protect Mil Brals, an old man with a head muddled by a lifetime of easy, selfish living. The Warrior cut down every opponent in between her and her target, but Mil Brals' fear for his own life was so great that not many guards ended up on that path.

When the Warrior met Basten Brals, he was huddled in a large bedroom next to a window overlooking Coria. From the door, the Warrior could pinpoint where her childhood home would be, if it was still standing out there in the cold dark. When Brals turned to the Warrior, he thought he had come face to face with a ghost. Her face and body were still covered in barely healed wounds from her brawl with Sophi Earlls' guards the other night. Her arms and legs shook, from climbing the castle wall and running through its halls.

Brals was unarmed, so the Warrior drew a second sword from the sheath on her back and tossed it on the floor in front of him. Then, she turned and locked the door behind her.

"Guards!" Brals yelled.

The Warrior shook her head. "Anyone who would come for you is dead. Most of them ran to protect your father."

Brals was incensed. "I'm his heir! He wouldn't dare."

"And yet, here we are," the Warrior responded. "I hear you have quite the reputation as a duelist. As it happens, so do I."

"Is that what this is about?" Brals asked with a smirk. "An attempt to impress me?"

"No. This is because you've steered countless lives into wreckage from behind these walls, and I want to know you'll see the justice owed to Aneir, and to your victims."

Brals snorted. "Victims? From what? I've never hurt anyone in my life who didn't deserve it."

The Warrior pictured the serving boy with a broken arm, downstairs. "You and Sophie Earlls began the processing of Adder Eye."

"So what?" He still didn't understand, or wouldn't admit to understanding, the ripple effect his pursuit of coin had on the poor in Coria. What it had been like being a child who rarely saw her fathers. When she had seen them, they were beat down and exhausted. Noticing something wrong over a stretch of months as their skin turned sallow and the cough got worse instead of fading away. Knowing the end was near when they were too sick to work at a job that never paid enough to see a doctor in the first place, but now even that meager income was out of reach. Having to pretend there was hope, when her living father began to develop sallow skin and a lingering cough.

"So what?" The Warrior was incredulous, the heartbreak of her childhood a fresh wound after all these years. "So, my fathers were the ones who did the processing. They died in poverty and left me alone, while the two of you grew richer than the deities."

"Oh, please. If you're strong enough to fight your way up here, you're strong enough to make money. I could pay you ten times what your fathers made, and that *mess* was a long time ago." Brals picked up a small bag of coin from his nightstand and tossed it at the Warrior. She let it fall to the ground.

"Do workers no longer die processing Adder Eye for you?"

Brals didn't respond, but his eyes flashed with a cold edge.

"Lift your sword," the Warrior commanded.

"What will you do?" he asked, a tremble of fear revealed through the crack in his bravado.

"Try to kill you," the Warrior responded. "I'm giving you a chance you never gave my family. They died choking on their own breath. Pick up your sword."

"Everyone out there has plenty of chances, you savage! What's to stop your fathers from buying the tools to process Adder Eye and hiring other men to do it?"

The Warrior clenched her teeth. "Your sword, lordling."

Brals picked up the sword, tested its heft, and took an offensive stance. The Warrior raised her sword in turn, blood running down her arm from a reopened wound.

The following morning, the guards were allowed to search the castle. Basten Brals was found dead with a sword beside him, the same as Sophia Earlls. The faint track of boots on the thick carpet marked a path from the locked door to Basten's window, now open and leading out into the wide expanse of blue sky and green land into the horizon. The serving boy with the broken arm left Coria that morning with a heavy bag of coin, one that bore a striking resemblance to the one Brals had tried to give to the Warrior the night before.

Chapter 18

Young Sif, the Destroyer
Ponda, the market-city

Ivon explains who Sunnhilde of the River is before Sif has a chance to ask. It turns out their new employer is not only skilled but quite famous, and even has a degree of wealth.

"She's the advisor to Queen Benedicta of Hvek," Ivon explains. "She won the position by figuring out how to divert a river in order to help a small town on Hvek's border grow crops more efficiently." Buri hums in a tone that makes it clear he doubts the story. One could no more move a river than a mountain. "I'm serious," Ivon insists. "That's not the only story about her. She once came to Heron-Muse and, within three days, half of the governors had been replaced, and the borders all had to be redrawn. The old head of the Thieves' Guild called her the most clever woman alive."

Sif and Buri don't take much stock in it until they meet her the next day at the border of Ponda, where a small caravan of big, finely crafted wagons pulled by tall, muscular horses awaits them. Sunnhilde is smoking from a wooden pipe and speaking with a few women dressed in the robes of Een, the deity of knowledge. Unlit iron lanterns hang from each corner on the wagons, brand new and carved out of a sleek, red-brown wood. One wagon is filled with supplies, and the other two with thick bedding and pillows dyed rich, royal colors. Despite the extravagant display of wealth, Sunnhilde wears the same shabby traveler's clothes she'd been wearing the day they met.

Sif plans to put her things on the wagon and sit down, but Sunnhilde waves her over. Sunnhilde's pupils are dilated and her gaze is unfocused. Sif smells the familiar scent of traveler's leaf.

"Ladies," Sunnhilde says, "you'll have to excuse me. My friend has just arrived and I have something for her."

The followers of Een nod politely, but it's clear they feel slighted. Once they're out of earshot they begin arguing in whispers.

Sunnhilde's robes rustle and jewelry clinks as she leads Sif to her wagon. The horses tied to the front of it snort impatiently.

"What was that about?" Sif asks.

Despite her words, Sunnhilde speaks joyfully and walks with a bounce in her step. "Oh, who knows? Something about some kind of fish that lives off of the west coast. The disciples of Een are always bothering me about some thing or another. Bunch of uptight fuckers."

"I'm surprised they weren't offended at you burning traveler's leaf in front of them."

"They don't have a choice. They can't tell me what to do. Nobody can." For a moment there is a hint of bitterness in Sunnhilde's voice, but it disappears as the alchemist grabs a small glass jar from the back of the wagon. "You know, you should be impressed, Keno Sif. I've been called the smartest person alive. Those disciples of Een say I'm a seer."

Sunnhilde looks down at Sif expectantly. Sif finds herself at a loss for words, completely unsure of if Sunnhilde is joking or not, when the other woman bursts out laughing.

"Sorry," Sunnhilde says, wiping tears from her eyes. "You made a face."

"No, I didn't."

"Yes, you did," Sunnhilde insists playfully. "You were trying to tell if I'm being serious."

"Are you?"

"Yes." Sunnhilde hands Sif the glass jar. "Here. Start applying this to your wound once a day. Can I see it?"

Sif peels back her bandage with a wince. Even now it stings badly. A cool wind rolls off of the grasslands to the far southwest and, even though the wagon blocks most of it, Sif still feels her skin prickle.

"It's looking so much better. Let's change that bandage, though."

Sif hesitates. Though she's rarely self-conscious, the worry that the gruesomeness of her wound might shock Sunnhilde clings to the forefront of her mind. Sif takes a deep breath and exhales slowly, a trick Buri taught her to calm herself that, so far, she has not mastered. Then, she turns her head to the side and up towards Sunnhilde's face.

"Why do you care?" Sif asks. "It's not like you burned me."

The corners of Sunnhilde's mouth lift into an elusive smile. "I already told you. I do what I want, Keno Sif."

The two sit in silence as Sunnhilde works, adjusting to each other's company under the blush of dawn. Sunnhilde keeps the pipe in her mouth as she inspects Sif's wound, smoke puffing from the corner of her mouth. "How's that feel?" Sunnhilde asks once the bandage is replaced.

"Better," Sif admits.

A short walk away, Buri and Ivon talk about their upcoming trip, but Ivon's mind is elsewhere. Their distracted gaze returns to Sif, one of Ivon's oldest friends, and Sunnhilde, the strange woman that the Mages' Guild wants them to help. Seeing Sif's budding interest in Sunnhilde, they can't help but wonder if they have done something terrible. In their heart, they feel a cold, yawning grave.

Chapter 19

In the miserable days that follow their arrival in Béma, Sif doesn't get better. Najah can tell, even though the older woman tries to pretend otherwise. Eventually, she doesn't even try to get out of bed. One gray morning, as the wind whistles through cracks in the wall, Najah approaches Sif with her fists balled up and expression set for an argument.

"I'm going to get you medicine."

Sif tries to speak, but a fresh bout of coughing rattles her stout frame first. Eventually she gets her rebuttal out. "No reason, kid. I already got medicine."

"I'm not stupid, it's obviously not working." Najah responds, beginning to pace the room nervously, clasping her fox pendant in her fist.

"I didn't say you were stupid," Sif groans, wiping sweat from her forehead. "I just don't want you to get hurt or captured."

Najah hadn't expected Sif to admit to any concern for her. Secretly, Sif hadn't either. Najah almost doesn't know what to say, but summons the words anyways.

"You're dying."

"Well," Sif grunts. "Maybe." If Sif is finally admitting to it now, things must be much worse. Najah knew something like this was coming, because yesterday Sif was joking that she might visit a tavern and do some drinking and gambling. Despite what people say about northerners, and how Sif herself acts, the old woman isn't dumb enough to leave their hiding spot just to go drinking. Najah knew it was being said for her own benefit. Like Sif didn't want her to be scared.

"So, what's the problem?" Najah retorts, raising her voice.

Sif tries to sit up but can't. "Naj, if you get captured everything is over."

"Just trust me for once," Najah insists. "I won't do anything that endangers the temple."

Sif laughs weakly. "I do trust you. And we both know the temple is fucked. I doubt it's even there anymore. Kisha's people probably burned it all to the ground weeks ago."

The thought hadn't ever occurred to Najah. The idea that Sif had been living with this and never shown any signs shakes her. At some point, Sif decided to go with Najah even if it meant sacrificing her home. Najah doesn't know what to say. She feels an unfamiliar emotion welling up in her throat and chest and does her best to push it back down. Then she begins packing.

"What are you doing?" Sif asks.

"Going to that doctor we met before," Najah answers. "Get up and stop me if you can."

A snort of laughter escapes from Sif's mouth. "I can't tell if I'm proud or pissed. Serves me right for trying to teach you something."

Najah sheathes her dagger and tosses an empty pack over her shoulder. She lowers her head bashfully, hoping Sif can't see her face. "You're a terrible teacher, but I guess we're already used to each other."

"Sure." As Sif speaks, though, Najah hears what sounds like the clang of armor down on the street. Like marching soldiers. She doesn't say anything, but Sif notices a change in her expression. "What is it?"

"You don't hear anything?" Najah asks.

Sif shakes her head. Najah feels the familiar well of anger and sorrow and grief open in her chest. Sif is going to die, she knows it. For as old as Sif is, she's never been so poorly attuned to her surroundings.

Najah smiles faintly. "Don't worry, I'll be back soon."

Najah pockets a few hauwlings from underneath the thin straw mat she sleeps on. She looks out the window before she leaves, once she is sure Sif can't see her. A line of paladins from the Church of Druga search the streets below—five of them, two with spears, two with swords, one wielding an executioner's axe. Their armor gleams uncommonly among the browns, tans, and grays of the city. Across the street the other day had been a flag of the country Ograna, used by locals who reject the Church of Druga and their attempts at colonization. It's gone now. Whoever lives there must have pulled it inside when the paladins began their search. Najah suppresses the urge to scream, and instead flings her left hand out in a rude gesture.

"Hey," Sif calls out. "Watch your back while you're out there."

"Sif," Najah says, trying to mimic the volume of the paladins on the street. Trying to test if maybe Sif *can* hear. The old woman doesn't respond.

"Yeah, I'll be safe," Najah says, louder.

She takes the back door to avoid being caught leaving the inn, and gathers a few stones from the wilting garden out back. She isn't fast, and can't fight much, but she learned to skip rocks last year when she traveled through the riverlands with her mother and can probably hit someone from a distance if she needs to.

Behind the inn is a winding series of fences and alleyways and shacks that feel small and separate from the rest of Béma; overgrown gardens, weeds pushing up from cracks in the stone, half-rotten wood, and clothes hanging up to dry. Even the sun seems less harsh in the shade of the surrounding homes. The musty scent of the inn is gradually giving way to a damp, floral one that isn't pleasant, but it doesn't weigh on her senses as heavily. A small dog stops digging to sniff at her and then trot away. The patches of thin, wavering plant life spark an energy in her—confidence, maybe, at seeing nature continue to find a place among the burden of civilization.

Back at the doctor's office, she tries to explain Sif's condition to the doctor. The man listens with unhidden impatience which makes Najah clench her fists. "Are you sure she was robbed?" the doctor asked pointedly.

"Uh, yes."

"Because if that isn't what happened, it would be important to know. Sometimes the Druga cul— er. . . the Church of Druga has soldiers who use a very specific kind of poisoned blade oil. Maybe the person who robbed her stole a blade like that?"

"Yes!" Najah can't hold back her relief. "The woman who robbed us definitely had one. It had the Virtuous Path circles on the hilt."

"Then that could explain it. Even if she is resistant to alchemy, the human body isn't made to fight off infection and poison at once. If I had known the situation, I would have prescribed her another medicine. Take this." The doctor walks across the room to a small wooden box and removes a clay pot. The pot is cool to the touch and a faintly herbal scent surrounds it. "She needs to take it as soon as you get to her, then again every morning for a week. Make sure she is getting rest and drinking water."

Najah's face goes slack. "Wait, what? You can't come to her?!"

"No. I'm sorry. The Church. . . Not all of us like them. But I have a husband and ch—" The doctor trails off, realizing he is talking to a child whose life is already in danger.

Najah frowns at him, then turns in a huff to storm out the front door.

"Wait! You haven't paid!"

Najah pulls a cloth bag from her belt and sets it down roughly. The impact of it shakes a small vase of fresh flowers.

The doctor stares at the door for a time, then gets up from his seat and shuffles over to retrieve his payment, which turns out to be a bag of small stones from somebody's garden.

Chapter 20

Buri the Giant
The road south

The night of the attack Buri is fast asleep, snoring heavily, and dreaming of one of his many lost loves, a man who has mostly faded from his memory but never from his heart. The sound of arrows wakes Sif first. She shakes Buri from his slumber as a wagon driver cries out in alarm.

"Wake up, Uncle!"

A flaming arrow shoots through the canvas, narrowly missing Sif's skull, and embeds itself in the wood. Without missing a beat, Sif yanks it from the wall and pats out the fire with the palm of her hand. Out across the grasslands, where pale blades sway under the moonlight, a choir of voices call out in the ancient tongue of Dead Tician. Sif and Buri both perk up immediately. In a continent as bloodthirsty as Atlas, there are many things a traveler does not want to hear or see. Masked hunters from the lost country of Ticia aren't at the top of the list, but they're high enough.

Besides them Ivon whispers, "Is that. . . is that Tician?"

Buri grumbles affirmatively.

"Shit," Ivon swears. "Somebody needs to protect Sunnhilde. If she dies, our job is over before it can begin."

Buri retrieves a sword and shield from the back of the wagon, keeping hunched over to avoid banging his bald head on the wooden beams above.

"She can take care of herself," Sif spits, taking cover near the entrance to the wagon as arrows continue to rain down from above.

"You don't know that, Keno," Ivon insists aggressively.

Buri's forehead wrinkles at their argument. Ivon has been unusually irritable lately. This is the longest they've traveled together at one time,

though, and the most trouble they've been in since Ivon was forced to leave
Heron-Muse. Buri's nature is to let people have their moments of pettiness, but
he also knows there is a world behind the one he can see, and something about
Ivon's behavior makes Buri worry there is more than simple fatigue or fear
affecting his friend.

"Listen, if she dies now, she was never going to make it through Agartha.
We protect each other first. Grab a weapon if you don't want to be embarrassed
when you meet Aneir."

"If, dear. *If* we meet Aneir," Ivon responds, removing a short bow from the
stockpile of weapons. Their feigned exasperation sets Buri's heart at ease,
although only a little.

Two Tician hunters appear behind the wagon as if out of thin air, their
loose, antiquated clothing fluttering with every movement. They approach on
horseback, wooden masks painted white with too many eyes, then leap for the
wagon. Sif swings out from cover and lets the hunter's momentum carry them
into her blade. An arrow from Ivon's bow lands in the other hunter's chest, and
when they drop their sword Sif throws them from the back of the wagon.

Sif shoulder slump disappointedly. "Is that it?"

"No," Buri responds. A breath later, swords tear through the canvas above
them. It's hard to tell how many in the dark, but Buri counts five for certain.

"Stay safe." Buri whirls around to see Sif wave goodbye and pull herself on
top of the wagon. The ring of clashing swords gets louder up above. Ivon fires
arrows through the canvas, hoping to hit flesh, while Buri swings at the
impression of a boot above him. A body crashes against the ground outside in
response. As he moves to follow Sif, the wagon comes to a slow stop.
Someone has killed the driver or the horses. Or both.

He steps off the back and is met by two women, one brandishing a sword
and shield, and the other a small bow. Maybe they intended to ambush him,
because as he squares off, someone kicks his right leg out from under him.

Pain shoots up from his knee as it slams into the ground. Hot air bursts from his lips and a gust of fresh air replaces it.

Knowing the move could cost him, he spins around to face his newest attacker just in time to block a horizontal swing. The woman behind him seizes her chance and leaps in. Buri rolls backwards, crashing into her and sending them both sprawling. Before he does, he just barely catches the sight of Sif fighting off her attackers on the wagon. Buri scrambles to his feet as two arrows *thunk* into the man who has kicked his leg out. He turns around and a piercing heat flares in his chest as an arrow from the Tician archer glances off of his ribs. The woman snarls something in her native language.

He reminds himself to stay calm. Consistency, control, and inner peace will win any battle. Outside, he bellows like a rabid beast, cuts down the swordswoman as she struggles to stand, and leaps at the archer. He dodges her next arrow, though only barely, and throws a handful of sand in her eye to prevent another. A simple stroke of his sword ends the fight. Behind him, the last of the hunters falls from the wagon, dead, and Sif stands in the moonlight, bathing in the rush of adrenaline. Ivon lets another few arrows loose into the distance and silence retakes the night.

Sunnhilde stumbles out from her wagon less than two dozen feet ahead of Sif and Ivon. Far behind them sits the final wagon, dead driver and horses all lifeless at its head.

Buri raises his voice to Sunnhilde. "Is your driver dead?"

She shakes her head, and as she gets close, he can see she is holding a curved dagger, slick with the same blood that covers her hands. She walks with a pained limp and her breathing is labored.

"Yes; I asked my driver to stop when I saw you falling behind."

"Bad luck for him," Sif comments, leaping from her spot above them and landing deftly in the grass.

Sunnhilde shrugs casually, but in the starlight a shadow of sadness crosses her face. "He was one of Queen Benedicta's," she says, as if that explains it.

"Are we going to kill all of her retainers as well?" Ivon asks, with a noticeable amount of concern.

"No, not us," Sunnhilde murmurs. Sunnhilde offers her hand to Sif. "Come on. We'd better get moving again. We still have a long journey ahead of us. I'm sure whoever hired Ticians to kill us would be happy to try again."

Sif and Buri trade a meaningful glance. Time is shorter than they thought if hunters from Dead Ticia are after them. Still, Sif thinks, it's nothing that time off the continent and a pack of ancient treasure wouldn't solve.

Chapter 21

Najah

Béma, on the banks of Fal River

Najah walks fast, in case the doctor comes after her for stealing Sif's medicine. She would've paid if he hadn't said what he did. Maybe she should have, anyways. The guilt and anger in her seethes at everyone who gets to live a life of mundane tragedies. She's been running for as long as she can remember and—

She wakes up with a headache somewhere outside of the city. She shoots up, eyes darting around incoherently as the fog of sleep lifts from her consciousness. She is in the back of a wagon. There are no buildings on the other side of the barred windows, only miles of grassland. From the placement of the sun, it's early morning. She's been out for hours. Sitting on a bench opposite of Najah is an exhausted woman in a tight bodice and a dress that is noticeably shorter than the fashion.

"Well, that's the first time I've seen someone get arrested while asleep," she says. "Are you okay, dear?"

Najah is hurled from sleep to panic and can't quite work out how to respond. She's been away so long, and now Sif will never get her medicine. Everything inside her crumbles and she bursts into tears. Her breath comes like an approaching army, louder and quicker every second. She digs her nails into her scalp and screams thoughtlessly that it's happening again, that it's all her fault, that she ruins everything. She punches the bench, but the pain feels like an added slight from the world against her, so she hits herself instead, though the physical pain is lost among the waves of suffocating heartache. Everything is fucked. She's alone again, and Sif is going to die just like her mother and Jinta and anyone else who was stupid enough to try and care about her.

"Oh. Oh no, uh, okay. It's okay." The woman switches seats to be next to Najah. Her voice is quiet and calm. Gently but firmly, she wraps her arms around Najah to stop the young girl from hitting herself. She strokes Najah's hair and whispers into her ear, "Shhhh. It's okay. You're safe. Just take a slow breath."

A dull sort of relief stabilizes Najah enough that she no longer feels like lashing out. If only she could also shed the embarrassment of having said all of that in front of a stranger.

"I'm sorry," the woman says, releasing Najah. "I probably should have asked before I touched you. Do you want me to stop?"

Najah looks up at her, hot tears flowing down her crimson cheeks, and answers sheepishly, "N-no."

The woman brings Najah back into her arms and strokes her dark hair. Despite everything, Najah feels herself slowly regain her grip. Her gasping sobs mellow out to a sniffle. Her shoulders relax. The woman smells like sweat and perfume, but mostly perfume. It's an overwhelming scent, but strangely comforting in the moment. Najah can't remember the last time someone hugged her.

"Are you an orphan, dear? Is there anyone who needs to know where you are?"

"I don't have a family anymore, but m-my friend is sick and I need to get some medicine to her."

"Okay. And what's your name?"

"Najah."

The woman knits her eyebrows. "My name is Tasoula. When the paladins open the door to the wagon, I'm going to tackle them. You just jump over me and run, okay? Just run and keep running."

"I don't think I can let you do that for me," Najah says, still sniffling. Her heart can't bear the weight of causing another nice person's death.

"Do me a favor, dear. Do you know of Asthia?" Najah shakes her head no. "Asthia is the deity of love. But for years now the Church of Druga has been arresting anyone who worships what they call the degenerate deities. Asthia, Siduri, Aneir."

"Saving me won't get you revenge," Najah argues.

"No, dear. Not revenge. But when I was younger, Asthia saved me when nobody else would. And I would dishonor myself if I let anything happen to you now." The woman's eyes shine with conviction. She's so sure of herself. So brave. In that moment, Najah wants to be like her. Wants to believe it's okay to rely on her.

"Are. . ." Najah fights against the urge to hope, but Tasoula is offering her a way to return to Sif before it's too late. The medicine is still tied securely to her belt. "Are you sure?"

Tasoula squeezes Najah again, long waves of dark hair tickling her nose. "Of course. You need to save your friend. Just promise me you'll get away."

"I promise," Najah says.

Tasoula stands up, takes a deep breath, and yells, "HEY! HEY! THERE'S SOMETHING WRONG WITH THIS GIRL! I NEED HELP!"

The wagon jolts to a stop. Najah can feel herself shaking with anticipation. The two nod at each other, silently reaffirming their plan.

Sooner than expected, the door in the back of the wagon swings open. In a blink, Tasoula leaps across the wagon and throws herself like a wild animal at three fully armored paladins. Najah yells at the top of her lungs as she vaults over them, landing awkwardly on one leg and falling to the ground.

Behind her, Tasoula is being beaten by two of the paladins, the third already heading towards her. She turns to run but is struck in the back of the head. The force of the blow crumples her back to the ground. The taste of blood and dirt fills her mouth. A sound like ripping earth and twisting wood erupts from the brawl beside her. It must be a monster, some horrible beast the Church of

Druga has enlisted to do their work. Najah braces for another blow, but it doesn't come.

Shaking, she lifts herself from the ground. Where her blood spilled onto the dirt is a small patch of wild flowers. When she turns to see what has become of her savior, her heart skips a beat.

The paladins have been lifted no less than a dozen feet in the air, arms and legs bound up by the branches of an oak tree. Leaves sprout from it quickly and spontaneously, like bubbles in a pot of boiling water. One leaf sprouts so fast it shoots right off the branch, falls slowly on the wind, and brushes Najah's shoulder. Tasoula is leaning against the wagon that held them moments ago, trying to stop her legs from giving out. Her jaw is slack in amazement. Her face is bruised but relieved. In the distance, Béma is still visible. The trees continue to grow as their eyes meet, making paladins groan in pain as the branches tighten around them.

". . .are you a witch?" Najah asks Tasoula.

She shakes her head. "That. . . that was *you*."

Najah shakes her head insistently. That's impossible.

"It's okay dear. It's okay." Tasoula stumbles to her feet, legs shaking and body bruised. "But we need to leave now and find your friend."

Najah nods slowly. Her body trembles with fear and adrenaline.

Leaving a wide berth between themselves and the trapped paladins, they climb the front of the wagon and take the reins. The horses that had been pulling the wagon are undisturbed by the change and, in fact, handle remarkably easily. Maybe the paladins didn't treat them well either.

"Your friend is back in Béma?" Tasoula asks.

"Yeah. She's really sick, she'll die if we don't help her soon."

"Well," Tasoula exhales and sets a look of determination on her face. "Let's hurry, then."

Behind them, the lush green of Najah's tree has already started to turn autumn-brown. A single, dying leaf snaps off of its branch and floats slowly to the ground.

Chapter 22

Young Sif, the Destroyer
The Rose Gold

Weeks after sealing their deal, Sif, Buri, Ivon, and Sunnhilde meet in Queen's Port on the west coast and begin boarding a barely disguised pirate ship named the *Rose Gold*. The ship is tall and proud, lovingly maintained by a crew that works carefully and talks joyfully. Word is the other two ships left port for Agartha already and that they would have to catch up. After that, it's just a simple matter of regicide and they can all make enough money to stay out of trouble back on the continent.

The captain of the *Rose Gold* is a tall, muscular man with long locks of black hair, and half his left arm missing. He introduces himself as Wahyu and offers each of them a kiss on the cheek in greeting. Sunnhilde passes, as does Sif, but Buri accepts it in the spirit of friendship and Ivon, clearly enamored with the man's physique, accepts it in the spirit of lust.

Wahyu proves himself to be good company, a charming conversationalist, and a decent gambler, although the last trait irritates Sif more than it endears him to her.

One night, after losing three hauwlings to Captain Wahyu in a game of Shen's Tower, Sif leaves Buri and Ivon in the captain's quarters to walk the deck and drink in the night air. She packs her pipe with traveler's leaf and, as she lights it, Sunnhilde appears as if summoned. The jewelry on her face and fingers sparkles in the starlight.

"Good evening, Sif."

"Hey, Sunnhilde."

Sunnhilde speaks with a comfortability that seems genuine, if also very practiced, all measured words and nervous hand wringing. Ten minutes into a messy, rambling story about a minor earth goddess celebrated in the southwest, Sif interrupts her. "Sunnhilde. What's wrong?" Her tone is unapologetic.

"I have to be honest," Sunnhilde starts. "I've been a little bit intimidated by you."

A single chuckle escapes from Sif's lips. Odd thing to say after how long they've traveled together. Then again, they haven't spent much time alone. "Why's that?"

"Well. . . I've heard tales about you and Buri."

Sif's heart sinks a little bit. "Ah, you're worried something will happen to you."

"No." Sunnhilde shakes her head. "The stories are really entertaining. I've loved hearing them for years. I feel awkward that our first meeting had to happen like that, especially since one of my swordsmen burned you so badly. I could never apologize enough for the pain you've been through."

"Guess I won't be winning any beauty competitions." Sif exhales a plume of smoke and watches it waft over the dark waters.

Sunnhilde shakes her head, curling locks of crimson hair bobbing side to side. "You'd be surprised."

A breath passes, then Sunnhilde asks, "Do you. . ."

Spurred by Sunnhilde's hesitation, Sif turns to face her. Sif's heartbeat quickens, even as she wishes it wouldn't. But the alchemist lets whatever she was going to say die on her lips as a mystery. The missing words are replaced by the sound of waves lapping against the wooden hull of the *Rose Gold*.

"Can I share your pipe?" she asks instead.

"Sure." Sif passes her the pipe and becomes acutely aware of Sunnhilde's fingers as they briefly touch her own. Sunnhilde says a brief prayer to Siduri and then inhales. The words of the prayer and smell of the smoke are an unexpected comfort for Sif; a reminder that it isn't just her, Ivon, and Buri against the whole continent.

"I've been meaning to ask. You seem powerful, why do you need us? Couldn't you just put Queen Benedicta to sleep and slit her throat?"

Sunnhilde coughs and laughs all at once. A thick plume of smoke escapes her lips. "I'm more of a lover than a fighter."

Sif swallows hard. Her throat feels very dry.

"How do you do magic, then?"

"It isn't magic. I have a pact with Siduri. I've always been smart. Too smart, really. I used to get in a lot of trouble. But now I'm much, *much* smarter."

"It seems like you still get in a lot of trouble," Sif remarks.

That makes Sunnhilde smile. "I never get in trouble now, because now I never get caught. Siduri has blessed me with an unnatural knowledge of many things, but especially alchemy. In return, I worship *feverishly*." Sunnhilde gestures to the pipe they share.

Sif raises an eyebrow. "What use is being that smart if the way you do it destroys your memory?"

Sunnhilde only nods. "That's the point. The knowledge can't be gathered and hoarded. I'll never be able to backstab my way onto a throne. Not that I would want to. I can know the world, and I can affect it, but I can't. . . hold it. Some things just slip through my fingers."

"Sounds sad."

"Nothing lasts forever, Keno Sif. The pact is a limitation, but it's also a blessing. I feel awake in a way I could never be otherwise. Do you remember a smell in the tower the night we met?" Sunnhilde doesn't wait for Sif to answer. "That was a formula I'd flooded the room with. It primes the command to sleep in anyone who's already tired. I wasn't sure if my bodyguards were trustworthy, so I had them meet me there at night."

Unexpectedly, Sif bursts out laughing.

Sunnhilde leans away from Sif, but only very slightly. "What did I say?"

Sif wipes the tears from her eyes. "No, it's just. . . Ejigu said something about that and I thought you might have controlled his mind."

A bubble of annoyance surfaces on Sunnhilde's expression, and suddenly it's like a bucket of cold water drops on their cheerful conversation. Sif opens her mouth to try and salvage it, but Sunnhilde puts up a hand.

"I understand. You don't know me."

The mood of the conversation has shifted, though. Bitterness is evident in Sunnhilde's voice. The silence is almost enough to make Sif apologize, when Sunnhilde speaks again.

"When I was a young girl, I had awful headaches. I couldn't sleep, couldn't study. The pain got so bad that I would throw up anything I ate. So, my parents took me to Siduri's temple in Traumbrücke, in the southeast, hoping that our goddess could relieve the pain."

Sif nods, although the name of the town or country doesn't sound familiar. "Not a bad plan."

Sunna smirks. "I'm lucky they thought of it. I'll be grateful forever. Something not many people know, though, is that Siduri is also a goddess of prophecy. The first time I took traveler's leaf, I saw my town destroyed and my family slaughtered by the army of Queen Benedicta's father. Not many people believed me, though. Nobody, actually."

Sunna wipes a tear from her eye with the heel of her palm.

"Sorry," Sif murmurs, giving her best approximation of a comforting smile. It's a cold comfort, but one Sunna is glad for.

"Seeing visions of Agartha is worse than any of that. I just. . . need it to stop. I need to dream about something else. It won't stop until Benedicta is dead and there is no chance of Agartha's magic reaching the continent."

Beside Sunna, Sif clears her throat awkwardly. She wants to ask Sunna what happens if they fail, but the words that come out are, "Do you. . . uh. . . want a hug, or something?"

Sunna sniffles. "Yes."

They embrace, awkwardly at first, until a faint yearning begins to glow in each of their hearts and the distance between the two of them closes into a connection. A tenuous connection, but enough that when Sif's arms tighten around Sunnhilde, the latter woman's usually mild laugh comes out as a loud snort. They both burst into laughter, tears collecting in their eyes, and Sunnhilde's arms tighten around Sif in return.

"Thanks, Sif."

"Sure, whatever," Sif mutters. Desperate to erase the bashfulness in her own voice, she asks, "Hey, you know how to gamble?"

"It depends on the game," Sunna responds.

-

Inside the cabin, Buri and Wahyu drink warm beer from pewter cups. The night has gone silent as most of the day crew has found a place to sleep below deck. Their absence, and the quiet rocking of the ocean, lends the cabin a contemplative air. Only the captain, who is known to keep odd hours, and Buri, who has no set schedule, stay awake. The conversation is mostly polite small talk. An excuse to stay and drink. Only, the longer the night grows and the more Wahyu drinks, the clearer it becomes that the captain has something on his mind. At last, he speaks.

"Later this week, we arrive at Titzi. Can you keep a secret?" Wahyu's steady voice has a taste of doubt lingering within it.

Buri grunts affirmatively.

"We'll be picking up supplies. Have you been to Titzi before?"

"No."

"It's important no soul in town has any reason to suspect we might be pointed towards Agartha. Nobody butchers magicians like Titzi and I almost wouldn't blame them, knowing what horror the Three Mothers have brought to Atlas. Except that in Titzi, they'll burn a whole village down if a single person in it is caught doing magic. They guard the seas heading to Agartha, and well. I'll let the rest of the crew know soon, but you should prepare for a fight, just in case."

The old man strokes his beard. His eyes are fixed on the warm, flickering tip of a nearly spent candle.

"That's your secret, Captain?"

"One more thing," Wahyu starts, "and I'm only telling you this out of professional courtesy. But our Queen Benedicta has asked me to kill you if you get out of line. Sif and Ivon, also. Sunnhilde, depending on the circumstances."

At that, Buri's beard twitches. "How do they know us? Isn't her ship ahead?"

"Not too far. The day we set off, I sent her a pigeon with an update. I didn't recognize your names. No offense. If I had known, I would've lied. Far as I'm concerned, us thieves have to stick together when we can."

"Appreciated, Captain." Buri lifts his cup for a toast. Amber beer spills from the cups. They make a dull clink.

Buri clears his throat. "If she dies, will you follow her order?"

"I don't know. Maybe. It depends. I have a ship full of people who deserve to be paid for risking their lives. Do you think you'll kill her?"

"Do you want me to answer that?" Buri responds, slowly.

"No." Wahyu looks grimly into his cup, watching his reflection in the ripples of dark liquid. "No, I don't."

Chapter 23

Najah

Béma, on the banks of Fal River

When Najah and her new friend arrive back in Béma, it is too late. They learn within minutes that Sif has been arrested. It's the talk of the town. Supporters of the Church brag about how easily she was captured; only Najah knows it's because she was so sick.

Najah spits on the ground in anger and hisses through her teeth, "Cowards!"

Her soul overflows with the urge for revenge, simultaneously energizing and repulsing her. Her mother's voice tells her this isn't the way to solve things, but part of her doesn't care. Why should violent men be allowed to escape violent ends? She draws her dagger and starts to stomp away when Tasoula stops her.

"What could you possibly do on your own, against a whole army?"

Najah deflates. She wants to assert herself, but feels stupid for her rashness and guilty for wanting to see anyone dead. "I. . . don't know, I guess."

Bending down to her level, Tasoula suggests something else. "Let me introduce you to a friend of mine. They know a lot about what happens in the region. If Sif is in the city, they can break her out, maybe. If she's left, they'll know where to."

"You promise?" Najah asks.

Tasoula shrugs. "Nothing in the world is certain, dear. But if my friend finds you interesting, they'll do what they can. If it doesn't work, you can still go stab someone. Although I'm sure your friend doesn't want you to get arrested, too."

Najah reflects on something Sif had said: *If we run into trouble, I'll hold it off. You just run.*

And her own response: *I was going to.*

So much for that.

Tasoula takes Najah down, down into the narrow, crooked alleyways of Béma, where the smell of food and sight of coin is replaced by smoke and dust. Roads are narrower and the people on them thinner, a little less at ease. Many more homes fly the flag of Ograna. Najah spots more than one image of a horn-headed sword-swallower, an allusion to Aneir. Outside a building missing its doors sit offering bowls to Saint Daado, Saint Buri, and Saint Teodore. Najah peeks inside the bowls curiously, finding satchels of herbs, split pieces of coin, and other odd trinkets. Nothing of real value. Nothing like the shrines to Saint Daado she's seen at the gates to most cities around the continent. Back at the half-rotten inn, Sif had said something about how every city is the site of a struggle for authority that ended in blood. If that's true, it's clear the residents of this neighborhood haven't yet had their day in the sun.

Tasoula and Najah are ushered through a winding building, then across the road into another, and through several makeshift doorways covered in dull cloth. The air takes on a hazy, golden quality as the light struggles to reach them between tall, close buildings. The route feels purposefully confusing, as if the two men leading them forward are obfuscating their path. She looks up at Tasoula, searching for an answer in her expression, and finding only calm.

The pair of them step unexpectedly into a large room covered in thin, colorful cloth and filled with plush crimson and gold pillows. Symbols of Aneir dot the walls and tables. A crowd of people of all ages, sizes, genders, and countries chat in low, friendly voices and spare only a casual glance at the two women as they enter the room. Through the doorways to adjoining rooms, Najah spies glimpses of alchemists brewing odd liquids, with acerbic smells that sting her nose.

A somewhat thin, aging person with a receding mop of blonde hair and a messy beard stands up to greet them. They're missing an arm and are hunched as if cradling some injury to the stomach. As they stand, the others in the room take notice. Najah gets the sense they're someone important, so when Tasoula offers them a slight bow out of politeness, Najah awkwardly attempts to follow her lead.

The one-armed person waves a hand through the air, like they're dispelling the formality. "Please. You're. . . Thalia, right? Mihail's granddaughter?"

Tasoula shakes her head. "You have the right grandfather, but the wrong granddaughter. I'm Tasoula, and this is my friend Najah."

"Uh, hi," Najah stammers.

The elder looks Najah up and down, humming. "I hope you aren't expecting work. The Union hasn't employed children for a long time. It's for your own good, dear. Thieving is a dangerous line of work. You can have any food you'd like for now, though."

Tasoula starts to explain, but Najah cuts her off impatiently. "My friend Sif was just arrested, and I need to rescue her!"

The one-armed thief reels backwards in shock, then smiles a wide, toothy grin. "The Destroyer? Keno Sif?"

"Yes; she's sick and the Church of Druga took her somewhere."

The aging thief motions at some of the others in the room. They stand up and rush away.

"Dear girl, I'm so glad you brought this to me. My name is Ivon of Heron-Muse, and I'd be happy to help you."

Chapter 24

Kisha of Feigrvoller

???

Kisha is wiping the blood from her sword when the news comes in. At her feet lay a half dozen priests of Aneir, mostly men, and many of them old. Since the worship of *degenerate* deities has been suppressed, fewer young people have found their way to the shrines of Asthia, Siduri, and Aneir. Salko, a young noble under her command, approaches her from behind, casually running a hand through his curling autumn hair. He examines the devastation before shifting his attention to the small temple of Aneir, barely more than a cave. The coppery scent of blood and the drone of flies already fill the air. These were not clean deaths. Salko isn't bothered by the idea that heathen worshippers died, or died painfully, but the excessiveness of it strikes him as unseemly.

"Was all of this necessary, Kisha?" he asks, with a tone that suggests more annoyance than concern.

"Somebody has to get their hands dirty. Maybe if you were a little less afraid of it, your daddy would have let you be in charge instead."

Salko's lips twitch into a brief frown, quickly replaced by a feigned indifference developed from years of observing his father in court. Besides, it isn't that Kisha has any real power, only that she has made herself a valuable enough weapon that she is allowed some additional liberties and resources. A stupid move on the part of the Church officials, Salko thinks bitterly.

"We received news that Keno Sif has been captured. There's a rumor as well that the girl was caught, but something may have happened while she was transported. We were right to search near the border of the desert."

"Where is she being taken?"

Salko produces a map from his satchel and points to a small town called Behno, almost halfway between Hvek's border and capital. "Right here. The town is nothing, but we have a fairly large prison for exactly this situation. You should know, though, that she's incredibly sick. Barely able to talk or move."

"Send a letter to Behno. If she dies before I get there, so will whoever is responsible for not saving her."

"It will take time for the letter to be delivered, Kisha. She could already be dead."

"I don't care," Kisha snaps. "Do it."

"Why? She's just a barbarian! Do you know how much time has been spent on your little quest? We should be focusing on the girl. You're lucky you weren't hanged after you disappeared."

If Kisha is offended by the use of the word barbarian to refer to northerners, she doesn't show it. "Think, Salko. Isn't that what you aristocrats are supposed to be good for? If Sif lives, she might tell us where to find Najah."

Salko doesn't believe her at all. Kisha is still after the glory of killing a legendary enemy. Or maybe she imagines doing the deed herself will earn her further liberties with the Church. Salko gestures accusingly to the needlessly dead priest. His meaning is clear. She's bloodthirsty, and if he gathers enough evidence, he might end up in charge, while she ends up in a shallow grave.

"They would've wanted it to be like this," Kisha responds.

"What?" Salko responds, taken aback by the absurdity of Kisha's response. No sane person would want to die, save maybe the priestesses of the Lunar Goddess of Death. Although whether or not they're sane could be up for debate.

"They worship the god of courage. They would've wanted to die fighting. Running would be cowardly."

"Is that why you made this mess?" he asks.

"It's not like it matters to them," Kisha deflects. Salko isn't sure if she means the Church of Druga or the Aneir priests. "Besides you should've heard the one with the red hair. *May your sword stay sharp,*" Kisha laughs. "What a stupid thing to say to an opponent."

Salko sighs. "The Church doesn't want a mess. Even an up-jumped mercenary can see that, Kisha."

Kisha bares her teeth at him. "Is that so? Well, why don't you stay here to help with the cleanup while I push ahead? Have fun."

Salko bites his tongue as she stomps off to the horses, gathering the few soldiers cracked or low-mannered enough to actually respect her. Together, they gallop towards the horizon, in the direction of the prison. Salko watches them disappear, then leaves the priests' bodies behind to rot in the sun.

Chapter 25

Young Sif, the Destroyer

Titzi, the gateway to the sea

Titzi is a welcome sight, despite its reputation. Uniform buildings made of bright stucco, rock, and seashell dot the city on either end of wide roads shaded by tall palms. The sky is a vast, shining blue. On their approach, the crew of the *Rose Gold* can smell food cooking at stalls set up just outside the port. The scent of it would be mouth-watering even if they hadn't subsisted on crackers and bone stew the past several days. Captain Wahyu doesn't even try to stop his crew from rushing to the stalls. It would be too cruel. Instead, he reminds them not to mention their destination, and waves them off with an order to return in an hour. A deluge of whooping pirates run and jump down the pier, practically throwing coins at the venders.

"I can't believe this. . ." Ivon groans. "I just saw somebody drop a whole lida. It rolled right into the water."

"Maybe there's time to jump in after it," Sif jokes.

Ivon starts to consider it when Buri put his large hand up against their chest.

"Wait," he rumbles. "Something's wrong."

Sif eyes Buri curiously, noticing his narrowed eye and tensing shoulders.

"Are you afraid, Uncle?"

Buri shoots Sif an annoyed glance. "Just cautious."

Sunnhilde, who has spent more and more time with the group lately, agrees. "They're watching us."

"Sure, we're customers—" Sif starts, but then notices it isn't just that. Passersby and port guards are stealing glances at the ship. From a rooftop across the street, a small group of children are laying on their stomachs and observing the whole scene. Is a single ship that unusual for a port city?

Sif blows a strand of hair out from her eyeline and shrugs. "Eh. . . maybe they just aren't used to foreign ships?"

"It's a port town, Keno," Buri reminds her gently. Sif grimaces.

"I know, Uncle."

"Well, I'm heading into town." Sunnhilde casually announces, parting the other three with her hands. Brass bangles on her wrists ring against each other.

"You're the one person who shouldn't!" Ivon practically yelps. "Who is going to pay us if you die?"

Sif punches them in the shoulder. The truth of Ivon's discomfort, their ultimatum from the Heron-Muse Mages' Guild, remains their own.

"I'll be fine if I have someone strong with me." Sunnhilde grins in Sif's direction. Sif feels her face grow hot. Buri and Ivon each hide a smile, trading a knowing look with each other. They're going to be insufferable later.

"Yeah, alright," she responds, trying her best to sound like she doesn't care one way or the other. Truthfully, after seeing all the attention they were getting in town, Sif had planned on buying a bowl of stew at the pier and then wasting away her time on the ship. Maybe try to win back some of the coin she's lost to Wahyu. As she accompanies Sunnhilde down the plank, she can hear Ivon murmuring to Buri in the tone they use when there is particularly scandalous gossip. In this case, Sif and Sunnhilde are the gossip.

They stop and get a skewer at one of the stalls, then walk into town. All the while, heads turn to follow the pair of them. The attention makes Sif's jaw clench, even as Sunnhilde floats along beside her, ephemeral, elegant, and unbothered.

Sif edges closer to Sunna, lowering her voice conspiratorially. "What are we here for, Sunna? Figure I should know what some of these folks are about to die for."

Sunnhilde arches an eyebrow. "That's very dramatic, Keno."

"It's Sif," she corrects, but almost doesn't. "I'm not dramatic, I've just been in enough fights to know when one is about to happen."

Sunnhilde loops her arm in Sif's. "Well, Titzi has an excellent tailor. . ."

Sif stops in her tracks, letting go of Sunna's arm. "Sunna, tell me we aren't shopping for dresses right now."

"Among other things," Sunnhilde confirms. "Why, what's wrong with shopping?"

"Nothing is wrong with it, but we're on our way to a murder. It's strange timi— oh." Sif pauses. Sunnhilde is barely able to conceal her smile. "You're messing with me."

Sunnhilde laughs musically. "Titzi does have a great tailor, but I just need a few alchemical ingredients."

Sif closes her eyes and sighs, running her fingers through her dark hair, and responds, "Don't joke like that. If someone separated us, I don't know if I could get you back. What if you got hurt?"

When Sif opens her eyes, it almost looks like Sunna is blushing. Before she turns away, at least. "That's sort of sweet. Although I can take care of myself. Still, after all that time in Queen Benedicta's court, it's nice to have someone I can trust."

"Sure," Sif mutters, still sore that she fell for Sunnhilde's joke. Although, it was kind of funny.

"Well, I guess it's better if you stay close, then," Sunna adds, turning just long enough to flash a charming smile. "After all, they did drug the food."

"Is that another joke?" Sif hisses under her breath, leaning in close.

"Come on, now you're joking. You really can't feel it? It's just a little somnafera to loosen our tongues."

Moist chunks of meat glisten on the wooden skewer in Sif's hand. She tosses it into a gutter on the side of the road. "I hate this place. Why would anyone use one of Siduri's gifts to uphold the law? It's obscene."

"Relax, you'll look suspicious. Besides, somnafera is nice. It always gives me a warm feeling in my chest. But we should hurry, in case one of the sailors says something they shouldn't."

"Great." Though Sif grumbles, a fuzzy warmth begins to spread in her chest. "You're lucky you're pretty."

Sunnhilde stops walking. "Oh, I'm pretty?"

The fucking somnafera. Sif plays it off like the admission was made on purpose, rolling her eyes dramatically.

"Come on," Sif mumbles. "I don't want to get killed over a shopping trip."

The alchemist's shop is located just off of the main road, although the sign reads "Exotic Herbalist." A variety of colorful flowers and tall, rambling ferns line the short walkway to the front door. Ducking under the leaves makes Sif feel like she is charting a path through a jungle. It brings to mind travelling with Ograna's self-proclaimed bandit queen years ago, before her execution.

The inside of the building is an explosion of flora that only heightens the sensation. The dense, musty aroma is overwhelming. The bright side is that the two of them no longer feel the eyes of the locals appraising them. The building is so full of plant life that a person could be forgiven if they forgot there was a store among all of the green. Insects buzz overhead and crawl through the dirt. Tinted light shines down from glass set—absurdly, to Sif's mind—into the ceiling. Years of traveling and Sif has never seen anything like it. From deep in the brush, an elderly man's voice calls out.

"Welcome! Make your way towards my voice, please."

When they find him, he is sitting on a stool, trimming the leaves from small succulents. He is short, even shorter than Sif, with thinning hair and a bushy, unkempt mustache that threatens to take over his face. His wiry glasses balance unevenly on his nose.

"Ah, Miss Jule, is it? Am I remembering you right?"

Sunnhilde nods politely. "You remember! Yes, I'm back in town and buying the same as before, if you have it."

Jule? Sif looks at her friend, hoping for an answer. A meaningful glance, mouthed secret, or a wink. But Sunnhilde doesn't give up anything. The woman is a natural actor. The shopkeeper hops down from his stool and strolls further into the room, calling back at them from behind a thin copse of small, fruit-bearing trees, "Yes! I got your letter and made sure to have it in stock. It's an unseasonably warm time of year, though. I nearly couldn't get my hands on it. This only arrived a week ago, by chance."

"Lucky me," Sunnhilde replies.

"Lucky both of us, Miss Jule. You owe me two lidas." The shopkeeper holds out his hand expectantly.

Everything about the transaction is odd. It's clear Sif knows very little about who Sunnhilde really is. She could be the princess of Hvek, or a changeling from an ancient, underground cult, to the god of spotted geckos, and Sif would have no idea.

"Jule?" Sif asks, once they're outside. The humidity of the alchemist's shop is gradually wearing off, but the crowd of busy shoppers glancing at them is working to replace it in terms of discomfort.

"Everyone has secrets, Sif." It isn't that Sunnhilde is wrong, but the response is unnerving. Because it isn't a real answer, and it implies the existence of other non-answers.

"Is that your real name?"

"Oh, no. I just needed a fake name and that's the first one I thought of. Can't let anyone trace us to Ag—"

Sif clamps her hand around Sunnhilde's mouth before the word *Agartha* can leave it. Sunnhilde's eyes flare with horror and confusion. Her hand rests tellingly on her chest, where the warmth from the drug emanates.

"It's not somnafera," Sif murmurs. Sunnhilde has had somnafera enough that it is familiar to her. It shouldn't affect her like this. Given how much it took for Sunna to convince everyone she isn't really a witch, she has the most to lose out of everyone if the people of Titzi become suspicious.

Sunnhilde shakes her head side to side. Nothing usual in a small dose should have loosened her tongue like that. Not anyone who follows Siduri. Whatever they've been dosed with is stronger than they thought. Goddess knows what it's done to the dozens of sailors who had eaten at the same stall. Sif curses her own short-sightedness. She knew coming into Titzi would be dangerous, but still underestimated the kingdom's ability to keep tabs on strange sailors. Sif slowly removes her hands from Sunna's lips. She can feel their impression on her palm.

"We need to run," Sif says, and her companion only nods.

The way to the docks is clear. The citizens of Titzi line the side of the road leading up to the *Rose Gold*, watching the newcomers. Most of the pirates are back on board, and even though there is no fight, the scene fills both Sif and Sunnhilde with a crawling dread. When they tell Wahyu about their suspicions, he has the ship back on the open sea within minutes, leaving behind anyone unlucky enough to have ventured out.

Chapter 26

Najah

The Great Desert

It doesn't take Ivon's network of thieves and beggars long to track down where Sif has been taken. So many soldiers all over the city are celebrating the capture and eventual execution of Keno Sif the Destroyer that Béma is bound to be drained of all its alcohol in half a week.

The trail leads to a town called Behno, in the part of Hvek's borders that aren't disputable. No Ogranan flags to hint at safety. It takes longer than Ivon promises to find a map that shows the town but, even though the wait is agony, Najah doesn't blame them for it when she learns why. Behno wasn't a notable town before it held the Church's prison, and so for most people there is no town at all—only a relatively new castle that seemed to suck in the political detritus from all around the region. Heathen worshippers, thieves, vagabonds, revolutionaries, undisciplined workers. Anyone who threatened the order that the Church of Druga fought so hard to win during the war of expansion.

Before they leave, Ivon procures Najah a change of clothes, something befitting the child of a struggling merchant rather than a wanted criminal. They also have a barber shave down her matted hair, which Najah doesn't like but does accept on the condition that it be quick so they can leave. After the haircut she runs to a stone birdbath outside the Thieves' Union to view her reflection, and deflates at her boyish appearance. But it'll be worth it if they can save Sif, and who would find the sight of a disabled elder and their young ward suspicious?

-

"How did you meet Sif?" Najah asks, bouncing on the back of an animal Ivon called a camel. At first Najah was scared of it, but has since realized it's essentially a strange looking horse. Ivon bought it two days prior from a merchant who admitted to knowing nothing of Sif's fate. An event that felt both troubling and soothing.

"Ah." Ivon chuckles, their remaining hand holding the reins. "It's a funny story. We both tried to rob the same person, who turned out to be a spirit with a habit of dragging people to their deaths at the bottom of a swamp. Although we didn't get along at first. In part because I saw Sif in trouble and tried to escape with more than my share of the cut. Sadly, I paid for that later."

"Is that how you lost your arm?" Najah adjusts herself on her seat and wipes the sweat from her forehead. In the distance, a falcon glides effortlessly through the clear sky, hunting for prey, white tufts of feathers visible on its stomach.

"No, darling. I primarily lost a bit of pride. But I was young at the time, and when you're young you think pride is important and imagine yourself invincible, so it seemed like a great loss. Now if you want to know when we became friends, it was when the two of us and Buri got together with a mage to try and break into a church in Heron-Muse."

Najah is enraptured. Despite their adventures, Sif is still a grumpy old hermit in her eyes. A hermit who can make a good campfire meal, and is occasionally a bit of fun, but still. These scraps of information are a revelation. "Why did you rob a church? What happened?"

"One question at a time, love. I did it for the coin, naturally. At the time I was in what seemed like a lucky situation as a thief who could take jobs from the Mages' Guild. Everyone else was too afraid. Sif, on the other hand, wanted to impress a famous poet to try and. . ." Ivon snaps out of their reverie, remembering the child listening, and quickly amends the story, "make a new friend."

Najah scoffs. "That doesn't sound like her."

"Well," Ivon says, hard-pressed to agree but wanting to avoid the topic of sex, "it's what happened, dear. He was a very well-known poet. And as for what happened, the mage died, and the rest of us were almost executed by a very angry noble. You know, you really shou—"

"Ivon!" Najah leans forward, pointing past Ivon at a small caravan that's appeared over a dune of sand. A group of about two dozen people mill about four wagons in loose, heavily embroidered clothing, unlike anything Najah has seen before.

"We just stopped this morning, dear," Ivon reminds her.

"But what if they know something about Sif?"

Ivon chews the edge of their tongue nervously. Najah has wanted to stop and ask about Sif at every sign of human life so far, but the more often they stop, the greater the chance Sif will be dead when they arrive. And though they wouldn't admit it, part of them doesn't want to stop, in case it means learning Sif is dead. Not when they've just learned she's still alive. "I don't know. We should try to make better time."

"I'll be quick, I promise." The hope in Najah's voice is too strong to resist.

"Very well. But I'm holding you to that. If you take too long, we're not stopping anymore."

Najah sits in her seat like she is ready to leap off of the camel as soon as they stop. Luckily for Ivon, the height of her seat on its back forces her to rethink. As they enter the camp, the inhabitants begin to whisper, trading uncertain glances between each other. An unspoken conversation. The clear consensus is that a crippled elder and scrawny young boy can't be any danger.

A muscular man with endless curls of long red hair approaches them. "Ho, elder. You're welcome to rest in safety here, but we have no food or water to spare, and nothing to trade."

Najah scrabbles down from her seat, Ivon not far behind but grunting with the effort. "We just want to know if you heard anything about a prisoner being transported through here."

The red-haired man puts his hands on his hips and stares skywards, combing through recent memories. "No. Well. . . could be. A large group of Druga cultists passed us going east two days ago. Maybe three. We stay clear of that type, but they had a wagon like a person could keep a prisoner in, with the barred door."

Najah's eyes spark with excitement. "That has to be her."

"Then we should go," Ivon gently suggests.

"What else did you see?" Najah asks the red-haired man, ignoring Ivon entirely.

The man strokes his chin thoughtfully. "Nothing much to tell. Typical group of soldiers. Used to be even bandits didn't wander out here much, now you're like to meet soldiers every few days. Going between the riverlands and central kingdoms, I'd guess. If I were you, I'd stay clear of them."

Easier said than done. Ivon pats Najah's back, encouraging her to saddle up. "We will, thank you."

As they climb the camel, the red-haired man watches them. Then, just before they head off, he calls out, "Wait!" They stay seated as he rummages through his wagon, then jogs over to them and presents a sleeve of water, kept shut with a bit of cork. "I apologize for not offering this to you sooner. It's been a hard journey. Wares from the east coast are harder to move since the war."

Ivon shakes their head. "You should keep it for yourself, friend."

The man practically shoves the sleeve into Ivon's lap. "No. If you will not take it for yourself, then take it for us. Unlike most of the world, we have not forgotten what Saint Daado and Shen teach. Travelers should watch out for one another. I only forgot for a moment."

Ivon looks at the man's gift as if it's a puzzle that needs to be solved.

Najah taps them on the shoulder. "We should go."

"Remind me, where does Shen bring his devoted followers after death?" Ivon asks.

"To the Everroad. An endless trek along breathtaking vistas, lined with fruit trees and within walk of cool streams. A perfect journey that never ends."

"Well, may you find your way there." Carefully, Ivon places the sleeve in their pack. "If you wind up in Béma, ask for the Thieves' Union. Maybe they can help move your goods."

The man grunts in response. Having received what they came for, Ivon and Najah set off. Once they're out of earshot, Najah leans forward to whisper, "That was weird, right?"

"Yes," Ivon responds, their clear voice tinted with unexpected melancholy. "Very."

-

Luck is a fickle thing. Just as the heat and travel begins to weigh too heavily on Ivon, a trading post appears on the horizon. The lunar goddess rises in the sky on their approach, unfurling her cloak of stars and stealing some of the brutal heat from the desert. Then, as they approach the trading post, comes a mass of rolling, gray clouds. The smell of rain. Najah's heart sinks, a ship wrecked in that sea of gray above.

"We can't slow down now. We're almost there, right?"

Ivon sighs. "We can't push on like this, love. I'm sorry. Maybe someone in town will know about Sif, though."

Despite her earlier attitude, Najah is much less interested in news than she is in their destination. It's one thing to make your choice when all options are available, and another to have a choice forced on you by fate or circumstance. At least the poor camel can rest.

The trading post is surprisingly lively, considering its remote location. Or maybe because of it. With countless miles of desert on either side, who wouldn't be tempted to stop at the only sign of food, water, and safety, especially with a storm on the way? The thought of a nice night in is almost exciting. Good food, interesting new people. A bed that is more than a roll of cloth. If it wasn't for the terrible urgency in Najah's heart, it would be the perfect thing after days and days of weary travel. As Ivon hitches their camel to a post outside a stable, Najah runs inside to inquire about Sif. Near the entrance is the stable hand, a young, heavyset woman shoveling hay.

"You're a little young to be alone, girl. Got a parent somewhere? Or a horse?"

Najah holds back her natural instinct to argue but is distantly pleased the stable hand has recognized she isn't a boy, despite her new haircut. "I don't need the stable. I'm trying to find my friend."

"Another little kid?"

Najah suppresses a groan. "I'm. . . not a little kid. And no, my friend is an old woman. Like, really old. She might have been traveling with some paladins."

"Ah," the stable hand responds hesitantly, her eyes turned away to avoid contact. She wipes sweat from her forehead and swats away a bothersome fly.

"What is it?" Najah asks, afraid of the answer.

The stable hand exhales deeply and runs her round fingers through her hair. "Unless your friend is a paladin, I don't. . . uh. . ." she gathers herself. "Look, they had an old woman with them, but she was either dead or most of the way there. I sent them to an alchemist, but who knows what came of it. We don't exactly have the same quality of items you'd get in Hvek or Ograna."

Najah clenches her jaw hard, trying not to let tears spill out.

The stable hand shifts her weight uncomfortably. "You okay, kid?"

Najah keeps her gaze on the ground as she stomps out without answering, but as soon as she passes the entryway, everything floods out. Hot tears spill down her cheeks. She bawls in a way that only the newly born and soon-to-be-dead do, burying her face in camel fur to conceal it from Ivon's concern. They reach out their hand to touch her, but she slaps it away. Even if it's unfair, Najah can't help but oscillate the blame between Ivon and herself. The camel is the only thing she knows can't hurt her. Unlike people, animals will never disappoint. They are always and only themselves, and never aspire to be anything else.

"Najah, what did y. . . what did they say?"

Najah takes a deep breath, wipes the tears from her red eyes, and turns to face Ivon. "Sif is probably dead already. Druga cultists took her to an alchemist, but I guess she looked really bad."

"Then we should talk to the alchemist, right? Who knows, we could get lucky." Ivon smiles confidently, but it's more an expression of will than belief. Their eyes betray a sense of exhaustion and desperation.

Najah remembers what Sif said in Béma. One of the last things she said.

I'm not going to die. I promise. Be. . . brave. For a little bit.

She could be brave. For now. After all, having to keep herself together is nothing new, and what could be more worth the effort than protecting a friend? Najah nods at Ivon, ready to embark, but when Ivon turns around their legs wobble beneath them and they nearly collapse.

"Ivon!" Najah rushes to their side.

"I'm fine." A sheepish expression flashes over their face. "Just my pride. You never really get used to being old. I just need to rest before we start moving again."

"I'll go find the alchemist while you wait," Najah suggests. It seems wrong to leave them here alone, in this unfamiliar place. Still, if there was danger, what could Najah do other than get in the way? She has a dagger but not the will to use it. All she has in this world is anger and fear, and the desperate urge to find anything that might quench it.

"Please, dear," Ivon says, standing to their full height. An unconvincing display of strength. Their brows are furrowed, words heavy with some emotion or memory that is lost on Najah. "I only need a moment."

"There's no reason I should have to wait here with you." Najah does her best to keep her tone level, but all she can think of is how desperate their situation is. How Sif wouldn't have tried to hold her back.

"It may not be safe." Ivon's tone is suddenly and uncharacteristically severe.

"I haven't been safe for years, and having you with me won't change that," Najah snaps at them. She has more words in her, ones that would break Ivon's heart. But she summons all the restraint she has and swallows them back, choosing instead to march off with or without Ivon's blessing. They don't call out to her.

Against good sense, Najah storms away without asking the bartender for directions, choosing to put as much distance as possible between herself and her conversation with Ivon. The trading post is relatively small, but in the darkness, what is merely unfamiliar becomes entirely inscrutable. Najah almost regrets not getting directions, but stubbornness urges her onward. Two men hold each other hands next to a stall where locals sell shocking quantities of water. They speak their burdens aloud in order to better share them. "We can't keep it in stock since the croplands were burned last spring."

"Burned for what? Seems like I was there so recently."

"The Church of Druga did it to stop the Celebrant Prince from marching west."

Further on, a group of drunk men in long white and gray robes gossip outside of conical tents set up among tufts of sandy grass. A pale lizard darts after gnats drawn by firelight. ". . .said she was setting off to the southeast to discover new lands."

"The southeast? I hope it works. My mother once told me the southeastern lands live in perpetual night, and instead of grass there is a flower that causes forgetfulness."

"Really? I hope that's not true. No disrespect to the lunar goddess, but there is a reason she shares the sky."

A harrowed woman sits on the edge of her carriage, tears drying below her bloodshot eyes as an old, genderless trader in a turban tries to comfort her. A paper lantern hangs from the corner of the carriage, its soft, yearning light too weak to fight off the darkness of the world.

Her voice cracks as she speaks. ". . .when they got there, the whole town was crushed. Crushed! Burned or abandoned I could understand, but this? Shen protect us from whatever demon could do something like that."

"Oh, I'm sorry. I know what that place meant to you. To all of you."

All these disparate people, brought together in a strange land, pushed by their past, pulled inexorably towards their future, struggling as the present attempts to devour them. The emptiness in Najah's chest could hold a whole cavern in it. Ivon put themselves at risk to travel with her, and she treated them like a passenger instead of like someone who also had a stake in the outcome. Who was also fighting with their past, present, and future.

"Fucked everything up again. . ." she mutters to herself.

A deep, unfamiliar voice answers from behind her. "Boy. What are you doing here alone?" Najah turns to see a man and a woman, both dressed in simple leather armor. On both of their belts hangs a scrap of fabric decorated with the symbol of the Virtuous Path. Soldiers for the Church of Druga.

"Is that a boy?" the woman asks, peering at Najah critically. After a moment, the soldier leans to her companion and whispers something in his ear. His eyes widen. The weight of Najah's dagger hanging on her side makes itself known, and despite the dread rising in her chest her eyelids become heavy. A whisper, barely recognizable as a human voice, hisses at her in the distance, and as it does a flicker of sharp pain rises and falls in the back of her skull. A heavy, grasping sensation rushes through her like rising water.

"Boy, look at us when we speak to you." The anger in the soldier's voice pulls her back to reality, if only a little. Najah struggles to raise her head and open her eyes, only to find the world in front of her has horrifyingly and imperceptibly changed. In the night, beyond the campfires and lanterns, bodies like fog undulate and seethe, trailing a sickly tide of gold behind them. Through some outpouring of dream logic, Najah can sense that the soldiers in front of her are not human. Though they appear normal in every way, a presence writhes within them, watching keenly through their eyes. Fear of the creatures in front of her prevents Najah from calling to the merchants for help, who carry on nearby as if nothing at all has happened.

"I-I'm sorry. I didn't hear."

"I asked where you're from," the man growls. The side of his face bubbles like something beneath him is pushing its way out.

"I didn't do anything, okay? I'm just looking for someone." Najah stumbles backwards. "Just leave me alone."

The soldiers reach forward, ready to grab her, when Ivon calls out from down the street. "Hello! Is there a problem? That's my grandson." Trotting along at their feet is, inexplicably, a hoary fox. Its dark eyes meet her own, an acknowledgement and something else less knowable, but as it does Najah feels a revitalizing breath enter her body and set her blood pumping again. When she blinks, the fox is gone and the world is back as it should be, filled with only the mundane sort of monstrosities.

This is your grand*son*?" The woman asks.

"Yes, my grandson Saed," Ivon continues. "We're heading into the civilized lands to live closer to the Church. Our home was razed by heathens, where my daughter and son-in-law were both lost."

This fiction cools down the soldiers somewhat. They step back from Najah, giving her room to breathe, hands further from their weapons and shoulders less tense.

"You two shouldn't be out so late. We've been left behind here in anticipation of troublemakers. You see why a child being out this late, alone and behaving with hostility, seems suspicious."

Ivon nods. "Of course. He was only looking for me. I insisted on going out alone to buy water, but I get confused. I suppose I haven't accepted my old age yet."

"Still, he can't speak disrespectfully to soldiers. That attitude will cause you problems in the central kingdoms."

"Apologize, Saed." Ivon's voice is harsh and commanding. Najah is so astounded she almost doesn't respond.

"Of course. I'm sorry." It's good luck that Najah is in such a shaken state. To the soldiers, she is the perfect image of a boy who realizes the trouble he is in and is grateful to be released from it.

"Saed has been troubled since his parents were killed. We only have each other now. I'm sure you understand what it's like to lose someone you love."

The woman softens immediately. "Who doesn't, in these times? Just go back to wherever you're staying as soon as possible. Don't leave your grandson's side again. Understood?"

Ivon nods. "Yes. Thank you for your kindness."

As they leave the soldiers behind and make for the alchemist, Najah finds herself in awe of Ivon, a person who doesn't need to fight in order to overcome danger. An elder who disarmed two young soldiers with only words. She has spent so much of her life running, that to simply walk away is a novel luxury.

"How did you do that?"

"Hmm? It was easy. I've talked myself, and Sif, out of far worse. Always remember, dear, in this life you must be either very honest and upright, or very charming. And since the former path is already closed to me, I choose to be charming. Besides, that woman had a tattoo on her neck of a name and a date. Since it seemed rather crisp, I assumed it was a recent loss. There are situations keen perception will get you out of that physical strength may not."

Najah hadn't noticed any of these details, but the burgeoning awareness of what is possible gleams in her mind like a rosy, golden dawn. As they make their way to the alchemist's shop, her perception of Ivon shifts. They seem less like a kind, if odd, elder, and more like a figure out of myth. If not a hero, at least quite heroic.

They find the shop quickly. It's near the edge of the post, hidden near where they'd entered before. It smells like cloying perfume and looks like the rotten end of a dock. Rather than the one alchemist the stable hand implied they would find, the shop is run by a man and woman, both wearing vibrant makeup and possessed of an unusual jitteriness that has them both frantically darting around the place. A patter of rain begins outside, just audible behind their footsteps.

When neither proprietor acknowledges their entrance, Ivon speaks up. "We're looking for a friend. She is about my age, but a little shorter, with brown skin and a burn scar along her face. We were told you've seen her."

"The Destroyer?" The woman asks, halting in her tracks as if she were pulled by strings. Until now, both alchemists had been moving at a breakneck pace. It is a small miracle every time they pass one another and don't spill the myriad vials and multi-colored herbs that are constantly ferried between different stations around the room.

". . .yes." Ivon admits with some hesitation.

"She left as she came," the man shouts, rifling madly through a pair of stout, wooden boxes.

"Is that alive or dead?" Ivon asks, their amiable demeanor taking on a gruff tone.

The woman is scandalized, eyebrows shooting up her forehead and eyes widening. "Alive or dead? Alive, of course. She looked half a corpse, but unless those cultists mishandle her, she'll live for a little bit, at least. Mind, they do tend to mishandle people."

"She's alive." Najah smiles cautiously, allowing herself a modicum of optimism.

"She's *probably* alive," the woman corrects. "The cultists do tend to mishandle people."

Chapter 27

Old Sif, the Destroyer
Prison

"Oh, good. You're awake."

Even through the pounding headache, blinding disorientation, pain and exhaustion, Sif recognizes Kisha's voice as if they had known each other as children. Sif's mind tells her to get up swinging, but her body is too weak to even move the shackles tying her down. The helplessness is infuriating, a spit in the face.

"Fuck you," Sif groans. Through her cracked eyes she can make out the canvas ceiling of a tent, but not much else.

"Can't hear you, Auntie. You're so weak, you need to speak up," Kisha teases. Sif's vision clears, revealing the glint of a knife in the younger woman's hand.

"Fuck you, Kisha." Sif intends to roar, to scare Kisha, to show herself and the world that she is still strong and capable. Her voice is just loud enough to hear.

Kisha laughs. "What a way to speak to the woman holding your life in her hands. Honestly, I don't get it. I could've killed you and that girl back near Mount Hoda. The only reason I didn't is because I respect you. Or respected what you were. This," Kisha motions at Sif's weakened form. "Is pretty sad. You're like a dog. No understanding of how the real world works, getting kicked around because you refuse to learn."

"You're the dog, Kisha. Running all around the continent at your master's word. Taking whatever scraps they decide you deserve."

Kisha frowns, lowering her knife so that it points at Sif. "I'm more powerful than you ever were. What's the point of any of this if not to get the things we deserve, huh? I would've done anything for stable coin as a kid, you know? It's not political, it's practical. The royals run the world. Nothing is going to change that."

"The royals are a bunch of freaks," Sif groans. As the pressure in her head fades, she becomes aware of the heat and the sound of boots marching outside. "They're all obsessed with who has the best blood. Might as well argue about the best dirt. The best vomit."

Kisha shrugs. "Well, they sent you into hiding, so they must be on to something."

"They won't tolerate you forever."

"You really piss me off, Keno," Kisha growls, grabbing Sif by her shirt. Then, suddenly thinking better of it, she lets go. "Just tell me where Najah is. At this point the cultists are going to kill you either way, but I can make it quick. Hells, I'll even make up a story about how hard you fought. Keep that reputation intact. You know in your heart that you were never going to be able to help her."

Something hidden in Sif's heart, a secret fear, dislodges itself and becomes known. Sif couldn't save Buri as a young woman, before Druga's cultists swarmed every corner of the known world. How could she save Najah now?

Kisha smiles unkindly. "You know I'm right, Auntie."

Sif's breaths come shakily and uneven. The heartache, the regret, the guilt, the fear. They all come so much easier with physical pain. Sif swallows them down, beneath the armor of her pride.

"Do what you have to. I'm not saying anything." Sif knows the temple is probably gone, and Ummun with it. Still, she pictures the lavender hanging on the door of her cabin, a sign she would return home soon, and her heart aches at the thought of not fulfilling that promise.

Kisha rises to her feet, scowling violently. "Old hag. You have no idea. I'm the only one here on your side. I wanted to make this easy. Not like some others." She stomps to the flap of the tent, peeling it back. Sif's head lolls to the side, following Kisha's movements. From outside enters a pale young woman with cold eyes, carrying a leather satchel. The smell of horses and distant rain float in behind her. "Oh look, here's one now. Bye, Auntie."

Chapter 28

Najah

The Great Desert

In the long, winding trail of desert grass and soil and sand, Najah and Ivon find constant signs of life, but very few signs of Sif. They see travelers like themselves, but also lichen and snakes, tall, pale cacti, and the hearth-brown wrens that eat their fruit. Ivon is horrified to find a spider among their belongings one morning. Najah lets the spider crawl into her hand and deposits it safely away from their camp. There are people here who would be horrified to find her among them, as well.

As they come ever closer to Behno, their relationship has reached a comfortable equilibrium. But it isn't the same as when Najah traveled with Sif. Ivon has their own reasons for helping, reasons they keep close to their chest, and a family to get back to besides. Sif may be a loud, drunken bandit, but she's also the first person since Najah's late mother who was willing to risk their life to keep Najah safe. Whatever flaws Sif might have, that means something. It means there is someone out there Najah can trust, but also that there is something in Najah worth protecting.

"You know," Ivon starts, breaking a long silence. "The other day you were asking me about Sif and I never finished my thought."

"I don't remember," Najah admits.

"It's fine, dear. I was going to say that you should ask Sif these things after we rescue her. I think it would do you both some good."

"No, she doesn't like to talk about herself."

"Hmmm." Ivon mulls that over for a while, then responds. "Try one more time. I haven't led you astray yet, have I?"

"Well, not yet." Najah says, a weary but genuine smile on her lips.

-

One dawn, when the sun rises in the east, Ivon ties the camel to a stake and joins Najah on a sand dune that rises over the small town of Behno and the large prison at its back. Behno itself seems impossibly fragile. It's hard to believe this town could withstand the desert on its own. It isn't big enough for trade, nor beautiful enough for visitors. Maybe that is why the prison has latched onto it. It's too remote for unwanted guests and too weak for an uprising of local peasants. Najah considers all of this and tries to anticipate what the plan will be.

They won't be fighting their way in, clearly. Even if they had two arms and no limping gait, Ivon doesn't seem like that kind of fighter, and *she* isn't a fighter at all.

Are they going to climb the walls? Ivon is old and missing an arm. She wouldn't put it past them to find a way, but it also occurs to her that climbing a sheer wall during the day would make them very visible.

Or perhaps they are going to pretend to be prisoners? Surely an extra set of captives wouldn't raise any eyebrows. Then again, the whole point of her journey with Sif was to avoid arrest. Although going by Ivon's stories, they've broken out of plenty of prisons in the past.

A lightbulb goes off in her head. They can pretend to be local workers. The prison is in the middle of nowhere; they would have to rely on locals for some of their supplies. Who would question an elder and their young helper? Najah makes their guess aloud, trying to temper their excitement at having seen their route.

"Very good guess, dear, but no. Behno is small, it would be clear that we don't belong. Besides, we would need to scout out the town long enough to know how and when to make our move. Time is a little short. Before the

Church of Druga began expanding, mathematicians from the desert kingdoms figured out how to ferry water around their cities. In Phosita, for example, is the floating aqueduct, which doesn't float as much as you would think. In Behno, they have an underground system that does some of the same work. We'll be sneaking through there."

-

The entrance to the waterways fills Najah with a dizzying sense of impending danger, from the distant roar of water, the cold and dark air, the bars preventing easy access. She doesn't want to run, but it makes her flinch internally. Somewhere in the back of her mind she knows this is the kind of place that monsters live. Her thoughts must be obvious, because Ivon's face lights up with a bemused expression. When Najah notices, she puffs out her chest, sets her jaw, and stomps most of the way to the bars at the mouth of the semi-circle entrance set into the hillside. The stone prison looms above her.

"So, what now?" she asks. "How do we get through the bars?"

Ivon produces a small glass vial from a pouch. The cork comes out with a pop, filling the air with an acrid, eye-burning scent that makes Najah wrinkle her nose and turn away. It's the same scent she caught in the Thieves' Union before Tasoula introduced her to Ivon. The bars sizzle on contact with the liquid inside of the vial, and a thick smoke carries itself into the air as evidence of their meeting before dissipating on the wind. Slowly, the liquid eats away at the metal. What wonder and awe Najah feels is somewhat dampened by her watering eyes. Ivon turns their head away, but continues to pour until the whole vial is empty, and shining, liquid metal drips like molasses down what remains of the bars. Ivon pops a second bottle.

"Won't someone see that?" Najah asks, holding her nose and waving one hand back and forth in front of her squinting eyes.

"There is nothing worth doing that doesn't carry some risk, little one," Ivon responds.

Najah groans impatiently. "How many vials will you need to get through?"

"Don't worry, dear. I've done this a hundred-thousand times. Most people are too lazy or afraid of trouble to investigate. Prisons tend to be rather noisy, and there is more going on to deal with. Besides, this is our quickest way in, and the faster we do it, the less time anyone has to show up."

"That's what *I* was just sa—"

A long shadow cuts across the ground between them, putting an abrupt end to their conversation. It's a rogue guard. Najah hears him only moments before he appears; the stomp of boots on loose soil and sand. The vague heaviness of a nearby body. The sour, curdling smell of sweat trapped under leather.

"Hey! Who are you?!" The guard has clearly not expected to see anyone here. Judging by the wine skin in his hand he must have snuck off to drink, rather than stumbling upon them while doing his duty.

Ivon adjusts their posture to more resemble a hunched, ailing elder. They place all of their weight on their walking stick. Their voice produces a new, warbling quality.

"I'm Safi of Béma, and this is my grandson, Saed. We noticed smoke coming from this area and—"

The guard lurches down towards them, drawing his sword. "You stay there! Don't move!"

Najah's heart hammers in her chest. This drunken oaf is going to kill Ivon, then she'll be alone *again* and she'll have no way to free Sif, and she'll be stuck here in the prison. The fear grips her imagination and squeezes until the world around her loses focus. She grinds her teeth and clenches her fists. Her breathing is fast and loud and she reaches for her dagger unconsciously. The soldier isn't paying her any attention at all. He stomps drunkenly towards Ivon, who is maintaining the façade. If Najah were clear-headed, she would notice Ivon's eyes on her, dimly reflecting fear at what she might be about to do.

Najah is barely aware of the roar that escapes her lips as she leaps awkwardly onto the soldier's back. She has no plan, but the fear of death is nothing compared to the fear of being alone, of watching her caretaker die. Again. The guard spins around in a bewildering motion and a splash of red catches Najah's eyes.

"Stop!" Ivon barks. They've never taken a harsh tone with her. The jolt of it brings Najah back to reality. As the soldier turns to attack her, Ivon drives their own blade up through the spot where the man's neck and jaw meet. A dazzling fount of bright blood flows down Ivon's blade and over their hand and forearm. Ivon releases their blade and lets the guard's body fall; as it does, Ivon's face is revealed, their lips and brows twisted in fury. Najah steps back, shame fluttering in her chest, then confusion, until her own anger bubbles back to the surface.

"What?!" she yells. Then, remembering where they are, lowers her voice. "I didn't do anything wrong!"

Ivon sighs, the anger draining from their countenance. "No, no you didn't."

"Then what are you mad for?"

"I was mad at myself, dear girl." Ivon pauses, collecting their thoughts. "You shouldn't have to burden yourself with violence. If this happens again, let me take care of it. I always have a plan."

They tap their index finger to their head, though this time Najah doesn't find it so charming.

"I'm already. . . *burdened*." she responds sullenly. "You don't know me, Ivon."

"Well, I can't say that doesn't hurt a little bit," Ivon admits. "Still, whatever you've been through, it can get worse. Please let me take the lead going forward."

Najah raises an eyebrow, a move Ivon feels strangely reminiscent of Sif. They feel a flutter of pain in their chest.

"You really think it can get worse than this?"

"I know it can." Ivon wipes their blade on the dead man's clothes and sheathes it.

"You mean like how you lost your arm?" Najah asks bluntly.

Ivon shakes their head. "No, darling. No, I do not."

Chapter 29

Buri the Giant
The Rose Gold

Lately, Buri has often found himself dreaming of his family in Feigrvoller. For the most part he lived with his two mothers in a cabin. His father was a hunter and was often gone, but would come back with food, coin, and stories every two to three weeks; sometimes longer, sometimes shorter. Then one day, he didn't come back again. One of his mothers, Vibeka, a tall, strong woman with long, wheat-colored hair, spent days crying inconsolably. Hlif, his other mother, masked her distress by doting on Buri and Vibeka constantly. Word came back months later that his father had been killed by soldiers on patrol to the south. They had mistaken the hunting party for a group of bandits and killed or arrested most of them. There was a narrow pass to the southwest of his home in Feigrvoller, northeast of the nation of Ograna, where the hunters had fled from the gang of soldiers, and where Buri's father had been killed trying to defend his friends.

Early one morning, Buri woke up to Hlif begging Vibeka not to leave. When he peeked out of his small room, he saw Vibeka adorned in fresh, bright steel and carrying the family sword. Only after Vibeka, reluctantly agreeing not to seek revenge, put down the sword did she begin to take Buri to Aneir's temple. For a long time afterwards, he held a grudge against Hlif for not allowing his father to be avenged.

Buri's dreams aren't always of his father's death. Sometimes they are of his first crush, a dark-haired boy from a nomadic clan. Sometimes they are of his mother Hlif trying and failing to teach him to cook. Sometimes they are of Vibeka's garden. But they always end the same way. With a memory of the day he lost his eye.

He had been drunk and angry, and caught sight of a man who vaguely resembled one of the soldiers who killed his father. The man was dead before he had time to gasp. When real soldiers appeared to arrest him, Buri could see Aneir's hands on their swords, guiding each stroke to their victory and his humiliation. He looked down to find his own hands held tight in the swordeater's massive palms, turning his blows feeble and clumsy, as if he'd never held a weapon in his life. His heart raced fearfully. The edge of his enemy's sword clipped his face and the last thing he had seen with both eyes was the face of an angry god burned into his mind.

When he was led away in chains, the message had been clear. He now knew what it was like to be helpless in the face of overwhelming violence. Aneir revealed his failure to him and gave him a choice. Accept this slap on the hand and become better, or continue down his current path and receive a punishment with weight. The dream is a reminder of his well-deserved correction.

He wakes up, face damp from silent tears, with only a distant sadness quickly fading in his heart. As he sits up in bed, feeling the waves rocking against the *Rose Gold*, he knows that Hlif had been right to stop Vibeka. Not because his father didn't deserve to be avenged, and not because the violence would be too much of a sin. But because the ability to do violence is a form of power, and the only true way to use it is with the knowledge of what that means, with a mastery of the self he had never managed to find in his youth. It must be tempered by clarity of purpose and a willingness to accept responsibility for its outcomes. Vibeka, much like his younger self, and sometimes like Sif, was too hot-headed. Maybe that's why Vibeka had taken him to Aneir's temple. Although whether it really had been to temper him, or to properly avenge his father, Buri cannot know.

What he does know is that the tears on his face aren't for the loss of his father, or his eye. They're for Sif. Because in Sif he sees a person who is skilled, funny, and kind, but who may still have room to be subsumed by the monstrous allure of thoughtless violence and power. To be the kind of person Buri was. The kind of person who, Buri suspects, the soldiers who killed his father were. People so consumed with fire that they risk being burned up without even noticing. Monsters.

He reminds himself that she is better than he was at her age. Still prone to rashness, and sometimes to cruelty, but also more courageous and generous. Under her mask of bravado beats a golden heart that he is proud to have seen forged. He breathes deeply, then exhales slowly. The smell of salt and the feeling of cool air gradually releases him from his anxiety and places him back in his own body. That is the comfort that allows him to, eventually, forget his nightmare, his sweat-damp skin, and the rocking of the ship, and fall back asleep.

Chapter 30

Najah

The prison-city Behno

Ivon and Najah follow the path of murky water underground until they're under the jail. The tunnel is cool, dark, and quiet, except for the sound of water sloshing around them. Najah cringes as it soaks through her boots and trousers, but the walk through the tunnel is about the only part of the trip that doesn't take an agonizingly long amount of time. Even still, her brain buzzes with anxiety over finding Sif. What if they've come all this way only to learn she is dead? As they approach the town, Najah sees a small graveyard behind the prison. Sif wouldn't want to be buried in a prison. The thought of the old woman spending eternity here makes Najah's heart ache, and a memory of the day her mother died burns through her mind.

Her mother's body, left at their campsite because soldiers and bounty hunters were never far behind and the frozen ground would've taken too long to dig through. Wanting to shake her awake, but the way she was lying making it obvious that she was dead. Her face looking like she was gasping for breath and got stuck. Having felt so out of control for so long that she thought it couldn't get worse, and then it did.

As they make their way under the prison, thin shafts of light trickle down from above. It's the sun, pouring between loose floorboards on the prison's bottom level. Suddenly the boards rattle, shaking down dust and small debris, as a deafening cacophony of horses stampede overhead into the prison. Sunlight beaming in through cracks in the floor flickers maddeningly as armored figures enter the prison. When it's over, dust and dirt from the crossing floats lazily in the golden slats of light. The two of them wait a few moments where a rickety metal ladder leads up to a conspicuous exit, bodies tense and minds racing, then push up the boards and enter the prison.

From their new location, Najah can see what is probably the front entrance to her right. To the left is a long hallway ending in a large, barred door with a courtyard on the other side. Nearby are two narrow stairwells on opposite sides of the room. Before she can take in much more, Ivon rushes her up a set of stairs, encouraging her steps with a prod from what remains of their left arm.

Once they're not completely in the open, Ivon speaks. "She should be up here. My contact said the guards keep the sicker prisoners upstairs. We'll make our way up slowly, stick to the shadows, and free her using the same alchemy that got us through the bars below."

Najah swallows nervously, then nods in silent confirmation of the plan.

Boot steps begin to echo from the hallway at the top of the stairs. The two of them double back, but the main door at the bottom floor begins to open as well, forcing them to reorient yet again. Ivon pushes Najah into a small corner where a trio of wooden barrels have been stacked. They're hidden, if only barely, from the front door and the stairs they just retreated from, but if anyone comes from the other stairway or the path leading to the courtyard, they'll be done for.

"Ivon. . ." Najah's voice wavers, pitched up by the urge to run.

"Shh! Stay quiet," they hiss.

The two approaching groups must have expected each other, because they stop to talk in front of the stairway. Najah can barely make out the very back of a boot heel from where she has ducked down.

"Took you long enough, Salko." Najah's breath seizes at the sound of Kisha's voice.

Whoever Salko is, he makes a displeased sound. "As always, I can only aspire to your single-mindedness, Kisha."

Ivon and Najah recognize Salko's words as an insult, but if Kisha notices she doesn't seem to care.

"I'm going to the courtyard to train. You and I will question Keno Sif tomorrow. I don't want you speaking to her alone. I'm keeping one of my men with you until then."

"And what should I do until tomorrow?" Salko asks, seemingly unconcerned. It wouldn't do for an aristocrat to show much emotion.

"Just stay out of my way and do what I say." Kisha's response is like a muzzled bark. Full of violence, but tempered by circumstance.

When Kisha turns towards the courtyard entrance, Najah is certain she'll be seen. Beyond the fear of death and capture, but worse, is a new emotion Najah feels burning in her chest. Humiliation. She doesn't want to look into Kisha's eyes and know that someone she confided in betrayed her so easily and got away with it. It's enough to turn her face red. Kisha strides confidently into the courtyard, one of her paladins rushing ahead to open the door for her, too busy with their duties to check around. After she disappears, Salko speaks to the remaining paladin.

"You're going to show me where Keno Sif is being kept."

"Sir, I can't. She'll kill me." The paladin's voice quivers, shockingly blue eyes wide behind the slit of their helm.

"She doesn't have the power to have you executed," Salko insists coldly.

"It doesn't matter. She's clever for a barbarian. People who have upset her have disappeared. Forgive me for saying, but some of my fellow soldiers. . ." the paladin shifts uncomfortably on his feet. "They've lost faith that the high commanders can protect us from her."

A burst of indignant rage disrupts Salko's cool exterior. "Why wasn't I told? I could have alerted my father!"

The paladin's silence speaks volumes. Nobody believes Salko could stop her, familial privilege or not. Or worse, maybe Salko's father already knows and doesn't care.

"We're not in the wilderness any longer," Salko continues, his voice regaining its disaffected refinement. "If I convince Keno Sif to talk, I can have Kisha taken care of. We'll be rid of two barbarians at once."

"But your lord father—"

"If my father will not remove her, I'll do it myself."

"Thank Druga. I'm sorry to say it, sir, but the church never should have put someone without noble blood in charge. It's an insult to those of us under her command."

"All tools have a use in their time," Salko responds, smoothing his shirt as he does. "Now lead the way."

Salko and the paladin walk up the other set of stairs, opposite from the set Ivon and Najah took, and before Ivon can stop her Najah is following silently behind. Ivon catches up quickly and silently, despite their hunch and reliance on a cane. The paladin unwittingly leads them down two corridors and directly to Sif's cell. From their spot in the shadows, Ivon and Najah can barely see her. She's alive. And looking better than the last time Najah saw her in Béma, even, although not by enough to feel true comfort. A ring of keys jangles loudly as the cell is opened and Salko walks in. Whatever is said is too low to discern, but Najah's heart alights at the sound of Sif's voice responding. She's really alive. In less than two minutes, Salko leaves. The paladin hangs their ring of keys back up on the wall and follows. The brevity of the conversation is striking. Salko doesn't even raise his voice, much less try to beat anything out of her. At least there is a quicker way to free Sif than Ivon originally planned.

"Come with me," Salko orders, speaking to the soldier. "I have a plan."

Ivon and Najah duck around a corner and, as Salko passes, he turns and looks directly at them. A wolfish grin stretches across his fine features. Ivon's breath catches in their chest. They push Najah behind them, ready to protect her with their life, but Salko does not raise the alarm. In a strange way, that disturbs Najah even more than the thought of being arrested. There are too many secrets in this world. People should live more honestly, she thinks, feeling a little ridiculous since Salko's honesty would land her in a cell. In moments Salko is gone, the paladin with him remaining entirely unaware of their presence.

The two of them creep closer to Sif's cell. The smell of mold mixed with sweat and waste turns their stomachs. Every padded footstep feels like cannon fire. Down the hall is the wet, sickening sound of vomit. Further away, cries of pain and the crack of a whip.

"Sif!" Najah hisses at the door to her cell.

"Well, damn!" Sif says happily. Then, when she notices Ivon, curses softly. "Oh, damn."

Ivon clears their throat. "Hello, Sif. How have you been?"

Sif blinks rapidly. For a moment she is speechless.

"Ivon, you look like shit."

Ivon feigns offense. "How dare you. Maybe I'll turn around and leave you here, hmm?"

Najah yanks the ring of keys from the wall and begins searching through them for the one that will free Sif.

"Humph! You're lucky she's here," Ivon continues, motioning at Najah.

"Really, where have you been?" Sif asks.

Ivon hesitates, brows tightening and lips pressed thin. The words they have to say are too big for what little time is available. They sigh and say, "Let's talk about it when we're out of here."

Sif stumbles out of her cell on weak, wobbling legs. Najah tries to help her walk, but Sif gently declines. The relief of their reunion is quickly overpowered by a voice in Najah's head that is screaming at her to run as hard and as fast as she can. She knows having two injured, older adults with her is slowing their escape. Sif's strength, she realizes, has been a greater source of solace than she completely appreciated. Najah takes a deep breath and tells the fear in her heart that she will not run. Instead, she walks ahead of her friends, quiet as a mouse and keeping a diligent watch.

The prison is eerily silent. The only sign of life is a jeering crowd in the courtyard. It sounds like some kind of game, and after a time the crowd begins to chant the victor's name. Najah can't help but wonder if Salko has cleared their route to aid in their escape. The idea that someone like him would assist her feels like swallowing back vomit. Ivon stares ahead nervously, eyes twitching across their path as if trying to find the seams in it. Sif, noticing Najah's disquiet, winks playfully, her bloodshot eye gleaming in a bruised socket.

Chapter 31

Young Sif, the Destroyer
The Rose Gold

Across from Keno Sif, the captain of the *Rose Gold* grins from behind his dark beard. The dim light reflects back at her from two gold teeth in the front of his self-assured smile. Around them both, a circle of pirates watches them through bleary eyes. Sif snorts loudly and spits into a tin.

"Come on, Sif. The future belongs to the bold," Captain Wahyu teases. He has room to be cocky, since he has won almost every round. Sif swears to herself she will win everything back from him and then never gamble again. What a waste of time.

Sif eyes the cards in her hand, then his face, and back again. Feels the smoothness of the card faces. Calculates her chances. It could go either way. The allure of a comeback is too much to resist.

"Damn it. Fine." She spreads her cards out on the worn tabletop. He flips his over. The crowd erupts into groans. Sif's streak of losses continues.

"Ah, fuck," Sif curses, running a muscular hand over her close-shaven hair.

The captain guffaws, raking in her coins with his hands. Shining lidas, hauwlings, and ifrids pile together in a haphazard rainbow of yellow brass, silver-purple, and brilliant gold.

"You did your best, Sif. Admirable work, considering your opponent," Wahyu jokes. "You can always bet your sword. I like that Assajian hilt. It's hard to find one without going pretty far inland."

"Yeah, I'll just ask you to borrow it every time I have to kill someone. I'll get that coin back." Her voice inflates with confidence, even though her pride is wounded. "How about we arm wrestle for it?"

Wahyu shakes his head, dreadlocks moving along with the motion. "Oh no.

I've heard some stories about Sif the Destroyer since you've joined us. Even if I had both arms, I would pick a game with better chances."

"Yeah, yeah." Sif rolls her eyes and stands up, drains the last of her drink and slams the cup down. "I'll just pick it off your corpse when we get boarded by real pirates."

The crowd jeers and boos as Sif leaves the game behind. It's all in good fun. Outside, Buri is speaking with Sunnhilde. It's an odd sight, but maybe the extreme dullness of being stuck on a ship has brought them together out of necessity. Sif has caught on to the fact that Buri would have preferred not to have taken the job with Sunnhilde. At first, she was annoyed he didn't say something, but the past is the past. Now she is just trying to make it through the humdrum voyage without going insane or broke.

Sif produces her pipe and joins the two of them. Whatever they're talking about must be serious. Buri's face is always grave, but Sunna is either cursed or blessed with a near perpetual aura of contentment. Now, though, she looks as if she's seen a ghost. Sif follows their gaze to a pair of ships on the horizon, behind the *Rose Gold*. They're flying the Titziri flag, a canvas of star-white with a gray shield in the middle and stripe of blood red on the far end. Sif lights her pipe with a match and takes her first inhale.

"Well, at least the day got a little more interesting. Who do you think told?" The glance she shares with Sunnhilde at the same time asks if it was the two of them.

"Most of them," Buri responds. Sunna nods, confirming it. Telling Sif not to worry.

Sif's gaze falls casually from Sunnhilde's eyes, to her hands, to her thighs. "You sure?"

Buri nods.

"Well, how come I didn't hear anything about it?"

"Too busy losing at cards," Buri jokes, although his tone is so grim and flat nobody could be blamed for thinking it wasn't a joke at all.

"Yeah, well, you taught me to play, old man, so who's really to blame here? Now that I think about it, you might owe me some coin."

Buri smirks.

"We found out by accident," Sunnhilde says, cutting in a space in the conversation for herself. "The crew is trying to hide it. Captain Wahyu would probably throw anyone who fucked up this bad overboard."

"No," Buri disagrees, remembering his night drinking with the captain. "He wouldn't."

"Well, we'll know soon," Sunnhilde says. "That ship is gaining speed quickly. They'll be on us by tomorrow."

"Why'd they wait?" Sif wonders aloud.

"To avoid a fight at the port, I'd bet." Sunnhilde puts her head in her hands and groans loudly. "I wonder if they'll try to parlay."

As if summoned by her words, letters begin to rain down from the sky—rolled up parchments tied in twine. Above them, a flock of carrier pigeons finish dropping the letters before flying back to the Titzi ships. Buri, Sunna, and some of the deckhands pick them up and begin to read. Sif can only wait with bated breath.

"What does it say?"

Sunnhilde clears her throat. Whatever is written on the letters is casting a shadow on her face. She seems much smaller than she did before.

"It's a letter from our pursuers, saying they will spare the lives of anyone who can turn this ship around, through sabotage or mutiny."

"They won't, though," Sif says. "Titzi is going to kill everyone on this ship if they can."

Sunnhilde nods slowly. Buri begins gathering the letters and tossing them into the sea, but the lamentation of crewmembers already on deck draws out everyone who had been playing cards inside. Sif snatches the letters from as many people as she can, but it's too late. The ship erupts into a furor of fear, anger, and paranoia. A fight breaks out within minutes. Only Captain Wahyu's stern command and the threat of being thrown overboard ends things before they go further. Nobody wants to tread cold, dark water as Titzi ships grow on the horizon. When the crowd disperses, Sif asks Wahyu who is keeping watch tonight.

"Same crew as always." His eyes are dark and his countenance is like a trap about to spring.

"People you trust?" she asks.

"Is there anyone you would trust in this situation?" Wahyu responds. His question is more earnest and less hypothetical than she expects.

"Yeah." Sif trusts Buri with her life. Ivon only somewhat less. She even trusts Sunna a little, and in this situation, a lot.

The captain sighs. "Well, ask them if they'll keep watch with me, and maybe we can stay alive long enough to have a fair fight." It makes sense. Presumably most of the crew is only here for money. Money that isn't worth losing their lives over.

Sif pats the captain on his back. "They've got two ships to our one, Wahyu. Don't you think they're a little outnumbered?"

The captain smiles, but doesn't laugh.

Chapter 32

Najah

Road from the Great Desert

Ivon leads them southeast from the prison, into the riverlands. Halfway there, they trade the camel to pilgrims heading in the opposite direction. It's the longer route to get to the ruins of Ravinser, but it helps them avoid patrols set up to catch them traveling. The value of the decision is quickly clear. During their first night at the border, resting under the thin canopy of cedars, they notice the torchlight of soldiers searching the road in the distance, flaring up at the bottom of the wide, dark sky.

A handful of days later, as the wide grasslands begin to meet ancient forest, Najah gathers the courage to take Ivon's advice. Partway through the day, Ivon suggests they take a break beside a stream to fill up on water and check Sif's wounds. Najah offers to fill up their flasks, buying extra time to steel her resolve. Sif is her friend. It's completely normal to talk about things other than evading death. They trust each other. She just saved Sif's life. It won't be weird.

Back with Ivon and Sif, she almost immediately proves her last thought wrong.

"So," Najah starts, unsure of how to directly ask a question to the woman she spends most of her time trading barbs with. The silence that follows is not encouraging.

Sif raises an eyebrow. "Yeah?"

"You drink a lot. And smoke a lot. I guess that's a Siduri thing." Najah does her best to push the conversation forward.

"Yeah," Sif admits.

"I think she is trying to ask you something, love," Ivon remarks, hiding their amusement.

"Right," Najah confirms sheepishly, pushing down the urge to cover up her embarrassment by starting a fight.

"Okay. What's on your mind, Naj?"

Sif, Najah realizes, is committed to making this difficult.

"Why do you care about Siduri? Doesn't seem like anyone else even *likes* her."

Usually, Sif laughs when Najah is rude. This time she doesn't. For a moment, Najah is worried she made a mistake.

Sif hums thoughtfully. "I guess I never thought about it. Siduri is perfect. She teaches us about freedom and fun. Takes away pain and boredom. I can't imagine travelling with a heavy pack and nothing to ease the soreness or keep me awake. Having to be prudent with coin and be a good worker or a modest woman."

"Right, but if you travel all the time, why not Shen? Or Aneir, since you're a fighter?"

Sif scoffs, not at Najah's question but at her options. "Shen is the god of the road, but I'm not interested in being friends with everyone who just so happens to be walking between two places. Besides, not the wisest course of action for a bandit. And Aneir. . . eh. . . I almost don't want to say. Buri worshipped Aneir, and so did my mother and most of my skill-fathers. But the whole thing feels stuffy."

Najah is surprised to hear Sif mention Buri. It's clear he was someone important, but the old woman has been reluctant to bring him up. "You are a fighter, though. Aneir is the god of war."

"Aneir is the god of *courage*," Sif corrects, not without a trace of mild annoyance. "And I don't sit around thinking about being a fighter. I like to fight, but I also like music. I like drinking and climbing and fuck—

uh. . . friendly conversation." A tone of wistfulness enters her voice unexpectedly. "You know, it used to annoy me that people called me The Destroyer. I wasn't even trying to hurt anyone when I got the nickname. Besides, King Ottson was a tyrant. Though I only killed him because I had a grudge. People talk like I pushed the castle down all by myself, but I was just trying to kill a beast that *he* summoned. He was as guilty as me."

Sif's openness is disarming. This is the most the old woman has spoken about herself in the entire time they've traveled together. Usually, they're arguing or trading half-joking insults. To feel trusted with a real piece of information feels like treasure.

I didn't know," Najah says. "You seemed proud of it."

"The name only stuck because the monarchists think northerners are worse than animals. But what good would arguing do? I figure, if they want to call me Destroyer, I'll wear it with honor. Make them know they can't break me. Better than begging for understanding."

Najah nods silently. Sif's words fall neatly into the context of Ivon's story about how they met. Najah can almost imagine Sif as a young woman, fighting against the world, laughing with a drink in one hand and a sword in the other. What would have caused someone like that to hide away on Mount Hoda, living as a hermit? What could send Keno Sif the Destroyer to live alone at the end of the known world?

-

A few weeks into the journey, the three of them run across a small encampment of nomads traveling south from Ograna. The camp is roughly two dozen tents and several uncovered wagons, and many of the nomads wear ceramic bands that seem to denote their prestige or authority. In the middle of the encampment burns a ritual fire in front of a small shrine to Nnedsu, the deity of change. A pot of tea cooks over the flame, letting off ash and the smell of spices and homeroot. The smell conjures memories of her sister, who took the same tea often, and Ivon, who only takes it on occasion.

A group of young priests, all wearing a stack of ceramic bands, greet them at the edge of the camp and, in exchange for a small fee, allow them to stay. Sif can't help but stare at Ivon as they walk to their tent and take a seat inside.

"What?" Ivon asks.

"What do you mean *what*? Why are you being so weird, showing up out of nowhere and paying for things? You don't pay for things."

"Maybe I do now, hmm? Ever think about that?"

Sif snorts. "Yeah right, you'll always be a cheap ass."

"Rude."

"Seriously, Ivon," Sif responds flatly. Najah leans forward from where she is sitting in their tent, pretending not to listen. The wind rustles the treetops high above.

"I. . . don't know what to say," Ivon admits. "I've regretted so much of what happened during our last journey. You two were my best friends, and I let my own fear build in my head until I was convinced I had the right to make the decision for all of us. When Najah appeared, I couldn't let you down again." Ivon feels tears threatening to pool in their eyes, and blinks them away rapidly. "Everything we went through was my fault. Buri—"

"Shut up," Sif interrupts, although not unkindly. "Don't be stupid. Me, Buri, Sunna. . . We all knew what we were getting into."

"Not everything," Ivon responds, their voice barely more than a whisper.

"Well, more or less. You told us eventually. I don't blame you for being scared."

"You did at the time," Ivon says.

"I. . . I was mad that you lied, not about Buri and Sunna. And maybe. . . eh, maybe I was a poor friend to you. You should have said something, but. . . ah, I don't know if I would have made the best decision if you had. I don't even know if there were any good decisions. Maybe one of us would have died no matter what."

Hearing Sif's words, Ivon finally breaks. Hot tears spill down their face, now decades older and somehow still unable to shake the trauma and heartache of their old life. "Keno, I miss him almost every day. It's like. . ."

"Like a hole in your heart that can't be filled back. Always there." Sif finishes.

Ivon nods. "Exactly."

Sif leans forward and presses her forehead to theirs. "He wouldn't want you to carry all that guilt around. He'd probably be mad at you for it." She laughs. "You know, something about how it disrespects Aneir, or whatever."

They lean away from each other. Ivon wipes their eyes and gives Sif a knowing nod. "You're right. When did you get wise?"

"When I got old, I guess," she replies. The moment is surreal for them both. Ivon's thick hair is thinning and their dashing, meticulously groomed mustache has grown out into a ragged beard. They're missing a limb and walk with a limp, and offer to pay for things like coins grow from trees. Sif is graying and wrinkled, missing part of a fingertip and a few teeth. And, apparently, taking care of children now.

Ivon chuckles. "It's good to see you again. I only wish Buri could be here."

Sif clears her throat. "Yeah, me too. I'm glad you're alive, though. Even if you're still a pain in the ass."

Ivon rolls their eyes playfully. "Just so you know. . . I have people I take care of now. I protect them, where I can. Everyone knows every detail about a job before they take it. I heard some of Aneir's priests started calling Buri a saint, for how many soldiers he killed before he fell. So we have an altar for Saint Buri now, too. It's a whole thieves' union, if you're ever in Béma."

"What, like the guild in Heron-Muse?"

"Not really," Ivon responds. "Better. We help each other like the guild never did."

"Eh?" Sif smiles. "I'd like to see it."

-

Najah listens to all of this, at first out of curiosity, but then out of distant fear. Ivon and Sif really had been close. Now she and Sif are close, but who's to say something won't tear them apart as well? Back when she was captured by the Church of Druga, her blood made flowers grow in the dirt and trees stretch up into the sky. How would Sif react to her doing magic, even if it was by accident? Najah doesn't *feel* like she did magic. She didn't make a blood oath to the Three Mothers of Demons. Still, there is almost nowhere on Atlas where someone would see what she did and not accuse her of being a witch. Even Najah's mother found the use of magic abhorrent, maybe enough to forget her pacifism. Something to do with magic split Ivon and Sif up for years. If Najah couldn't be sure of her mother's reaction, and Sif and Ivon fell apart after all their time together, what are the chances that Sif would accept and believe that Najah is innocent? Najah looks at the older woman intensely, trying to gauge whether she is capable of abandonment. Her heart says that everyone is.

"Hey, quit staring," Sif says.

"Have you taken your medicine today?" Najah deflects. Sif had been getting a steady dose in the prison, on Kisha's orders, to ensure Sif was alive to kill later. In an odd way, Kisha's saved Sif's life.

Sif snorts. "Goddess, you worry a lot."

Najah scoffs. "No, I don't. You just don't care about anything but drinking and getting high. If the prison had a tavern, you'd still be there now."

Ivon chuckles and gets to their feet. Sif reels back and says, "What the fuck? I care about things. I care about you two." Then, after a pause. "And drinking and getting high, also."

"You didn't answer my question," Najah reminds her.

"I haven't taken it yet. My fucking back is killing me."

Najah sighs and rummages through their belongings for Sif's medicine, as well as a pipe and some traveler's leaf for the pain, all the while muttering to herself about Sif being too stubborn; mostly in good fun. Sif smiles gratefully despite it.

Ivon stands up, chuckling as they pull back the flaps to the tent and step outside. A cool breeze enters as they exit. "I'll leave you to it for now."

Najah opens her mouth to speak, but Sif cuts her off.

"Hey, you want to learn how to fight for real or what?"

Najah's time separated from Sif had been difficult. Something in her heart has changed, possibly for the worse. She'd been willing to kill the guard who found her and Ivon, and has put off considering what it meant that she was willing to kill someone. In truth, she doesn't want to hurt anyone, but she worries the choice has been taken away from her. The echo of her mother's pacifism reminds her that the violence was motivated by fear, and something about that feels dangerous. She is stuck in a situation with no easy answer, where walking the right path would be like balancing on the edge of a razor blade. Assuming she can find the path at all.

Sif senses her hesitation. "Never mind, forget I said anything."

"No," Najah insists. "I want to learn."

Sif presses her lips together uncertainly.

"I mean it, alright?" Najah says. "I don't want to kill anyone, but I don't want to have to rely on other people, either. I guess if. . ." Najah pauses, realizing what Sif meant so long ago, on the boat. When she spoke about the inevitability of conflict, and the importance of knowing what you believe and being responsible for it. "If we have to fight no matter what, I think I shouldn't rely on other people to keep me safe."

"I could still keep you safe," Sif says. Najah is surprised at first, until the old woman continues. "Would've kept you safe, if you weren't so intent on coming after me."

Najah realizes that Sif doesn't know she was arrested, not long after the old woman had been herself. She brushes past the thought and replies, "Too late to back out now, Aunt Keno. You better not be lying to me about teaching me to fight."

"I haven't lied to you yet." Which is true.

"You said you weren't going to die."

Sif spreads her arms out, showing off how not-dead she is. "I didn't."

"Well, you didn't do much to help keep you that way!" Najah shouts.

-

That night, they wait on the edge of the camp with a map old enough to show Ravinser's true location. Behind them, horses and sheep graze contentedly on long stalks of dewy grass. Crickets sing sweetly from out in the brush. Ivon confirms Kisha did tell the truth about Ravinser being burned down. Sif sighs loudly, but doesn't say what she is thinking. This is all they have for now.

The map is from before Hvek first funded the Church of Druga's expansion, before the desert kingdoms redrew their borders, and before the Church's campaign to unite Atlas under a common faith—Druga at the top, acceptable other deities in secondary positions, and the barbarian deities of Siduri, Aneir, and Asthia banished from the public eye. Sif frowns. It seems order always seems to mean one culture, nation, or class consuming the others. The monarchists call it peace, even though the fighting never ends; nobody with any self-respect would accept a life under a boot.

In any case, Sif thinks, most of the map won't be very reliable. Atlas has changed a dozen times over since it was made, and any number of places could have been built or destroyed since. The safest bet might be to find a river and follow it as closely as they can. Rivers usually mean villages, plus access to water. But maybe that would be what Kisha expects.

"Why are you making that face?" Najah asks, apparently having snuck up on Sif while she was deep in thought.

"Fuck off, I'm not making a face."

"Yeah, you were. You were looking at the map and doing this." Najah does her best impression of a very serious adult being very dour.

Sif snickers in response and says, "I'm trying to figure out our path to Ravinser. By a road that might not exist, or by river. The road might make it hard to get water, if some of these towns aren't still around. The river might get us caught."

"Why?"

"It's an obvious route," Ivon responds.

"Let's use the old road, then. I'm good at finding food and water. It's my skill." And maybe summoning trees, Najah thinks.

"Didn't want to mention this before now?" Sif asks.

"It wasn't important until now. Me and my mom had to live in hiding tons of times, and I always found water and food. I have a sense for it."

"Settles that, then. We'll keep to the old road."

"Perfect," Ivon chirps. "I bought you a horse, by the way. His name is apparently Russet, although if you ask me, he deserves a better one."

"Why do you sound like you're not coming with us?" Najah asks. The hurt is evident in her eyes. After everything they've been through, Ivon is just going to leave? Then what was all of this about? Najah wants Sif to say something to back her up, but the old woman is just as taken aback, her jaw slack and eyes wide.

"I'm sorry, dear one. I'm too old for the journey you're on. I know I do a flawless job at hiding it, but the travel has been difficult on me. I'm in a lot of pain. And I have a community at home that needs me."

"Ivon. . ." Sif starts to say, but the words die on her tongue. In the dim moonlight, she can see on their face how hard it is to part. It's obvious that Ivon wouldn't have chosen to leave if it wasn't important. Sif has been so glad to spend time with her old friend she hasn't even thought to ask what it was costing them to be at her side.

Sif clears her throat. "Well, you never were the strongest fighter. I don't want to have to watch out for both of you."

Ivon scoffs. "Please, if I had a hauwling for every time I saved your life, I'd be able to buy a title and live in Hvek."

"Yeah, you could be called Noble Ivon of Heron-Muse and have a battalion of servants spitting in your food."

"I'd be a very dashing noble," Ivon muses.

"You're a more dashing thief." Sif smiles, wrinkles collecting in the corners of her eyes. "Be safe, alright? I'm going to visit you in Béma."

"Of course. I'm too beautiful to die, Keno. The Lunar Goddess would send me right back."

Ivon stumbles backwards as Najah wraps her arms around them and buries her face in their chest. No sound escapes her lips, but Ivon feels the warmth of tears on their shirt.

"Oh, uhm. . . There, there." Ivon pats Najah's head awkwardly, unsure of how to respond.

-

The next morning, they part ways. Ivon rides back to Béma through the riverlands, eventually cutting through Ograna. Sif and Najah ride southeast into land that, like the camp, is largely unclaimed by any kingdom. Soon they leave the riverlands completely. The sound of running water and smell of moss and rain fade away, replaced by long stretches of dusty, ruined road and dry, brown grass. As the tree line recedes, a large catapult comes into view, slowly rotting outside the ruins of a town it demolished decades ago during the War of Expansion. In the far distance is a tall black obelisk, a remnant of the old kingdoms. Najah can't help but imagine it watching passively as the war burned across Atlas. She can't help but imagine it still watching now, silently tracing her and Sif's path to the south. The sun above them lingers alone, having burned away the clouds and left only a blue sky. In that moment, Najah feels very exposed.

She tightens her grip on Sif.

"Thank you."

"What's that?" Sif yells back over the sound of hooves pummeling dirt.

"Nothing. Keep your eyes on the road!" Najah yells back.

Chapter 33

Buri the Giant
The Rose Gold

It's been a long time since Buri has been unnerved by the quiet. Reflecting on his youth, he often thinks maybe that's why he acted like he did. He was a young man who was so afraid of the quiet that he tried to live his life burning through everything around him. Now he's the opposite. In everything, he yearns for the peace that comes with simplicity and reflection. But even still, walking the dark paths of the ship's bowels isn't the same. It's a kind of quiet teeming with panic: Whispers behind doors, the sounds of weapons being sharpened. The night buzzes with an ominous energy. The sea, dark and obscure as oil. While Buri is not afraid to die, this scene fills his heart with sorrow. If tomorrow is their last day, tonight shouldn't be spent indulging in paranoia and cowardice. The crew would be better off preparing to meet whatever deity they worship with dignity.

From behind him a voice speaks out, brittle but deadly. Like walking along a frozen lake and hearing the ice begin to crack.

"Buri the Giant. That's you, right?" Buri turns and recognizes the speaker as one of Wahyu's crew. They're of medium height, with skin that is either very tan or brown, but shrouded slightly by the blue-black of the night. They wear a short, androgynous haircut and have a sword on each side of their waist.

Buri nods. "It is."

The speaker approaches him cooly, until they are standing chest to chest. "I challenge you to a duel. If we don't die tomorrow."

Buri is surprised. "Why not now?"

"Would you fight me now?" Their tone says they know the answer, and that the question was pointless.

"Hmmm. . . depends."

They roll up one sleeve, revealing a tattoo on their arm of a man swallowing a sword. Aneir. "I don't have a grudge with you. I just need to know."

Though Buri first read this person as cold and calculating, now he notices their hands shaking, and hears the slight quiver in their voice. They want to say they fought him, and they're worried they'll die without knowing if they had the courage to try.

"I see. I'll find you later, for our duel."

"Stay alive, giant."

Buri nods wordlessly as the speaker passes by them and disappears in the ship's ribcage, off into the night like a ghost, into the kingdom of disaster that the *Rose Gold* has become. As their footsteps fade, other sounds rise from the background. The noises Buri had taken to be any number of threats against the ship weren't just that. All around him, people were spending what might be their last moments doing things they had put off. From all around come murmurs of tears, comfort, nostalgia, lust, and joy. Down a level, two men kiss each other hungrily outside of an empty room, before one drags the other inside. Perhaps, Buri thinks, he has made too grim an assessment of the situation.

Back on deck, Buri meets Ivon, who has had a visibly different experience. The cracks in their typically jovial attitude are evident. A bruise has spread across their face, and their hands are stained red with someone else's blood.

"I've had to stab two people in the last hour, Buri. I thought there would be some honor among thieves, but apparently not. Is nothing sacred?"

Wahyu sits on the deck railing above them, near the steering wheel, eyes lost among the distant waves. Sif and Sunnhilde are nowhere to be seen. Glittering points of starlight dot the vast, bruised sky above. He wraps his arm around Ivon and squeezes them lightly.

"Captain," Buri calls out. "Don't worry. There is always hope."

Wahyu smirks. "I appreciate it, friend. I'm not giving up yet, just taking a moment to feel melancholy. It's not every day a man has to kill some of his friends to save the rest. Luckily, we're only two or three days from where Queen Benedicta hopes to find Agartha."

"Odd definition of friends. One of these bastards tried to slit my throat," Ivon mutters, sadness and betrayal clouding their features. They shrug Buri's arm off of them and walk to the edge of the deck. Buri frowns. Despite his sense that things are not as bad as they seem, a growing piece of him feels this night is the start of something long, terrible, and lonely. He wishes Sif and Sunnhilde could join the rest of them on the deck. He sighs, feeling somewhat foolish for letting himself dart between hope and despair instead of deciding to be brave, regardless of what the future holds. Then the ship rocks violently with the force of an explosion below deck. That feeling of foolishness is immediately dashed, replaced with a grave concern for the life of his oldest friend.

-

A level below, Sif and Sunnhilde pace the bowels of the ship, checking for signs of sabotage or mutiny among the cargo. So far, it's been a peaceful watch, and Sif expects it to stay that way when she feels a set of fingers interlock with her own. The sensation is so foreign that she almost snatches her hand away, before she realizes it is only Sunna. Unsurprisingly, the brilliant woman walking with her picks up on that.

"Is this okay?" Sunna asks.

Sif nods, trying to maintain her cool. She feels off balance, though. She's had plenty of flings, and even a few romances. When she was just a bit younger, separate trysts with a male and a female priest at the Temple of the Wolf had even led to the two priests challenging each other to a duel. Despite being wanted on half of the continent, Sif has managed to become either a heartbreaker or a fond memory to dozens of people, most of whom she can no longer name. For some reason, she desperately wants Sunna to be impressed with her. She wants to hear Sunnhilde talk about all the places she's been, all the places she wants to go. Sunna lets go of Sif's hand, putting some space between them, and it makes Sif's heart fall into her stomach.

"What?" Sif is painfully aware of the way her own voice pitches up.

Sunna smiles, but some of the warmth is gone. "That didn't seem like a very sure response."

Before she knows what she is doing, Sif takes Sunna's face in her hands and kisses her deeply. She can feel Sunna's lips curl into a smile against her own. Her heart beats like a stampede, and a gust of adrenaline rushes through her body. As they part, their eyes meet in the dim light. Sunna opens her mouth to say something when the roar of an explosion grabs their attention. They both lurch off of their feet, sprawling across the ground, and then the only thing they can hear is the sound of rushing water quickly filling the *Rose Gold*. Alarm flashes across Sunna's face, beyond anything Sif has seen in her. It's the look of someone who expects death.

"Come on!" Sif yells, jumping to her feet and holding out her hand. "We have to help!"

Sunna grabs her hand, but stops her from running off. "No, Sif. Stop."

"What?!" Sif yells over the sound of cascading water. "We need to move before it's too late!"

"It's already too late." Despite the noise, Sunna isn't raising her voice. Sif can barely hear her, and is torn by the twin impulses to stay and to leave.

"It's too late to save the ship, Sif. I'm sorry. I didn't want this to be the way it happened."

"What are you saying?" Sif asks desperately. "You knew this would happen?"

The roar of the ocean grows louder. Water begins to pool at their feet.

"I knew it could. I've known a lot of what has happened. I told you I have. . . unnatural knowledge."

Sif shakes her head and tries to remember exactly what was said. Sunna said she had an unnatural knowledge of *alchemy*. Right? Or was that just part of it? Sif can't remember. It's impossible to concentrate while everything is falling apart.

Sunna takes Sif's head in her hands, much like Sif did before. "Everything is going to be okay. Just keep swimming. Don't stop, no matter what."

For the first time in a while, Sif is speechless. In Sunna's eyes is a reflection of her face, mutely bearing the shock of betrayal. Sunnhilde meets her glance with grim determination. Sif's blossoming affection quickly wilts into paranoia. If there was time, Sif maybe could pick things apart from Sunnhilde's words or expression but here, at oblivion's crest, the other woman is almost completely inscrutable.

The orchestra of destruction reaches its height, too loud to hear anything else. Sunnhilde is yelling something, but between the noise and the movement, Sif can't make any of it out. It's too much to process at once. Sif is knocked off her feet. Sunna slips away from her, and is lost in the cold, dark ocean. The taste of salt, then blood. And after a moment, everything goes dark.

Chapter 34

Old Sif, the Hermit
The road to Ravinser

There is no shortage of towns abandoned or razed during the war. From Sif's admittedly limited knowledge of the area, she expects the first town they come across to have been long emptied of people and reclaimed by nature. She is half-right, in that there is nobody alive. She is wrong in that there should have been. What they find is a village that seems to have been populated recently, but has now been reduced to a burnt-out shell of what it was. Najah's eyes dart fearfully around, trying not to linger on the corpses. Sif scans everything for signs of an ambush. Russet whinnies nervously and Sif has to encourage him to continue on. Judging by the state of the still-smoldering buildings, the town could have burned down that same day. A handful of bodies lay in the streets, either cut down or turned to a crisp by the fire, but otherwise it is like most people had gotten up and left all at once.

"Probably bandits, or some minor regent looking to expand their borders. Nobody loves digging in other people's dirt as much as someone with a crown."

"I don't think so. . ." Najah responds, stare fixed on the face of a dead man. His eyes are wide. Too wide. His face is paralyzed with horror. Beyond his glassy eyes, something alive is peering back at Najah. A distant wave of gold. The grass beneath him withers as if touched by an invisible flame, but when Najah blinks, everything seems normal again.

"I don't like this," Najah says, making a face what is somewhere between eating a whole lemon and about to lose the contents of her stomach.

"It'd be weird if you did, kid." Sif slides out of the saddle to check bodies for food, drink, and valuables. She doesn't have much luck looting, but finds a mostly-full wineskin and drains it in one go. Siduri wouldn't approve of the waste. Sif bows to the corpse she took it off and tosses the wineskin over her shoulder.

Najah shakes her head. "No, I mean I feel strange." She cannot shake the sensation of being observed. The air around her shimmers like the surface of a lake, causing the village to warp in unnatural ways. In between blinks, she sees flashes of sickening light beaming through the forest around them. Searching.

"Like *tired*, strange?"

"I don't think so. But. . . do you see anything weird?"

"Yeah, Naj. We walked into a massacre, it's all weird."

"Maybe we should leave." Najah shuts her eyes tight and breathes deeply, hands gripping the saddle like she expects to fall off. Russet whinnies nervously.

Sif shrugs. No harm in abandoning a place with so little to pick clean.

The smell of smoke lingers in the air, charged with an eerie sense of danger. Flakes of ash waft from a small fire, still burning homes that are already lost. Outside of town, the two find what happened to everyone else. They must have turned on one another. It was a massacre, and from what Sif can tell it looks as if everyone abruptly decided to grab whatever was nearest to them and start cutting and beating each other down.

Carriage tracks roll over the scene, breaking bone and tamping down dirt. The driver must have either been in a desperate hurry or completely unbothered by the aftermath. As the carriage rolled on, it left a thick trail of blood behind it. Sif clenches her jaw. She's seen something like this before. These were people who saw something magical, beyond the limits of human understanding, and whatever they saw had seen them back, reached inside their minds, and unraveled them. Like pulling on a loose thread until the whole garment is undone.

Sif turns to Najah, suddenly worried for her safety. The young girl stares ahead, face slack and expression blank, then turns to Sif and says, "Agartha is a city in a hole in the sea."

Her jaw drops, mouth gaping in pure terror, as she falls from Russet's back and collapses unceremoniously into the dirt.

Sif is too startled to catch her in time. She scoops Najah up in her arms, checking her for injuries. Her eyes dart maddeningly between the burnt town, the piles of bodies, and her unconscious ward. It is all she can do to not lose her senses in the devastation of the world around her, and under the weight of hearing the name *Agartha* come from Najah's mouth. Her chest heaves with panicked breaths as scenes from the past blaze through her mind.

-

Two days pass before Najah wakes up again. She does it at an inopportune moment, as they run across a small campsite on the side of the road littered with bodies in the same way as the last town. The carriage's path has left a faint depression in the dirt. Whether it's from her unnatural sleep or something else, Najah is in a daze until the campsite is far behind. Sif tries to question her about Agartha, but Najah doesn't know what she means.

In a woozy voice but with distant, fearful eyes, Najah says, "Saw an insect crawling upside down on the night sky, but moving all wrong. Like maybe it wasn't on the sky at all, but inside my eye, and I only noticed when I looked up. Women like flower petals, all joined at the stem and moving like pale honey. The sound of wind through grass, echoing from an old well."

Sif's eyes widen. The concern is evident in her voice. "That's what you dream about?"

Najah blinks rapidly, and the fear in her eyes is replaced by deep exhaustion. The odd quality in her voice is gone, swapped with that of a normal young girl. "What's what I dream about?"

Sif's jaw hangs slack as she tries to find the right way to respond, wanting to address Najah's disturbing words without scaring her or hurting her feelings.

Before she can, Najah points ahead of them on the trail, voice slurring feverishly. "Look, a fox."

Sif's reply is nearly a whisper. "There's no fox, Naj."

-

A day later, they arrive at another town. Here too, bodies thicken the streets and foul the air. It's all Sif can do not to vomit. Russet fights her every step of the way, until he bucks so hard that Sif and Najah have to get down to avoid being thrown. As they walk on, Najah continues to lapse into a stupor, speaking in a way that makes Sif's skin crawl.

"Pathetic," Najah says, eyes glaring at a charred body left on the ground after having crawled halfway out of a burning home. She spins around to Sif, face wide with guilt, eyes tired and fearful. Her voice is a blubbering croak. "I didn't mean it! Why did I say that? I promise I didn't mean it."

Sif doesn't want to tell Najah to keep quiet, but the young girl's words make her uneasy. The horse isn't doing much better. Russet rarely eats or sleeps anymore unless Najah is awake and lucid.

In the middle of the town Najah seizes up, limbs gone completely rigid, then crashes to the ground asleep. It's so much more violent than the curse's normal effect on her that for a moment Sif worries she may be dead. It's four days until she wakes again, the longest she's been asleep so far, and every day the dread in Sif's heart grows. The only spot of good luck is that Najah had been right about her ability to find water and food. When she is awake, at least. When Sif sleeps, or *if* she sleeps, her dreams are gruesome beyond compare and set her heart hammering upon waking up.

Several days after Najah blessedly awakens again, they finally come across a surviving town. During each step of their journey, Sif's eyes follow the tracks of the carriage, and her heart skips a beat when they disappear off the road and into the woods. Sif can't help but feel eyes looking back at her from the deep green. Then, from around a bend, come a young couple holding hands and laughing, followed by a hunter and dog further down the road, before an entire town blossoms ahead through the trees.

Despite the horror they'd experienced on the road, this new town, called Barburha, is a comforting reminder of life. Children run and play in the streets. Crowds of people laugh and kiss and fight. The smell of warm bread and stew wafts through the cool air from houses glowing with golden light. Sif breathes a sigh of relief. "Finally."

She expects a similar sentiment from Najah, but the young girl does not respond. Her gaze is locked in the middle distance, shoulders hunched and fingers closed in a fist around the pendant at the end of her necklace. A faint drizzle of rain patters down on them from the blue-gray sky above.

"Hey," Sif says, trying to catch her attention.

"Huh?" Najah makes a small noise of acknowledgement.

"What's on your mind?"

"I don't want to be here."

"Seeing things?" Sif asks.

Najah stares at the ground, thumb rubbing against her pendant. "Only when we arrived."

Sif squeezes Najah's shoulder. "Let's find some shelter. We can sleep out of the rain, get some decent food, and be back on the road."

"How long is that going to take? What if it rains for a whole week?"

Sif shrugs, trying to cover up her frustration. The endless march between disasters has taken a toll on her morale, but also on her body. Her joints and back are in agony, limbs stiff and uncooperative. She feels none of those years in her heart, but although she has gained back a lot of the strength she'd lost living on Mount Hoda, she is still an old woman. She looks down at her hands, weathered beyond recovery, and thinks ruefully on everything she used to be.

"If it's still raining tomorrow, we'll head out anyways."

As they walk down the lightly paved roads, leading Russet by his reins, local chatter filters into Sif's awareness. There are two threads of gossip on the lips of everyone in town, and Sif counts herself lucky that Najah latches onto the second item rather than the first. The first is the rumor of monsters appearing at the edges of the riverlands and the lands to the east of the desert. Some talk is of something sluglike and massive, easily dwarfing a building, with a thick, ridged carapace and thousands of flailing corpse-like limbs holding rusted tools and weapons. Or tall and many-eyed, with fingertips that graze the bottom of the clouds as it swings its colossal arms, and followed by an army of scavenger-birds that pick clean the bones of the people crushed under its impossible weight. Another claims it is a thick fog, imitating human cries for help, and with the ability to render long, crooked and spider-like limbs to grasp and corral lost souls, then devour them. A final story claims it is a set of four bone-thin women, all stuck together and folding out from each other like petals in a fleshy flower, and whose touch can mold skin and bone like hot wax.

The second point of discussion is a visiting troupe of actors. Najah is immediately fascinated. Sif is glad for anything that will distract Najah from her dourness, and is willing to bet the contents of her purse—what little there is —that the actors are spreading rumors to drum up excitement for their show; it's supposedly quite the tale of terror. She and Buri traveled with an acting troupe decades ago, and nothing livens up the imagination of a small, isolated community like the arts. The man who helped them in the farming village up north, shortly after she and Najah set out, had mentioned demons and spirits as well. But people have been saying that for decades now.

-

The gray, rolling sky above threatens to open up any moment and soak them through. Sif's things were mostly confiscated when she was arrested, and since Ivon had been paying for everything, she hasn't had a reason to think about coin until now, when a storm threatens to drench all of their belongings. Maybe it's for the best that they not stay in an inn, anyways. Even though a warm room and nice bath would feel like coming back to life, it could also put them in front of untrustworthy eyes. Reluctantly, Sif and Najah spend the night in an empty stable. The owner allows them to, on the condition that they pay to board Russet and would have to find somewhere else to sleep if the stables become full. The smell of horse and moldy hay is thick in the air, but the two spend their afternoon training outside. Najah focuses on her dagger and Sif promises to steal her a real sword soon. It'd be a lie to say Najah is a quick learner, but she is a surprisingly determined one.

Taunting them from across the dirt street is a fabulous inn. Two stories of glorious mid-continent architecture. It isn't large but it has dignity, and they can see flashes of the acting troupe setting up inside. A large, muscular woman collects entry at the door. As night falls, the inside is illuminated by the warm glow of candlelight. Inn workers chat with patrons and serve warm food and drink. In the cold and rain, sitting on hay and smelling horse leavings, it's an image out of a fairy tale.

"Hey, Auntie. I'm going to ask the woman at the door if she'll let me in."

Sif opens a single eye from where she has been sitting in the corner. "Someone could see you."

"Can I go? I promise I'll be careful." The young girl's voice carries an unusual mania, but if there is one person unsuited to predicting the moods and habits of children, it's Keno Sif.

Sif is surprised that Najah would ask for permission. "I'm not telling you what to do, I'm letting you know what might happen."

Najah looks like she might stay after all, but the allure of comfort and entertainment is too strong for her, especially now that she is used to whatever it is about Barburha that upset her previously. Before she goes, Najah collects Sif's pipe and traveler's leaf, and presents it to her.

"Now if your back or knees start to hurt, you don't have to get it yourself."

Sif smiles, but doesn't respond.

The woman at the entrance to the inn turns Najah away. Who would let in an unattended child who smells like horse, can't pay, and is traveling with a barbarian? The riverlands aren't as insular as the central kingdoms, but prejudice against northern barbarians is strong. The woman looks her up and down, follows Najah's path back to where Sif sits, then shoos Najah away unkindly. Najah swears loudly at the woman, throwing up rude gestures with her hands, and walks around the side of the inn. She smells her clothes, cringes to herself, then realizes she can watch the play through the window. The overhanging roof above her blocks most of the rain, except a few drops that occasionally hit her neck and run down her back.

Across the way, Sif keeps an eye on Najah. Her ward is on the tips of her toes, face up against the glass, her breath fogging up the window. It makes Sif smile, even though it is a little confusing. At Najah's age, Sif had already left Ummun and had been making her way around the northern regions of Atlas by stealing and fighting. She hadn't settled on Siduri's path yet, but felt stifled by life at home. Seeing the world had felt like the only beautiful thing in her life. Maybe that's what this play was to Najah, who had traveled the continent out of necessity rather than choice. Something beautiful to help forget the dullness and ugliness she's already encountered. Sif imagines Najah as a young woman, watching the play from inside, and then drifts to sleep without realizing it.

Inside the inn, the actors begin to take the stage. A handsome man takes the center stage for his opening monologue. He looks carved from marble, possessed with an unreal beauty. It's hard to tell what he says through the thick glass, but Najah is equally fascinated by the shock and amusement on the faces of the patrons. It must be something mildly scandalous. Probably something Sif would find funny. Najah wonders what it is.

Najah sighs and lowers herself back onto the flats of her feet. Watching the play from outside is completely unsatisfying. Like chewing food that can't be tasted. A growing whisper in her mind urges her to find a way inside, and despite agreeing with it, Najah finds the voice uncomfortable, like the prick of a thorn. Slight, but alarming. She shakes her head gently, face cringing and eyes shut, trying with only modest success to quiet it down.

Careful not to be seen, Najah eyes the woman at the door. No reaction. Slowly, she creeps toward the back of the inn, and begins checking windows to see if any can be opened. Behind her is a patch of woods, oddly quiet except for the distracting, high-pitched yip of a distant fox, which Najah ignores in favor of her task. She has no luck with the windows, but eventually notices that the roof hangs further out from the building in back than it does at the front, and a wooden pole has been added to support the extra weight. Najah looks side to side, now soaked through by the rain, and then gets as good a grip around the beam as she can. She climbs it awkwardly up to the balcony, grunting with exertion and trying to blink the rain and wet hair from her eyes. At the top she sets a foot down, breathing heavier than she expects, and enters the second story through an unlocked door. The hinges creak loudly as Najah slips inside, but even if there was anyone around, the room itself is almost completely dark. The second floor consists entirely of a balcony overlooking the first floor, and the dim fingers of light reaching up from below shape the outline of the railing and furniture in front of her. She has to walk carefully in the dark to avoid tripping over crates, vases, and lengths of rope piled along the back wall.

Najah settles into a hiding spot and tries to watch the play, but the actor's lines barely reach her from where she is, and what she can hear doesn't make much sense. That same whisper in her mind urges her forward. Keeping low, she moves ahead and around the corner until she is close to the top of the stairs going down to the first floor and can see the stage in full view. She was hoping for a comedy, but the scene in front of her now is extremely different than the one she saw from outside, or even the one she thought she heard moments ago.

A figure in a tattered golden cloak finishes speaking in a hissing language. They hold an antlered skull aloft. From her spot on the balcony, she can just make out groupings of runes carved into the pale, yellowed bone. A bright blue material fills the engraved lines, giving the impression of water flowing across the bone's surface. On stage are small braziers burning long sticks of some mineral that fills the air with a deep, drowsy scent. The painted background is of a drowning city. The scene fills her with a sense of déjà vu. A sense of doom rises in her chest.

When the next actor appears, Najah clamps her hands over her mouth and holds her breath to stifle a shout. The figure is swollen, fever-pink skin stretched tight over a form that bulges unnaturally, like a large body shoved into a much smaller one. They wear an assortment of rags, and their body is run through with a dozen swords glistening at their points. The pallor of their skin suggests a deathly infection. A voice in Najah's mind, different than the whisper that led her here, tells her to flee, but she does not, and neither does the audience. Rather than fear or disgust, the people below are silently enraptured. Below Najah, at the table nearest to the stairs, a fly lands on a woman's glassy eye. She doesn't blink.

The run-through figure begins to speak. His voice is a rough, baritone gargle that booms across the room. "The voice of The Mothers is upon us. The hand that turns the key. The eye that peers beyond the waking world. By His hand Their children will walk this plane. You will know them as The Flower of Despair, The Blind Behemoth, The Husk of a Thousand Dead, The Grasping

Fog, and endless, eternal others. The moon, the sea, and the dirt will break beneath them. Know now the freedom of the shackle, the unity of the gate, and the equality of the throne. Praise His works and weep with joy, for you will now witness the fire and blood of the dream. All hail The Wretched King!"

As the speech ends, the Run-Through Figure motions to their master, the gold-cloaked figure called the Wretched King. As the play proceeds, the Wretched King, commanding an army made of burning light, presses into the wilderness on a mission of conquest, to destroy the deity of the forest. Between the odd prose and unusual premise, Najah has a hard time following the play. The scent from the braziers makes her feel foggy and the actors deliver their lines in an antiquated and winding fashion, a version of Found Tongue cut with ancient words and strange pronunciations. Chasing the words makes her feel like she is running after something elusive, always a few steps ahead of her but never out of sight. Despite the warning in her heart, Najah creeps forward, hoping to get a better look. Slowly, shakingly, she forces herself to watch, even though the sight of the Wretched King and the Run-Through Figure sends a shiver up her spine.

There is a bright flash as sparks fly from the stage and the Wretched King loses His golden cloak, revealing His true form—a crooked terror of thin, knotted flesh and agonizing gaze. The sight of it makes her ill. It is by far worse than any costume she could imagine. She sees, or imagines she sees, a thin yellow ichor collecting on the Wretched King, slowly running down in between the cracks in His stretched skin.

Najah is struck by the awful recognition that she has seen Him before. Each time she succumbs to her curse, the Wretched King is whispering to her in her dreams. It comes to her in broken pieces. Her mother's voice, crying out. Embers of a forest turned to ash. The stark silhouette of a tower built on the back of a writhing monstrosity. A soul older than the whole continent, whispering into the minds of the priests and soldiers searching for her. And whispering into her own mind, as well. In the months of nightmares since her mother's death, as she and Sif have crossed the continent, a fragment of the Wretched King has been traveling with them. The memory stretches on and on, an endless and torturous awakening to a part of herself that had been locked beneath the veil of sleep.

A cry escapes from her trembling lips, that she only recognizes because of the sound that overtakes it. A faint, high pitched whine rises so slowly that Najah can't tell when it started, and for a moment doesn't realize it is coming from the audience below. The dozens of bodies below are paralyzed by horror, unable to turn away or blink. One by one, mouths are wrenched open by invisible hands and another voice is added to the shrill, collective cry. Then, at the front of the stage, a man goes up in a pillar of flame. It takes less than a second for him to be completely devoured by the flames, yet he only stands still, swaying sickeningly, whining with the rest of the audience until the smoke and flames strip his voice into something hoarse and guttural. This horror can only be the work of the Three Mothers of Demons. And so must be the trees that sprouted from her blood and saved her from the paladins. The Wretched King has infested her soul and poisoned her blood.

Below Najah, the Wretched King and the Run-Through Figure deliver their lines as if nothing has changed. They pose and orate with the appropriate dramatic sense. But in her heart, Najah knows this is some sick game. That this was all orchestrated to draw her in. That the dizzying words are being recited to her. To show her that struggling is useless.

Two more gaping audience members go up in flames. Najah screams without realizing it, scurrying back to where she entered the inn, tripping and stumbling in the dark. Tears stream down her cheeks. Her mind races with such singular focus that she almost doesn't hear Sif kicking down the front door.

It is impossible to say if the spell is broken or made complete when Sif enters, but the audience rises from their seats and begins to tear each other's throats out with animalistic fervor. Even the men on fire take slow, torturous steps into the brawl.

Sif cries out for her friend. "Najah!"

"Keno! Help me!" she screams.

The King of The Tower hisses an eldritch command, and the crowd divert their attention to Sif and Najah. Though most of them turn their eyes toward the front door, a few bound up the stairs after Najah. Sif feels her heartbeat in her ears. Her gaze touches the Wretched King, and His finds her.

Thump

Thump

Thump

Chapter 35

Young Sif, the Destroyer

An unknown island

Sif has heard stories of people who, after being shipwrecked, wake up on a distant island. When she and Buri traveled with an acting troupe, a large genderless actor named Parishwar used to tell the same four, overexaggerated tales of castaways washing up on ancient islands, coughing up water and then coming back to life. With the wreckage of the *Rose Gold* sinking behind her, Sif understands the absurdity of it better than ever. She would only survive if she could power through and, more than that, get extremely lucky.

Sif has never put much effort into swimming, but what she lacks in experience she makes up for in strength, stamina, and force of will. The waves fight against every move she makes. Wreckage and artillery crash against the freezing water all around her. She stays under as long as she can, then bursts to the surface, taking deep, frantic breaths. The water deity Lyr must favor her, because the dim shape of an island blotting out starlight catches her eyes. The Titziri ship is further behind her than she expects.

"Uncle!" she screams, hoping beyond hope that Buri will hear her. "Ivon!" And, in a moment of conflicted desperation. "Sunnhilde!"

She feels the strength leaving her body every passing second. All she can do is hope they heard her, or that they spot the island as well. She paddles in the direction of land.

She pushes forward through the waves, the cold, and the darkness with nothing but blind, stubborn persistence, until every muscle aches and screams and her thoughts are just darkness and void. She expects to pass out, but a strange calm sets upon her. Her mind is empty, with nothing guiding it but a black spot on the horizon. Sif makes it to shore, alone, but she never entirely loses consciousness. Eventually, some dim awareness flickers in her mind as the gradient between freezing water and wet sand begins to favor the latter. Every fiber of her body burns with agony. She is safe for now, but Buri is gone, and so are Ivon and Sunna. By the time she can sit up, the Titziri ship is barely even a dot on the horizon. She wants to cry, but doesn't know how.

Since she was a kid Sif has been self-assured, sometimes to a fault. Even among northerners, Sif is a prodigy with a sword. A gift for someone without the temperament for a regular occupation, though it's landed her in much more trouble than farming would have. But even the trouble has been fine, because until now she has always had the strength to set her own path. Even with her mind emptied from exhaustion, she knows this is different. There is no path. She is alone. She curses herself for not looking harder for her uncle, but by the time she made it out of the ship, she barely knew which way was up. Maybe that's how it was for the others. Maybe they were picked up by another ship and are safe. Or maybe they would swim up to her soon.

But they don't. Sif barely musters the energy to drag herself under the shade of a strangely hued palm tree before she falls into a deep, restless sleep.

Agartha is a city in a hole in the sea
At the end of the world
In the pitch of a dream
The prison of hope
The gnashing of teeth
Agartha is a city in a hole in the sea.

-

She wakes up feeling like a pack of dogs has torn her apart. Sand and salt stick to her skin and rub her raw under her clothes. The air tastes like smoke, although none is visible. Her head feels like it's filled with broken glass. Even her lungs hurt, laced with a dull ache deep in her chest that tightens whenever she breathes. She spends the first few hours of her day sitting listlessly on the shore, searching for any sign of her friends, but none appear. Every so often she thinks she hears the echo of someone shouting, but no matter how fast she snaps her neck around there is no one visible, and no further noise. There is nothing left to do but trust in their ability to survive, and that one day they'll meet again. If not in this life, then in death. The thought doesn't quell the simmering fear inside of her.

Above her, the sun is a slowly drifting haze, and beyond it the sky dreams a delirious, cloudless blue. The air is bright, hot, and feels foreign in her lungs.

When she begins to drift off, a low, hissing voice rises in the periphery of her mind, calling from the forest where she can't help but feel countless eyes passing over her. Exhaustion and grief make an easy catalyst for fear. She flinches at sounds both natural and strange. Then a bolt of irritation strikes the tender of her heart and catches into rage. Whatever is in the forest, it either intends to scare her into submission or draw her into a trap. But if there are two true things about Keno Sif, they are that she will never let herself be hobbled by fear and that there are very few, living or dead, who can match her in combat. Sif wipes the sweat from her brow and summons all of her courage, determined now to catch or kill what hounds her.

A few miles into the canopy of forest, Sif is on the verge of accepting that the island is uninhabited when the smell of meat over a fire reaches her. She lifts her nose up and sniffs the air greedily, stumbling after the scent into a small camp built next to a shoddily constructed shelter. A thin, shabbily dressed old man walks up behind her as she inspects the site, and when he speaks, she has to stop herself from swinging at him in surprise. He is short and wearing the very grimy remnants of a red military uniform that Sif vaguely recognizes, but couldn't tell what country it belongs to.

"Goddess's song, old man. I could have killed you. Don't sneak up on me."

"You're in my home, young woman." His demeanor is flat, but not hostile. He looks well, for a man living in these conditions. He speaks in Found Tongue, same as everyone else, but with an accent Sif cannot place. It is a voice extremely different from the one that whispered to her before.

"Yeah," she admits. "Fair enough. Is there a town nearby? Are we on Atlas?"

The old man laughs ruefully. "Oh, you are far from home. I've never heard of Atlas. This island doesn't have a name. Not many people have lived here long, and none of them on purpose. How did you get here?"

"Shipwreck. Although, before that it was my taste in women, I guess," she mutters glumly.

"You need to stay on your toes as you journey inland. The spirits here are restless. Something about this place attracts those lost at sea, but none have survived as long as I have. So, take my words with the weight they deserve, hmm?"

"We'll see," Sif responds. "Why doesn't anyone last long?" Sif takes a seat next to him by the flame, secretly glad to get off of her feet. He adds wood to the fire and stirs up the ash. From the trees come the clicking and buzzing of a hundred insects, multiplying in the humidity.

"Many of the spirits here don't know they're dead. You don't want to be around them when they remember. The ones that always remember are worse. They're cunning. They can read your mind and control what you hear and see to trick you. I survived because I assume nothing. If we separate and I see you again, don't be offended if I ignore you. Or be offended. There aren't many ways to tell what is real, and I won't die out of politeness."

"Yeah? Maybe I'm a spirit now, then."

The old man scowls. "I have charms in the trees around us. Spirits can't enter the campsite as long as they hold." They must be well-hidden, because

Sif doesn't remember seeing any. Although she isn't at her best. A pack of three-headed serpents could have crossed her path for all she knows.

"So," the old man continues. "What were you doing before misfortune brought you here?"

Sif spits into the fire. "I was supposed to be going to Agartha to do a job."

The old man is quiet for a long time before he responds. "People don't go to Agartha. They're brought there."

"How would you know?" Sif scoffs, mostly joking.

"Because Agartha is nearby."

Sif would've leapt to her feet if every muscle wasn't screaming for rest. "The ruins are on this island?"

The old man shakes his head. He is avoiding looking at her. "No, no, no. The ruins of Agartha are miles from here, completely underwater. You've heard the song, right?"

Sif sets her teeth anxiously. The memory of the song and the moon-cursed dead weigh on her soul. ". . . yeah. Agartha is a city in a hole in the sea—"

"—at the end of the world, in the pitch of a dream," he completes. "You can see the ruins of Agartha under the sea if you sail far enough out. But you can only truly *get* to Agartha through the dreams of the cursed dead. You need to fall asleep where those who fled Agartha first died."

Sif pats herself for her pipe but can't find it. Only a bit of water-logged wax moth, wrapped in soggy, torn paper. The substance is usually a deep golden-brown and tough, but now it's taken on a pale yellow hue, and softened. Sif peels it off the paper and takes a bite, forgoing the normal consumption ritual for wax moth in favor of not being cursed by Siduri for excessive sobriety. Jeweled sunlight shimmers in between the trees, clarifying an inexplicable mist of water that carries with it the smell of the sea and the faint sound of a waterfall.

"Really hate to hear you say that," she murmurs through gritted teeth, fighting the urge to throw or break something. What is there to throw or break? The old man barely has a house, and even if she had the energy, it would be a miserable thing to take from him. This situation is already miserable enough. "Can you point me in a good direction?"

The old man nods grimly. "I can. But we should leave soon, while it's early. The spirits are worse at night, when the moon overhead reminds them they're no longer alive. They're still upset with the lunar goddess for not offering them a path to a true death."

Sif has seen the moon-cursed dead, at least in one form, and doesn't blame the spirits for wanting out. Life is for using up and casting aside. Hanging on to a facsimile of it is a much worse fate than simply dying.

The old man finishes cooking his meal and, rather than eating it, stores it in his home. Though from what Sif can see, it was a bit old to be palatable anyways. Sif turns away as he lifts the canvas flap to go inside, wanting to avoid the feeling of invading his privacy. In the few moments he is gone, Sif feels the lull of slumber wash over her like a flood. Her eyelids flicker heavily, drawing her deeper in, until the sound of rocks falling like thunder erupts from the trees in front of her. A cloud of thick dust obscures the air and seizes in her lungs. Sif coughs violently, swatting in front of her. Cries of pain and horror escape from all around her.

"Are you ready?" The old man asks, oblivious to all of it.

When Sif turns to face him, the vision is gone. Her lungs are clear and her vision is as sharp as ever. There are no voices and no collapsing stone. Sif feels wide awake, but can only assume she must have dozed off standing up and the force of the nightmare brought her back. Touching her chest, her trembling hand can still feel her heart hammering away.

"Yeah, I'm ready," she murmurs. "Thanks."

Afterwards, they begin their march further inland, where the flora has discarded its peaceful arrangement to focus its energy on grasping and clawing across any potential walking path. Walls of thorns and thick brush impede them at every turn, cutting her skin to ribbons with each step of slow progress, though if her guide feels the same way he doesn't show it. He nearly glides along the ground and slides past obstacles with little effort. For a starving man, he's remarkably resilient. She wipes sweat from her eyes and curses the humidity. A plant brushes her neck and feels like swollen fingers, the nails scraping her skin as they pass. The old man presses on wordlessly.

"We're looking for a ship," he eventually says, just before the birds and insects grow quiet.

"Inland?"

"Far inland. This ship was one of the last to leave Agartha before it fell. Afterwards, it crashed here and Lyr, the god of the ocean, pulled the sea back from the ship, ensuring that they would never bring the rot of Agartha to other shores."

"I know who Lyr is. So, he hates these particular sailors, or what?" Sif tries to joke, but the old man doesn't laugh.

"Yes. The deities of the sky and sea were so revulsed by Agartha that they buried it beneath the waves, where no living soul could reach it again. The dead, though, can never leave."

The song suddenly makes more sense to Sif. A city in a hole in the sea, and the pitch of a dream. In the pit of her stomach, she begins to believe the words the old man said. That people don't go to Agartha, Agartha calls people to it. Did she get Buri and Ivon killed? Was it some spell that drew her to Sunnhilde? The doubt breeds disgust in her heart. Not at herself, but at whatever force is trying to control her. Sunnhilde, Agartha, or fate. She swears to herself that she'll get her revenge in time. Keno Sif is nobody's puppet. She emerges from her self-reflection as the path ahead ends, revealing a monumental wooden boat sunken into the side of a hill, among a copse of palm trees. The old man is shaking.

"You alright?" she asks. The sky above is a dreamy, vibrant blue, with clouds that swirl maddeningly, far quicker than is natural. The smells of smoke and saltwater rise again on the breeze.

"I. . . haven't been back here in some time," the man admits. He is facing away from her, but Sif hears him choking back a sob. "I was forced from my home, with many of the people I'd worked with. It was either offer our souls to the king's vile magic, be killed in the violence that followed, or escape and hope we could find safety. We thought landing here would keep us safe. But apparently, it was too late."

"Hey, go back if you need to," she offers brusquely. He mutters something and keeps trudging forward, having lost the speed and grace from before.

The wooden boards that make up the Agarthan ship's hull have been torn, smashed, or rotted away against the hillside. The island pushes up here, reclaiming what little ground it's lost to human interference. Weeds and flowers and vines curl around a makeshift entrance in the ship's hull where a tree collapsed it in. The stems writhe and buds open and shut like mouths, only reverting to normal when Sif looks directly at them. Snapped planks of wood and fragrant plants frame the darkness of the ship's interior. The wax moth she ate earlier makes itself known, as a hazy, iridescent sensation fogs over her vision and settles behind her ribs. Her exhaustion retreats, but only slightly. The animal half of her brain tells her to run, but the woman half tears the fear into shreds, feels the blood and bones in her teeth, and lets it fuel her march forward.

Beside her, however, the old man breaks into tears. Soft, grief-filled, body-shaking tears. She turns to face him. He wipes his face with the palms of his hands. "I'd forgotten all of this. All of it. I should've seen what he was doing sooner. I'm sorry. I'm so, so sorry. . ."

"Uh, hey. . . It's okay. Listen, just go back home. There's no reason for you to get involved." Sif isn't sure what to say to him. She's never been adept at dealing with other people's emotions.

The old man puts a hand on her shoulder, tears collecting in his red-rimmed eyes. "Go ahead. I'll meet you on the deck."

"There's no reason we need to go together," Sif insists, this time with an edge in her voice. The hissing in her head picks back up, now sharp and frantic but still indecipherable.

"If there was a choice in the matter, do you think I would stay?" The old man roars back at her. The question echoes far into the distance.

The urge to fight almost overtakes her. Sif knows the island is getting under her skin, and although the temptation is there, she sets it aside for the sake of. . . of what? For the first time, it occurs to her that she doesn't have to go to Agartha. There is no reason to assume her friends will be there. It's as if she felt called onward, despite all reason. The old man said Agartha calls people to it, but even as the memory of those words repeats in her mind, Sif knows she won't turn back. If this is a trap, it's a perfect one.

"Whatever you say. I'll see you up top." Sif turns, hoping to leave in a hurry, but as she steps inside the boat, the old man says one last thing.

"Don't die here, Keno Sif," he whimpers. "This is a bad place to die."

She never told him her name. When she turns to ask how he knows it, the old man is gone. There is no rustling of leaves or chirping of birds. Even the wind is silent. Suddenly her spot between the woods and the ship seems colder than it did before.

She climbs the stairs inside the hull, and with each step her limbs become heavy and eyelids droop. The call to sleep is almost overwhelming. On the deck lay a dozen or so bodies. Sif can't help but notice none of them have been picked clean. Every one of them wears a red uniform closely resembling the old man's and, behind the wheel, she finds the one that matches perfectly.

Many of the spirits here don't know they're dead.

That's when she realizes why the red uniform feels familiar. They've appeared in many of the dreams she's had since she came across the moon-cursed dead in those desert ruins, all that time ago. Efa had said dead men in red uniforms killed her comrades. Ever since then, Agartha has been calling to her from her dreams.

Sif feels she should do something, but there is nothing to do and she is so, so tired. Whatever the dead men were involved in, it was abominable enough that Lyr killed them and the Lunar Goddess of Death refused to let them rest in the cloak of the night sky.

Sif crumbles to the deck beside the corpse of the old man, one hand on the hilt of her sword, and closes her eyes. She means to say a prayer for his soul, but her energy is completely gone. Even the sounds of crumbling stone, crashing water, the slaughter of countless innocents aren't enough to raise her from the deck.

And in the dim road between the land of the living and the land of sleep, a choir of the dreaming dead and their wretched king sings Sif's body down into the ruins of Agartha.

Chapter 36

Old Sif, the Hermit
Barburha, a town in the riverlands

The sight of the Wretched King is like dry brush to the flame in Sif's mind. In the decades since they first met his face has not left her mind, and even though it is different now than it was before, she knows it immediately. She roars at the top of her lungs for blood and revenge. In that moment anybody could be forgiven for thinking the Keno Sif of legend had made her way into the modern world, full of the same strength and energy she had in her youth. She cuts down the villagers in her way as if they're nothing, even as they scratch and gouge and pummel her.

Najah watches in mute horror, tears rolling down her face. All of it—the play, the magic, the violence—is too much. The moment strikes against her mind like flint, illuminating into horrible clarity. The only choice is to fight or die. It's the moment she knew would come for her ever since she and Ivon broke Sif out of prison. She draws her dagger and faces the creatures ahead of her. Her hand shakes, but Sif's bellowing from below stokes a flame in her heart and a cry erupts from her own throat in response. She leaps at the nearest man, grasping the collar of his shirt with one hand, stabbing clumsily with the other. His reaction is slow, as if he doesn't know what is happening to him until after it has happened. A low, sludgy moan of pain gradually works its way out of his lungs. Dark blood spills from his chest. Najah stumbles back in dismay as it rolls over her skin.

Below, Sif carves her way through a wave of bodies crashing against her in unnatural synchronicity. Arms reach out to grab her and pull her under, off her feet, or strip her weapon from her hands. The sight of the Wretched King pulls out feelings and memories that Sif has stamped down for decades, and once the gate of her soul has been opened there is nothing she can do to stop the torrent overwhelming her. Despite everyone she has cut down, the audience of walking corpses only grows in size.

Sif is rocked by the sway of bodies around her. When she puts one down, it takes only a moment before it rises back up. When she saw the Wretched King's grotesque face again, she acted before she thought. It was a mistake. But Sif has dreamt of this moment more times than she can count. She can hardly blame herself for being eager.

The Wretched King stares into her from the stage, wearing a cruel smile, unafraid of her anger. Through His loathsome gaze, Sif understands what He wants from her. He wants her to struggle and flail and rage, like an animal caught in a trap. To let the crowd around her absorb all of her energy until she has none left with which to fight. So. . . she stops. Her mind drifts to one of Buri's many lessons, one that had never completely sunken in. Rather than raging mindlessly, she lets herself be calm, directing herself mindfully and with clear purpose.

She takes in a deep breath, feels it travel to her lungs and back, and exhales slowly. Her mind clears. The burning anger fades, only a little. Just enough for an idea to take its place. The hands of the deranged villagers drag her downwards and, when the light above is blotted out, Sif swings her sword in a wide arc, cutting as many down at the knees as she can. She wrestles her way back to the surface and, with new room to move, runs and leaps at the Wretched King. But before she can reach Him, the candlelight is extinguished with a wave of His hand. Although Sif knows in her heart where He should be in the dark, there is nothing to cut down when she lands on the stage. Only thickening darkness.

Sif's breath, and that of an unseen other, are all that make a sound in the pitch-black room. She swings her sword around her, spinning on one knee, hoping to catch the Wretched King off guard. But He is gone.

With a flash, the light comes back, and Sif is in a burning inn, surrounded by a half-dozen slain villagers. At her feet is the handsome man Najah saw at the start of the play, possessing a normal human frame, except for his broken bones and flesh stretched out as if something too large had inhabited it before him. He gurgles something inaudible, pleading, before he dies. The golden raiment of the Wretched King lies on stage, resting on a pile of ashes. Sif frowns. Of course this wasn't the real Wretched King. It's just some sort of sick joke, like He's finally made it to Atlas only to toy with her.

Najah is on the second story, holding a bloody dagger, standing over her opponents. Her body is trembling, face still damp with tears. "Keno. . ."

Sif holds out her hand, offering it to Najah from across the room. "You're safe, Naj."

The two escape through the front, into the cool night air. The rest of the village is safe. A few charred bodies lay dead in the road, but there are no other signs of fighting or fire. In the distance, a crowd is gathering with buckets of water from a well in the center of town. Huddled against her is Najah, still wide-eyed and clutching her dagger.

"Hey, put it away. Before someone sees."

Najah's shoulders lower and she sheaves her weapon. The violence and fear in her eyes have been doused, leaving only grief. Sif expects Najah to ask what happened, but instead, she buries her face in Sif's side and blubbers incoherently.

"Am I awake?"

"What?"

"Am I awake?!" Najah's shriek is like breaking glass. Like a cold wind through dying trees. Like limbs thrashing under lightless waves.

"Yeah, of course." Sif slowly lowers her arm around Najah's shoulders, hoping it's a reassuring gesture, but feeling that it isn't. "What do you mean?"

"No, no, no, no. . ." Najah weeps.

"Yeah," Sif responds, not sure what else to say. The day she had met the Wretched King had led to the worst day of her life. She couldn't blame Najah for having the same reaction. Except then, the girl says something else that sends a chill down Sif's spine and seizes her heart.

"He's supposed to be a dream. He's only a dream. He's only a dream."

Sif opens her mouth to speak but can't find the words to say. Villagers rush by them with buckets, desperately trying to save the building, and all Sif can do is stare at Najah in dumbfounded silence, feeling like both of their already-difficult lives have truly gone up in flames. She doesn't have the heart to tell Najah that the king they saw wasn't real. That the Wretched King Himself is far, far worse. She bends down and wraps Najah in her arms, feeling the young girl's tears soak through her shirt.

Chapter 37

Young Sif, the Destroyer

Agartha

Sif can hear the roar of an immense waterfall in the far distance. As far as she can see, the waterfall forms a ring around the city. At this time of day, the height of the falls blocks most of the sunlight from the world above, casting the city in long shadows. Behind her, resting on a cool marble floor and shaded by a wave of delicate vines grown from a trellis roof, is a small shrine. The shrine is little more than a square hunk of marble with an offering box, but atop and next to it is a beautiful masculine figure, in a pose that suggests parental care. The top half of the figure now rests broken on the granite floor next to the shrine, laying on a thick coil of rope as if somebody pulled it down in anger. The figure wears a crown of antlers, some of the points broken off where it cracked against the floor. One arm is wrapped around a lamb, holding it close to their side, and the other is extended outward, holding a sheaf of wheat. The bottom half, still anchored on the shrine, is little more than a pair of sandaled feet planted beside a fox, unusually regal in its presentation and positioned as if on watch.

"Druga," Sunnhilde says, from behind her. "People don't sculpt them like this anymore, but this was the popular way to do it a few centuries ago."

Sif turns with a start. She isn't sure whether to be relieved or upset at Sunnhilde, but Buri and Ivon are there as well, and the sight of them almost causes her to cry out. All three of them are haggard and bleary-eyed, but smile warmly. Ivon's face is bruised deep purple and Sunnhilde's dress is stained dark crimson with blood at the hem, but Buri is completely unchanged. Overwhelmed at the sight of her friends, she rushes forward to greet them, planting a sloppy kiss on Ivon's forehead and wrapping her uncle in a hug. He smiles and returns the hug. A quizzical look passes over Sunnhilde's face when Sif doesn't acknowledge her.

"I thought you were fucking dead!" Sif yells.

"I've told you before, Keno, I am too beautiful to die. The deities would never let it happen," Ivon responds, faking offense.

"How are you here?" she asks, grinning widely.

"Simple," Sunnhilde begins, before Sif interrupts her.

"I was asking Ivon."

Ivon laughs awkwardly, then answers, "Well, dear. The Titziri ship came to check for survivors. Sunna somehow managed to gather the both of us, Captain Wahyu, and a few pirates, and pointed out how we could climb the ship without being noticed. Naturally, we slit their throats while they slept. Except for Buri, who refused to help, but didn't stop us since our ship was hardly sunk by fair means. We met Benedicta's flagship anchored above the ruins of Agartha which, let me tell you, is an absolute dread."

Everything comes back to Sif in a rush. The island, the spirit of the old man, the Agarthan ship that was beached trying to flee its home. She fell asleep on its deck and woke up here, in what must be Agartha. With two of her closest friends and a woman she doesn't know if she wants to kiss or fight, but is more inclined toward the latter.

"Did you see a spirit too?" Sif asks.

"Love, I *wish* we saw a spirit. We heard a whole chorus of them from underneath the water, louder than anything I've heard since we escaped Heron-Muse, and were almost crushed by that falling tower. Sunna had to give Wahyu and his crew an absurd amount of alchemy just to resist the drowsiness and the hallucinations." The energy in Ivon's voice dies abruptly. "I . . . honestly may not forget that for some time. I hope we don't have to go through it again when we wake up. I think this was a mistake."

Sunna steps forward, raising her voice's octave just a touch, a sign of her anxiety but also her hope. "Before it gets too late, we should talk, right?"

Sif frowns. "You tell Buri and Ivon what you told me?"

"Yes, why wouldn't I?" Sunna asks, brows drawing together. Her hand rests on her chest, evidence of the wound Sif inflicted.

"Well, you didn't before, and it feels pretty important that we're travelling with a witch."

"Are you serious?" Sunna snaps at her. "That's not what I said. I don't even want these visions, Sif." She draws back, a fresh wound opening in her voice. "I told you about my home."

Sif rolls her eyes. "You told me you can see the future, Sunnhilde. And then you hid it from me when it could have gotten us killed. For all I know, this is just some game."

"You've never seen things, Sif? Never had dreams about Agartha?"

Sif clenches her teeth. "You've been in my mind?"

"No!" Sunnhilde responds. The horror of the idea is obvious on her face. Obvious to everyone but Sif. "I wouldn't, even if I could. You talk in your sleep."

"It doesn't matter. We're here to kill Benedicta. Let's do it and go."

Sunnhilde stares at Sif disbelievingly. The silence lingers heavily in the air. "Fine," Sunnhilde murmurs angrily. She takes a deep breath, reorienting herself, and says, "Queen Benedita Yden is here because Agartha is a legendary site of magical power, and because the people here worshipped Druga." She motions to the statue.

"In the queen's mind, this is a sign the power here is a blessing from Druga. But it's not. It's a curse. Magic from the Mothers of Demons. No power here can be used without harm, and if the king's influence reaches the waking world, there's no telling what might happen. If we're lucky, it might only affect us like it has Agartha."

"Fine," Sif responds.

Sunna's eyes flash with annoyance. "You really don't have questions?"

"I have a lot of questions, Sunnhilde. But I'm already here. Let's just fucking kill her already, so I can get paid and go home. Or, I guess there's no pay either, is there?"

Sunnhilde glares at Sif. "There is treasure on Benedicta's ship that has not been tainted by Agartha. She brought it so she wouldn't have to pay Wahyu with anything too valuable."

Sif scowls. "Another little lie."

"Uhh. . . okay, ladies," Ivon says, speaking solely to break the discomfort of the moment. They run their fingers through their blonde hair anxiously, eyes darting between their friends. "Let's focus on getting out of here alive, shall we?"

Sunnhilde acquiesces. "Right. The queen is holding a meeting with Agartha's king now. She is trying to bargain for the secret of their power by offering him a pact."

"Great," Sif responds dully. "I'm on an island in the middle of nowhere, though. Pick me up, and I'll kill her while she's asleep."

"If it was easy, we'd do it ourselves," Sunna responds. "You're not wherever you fell asleep. You're in the shared, eternal dream of Agartha's death. A time so profoundly traumatic that the dreams of the dead here seep into the world. Even if we could pick you up, Benedicta wouldn't be on her ship when you get there. We'll have to get you once we're done here."

From the expressions on Buri and Ivon's faces, Sif can tell they've already reckoned with this. Mostly. Buri is somewhat tense, but otherwise as even-tempered as ever. Ivon, on the other hand, appears increasingly nauseated. Much of the color has drained from their face, and they stand with arms crossed in an unbelievable play on indifference.

"Keno," Buri starts, "the fall of the city is now. We should do what we came here to do and leave before Agartha is swallowed by the ocean."

Sif looks past Buri and, for the first time, really sees the city of Agartha. Pale white stone accented by ornate columns. A system for moving water through a series of intricate sluices that surpasses what the desert kingdoms of Atlas use. Lush plant life grows in abundance. Before the fall, it must have been quite serene. Now, it's pocked by flame and violence, and in the distance sounds a guttural howl that seems too human, too forlorn, to be a creature, but too bestial not to be.

"You're right, Uncle. Let's kill Sunna's queen and go home."

Sunnhilde is visibly annoyed. "Yes, please."

"Very well," Buri says. "You two go on, Sif and I need to speak."

Sif cocks an eyebrow in Buri's direction, but he doesn't give anything up. Sunnhilde leaves without a word. Ivon frowns and encourages them to hurry up once they're done. Sif watches them leave, but Buri keeps his eye on her. As soon as they are out of sight, he puts both hands on her shoulders and says, "This is not wise."

Sif shrugs. "We came a long way not to finish the job."

"No. Your feud with Sunnhilde is not wise." His rebuke is practically a bark.

Sif reels back in frustration and surprise. She starts to shove a finger at him but thinks better of it. "Of all people, Uncle, you should understand."

Despite her anger, Buri is outwardly unaffected. "I understand much better than you, Keno. Look at the uniforms of the Agarthan soldiers."

Sif knocks his hands from her shoulders. "So what? They wear red."

"They wear red," he agrees. "They wear red like the moon-cursed dead we came upon in the desert. Where your nightmares began. Should I take you for a witch?"

Sif freezes, realizing what he is getting at. A pinprick of shame blooms in her chest, for one of the only times in her adult life.

When she doesn't speak immediately, Buri continues, "You didn't choose your dreams of Agartha. Should I continue my line of reasoning?"

"I didn't lie to anyone, Uncle."

Buri puts a hand on her shoulder and squeezes gently. "I know, Keno. But Sunna has helped us so far. She saved Ivon's life on the boat. They were nearly beaten to death. She has earned enough trust to be considered an ally, at least. Whether or not you want to that to change can wait until we're safe."

Sif pictures Ivon's bruised face with renewed concern. She hadn't thought to ask. If Sunna is the reason Ivon is still alive. . . that means more than Sif can put into words. She sighs, embarrassed at her own foolishness. "I get it. Thanks, Uncle. I guess."

Buri grunts in response and, with nothing left to say, the pair follow after Ivon and Sunnhilde.

-

Their walk to the palace is a museum of human misery. Agartha had been a bustling kingdom in its prime, but now the streets are mostly empty. The wide, barren streets only heighten the city's sense of desolation. Families hoping to flee run barefoot to the edge of the city, where a machine lifts them to boats at the top of the waterfall. Armed guards in red uniforms fight against unarmed prisoners hoping to reach the ships. Buri finds the sight offensive. He raises his hammer and moves to attack the guards when Sunna reminds him that all of this has already happened. These are only ghosts, replaying a dream of their past.

"You're all still alive though, so be careful," she reminds them.

"Aneir's rings, what have I done. . ." Ivon moans softly. They should never have kept their contact with The Mages' Guild secret. They're too smart to have assumed this job would be palatable, but they had hoped to save everyone some grief by avoiding as much exposure to magic as possible. This couldn't possibly have gone worse.

Sif cocks an eyebrow, a little disappointed in Ivon for, to her mind, showing such fearfulness.

They find the palace near the center of the city, on a small hill. It isn't as large as Sif expects from the palaces she has seen before, but it is far more ornate. Gold and pearl accent the embellished steps up to a grand entryway. High spires fly colorful flags that whip around in the cold wind. Despite everything, Sif wishes for a moment that she could have seen the city before now. Poised at a set of stone doors is half of Queen Benedicta's retinue. Easily thirty people of all and no genders, standing mostly at attention.

"Here is the moment. Finally," Sunnhilde says breathlessly. "It's been so long." From her satchel, she produces a fine cloak, similar to what a well-regarded soldier might own. "Sif, put this on and cover your face. I don't want Queen Benedicta to recognize you. Ivon, follow us out of sight. Buri, please stay here until the fighting starts inside. Everything from here on out depends on this going well. I know none of you wanted this, but for some reason we all wound up here together. Benedicta has to die. Agartha cannot escape the dream."

Sunnhilde and Sif lock eyes, but only for a heartbeat. Sunnhilde looks away quickly. She seems tired. Homesick. Sad and scared.

The four of them trade glances and nods, confirming that everyone is willing to see this through. Neither Sif, Buri, nor Ivon have any objections to following Sunnhilde. The only one Ivon mistrusts is themself. All there is to do now is hope that when the dust settles, everyone is still alive and they have proven themselves worthy of the trust their friends place in them.

As the four of them split, Sif stops Sunna. "Wait."

"We don't have time, Sif." Sunna won't even glance in her direction.

"Just listen, damn it!" Sif snipes, immediately regretting it.

"What?" Sunna growls, eyes wild.

"I'm sorry," Sif says, hoping her expression conveys her sincerity.

Sunnhilde eyes her carefully, but not for long, then turns away without a word. Sif sighs and follows behind her dutifully. She can't force Sunnhilde to feel how she wants her to, and wouldn't if she could. Better to focus on the task at hand. It was a mistake to talk about this now.

With Sif disguised in a cloak, and Sunna recognized as Queen Benedicta's court advisor, the two pass into the palace without a problem. The guards part to the side and bow to Sunna as she passes. Sunna lifts her chin slightly and feigns the same casual disregard that nobility wears the world over. Sif wonders if she should do the same, but faking it feels unnatural, so she opts to stay true to herself.

Inside of the palace, Queen Benedicta Yden and the rest of her guard are spread across the shining marble floor, entreating Agartha's king. The guards stand with their weapons up, a show of force that doesn't threaten violence but implies the ability to carry it out. The queen is a beautiful woman of average height and a dark complexion. Her black hair is braided and pinned up in an intricate, fashionable hairstyle. Rich, brown eyes sit over a prominent nose and cheekbones. She is wearing an elaborate blue dress under a short, fitted coat. A long rapier is sheathed at her side. Sif's eyes move past her and to the king, then freeze.

On the throne is a man in a gold cloak, with a strong jaw and wiry build. His expression is haughty, with a perceived benevolence. Not dissimilar from the look Sunnhilde adopted to fit in at Queen Benedicta's side. Behind the king is a grisly mirror-image of the same man, with the sunken face of a corpse, wearing a tattered version of the same cloak. The former king seems regal in his crown, but on the latter, it is a strange, sick joke. Sunna strides with Sif between rows of soldiers, all staring at the tattered image of the king with intense disquiet, and takes her place by Queen Benedicta's side, once again playing the dutiful advisor. The occasional faint whimper or muffled sob of a soldier punctuates the stillness of the room.

The human king opens his mouth to speak, but freezes as if choking, and his soft, stern voice comes from the Wretched King's drawn husk of a mouth. "I thank you for your offer, Queen Benedicta. Truthfully, there is nothing to save. Agartha is not dying, it's going to sleep. But I will need your help to wake it up. And in return, I am happy to share what I know. My servants tell me you're a disciple of Druga, but I'm curious if you know their real nature. Before I met Mother Fog, I thought I understood Druga. But I was wrong."

Sif tenses up at the name of Mother Fog, one of the Three Mothers of Demons. The kind of name you could be killed for speaking openly on Atlas.

"Druga is the deity of order. They keep things, places, and people where they belong. They bless us with law and government, to keep us from behaving like animals."

Sif scoffs at this. She's seen how governments treat their people. The fact that they call it order is only proof of the rot that afflicts all monarchists. Queen Benedicta turns to Sunna and hisses, "Keep your woman on a leash or I'll have her executed."

"Very close guess, Queen Benedicta," mimics the emaciated corpse of the Wretched King. "But the key to it all is the Virtuous Path. We gain power in Druga's name, to create order in their name. Then we are blessed with peace, which leads to prosperity, which grants us more power. Power, order, peace, and prosperity, in an endless cycle. When you leave here, will you take these words with you? If so, I believe we could work out another deal."

The queen is enticed by his promise, but disturbed by the reality of Agartha's state. What peace and order could exist in a sinking kingdom? The man may be insane.

"Sir, I will. Forgive me for asking, but. . . your streets are in chaos. Most of your citizens have fled."

The corpse of the Wretched King laughs. "It's only some bloodletting to promote future health. The same way a physician might use a leech to better balance the humors. A small prick now will carry our dream to a better future." The queen must have made a face, because the Wretched King says, "Oh, did you think I didn't know? This is my dream first and foremost, Queen Benedicta. I ruled over Agartha in life, and now I carry it in my long, long sleep. Will you turn from Druga's light for something as inconsequential as the deaths of those already gone for hundreds of years? I'm not being cruel; I died here as well."

The queen shakes her head, but has trouble getting the words out. "No. No, I will remain faithful through this trial." Her guards shuffle uncomfortably. "What should I do?"

"Only come here and take my hand. I will grant you the same power I have now, and as you grow into it, the future of both of our countries will be secured." The Wretched King adopts a warm, paternal tone at shocking odds with his appearance. "Only you can help me correct all of this and save the people of Agartha."

The queen is about to ask which set of hands she should take when the still-living form of the Wretched King, sitting on his throne, is hit by an arrow. From the entrance to the palace, soldiers in red uniforms swarm the throne room. Gasps fills the room as the ghosts of Agarthan soldiers try to avenge their sinking home by killing its king.

The Wretched King steps past His own body and casually waves His clawed hand in the direction of the rebels, as if absent-mindedly swatting at a fly. The air shimmers briefly before the rebels explode noiselessly into a rain of bone and viscera. Queen Benedicta's guard cries out as a small portion of their side is caught in the spell. A grotesque sleet of gore patters on marble flooring and iron armor. The smell is nauseating.

Sif's breath catches in her throat, eyes and mind transfixed on the scene. A terror she has rarely ever felt takes root in her heart; one she already knows will take the rest of her life to weed out. The queen winces, desperately pretending to be oblivious to the brutality around her. The mist of blood pointedly misses her pristine gown as she glides across the marble and up the stairs towards the Wretched King.

"Now!" Sunna yells, redirecting Sif's attention away from the horror in front of her and towards their target. Sif draws her sword with shaking hands and clumsily runs after Queen Benedicta. Her legs feel like rubber, and her heart pounds in her chest with dizzying speed. Every breath carries with it the taste and scent of warm iron as the rain of blood continues. Sif leaps forward and drives her sword through Queen Benedicta's back. The queen gasps, then stumbles over. Relief floods Sif's body. It's almost over.

The Wretched King grins at Sif through rotten and missing teeth. He isn't worried at all. Sif's relief dies just after it was born. She raises her sword to the Wretched King, trying to summon a fire inside of her that will burn away the fear.

"Hey!" Ivon yells from a high window. As the Wretched King looks up, Ivon's dagger embeds itself in His face with a *thunk*. The Wretched King pulls the blade from Himself effortlessly, with neither a cry of pain nor release of blood from His sunken visage. He waves His clawed hand towards Ivon. Sif's muscles tense, and she leaps for the king, hoping to strike Him down before He can do to Ivon what He did to the rebellious army of Agartha. Ivon leaps back, but not in time. In their wake, Ivon leaves a spray of blood and wail of agony; at the same time, a cry of grief and fury erupts from Sif's lungs. She drives her sword into the Wretched King's chest. Unbothered, He raises His free hand. With it, Queen Benedicta regains her footing, whole and uninjured, and begins her march to the throne again.

Sunna runs up next to Sif and tries to help pull her sword out from the Wretched King, but it is immovable. Something inside Him is holding it in place. The sensation of it makes their skin crawl.

"Uncle!" Sif yells. The only chance they have now is for Buri to join the fray. The three of them combined can't be beaten. But Buri doesn't call back.

"Hurry up, old man!" she yells frantically. Sif and Sunnhilde are both being pushed backwards by the march of the Wretched King towards Queen Benedicta. Every moment, a palpable sense of hopelessness grows. Still, Buri doesn't respond. Sif eyes widen, heart hammering in her chest and teeth grinding against each other, her whole body fighting to hold faith that victory is possible.

"Sif, the queen." Sunna's voice is calm, but her eyes betray a deep sorrow. Whatever Sunna has seen, she doesn't believe now that they will make it. Still, she is willing to hold back the Wretched King on her own. Sif's affection for Sunnhilde grows into admiration. How could she have ever doubted her?

Sif lets go of her sword and rushes Queen Benedicta. She pulls a dagger from her boot and slits the queen's throat. Benedicta Yden barely puts up a fight. In the distance, Buri fights the remaining guard. He is covered in deep wounds, eyes bright and wide, never giving ground but, at this point, not strong enough to keep taking his own.

"Run!" Sunna yells.

Sif turns to see the Wretched King reaching His hand out for Queen Benedicta. In a moment, He may bring her back again. Sif carries the woman's corpse over her shoulder and starts to run, but He already has the queen's wrist in His grasp. Sif feels the queen begin to stir in her arms. In one smooth motion, she turns and severs the queen's hand at the wrist. The queen cries out in pain, her warm blood cascading over Sif's shoulder and back. Sif sprints past Buri, leaping over the fallen guards, away from the unholy sound ringing out behind her; she doesn't turn to see what it is. Bright red blood spatters on the marble floor as she runs from the palace, leaving Buri, Sunna, and Ivon behind.

This is why Agartha is forbidden. It is a literal nightmare invading the waking world. Sif chastises herself for almost every decision she's made over the past month. She shouldn't have let her bounty get so high. She shouldn't have run into the desert. Shouldn't have taken the job, shouldn't have doubted Sunna. All she knows is that if Sunna was right, then letting the Wretched King get His hands on Benedicta would bring a piece of Agartha to her home on Atlas. Sif doesn't want to live through that, and refuses to die.

"Let me go. . ." Queen Benedicta gurgles. Sif clenches her jaw. She hadn't realized Benedicta was still alive. Or had been brought back.

"Fool. Nothing about this pact can benefit you. Mother Fog? Death would be too good for you."

"Benefit me?" The queen laughs bitterly. "You don't care about me. You're doing this for yourself. All you've ever done is make life harder for loyal citizens of civilized nations. I recognize you, Keno Sif. The Destroyer."

Sif vaults over stone railing and out into Agartha proper, away from the palace. "Yeah, so I am. So fucking what? Why do you and Agartha's king get to cause all this destruction for yourselves, and I have to live meekly under the shadow of your boots?"

"It's the natural order, barbarian. Druga assigns us the places that will let us benefit humanity the most. Apparently, they didn't account for *you*."

"Right," Sif grits her teeth as she leaps from the end of a street to an adjacent rooftop, where the ground slopes downwards dramatically. "Easy for you to say. What were you going to do with Agartha's power anyway? Bigger home? Fancier throne?"

Benedicta bares her teeth. "I will use Druga's power to protect my country from the jackals that stalk its borders. From people like *you*."

Sif stops at the edge of the roof. She lowers Queen Benedicta from her shoulder. A cold wind whistles over the rooftops, prickling her skin. "Better to be a jackal stalking the borders than a vulture circling above them."

Benedicta meets Sif's gaze, eyes blazing indignantly. "The people of

Agartha deserve to be saved."

"They're already dead!" Sif yells. "You're just like that *corpse* on the throne back there. You can say it's all for peace and safety, but we both know you'd never give up your throne and live like the peasants you rest your boots on. Your life won't be the one ruined by whatever that monster has planned."

Benedicta spits in Sif's face. Sif flinches, then with a gentle push, lets the queen's body fall to the street below. The queen lands with a gruesome thud.

"Let's see the Wretched King bring her back from that in time." Sif scans her surroundings for pursuers as the waterfalls ringing the city roar in the background. Then, as if on cue, the sea makes its last attack on Agartha. The machine carrying away refugees crumbles. The ship waiting on top goes over the falls after it. Stone dust and rubble explode into the air as the ships crash into the city. Agartha falls away from the sun as the streets are swept away in a torrential flood. Sif looks back to the palace of the Wretched King.

"Wake up," she murmurs.

"Wake up. Wake up. Wake up."

Chapter 38

Old Ivon, the Master Thief
The road to Béma

Ivon is resting by a small fire in the riverlands, southeast of Ograna, when a cadre of church soldiers happens upon them. In their youth, Ivon could never have been surprised like this. Unfortunately, their hearing and focus are both not quite what they used to be, and the soldiers are wearing scouts' leather armor. Unlike metal, the leather barely makes a sound, and the natural breathing of the forest drowns out their approach.

"You there! Put your hands up," one of the soldiers calls out. Ivon complies, standing up slowly.

"Whatever you say. Although, I only have the one."

The soldiers whisper conspiratorially at the sight of Ivon's face. It isn't hard to figure out what about. Someone must have seen Ivon's face around the time of Sif's prison break. It isn't a surprise; Behno is a small town, and a one-armed stranger walking in from the desert would be notable.

"What's your name, elder?" a soldier asks.

"I'm Elin of Phosita. Traveling north to see my sister in Ograna." The path from Phosita to Ograna would take a person through these woods. Even still, Ivon knows they'll be arrested. The Church of Druga isn't an understanding organization on the best of days.

"Give me your right of passage," the same soldier commands.

Ivon frowns. Phosita must be issuing its citizens papers before they travel. It makes sense. Outside of Hvek, Phosita is the Church's next biggest supporter.

"I'm afraid I lost them crossing a river to the south."

"Take them," one soldier says to another. All three of them approach Ivon, ready to draw their weapons. Ivon knows that if they get themself arrested, they can probably escape in time to avoid execution. If they fight, they can buy time for Sif and Najah. But they won't win.

"So be it," Ivon murmurs aloud. With a flick of the ankle, they catapult their staff into the air and grab it with their hand. Wielding it like a club, they strike the first soldier in between the legs, then use their body weight and the staff as a fulcrum to send the soldier to the ground. The soldiers still standing draw their weapons, fresh swords gleaming in the sunlight.

"Don't make us kill you, elder. We know who you are. You can make up for your crimes."

"There are worse things than dying, dears. I'm not afraid to die if it means Najah will be safe. You two should listen to me when I say that serving a master will only bring you misery. The only dignity we can have in this life is in following the call of the heart."

"You can't talk your way out of this, elder. Serving Druga is the only path to peace. Give up now while you can still repent."

Ivon shakes their head sadly. "Maybe you don't have a heart after all."

The fight is short. Ivon blocks the first sword, but the second knocks their cane from their hand. By then, the soldier who had fallen over is back up and joins their comrades. Ivon draws a dagger from their belt and throws it, praying to Aneir that it strikes well. It strikes the middle soldier in their gut. Not enough to kill now, but maybe enough to kill them later. It's enough for Ivon. No matter what happens now, they've bought Najah and Sif time, and stopped one more pursuer.

Suddenly, arrows fly from deeper in the forest and strike down the remaining two soldiers. Ivon gasps in shock and relief, hand up to their heart. From between the trees emerge three figures. One of them, a tall, pale-skinned man with blond hair, runs to Ivon and falls to his knees, wrapping his arms around Ivon's chest.

"Aneir's name. . . I thought you were dead." His words come out in between gasping sobs. "How are you here?"

Ivon places their hand gently on the man's head. "Oh, dear. I'm sorry to have worried you, son. I had to leave quickly. I did leave you a letter. . ."

Ivon's son wipes his eyes and stands up. "Father is inconsolable, and Kariva is trying to help run the Union in your absence. What do I need to do to help you return home?"

"Nothing, son," Ivon replies, mustering a smile. "Just walk there with me. How did you find me? If it was through tracking, I'm very impressed."

"My new friend here, a sage, approached us in the Union, saying you were in danger. All she wanted in return for leading us here was to speak with you."

From behind him, a cloaked figure steps forward and speaks with a voice like honey. "Hello, Ivon. It's been a long time. I believe you have information I need."

Chapter 39

Old Sif, the Hermit
The road to Ravinser

Since seeing the Wretched King again, Sif hasn't slept much. Najah does, but only fitfully. Sif tries to ask her what she knows about Him, but Najah doesn't have answers. Sif is torn in two, between the parts of her subsumed by old fear and anger and regret, and the part of her that just wants the child in her care to be safe and strong.

"You really haven't heard of Agartha?"

". . .I already said no."

Najah has regained some of the timidity she had when they first met. She is quiet and emotionally distant, but rarely wanders far from Sif's side.

At the border to Ikeoba, a small kingdom in the southern riverlands, the Church of Druga has set up a checkpoint and patrols of soldiers. Somewhere past here is Ravinser. Sif thinks she sees Kisha the first day, riding south through the pines. While Sif works out how to pass the border, she and Najah have been camping on a ridge, careful to keep cover under the trees and away from the rocky edge.

"Have your parents been to Agartha?" Sif asks, grasping at straws.

"Not as far as I know. I only knew my mom, though. What is Agartha? Why do you keep asking me about it?" Najah strokes Russet's side absent-mindedly. For his part, Russet seems glad for the attention.

"It's where the man in the golden cloak is from. I. . . met Him once. Would your mom have gone there before you were born? There were a lot of soldiers with me when I went."

"I don't think so. My mom hated violence; she would never have been a soldier. I'm surprised she thought someone from Ummun would help us." Sif shrugs. It is odd, even if Najah's mother was correct. "Who is He?" Najah asks. "I don't really remember much when I wake up. Some of it's come back to me since we saw Him."

Sif sighs. The leaves underneath her feet crunch as she adjusts her stance nervously. "The King of Agartha. He was a magician and a monster, unsurprisingly. Fucked His kingdom up so bad that the people who died dreamed of it even after they had passed, and dreamed so long and hard that sometimes their memories can still reach us."

"That's why I can see Him?"

"Maybe," Sif says doubtfully. "When I was young, dreams about His country reached me because I fell into some ruins where people from Agartha died. But I still never saw Him. Maybe you got bad luck."

"He doesn't seem like a king. In my dreams, He's always in this tower, in the middle of nowhere. All the land is this red clay, without any plants or other buildings."

"Sounds scary."

"Yeah. . ." Najah agrees. Her voice has a forlorn quality. She's lost a lot of her faith in their goal. Sif hopes she can restore it, but doesn't know how.

Sif hums thoughtfully. Below them, three soldiers are chatting it up over tin cups of coffee. The smell doesn't reach them, and Sif finds herself feeling a little jealous. She would give anything to rest with a nice cup of Syrisian coffee after a long, quiet sleep. Sif sighs and tilts her head skyward. When she was a kid, Buri had been her mentor. She never felt unsafe with him. Not really. Maybe she should have, since he always used to chide her for being too foolhardy. But really, nothing like this ever happened to them. Sif's mother, skill-fathers, and sister were all safe in Ummun. There had been no fanatical, imperialist army of Druga yet, just occasional kingdoms dotting the continent. The worst thing that happened to them, before Sif was an adult, was the time she got caught stealing and almost lost a hand. Sif wonders if she is doing something wrong that Najah feels—and is—so unsafe. Would Buri have done better, or is all of this beyond even him?

In her heart, she hears her old mentor tell her to trust herself.

"Najah," she starts, "I won't let anything happen to you. Keep being brave. We can do this."

Najah smiles feebly. A spark of courage alights in her heart, but it doesn't catch fire yet.

After a moment, Sif absent-mindedly says, "Sunna had dreams, too. They helped her a lot, but they were also a burden on her soul."

"Is that your wife?"

Sif smiles. Hidden beneath that smile, Najah senses a distant sadness. "Yeah, that's her."

The two of them settle into a comfortable silence. The only sound on the ridge is the treetops rustling in the midday breeze.

-

On the east end of the roadblock, three paladins change guard. In the low moonlight, Sif and Najah sneak through a gap in the coverage. It is maybe two days walk to Ravinser, if they're lucky. Despite knowing Ravinser was always a guess, Sif feels a lightness in her steps and her heart, a truer version of what she felt when she stepped off the mountains with Najah forever ago. They move swiftly through the safety of darkness, thankful for the cloudy night above them. They pass one of the Church's encampments, where a small cadre of soldiers is drinking and cooking and laughing. Easily a dozen prisoners hunch in nearby cages, too many of them to lay down, but the cage too small to fully stand. Najah mutters curses at the jailers as she passes. She makes a promise in her heart to come back and free them when she is strong enough. A promise made in earnest, but still a victim of her naivete. None of these prisoners will live much longer.

By the time they leave the blockade behind completely, they are in marginally better spirits. In the relative ease of the moment, neither of them see Kisha before she leaps down from the canopy and cracks Sif across the head, sending her tumbling from Russet's back.

Kisha lands with a thunk, rolls to her feet and draws her sword. "Hey, Auntie. Sorry for the sneak attack, but I felt like I owed you one for last time." Kisha turns to Najah and waves. "Hey, kid. Ready to ditch this old hag? She's just going to keep walking you into traps."

Sif picks herself up from the ground and draws her sword. Bright red blood runs down her face. "Just run, Najah."

Najah leaps from the saddle, drawing her dagger. Kisha guffaws at the sight of the young girl brandishing a weapon. "Wow, guess Sif turned you into a killer huh? Just like me. Bet I can cut you first, though."

Najah runs through everything Sif taught her about how to fight, but holding her dagger still feels stiff and graceless. Panic and adrenaline sprint through her veins. "If you just wanted me dead, you would have killed me when you sucker-punched Keno. I think you can't kill me. I bet you'd get in too much trouble."

Kisha snorts as if Najah told a joke, but her eyes and lips make it obvious that Najah has hit a nerve. "Real smart, little girl. But the cultists wouldn't mind if I just took a few fingers. Enough that you can't hold a weapon. They'd probably prefer it."

"What is wrong with you?!" Sif barks. "You're from Feigrvoller. You know these cultists won't stop. What is the point behind all of this misery?"

Kisha jabs with her sword, testing the distance between her and Sif as the two circle each other. "What is the point? I am ashamed of you right now, Auntie. This is why you'll never be truly great. The Church of Druga has *money* and *power*. Doesn't matter how you swing a sword if you don't have that. You probably could've been a queen if you'd had the guts to take what's yours before your bones got brittle."

Sif spits in disgust. "You're sitting on a pile of bones and telling me it's a throne."

Kisha jabs again, a playful smile plastered across her face like she can't lose. "See, that's what you'll never get, Auntie. If you leave enough bodies behind, you can make anything a throne."

Sif rushes the younger woman, hoping to overwhelm her and break through her defenses before she can call for help. Kisha doesn't underestimate her this time. She deflects every attack with graceful ease. Najah stays back, searching for the perfect time to intervene.

"Just run!" Sif demands. She can't let Najah be captured after all of this. She'd rather die. Seeing the Wretched King again has opened up her memory of Buri like a fresh wound, and her whole heart is tangled up with the pain of that loss and her desire to protect Najah.

"Fuck off!" Najah yells back. She is tired of making herself small. Tired of running and feeling defenseless and worrying about being abandoned by whatever person fate decides will protect her until they either die or give up. "You don't get to tell me to run!"

Kisha laughs. "Come on, Keno. The girl wants to see you die. Just stand still."

Najah runs at Kisha, dagger pulled back for the plunge, screaming at the top of her lungs. Kisha turns and kicks her in the stomach. Najah tumbles backwards, legs over her head, gasping for air. The dagger rolls away from her in the dirt. Without missing a beat, Kisha deflects two more of Sif's attacks, then picks up the dagger and slips it into her boot. Najah feels hot tears spilling from her eyes. She isn't good enough, still.

"This is sad, Keno," Kisha says, ignoring Najah on the ground nearby. "Truly pathetic. You were my hero as a kid. I think after I kill you, I won't tell anyone how weak you've gotten."

Najah gasps in the dirt, tears and mucus streaming down her face. "It's S-Sif."

"What are you saying?" Kisha growls.

Najah wraps her arms around Kisha's leg, stopping her from moving. "Her name is Sif. You don't have any right to call her Keno. You're the pathetic one. You don't stand for anything. You just help the Church of Druga because it's an easy way to fake being someone who matters."

"You little bitch!" Kisha growls, trying to kick Najah off of her while deflecting Sif's attacks. She is upset. Distracted. It's the perfect moment.

Sif throws caution to the wind and darts in close, trusting Najah will do what she needs to. She makes wild swings at Kisha with all of her rapidly waning strength. Kisha narrowly deflects the flurry of blows, but has completely lost focus on Najah. Bracing herself to cross a line from which there is no coming back, Najah pulls her dagger from Kisha's boot and drives it into the older woman's leg. Kisha goes down hard, screaming and cursing.

Kisha, sensing she has lost her advantage, yells at the top of her lungs for help. "They're over here! Sif and the girl!"

Sif drives her sword downwards for a killing blow, but Kisha rolls out of the way, punching Najah hard across the face as she gets back to her feet. Blood spills from a gash on Najah's cheek. She watches in horror as the droplets land in the grass and weeds. Dozens and dozens of thin branches shoot from the dirt and wrap around Kisha. Buds on the branches sprout into big lilac flowers.

Kisha and Sif both stare at Najah in horror. Najah only sees Sif.

"Don't be mad," Najah pleads.

Countless boots stampede towards them from the camp nearby. Sif's eyes dart towards the sound, and then back at Najah. "I'm not," Sif says. "'I'm not mad."

Sif grabs Najah by the hand. They jump back into the saddle and ride into the darkness, leaving Kisha behind. In only moments, the safety of the night is interrupted by the persistent glow of torchlight behind them, and the clattering of armor and weapons. Eventually, the barking of dogs and pattering of other horses' hooves join the chase. Avoiding the road isn't enough, anymore. Every bit of ground they gain is lost by unfamiliarity with a territory the Church of Druga has been scouting out for weeks. Sif wouldn't be surprised if Kisha sent birds up as soon as she got free.

They flee for half an hour through the thicket, over streams, and up hills until they finally come across a moonlit clearing. In the middle of it is an elderly, dark-skinned woman, sitting on a stump. She perks up at their appearance, as though she'd been waiting for them. With the help of a branch she is using as a cane, she rises to her feet and says, "Hello, ladies. Is one of you Najah? I believe you're in need of some help."

They hesitate, unsure whether they can trust the woman, but short on time to decide. She doesn't dress like she works for the Church. If she does, it won't be hard to resist her. Still, Sif is about to decline when Najah makes the decision for them. "Yes. Please help us."

The woman smiles. "Of course, follow me. I've been expecting you for a long time. A long, long time."

She leads them across the meadow and past a shallow river then, shockingly, beneath the roots of a tall tree. The descent is steep, and almost too narrow for Russet's muscular frame. The spread of the roots obscures the passage, and they quickly lose what little illumination they had. However, when they arrive at the end, they find a very large and cozy home. They can still hear the cries of scouts, soldiers, and paladins hunting them down, but their voices are distant now.

"Where are we?" Sif asks. The smell of wood and dirt is overwhelming. She stumbles slightly as she walks over small roots that trace the ground. "Who are you?"

The woman lights a candle, illuminating the small, dark room with orange light. "My name is Aseli of the Wood, and you're in the last, true shrine to Druga, my dear. You'll be safe here."

Benedicta Yden and the Deity of Peace and Order

A history recounted by Aseli of the Wood

Benedicta Yden was no stranger to death. In the glory of her faith, she had been resurrected again and again. Painfully, each time. It was a burden she was grateful to bear if it meant maintaining peace at home. When she was shoved from the dream of Agartha and into the real world, she almost died again. Of thirst and exposure. Of exhaustion. When she was rescued, she saw it as another link in her chain of miracles. Chain was the right way to think about it, although 'miracle' ended up being an unfortunate falsehood.

Her spouse, Regent Jamil Al-Ghanem, was out on a campaign of conquest, but had sent servants, doctors, and knights to pick her up from the port where she landed. She was back in the kingdom of Hvek faster than anticipated, considering her injuries.

Word of her struggle to get home spread throughout the kingdom: The woman who died and came back again and again in the service of Druga. The woman who divined the words to the Virtuous Path—from power, to order, to peace, to prosperity. But Queen Benedicta left out the Wretched King, knowing the common folk wouldn't understand. The barbarians and the witch killed some of the knights; why not just say they had killed them all?

Regent Jamil, who had always felt comfortable with their position as a leader and a person of faith, grew noticeably weary and paranoid over the next years. They had shored up their power for the creation of peace, and shared that authority with their new Church of Druga. It created, both in the Church and in

Jamil, a passion for punishment that was sometimes unnerving to the queen.

Over breakfast one morning, Jamil commented, "Peace must mean a full prison." It was a sort of a joke, but not enough of one, and the queen wasn't sure whether the sentiment was funny or sad.

That week, Regent Jamil was injured by a rock thrown from a crowd, and although the initial injury wasn't bad, they had seizures for the rest of their life, which lasted only a meager three more years. Benedicta Yden attended the funeral with her infant child, and upon returning to the palace, found the Elders of the Church had staged a soft coup. They presented her with a plan for dealing with the unpopularity of the monarchy, which involved officially ceding some control to the same Church she founded and had served as a matriarch for. Between the new baby and Jamil's health, she had lost more ground than she knew. It was clear that the offer was actually an ultimatum. Either she submitted, or the soft coup would become a hard one. Though support for the monarchy had grown due to the sympathy the common people had for Jamil's death, Benedicta worried it wouldn't be enough to ensure her child's safety.

When her daughter turned three, Benedicta Yden finally understood how much of her life had been a trap that was now springing shut. Hvek must have been at peace, because the prisons had never been fuller. That was when the Wretched King began to visit her again, in her dreams. His requests chilled her to her soul.

The Church of Druga had been waging a war of peace, consolidating power across the continent in the name of Druga and the Virtuous Path. The Wretched King wanted to use that power. He wanted blood magic. He made threats as to what would happen if she didn't obey. He let her know that, since the moment He grasped her hand, He had been waiting inside of her mind for this day. He assured her that if she disobeyed, it would not stop Him. She heard His voice underneath the voices of the Church officials who kept watch on her, and it dawned on her that the journey to Agartha had been a terrible mistake.

As a last resort, the queen hoped to use what little authority she still had to try and disband the only mechanism capable of completing His requests—the Church of Druga that she had founded years ago. It was a plan she never had much hope in, but when the only tool one had been taught to use was bureaucracy, it was hard to see other paths to power. She would have been added to the prison's population, if a servant hadn't helped her and her daughter escape.

She had spent years building the structures of the kingdom, planning for how best to use them, but she was never meant to hold the power she had built for herself and her family. She had just been carrying the Wretched King's virus for him, creating a world that would eat itself the same way Agartha had.

My parent, Druga, met Benedicta shortly afterwards. They told me they had been looking forward to meeting her, although I was at a loss as to why. Druga often holds strange, seemingly paradoxical stances. Maybe it is the nature of their domain. Then again, I've said similar things about Siduri and Aneir. Perhaps it is in the nature of all the deities. In any case, Druga was horrified by the things Benedicta had done, but didn't seem to take it personally, despite the spread of the Church that carried their name and had such a negative effect on their own health. Druga could have sought revenge, but they did not.

Druga appeared at the time as a tall, lithe figure, almost human except for the bark, twigs, and leaves that made up their body. They encountered Benedicta as she entered our forest, chased by paladins from the Church. Druga raised a line of trees and thorns to cut off the paladins' path, and to give them time to speak with the disgraced queen of Hvek.

She recognized Druga immediately. They tended to have that effect on people they were interested in. Of all of Druga's children, only I thought that Benedicta would have fallen so far from grace and reason that she wouldn't recognize our parent.

The mistake isn't anything new. Humans have always heard "natural order" and, instead of placing themselves within that order and equal to it, they begin concocting schemes of hierarchy—which kind of human is best, which kind is worst. And they call this the natural order, even though it is neither order nor nature. When they're so willing to look upon other humans as less than people, it is no surprise they view the natural world as even less deserving of respect. The more these ideals spread, the less power Druga themself was able to wield. But I'm getting away from the point.

Druga offered Benedicta and her daughter a deal. They could stay in the forest, in a town called Ravinser, and be completely invisible to the eyes of the Church. In return, Benedicta would be a dutiful disciple, for once. And when the day came that the imbalance of the world needed correcting, Benedicta's daughter would be the mechanism to correct it. Benedicta accepted the offer gratefully, although she took a long time to purge herself of her old biases.

To her credit, though, she fulfilled her role dutifully. But it wasn't enough. The Wretched King's poison had already spread so far, and with each step the Church of Druga took, they spread conquest and misery and strife. Druga's influence waned, until one day there was barely anything left. To protect themselves, Druga had to retreat from the world, so that everything left of them was in the land around Ravinser and in the daughter of Benedicta. Without Druga's protection, the Wretched King pierced the forest, and His paladins burned Ravinser to the ground. My siblings, the spirits of the forest, watched bitterly. We wept for our lost home and for our missing parent. Many of us cursed Benedicta, and her daughter, and all humans. We were beginning to lose everything. Much of my heart felt the same, only I couldn't help but wonder whether Druga's gambit would pay off.

Chapter 40

Young Sif, the Destroyer
The ocean above Agartha

The fall of Agartha is the breaking of stone and the splintering of bones in the cold, brutal ocean. Sif remembers being swept from her feet and then, as quick as waking up, she is floating in the middle of the ocean under the clear blue sky. She wipes the hair from her eyes and looks around to find two boats, a royal vessel from Hvek and a military ship from Titzi. She holds her breath and goes back under the water. It's hard to say if she can make out anything below as the blue turns to black. The depth is so great her mind struggles to parse it, and her skin crawls with the unsettling feeling of being exposed.

Sunna and Buri breach the water next. Ivon is in Buri's arms, bleeding freely into the ocean. Sif screams their name. "Ivon! Are they alive?!"

Sif begins paddling to the Titziri ship, but Buri directs her to Queen Benedicta's vessel instead. It'd be the better-stocked ship, and it still holds the treasure Benedicta Yden brought as payment. Buri changes direction and hauls Ivon up as quickly as his aching bones can manage. Ivon writhes painfully, which may be a good sign. Better than not moving at all. Sif feels an emptiness in her chest as the two of them scale the side of the ship. Ivon is missing most of an arm and has a deep gash across their gut; the pain from floating in the salt water must be unimaginable.

"Don't worry," Sunna says softly. Sif hadn't noticed her surface. "I used to be a priestess. I can help with their wounds."

Sif doesn't know what to say. She's glad Ivon isn't lost, but can't help wondering if everything that happened, all of that horror, is going to end with them just. . . sailing back. Finding a port and heading out, like none of this ever happened. Wahyu greets her aboard Queen Benedicta's ship with his men, already counting their cut. As they sail off, Sif can't help but notice bodies surfacing in the water behind them.

Wahyu and Buri trade a knowing glance as they pass each other on deck. Wahyu notices Sif trying to decipher it and responds with false cheer. "Don't worry, Sif! I know a beautiful port in the south that will scrap this ship. So, you can finally get back all the money you lost playing cards against yours truly."

Sif only scoffs and walks away.

Buri and Wahyu meet each other's gaze seriously. Buri opens his mouth, but Captain Wahyu speaks first. "I hope you appreciate the risk we took for you. Killing you would've kept our pockets full for years, and if you'd failed, we'd all have been charged with treason."

Buri grunts in the affirmative, although he finds Wahyu's opinion to be grating. Did he really not consider Queen Benedicta's plan to be the greater danger? Or was he only leveraging his support, which he would have given anyways, for some future payment?

The two lock eyes intensely. Buri is waiting for Wahyu to say what he really wants. Wahyu is waiting for Buri to admit what he really thinks.

"Ah, fuck it," Captain Wahyu says, with a shrug. "If there's no honor among thieves, then what do we have?"

Buri is pleasantly surprised.

-

The days pass by in an insufferable, slow, slow haze. After the dream of Agartha, everything feels like a pinprick. A dream that keeps hurting after they've woken up. Sif worries that she will fall asleep and wake up there again. Which she does, but there is no mistaking it for the real thing. It's a very slight concession, but one she is happy to take. Sunnhilde, true to her word, does stabilize Ivon. And unlike Sif, they are immediately back to their old self.

"Hmmm," they muse. "Well, I guess I'll have to relearn some things. I hope I can still ride a horse. I've always been very good at it."

"You can't ride for shit, Ivon," Sif jokes.

"Well then, it's a good thing I'm so dashingly handsome."

Sif chuckles. "Yeah, that you are."

But when she looks back, there is a sadness in Ivon's eyes that hadn't been there before. Then they notice Sif's attention, and it immediately sinks back into the autumn greens and browns of their eyes.

-

At long last, the journey ends where Wahyu said it would: among a small chain of islands, in a port city named Red Cay. There, Queen Benedicta's ship is stripped, and the spoils divided mostly evenly. Wahyu's crew does take a larger cut, but to his credit, Wahyu doesn't take any extra for himself.

All four of them rent rooms in an extravagant inn built overlooking the rocky gray water, on the side of town where firelight sparks off of the rolling sea at night and packs of artists roam the streets drinking and singing. Afterwards, though, they drift apart. Buri spends his first several nights with an unknown man, but his naturally private personality means Sif, Ivon, and Sunnhilde don't hear any details.

Even after Ivon recovers, they're reluctant to go out carousing. Sif tries to be friendly with Sunna, testing to see if she is warming up. Sunnhilde is friendly, but not warm. Sif is not afraid of spending time with strangers but, with Buri occupied, Ivon acting withdrawn, and Sunnhilde still angry with her, a creeping sense of loneliness worms its way into her heart.

One day, under the amber light of early morning, Sif finds Sunnhilde on the bottom story of their crooked, wooden inn. She seems packed and ready to leave, without even a goodbye. As Sif walks quickly down the stairs, Sunna turns towards her, as if she had been waiting. Along the outside of the tavern, a riot of lavender sways in the breeze.

"Are you leaving?" Sif asks.

"Yeah. I've spent years of my life preparing for that trip, and now it's over. It'll be nice to live without the nightmares and the responsibility. Spend some time alone."

Sunnhilde's last sentence spears Sif in her gut. She turns her head, pretending to watch the flowers. "I see. Well, where do your visions put you next?"

Sunna shrugs. "I haven't had any."

"Just like you were hoping for." Sif tries on a smile, but it hangs awkwardly on her lips.

"Just in time. I don't think I could've kept going much longer."

"I didn't know," Sif replies sympathetically. Other than the night she told Sif about her home, Sunna had always seemed very at-ease.

"Well, you gave me a pretty good reason to stop opening up. Besides, we were already carrying so much on our backs. If it wasn't for the alchemy, I'm sure I wouldn't have slept a single hour."

A natural lull in the conversation signifies its end. Sunnhilde will be walking away soon. Fear cuts through Sif's heart. What can she say to make this last just a little longer? They meet each other's eyes and Sif's heart drops into her stomach.

"I should be going, Sif." Sunna says.

"Wait," Sif blurts. "Hold on."

Sunnhilde turns back to Sif, arching an eyebrow.

"Yes?" Sunnhilde asks, when Sif doesn't answer.

"I think I should apologize to you," Sif responds.

"Okay, then do it." Sunnhilde says.

"I'm sorry. You didn't. . . um. . . deserve that. What I said. You've proven yourself. I should've seen that."

Something tugs at the edges of Sunnhilde's mouth, but Sif doesn't notice.

"How have I proven myself?"

Sif frowns, clearly uncomfortable apologizing, and even more uncomfortable paying someone a direct compliment. "You're brave. And smart. And trustworthy. Braver than I was, going into Agartha, knowing what you'd see. You could have hidden away somewhere and let things play out, but you didn't. It's probably the only reason we're not stuck in a nightmare, too. Will you forgive me?"

"Swear to me that you will be better than that."

"What?" Sif asks, taken aback by Sunna's directness.

Sunna takes a big step forward. "Swear to me that you will not make that mistake again. With me or anyone else."

Sunna's gaze is all steel and burning intensity. Sif feels off-balance, like her shield has been splintered. "I swear," Sif murmurs.

"Now tell me what you want from me," Sunnhilde says.

"I want you to come back to me. When you can."

Sunnhilde's eyes widen in surprise, but a smile forms on her lips. "You don't want to ask me to stay?"

Sif shakes her head. "I won't ask you to do something I know you don't want to."

Sunna steps forward and runs her fingers fondly along Sif's face. The rapturous look in her eyes doesn't dim, even as she traces Sif's burn scar. Sif's breath freezes in her lungs. Her limbs and tongue feel heavy. She leans forward with a grin, feeling Sunna's warm breath on her lips. The scent of lavender envelops them both.

Chapter 41

Old Sif, the Hermit
The last, true shrine of Druga

Sif is awestruck at Aseli of the Wood's admission to being a priestess and child of Druga. While Najah is simply speechless, a passion and hatred that Sif had thought she was numb to reawakens inside her, building with each mention of Queen Benedicta's name. Najah said her mother had been saved by someone from Ummun, but that can't have been true. Or had Benedicta changed so much after leaving her kingdom that she had considered Sif an ally? It is too much to reckon with; all Sif can manage is to blurt out the first objection that makes its way to her mouth.

"You're just a crazy old woman," Sif spits out. "Druga is the deity of order. Every place their worshippers touch becomes less wild."

"Young human, you really thought there was a deity of courts and borders and trebuchets, and that they would also be the deity of peace? Are you an atheist?"

"No," Sif grumbles. "I follow Siduri."

"Then you know the temperament of the deities. They may be flighty and capricious, but which one of them doesn't care for their creations? If not love, they at least have a passing interest. It's why Aneir does not stand with the bloodthirsty, Siduri with the greedy, Een with the prideful, nor Asthia with those who are careless with another's heart."

Sif throws her hands up. "All I know is that the continent is teeming with soldiers who worship Druga, and they're all after Najah. If she's the daughter of the Church's founder, why would they be tracking her down? It's bullshit."

Aseli shakes her head. Worn nubs of horns peek out from her gray hair as she does. "Did you not listen to my story at all? Mother Fog and the King of

Agartha gained a foothold into our world through the late queen. They've taken advantage of your species' inclination towards violence and hierarchy to amass an army. They're after Najah because she has a piece of Druga inside her, from her time here in Ravinser, and because she has a piece of the Wretched King, transferred to her when her mother died. I'm sure there have been some symptoms of both."

Najah stares at Aseli, silently overwhelmed. The flowers growing from her blood. The cursed sleep. Her eyes are wide, arms close to her chest as if to protect herself. Sif, by contrast, looks like she might break something.

"I believe you," Najah says to Aseli. "I never knew my other parent, and my mom was always sort of weird about her life before." She turns to Sif and continues, "I didn't mention it before, but some things happened that kind of make sense with the Druga stuff."

"Yeah?" Sif asks, visibly annoyed at learning there is more being withheld from her. She can barely look at Najah knowing she is Benedicta's daughter. She knows it's irrational to feel betrayed; Najah had no way of knowing what happened between Sif and Benedicta. Still, after everything Benedicta did following Agartha, Sif can hardly stomach knowing that she has been protecting Hvek's one-time princess.

"There wasn't a time it felt important enough to bring up," Najah replies, seeing Sif's expression, but misreading its full source. "I sort of spoke to your goats. They said you were only pretending to be mean. I can hear animals sometimes. It's how I know where to find food when we travel."

"Fuck, Najah. You spoke to my goats?"

"Yeah. You should be glad, I was about to run, but they told me you were nice."

"Well, they lied," Sif grumbles. "Anything else you want to get off your chest while we're here?"

Najah frowns. She wanted to tell Sif about plants growing from her blood, but now she isn't sure. "No, Keno."

Aseli speaks up, breaking the tense silence. "There is a large well in Ravinser. The town was burned, but if you follow the new growth forest you will find the well in the center of it. That is where the rest of Druga has been sleeping. You need to go there and meet them. They will help you separate Najah from the Wretched King."

Sif shakes her head. It's clear her focus is elsewhere. "Kisha will be there. It's a bad plan."

Aseli interrupts. "It's the only plan. This was Druga's intention in blessing Benedicta's girl. The only way to protect her is to go to the well, release Druga, and break the curse."

"What the fuck does this well have to do with anything, spirit? You might as well ask us to go to a brick layer in the City of Roads."

Aseli gives Sif a patronizing glare. "Water is the barrier between the land of the waking and the land of sleep." An image of the ocean crashing down on Agartha flickers in Sif's mind. "It's the only place where Najah can reawaken Druga, return the part of them that sleeps in her, and correct the path you humans have started us on."

"Benedicta. . ." Sif murmurs, gaze flickering towards Najah. She recalls Najah saying her mother only had one hand. She pictures herself killing Queen Benedicta, then again, then again. Najah notices Sif staring at her and cocks an eyebrow.

"What?" Najah asks.

Aseli watches Sif closely, taking measure of the old warrior.

Sif shrugs and lights her pipe. Her voice is gruffer than normal. "Nothing. Just thinking."

Aseli snorts derisively. Sif side-eyes her but doesn't say anything. What does she know? It's easy to judge after she's spent years hiding from the world, where her hands never have to get dirty. Sif exhales a cloud of smoke and when it clears, Aseli is still staring.

"Got something on your mind?"

"Yes. You two can sleep on the floor here tonight. In fact, you must. But as soon as the sun breaks through the canopy, you will leave. Tonight, the woods will be swarming with paladins."

Najah grunts, and the chair under her creaks loudly. She slumps over, asleep, already twitching with nightmares of Agartha. The sight of Najah's curse has always been troubling, but knowing who causes it makes things a thousand times worse.

Aseli turns her attention to Sif. Her eyes are sharp, and in being seen Sif feels as if she is a rodent in the sights of a hawk.

"You should know by now, Sif the Destroyer. Your heart is there to help you live in truth, and not in a dream."

"So, you do know me," Sif says, pretending to be unbothered.

"I put it together as you spoke earlier. Benedicta mentioned you. Although, I could never tell whether she hated or respected you more. And now I find you're the one guiding Najah Yden. Seems dangerous to leave you with her. I'd be lying if I said I wasn't tempted to have the soil drag you down. I could tell Najah you left, and escort her myself."

"You don't have to worry," Sif hisses through clenched teeth, finally letting the anger inside her flood out now that Najah can't see it. Her whole body is tense, fists clenching so hard they shake. Her nails dig into her palms.

"You don't want revenge?" Aseli asks knowingly.

"Of course I do!" Sif shouts, jumping to her feet. She looks over at Najah sleeping and then sits back down, lowering her voice. "Of course I want fucking revenge. I want to see every kingdom in this world burn to the fucking ground. If every Druga cultist died, it wouldn't be enough. If I have one regret, it's not killing Benedicta permanently when I could. She must have been mad to think she could come to Ummun for help."

"Not to Ummun," Aseli says. "To you."

Sif seethes, blinking back tears. "I would have killed her. It's her fault Buri is dead and I let myself waste away on Mount Hoda. Foolish."

Aseli nods, contemplating Sif's words. "Maybe so. But her feelings towards you were more complicated. If it wasn't for you, she would have been completely in the Wretched King's grasp. Then Najah would never have been born."

Nearby, Najah snores and twitches. A thread of affection tugs at Sif's heart, threatening to unravel it. Just like her, Najah is brave and funny, full of guilt and disappointment and anger. Both of their lives have been ruined by the hubris and greed of monarchists in Atlas and Agartha. The only real difference is Benedicta, who is dead anyways. Sif exhales shakily, resting her head in her hands. While her bitterness at Najah's family will probably never fade, it wouldn't be right to hold it against the young girl.

"I would never hurt Najah," Sif insists, meeting Aseli's judgement head on. "I'll get her to Ravinser."

"Will you tell her you fought her mother?"

Sif's pauses. In her anger, she hadn't even considered what that could mean. Maybe Najah would try to leave, knowing that it was Sif who took her mother's hand. Sif is revulsed by the part of herself that worries it would be another thing that Benedicta has taken from her. Still, she knows she has to be careful. "I'm going to tell her eventually. Now's not the right time. What if she gets upset and leaves before we get to Ravinser? This can't all be for nothing."

"Humph!" Aseli exclaims. "So, your fear is in charge of the truths everyone around you is allowed to know? Interesting."

"Don't be naïve, spirit. It's the lesser evil."

"How convenient for you that you won't have to test that theory by letting her choose."

Sif freezes. White wisps of smoke curl out from the bowl of her pipe. Her face is expressionless, but her eyes are shot through with red, staring into the unseen distance.

"She might regret being given the decision at all," Sif mumbles, surprised to hear words come out of her mouth that would have disgusted her in the past. "I wish nobody had given me the choice to go to Agartha. Not with everything that happened after."

"Even if that is true, does the girl here look like Keno Sif?"

Is Najah like her? In Sif's heart, she doesn't know, exactly. Najah certainly doesn't seem like the same scared girl that Sif met near Ummun. She's brave, and smart, and a little funny. Not like Sif, but sometimes a little bit like her. Still, Sif turns to Aseli and says, "No."

"Then you don't get to make her choices for her."

Sif nods silently in agreement, even as fear of the future and pain from the past stampede through her heart.

Chapter 42

Young Sif, the Destroyer
Travelling north

Sometime after their voyage ended, Ivon, Sif, and Buri take shelter in an abandoned farmhouse to the north of Ograna, in the northern lands no kingdom has yet claimed. A violent storm has overtaken the skies. The three friends race through long stalks of grass that whip back and forth like waves. Sheets of dark water crash against the farmhouse walls as they crash through the front door. Buri breaks some of the furniture inside and uses it to start a fire as they strip off their wet clothes. Less than an hour later, there is a furious knocking at the door.

The three of them exchange a glance. Buri and Sif head for the door with their weapons, as Ivon moves to a corner obscured by shadows. Buri opens the door as Sif pulls her sword back.

"Shit!" Sif exclaims breathlessly.

"Are you going to let me inside?" Sunna asks calmly. Sif grabs her by the arm and ushers her inside, clearing off an extra space by the fire.

"What are you doing here, Sunna? How did you know where we are?"

Buri grunts in agreement.

"I gathered a lot of contacts during my time with Queen Benedicta. You three don't travel very quietly."

"Still. . ." Ivon remarks, amazed to see Sunnhilde in front of them.

"I've missed you," Sif says.

"I missed you too, Keno," Sunna says with a smile, "but that's not why I'm here. Queen Benedicta is alive. She didn't die in Agartha. Apparently, she's been recovering, and kept her return a secret."

"For what?" Sif scoffs.

"Us," Buri intones.

Sunnhilde nods. "We've made the top of her list. Hvek's church and royal family have hired whole companies of mercenaries and sent a vast portion of their army as well. They know you're here. We need to leave now."

Ivon is pale as a ghost. "To where? How long do we have?"

"Anywhere," Sunna says. "Leaving now is too late as it is."

"No need, I can hide you here," speaks a calm, cool voice from the rafters. Only Ivon recognizes the voice. It is the mage who paid him a visit in the desert, before the trip to Agartha began.

"Ivon, I believe you owe me something. Give it to me and we can call it even. I'll even shield you here until the danger has passed. As a token of goodwill."

"Who the fuck are you?" Sif barks.

"I am with the Heron-Muse Mages' Guild. Ivon is a friend of mine."

"Ivon?" Buri asks, eye wide with betrayal. Ivon's face is flush with anger and shame, but they don't say anything.

"Hey, Ivon! Say something!" Sif snaps.

"I don't have anything for you," Ivon hisses at the mage. "It was an impossible task. Not my fault."

The mage frowns deeply. Too deeply. Their mouth stretches in a way that borders on inhuman. "You expect me, and the rest of the Guild, to believe there was not a single magical object in all of Agartha?"

Everyone in the room turns to Ivon.

"Agartha doesn't exist anymore. The whole country is trapped in a dream. There isn't anything real I could have brought back. Even if there was, you didn't see Agartha. Trust me, dear, you would not want anything that had been found there. I would rather hold a burning coal than a piece of that place."

"Unfortunately," the mage starts, "it isn't about what I want. It's about what the Guild wants. You were supposed to take these barbarians to Agartha and come back with something for us. There are no more chances, Ivon."

"What?!" Sif roars, glaring at Ivon.

Buri clenches his jaw. His chest heaves with deep breaths, but his voice is mostly even. "Is that true?"

Ivon shakes their head, pleading. "I wanted to tell you, I swear. But then you would've tried to fight them, and you know what they can do to people. I didn't think Agartha would be that bad."

"Bastard!" Sif growls.

Buri says nothing, but the disappointment on his face is far worse than anything he could have said anyways.

"You may as well save your energy for the soldiers and paladins headed your way," the mage comments. Their voice is cool and smooth and fresh ice.

"Forget it, we need to leave now!" Sunna yells. Ivon grabs their wet clothes and bag, eager to leave, but the mage doesn't allow it. He speaks a spell in a hissing, ephemeral tongue that causes Ivon to become dizzy and nauseated. They fall to their knees, leaning drastically to one side, before they crash into a pile of matted hay and puke violently.

Sif raises her weapon, but another word from the mage turns the metal searing hot. Sif drops it with a yelp, the glowing orange blade lighting a small fire as it lands among the detritus on the floor. Buri hurls a clay bottle, but it shatters in his hand as forcefully as if it had hit stone, cutting him deep.

"Buri, stop!" Sunna commands. "Just tell us what you want."

The mage pauses for a moment, then says, "Oh, that should be enough. In an ideal world, these other three would be tortured and enslaved by the Guild. But I can't leave here with all of you. The army is close enough now, though, that you can't escape with two wounded. Sunnhilde of the River, you should do the smart thing and leave them to die. The Guild doesn't have anything against you. Personally, I rather appreciate your work."

"Fuck you," Sunna snarls. "I won't leave any of them."

The mage shrugs and then, quick as a thought, is gone.

-

The four of them run desperately through the rain and mud, having left so quickly that they're unequipped for both the rain and the cold. Thunder bellows from overhead, lightning only briefly illuminating the path ahead of them. Buri carries Ivon in his arms, despite the blood pouring from his hands. Sif is trying to chart a path ahead, based on what little she remembers from the area. She hopes to lead them through the mountains ahead and to the safety of Ummun. Sunna helps her keep an eye out for landmarks, although between the darkness and her unfamiliarity with the land, it is near impossible to be of any real help. In time, they can hear people approaching from behind. Hard to say who, except that they won't be carrying good news.

A small group of mercenaries cut them off on the path ahead. Sif draws her sword and fights through the pain, joined shortly after by Buri. It is a narrow victory, with each of them barely able to hold a weapon. Sunnhilde's hands shake fearfully, and she wonders if she traveled all this way only to watch Sif die. A strike of lightning reveals the path she had been hoping for. A narrow path in the foot of the mountains. They could fit through, but an army would take time. It may buy them what they need to escape.

Sunna grabs Sif by her shirt and points in the direction of their escape. As they walk between the stone walls of the pass, the sound of rain is dampened by the mountain overhead. For the first time in hours, they can hear each other. Ivon is groaning painfully. Buri's breath is deep and his face reddening, the effort of their escape exacerbated by his age and having already spent the day traveling. His chest heaves and his skin has blanched. He seems on the verge of passing out. Sunna is the same, being less used to extended physical activity, and although Sif feels better than them both, she would be lying if she claimed the day has not taken a toll on her. The cold has passed to her bones, her boots are filled with water, and she is covered in bruises and scratches from their flight.

"I've been here before," Buri says with a start. "Can't remember when. If we make it through, I may be able to guide us."

Within minutes, though, the small crack of light from above fades, obscured by rocks or roots.

"Fuck," Sif gasps out. "I can't see ahead."

Buri tries to answer but cannot catch a breath. "Push ahead slowly, we can guide ourselves by feel."

Another bolt of lightning illuminates the way, but in a twisted condemnation of their previous luck, it strikes a tree. Its wooden trunk splinters, toppling it over and down the pass. It carries with it a wake of dirt, stone, and flora, crashing with a horrid thud and crack, preventing their only way forward. Sif can only watch helplessly.

Buri sets Ivon down on the ground. "Sunnhilde, I need your help."

She turns toward him, shaking from the cold and the stress. "Y-yeah," Sunnhilde says. "What can I do for you, Uncle?"

"You carry strips of cloth and painkillers." It is a statement, not question. She pulls both from her sack, but the cloth is soaked through.

"I don't know if this will help, Buri. The cloth is already wet and the traveler's leaf will make you sick unless you smoke it."

Buri wraps the cloth tightly around his hands and eats the traveler's leaf. "Keno."

Sif turns around at the sound of her name and catches a handaxe thrown to her.

"You will begin clearing a path as I hold back our enemies."

"Got any more of that leaf?" Sif asks. Sunna nods, and feeds Sif a small amount. Sif smiles wearily at her as rain cascades down both of their faces.

Sunna cups Sif's cheek in her palm and whispers, "Hurry, my love."

Sif nods and begins the work of clearing their path. The work goes uninterrupted for longer than they expected, in part because the darkness and size of the path they had come through make it difficult for others to discern as well. Buri defends them against a half-dozen attackers, most of them cut down before they even see him in the low light. Eventually though, a horn blows nearby. Someone of importance has found the pass, and is directing the others towards it. Sif roars in a fit of rage, smashing the blade of the axe down in a flurry of emotional blows. There is a path through, but it isn't big enough for all of them. Ivon is thin, and Sif is short. Sunna is taller and has a roughly average build. But Buri is unusually tall and muscular.

Buri eyes Sif's progress and knows it won't be enough. A slight, melancholy smile passes over him.

"Go."

"Fuck you!" Sif screams at him. She turns around and resumes hacking away with her now half-blunt instrument.

Ivon gets to their feet, but only barely. Their legs shake violently with the aftereffects of the spell. "Buri, don't do this. I can help. I can buy us time."

Buri walks over to Sif and puts a light hand on her back. She throws her shoulder back, slinging his hand away.

"Stop it, Keno. You need to go before it's too late."

"Shut up!" Sif yells. "Shut the fuck up! I'm trying to concentrate on this damn tree!"

Buri takes a step back.

"Sunna," he murmurs. She meets his gaze, and despite herself, tears begin rolling down her cheeks.

"Sif won't forgive you. She won't forgive either of us."

Buri grunts. "Yes, she will."

"I don't—" Sunna starts to argue, when Buri cuts her off.

"It doesn't matter."

Sunnhilde stares at him pleadingly. Past Buri, Ivon has fallen back to their knees and is struggling to stand again. From the pass comes the sound of armored soldiers marching closer. "Fine. . ." she whispers.

Buri nods and walks over to Ivon, kneeling down to meet their gaze. "Ivon, my old friend."

"I'm not going," Ivon rasps. "Don't even ask, dear."

"Yes, you will. When you do, split up from Sunnhilde and Sif. You're better at this than them, and Sunnhilde can't carry you both."

Desperation burns in Ivon's eyes, but they do not argue any further. Silently, they lean forward and kiss him on the cheek. "I'll miss you."

"We will see each other again," he grunts.

Sif turns and faces him. Even in the rain, she is blinking back tears. The handle of her handaxe broke some time ago. She's holding the head of it in her hand. "I won't leave you behind," she says.

"Keno. You're like me. We burn so bright it is hard for other people to understand. And since you were little, I've seen that part of myself in you and worried one day you would burn so bright that you would burn up completely and not even notice." Buri runs a finger along his leather eyepatch. He hasn't spoken much about the day he lost his eye. Only that he acted in a way that he is still ashamed of, and that the eye was his price. "Violence for the sake of violence will destroy your heart. It will destroy who you are. I'm lucky all I had to give up to regain myself was an eye. Promise me that you will not become like the rest of the world, confusing violence and power with strength. Confusing peace with cruelty. You are better than that."

"I'll promise anything you want, Uncle, but I'm not going to leave you. We can hold the army back as Sunna and Ivon esca—"

Sif is knocked unconscious by a well-timed blow and never finishes her last protest. Buri catches her and sets her down near the hole she has made.

The horn sounds again, this time louder.

He looks up at Sunna, his single green eye shining in the darkness.

"Go."

Sunna sniffles and nods. "Goodbye, Uncle."

Chapter 43

Buri the Giant
A narrow pass

Waves of bodies crash against Buri's sword. Blood sprays through the air, only to be washed away in the storm. Spears and swords pierce his flesh, endless mountains of anguish. Rocks from slings crack his bones and skull, every impact a shock of disorientation and nausea. And whether it's delirium or truth, in the middle of the struggle Buri understands where he is: a narrow pass to the southwest of his home in Feigrvoller, northeast of the nation of Ograna. He visited here as a young man, wanting to see the place his father had died, hoping for closure. The place soldiers had cut his father down for being a so-called *barbarian*. The place his father had died trying to allow his friends time to escape, because they were only hunters and had not left the northern reaches looking for a fight.

Buri feels a sword slide into his gut, glancing off a rib.

Rather than closure, Buri had felt a loss inside of himself that for a long time he could not fill. Those years were filled with some of the strongest regrets of his life. It was only with time and introspection that he began to understand why.

The push is too much. Buri stumbles backwards, keeping his feet but allowing soldiers to pour out of the pass and surround him.

The loss of his father was exacerbated by his loss of self. By living with disregard. By becoming part of what he hated—someone who was cruel and who created more cruelty. Like the soldiers who killed his father. Like the soldiers he fights now, who don't care what happened on Agartha, if they even know. Who don't care about the damage their monarchs will do. Who only see the opportunity to collect a reward, jump up in fame and glory, and hoard wealth.

He remembers the night he lost his eye. The man he'd killed in cold blood, because in a drunken rage he had mistaken the stranger for a soldier. The fear and shame he felt under the gaze of his mother's god. Sif will never be like he was. She will succeed where he failed.

Buri is surrounded, peripheral vision now narrow and uncertain. His enemies circle him, taking careful swings. Broken bodies lie at his feet, both a warning to any direct challengers and a hindrance to his own movement.

He slides his sword into the guts of a soldier at the same time as the man's sword cuts into him. They both fall into the mud and rock below. The soldier cries out in pain, writhing as he is trampled by the boots of his comrades. Buri stares blankly into the darkness above, hearing nothing but his own breathing and heartbeat. The agony of his spilled guts, broken bones, and crushed skull fades away. The rain falls gently on his skin. His lips twitch in a way that, to almost anyone, would be no different at all from his usual grim expression. In the eyes of his friends, it would be a smile of joy. Of victory.

In moments, he is gone.

Chapter 44

Old Sif, the Hermit
On the road to Ravinser

The next morning, as the road becomes narrower and less traveled, Sif and Najah arrive at the outskirts of a small village. A cluster of tall striped maples borders the edges, freshly green leaves broken up by the occasional shock of sunset fluttering in the evening breeze. Past the homes is an apple orchard, picked clean from the previous fall.

"Najah, wake up."

Najah stirs on the back of the horse, blinking drowsily. Her awakening is a relief every time it happens.

"What is it?"

"We're going to sell the horse. The road'll be narrow from here on. Better to go on foot in case we need to abandon the path."

Najah's eyes flash unhappily. "Russet? We can't! Ivon bought him for us!"

Sif frowns. She had worried this would happen. The past few days of travel, Najah had grown attached to the beast. Maybe the result of not having to hide her talent for communicating with animals.

"Ivon would rather us have the coin than be gutted when soldiers see or hear us riding by."

"No." Najah is unwavering. As she raises her voice, Russet shifts his weight nervously beneath them.

Sif pats Russet's side. "Naj, you're spooking him."

"We can't just sell him to some random people because he's inconvenient."

Sif gets down from the saddle, groaning from the pain in her knees and hips. It hadn't occurred to her how sensitive Najah would be to something like this. The horse is not only a gift from a friend, but the young girl probably s some of her own situation in Russet's; being without a home, traded between different people when her care became a burden. "What do you want, then?"

"We can let him go. We'll sell the saddle and reins."

"We could use the extra coin," Sif argues. "Horses are expensive."

"The people we sell him to would put him to work or eat him. Animals want to be free, just like people." Najah scoots forward and wraps her arms gently around Russet's neck, heartache heavy in her voice.

"Shit," Sif swears, spitting in the dust. The canopy of maple leaves above them waves gently under a cool, blue sky. The coin would be useful, but Sif has always hated people who put coin above everything else. Najah would know better than she what the horse prefers, and she's probably right about it being eaten. Sif looks into Russet's big brown eyes. He *was* a gift from Ivon. And a good companion. She reaches forward and strokes his muzzle. "Guess there won't be many shops in between here and Ravinser. Besides, animals had the sense not to invent money, it wouldn't be fair to get Russet involved in it now. Let's take off his saddle."

"Yes!" Najah shouts. She climbs off Russet's back and wraps her arms around Sif happily.

Sif smiles, wrinkling the corner of her eyes. As Najah removes Russet's saddle, a memory of her own childhood grows in her mind. Most of her arguments with Buri had been over her hotheadedness or recklessness, and Sif can't help but admire Najah for drawing her own line in the sand over an act of kindness. Sif was never able to be open like that. Buri was. He would be proud to know Sif's protégé is brave, thoughtful, kind, and reluctant but not unwilling to fight. An errant bark of laughter escapes her lips at the realization that the daughter of Queen Benedicta would have impressed a saint of Aneir. Buri would gladly have given up his life to protect a young, courageous fighter like her. In fact, he did.

With a shock, Sif suddenly understands why Buri sacrificed himself for her. Why he tried so often to protect her, even after she was the stronger fighter. With new clarity, she can see that even if it costs her life, she will do everything she can to save Najah. A small part of her, the part that remembers being a hermit on Mount Hoda, is troubled by the realization. A greater part finds solace in it, because now Keno Sif can feel the hole in her heart filling in, if only a little.

-

Before they left, Aseli had said Ravinser would be easy to find. Even still, they hadn't expected tracking the village to be as simple as it is. In the southeastern forest is a sudden break in the old growth, where the plant life becomes young but strange. Countless varieties of ferns shoot up from the soil, a fresh, bright green. Pines too tall for how thin they are reach for the sky, swaying in the breeze, mingling with stout oaks where dozens of brown finches coalesce and call loudly to each other. Wildflowers populate the steady rolling hills like a congregation. All of it is newer growth, prospering under the influence of Druga's sleeping soul.

"Wow. . ." Najah comments, transfixed on the plant life overhead.

"Yeah," Sif agrees. To the east a river cuts a shallow ravine through the landscape, and a dozen ghost-white birds fly silently around the bend, wings beating in unison.

"This way, I guess." Najah jumps over a log. On the other side, a bright red cardinal is spooked by her approach and flees from where it had been eating blueberries off a bush that sags with the weight of its fruit. Najah opens her pack and fills it with as many berries as she can take.

"You recognize where we're at?" It's all just forest to Sif, albeit a very odd one.

"No," Najah replies, mouth partially full, juice running down her chin. "But if we follow this area to the center, it'll be where the fire started right? Isn't that Ravinser?"

"Sure," Sif shrugs. "Lead the way."

Thick branches wave lazily over patches of weeds and wildflowers. Squirrels and birds speak their secret languages in the canopy as insects buzz loudly from some unseen pocket of flora. Najah marches with a determined grimace on her face. Watching her, Sif wonders how much of their trip has been about revenge for her mother. She knows what it is like to lose loved ones. So, if Sif admits to having fought Benedicta Yden, how will Najah react? Will she want revenge on Sif as well? Anxiety burns in her chest. She feels small. She wants someone to slap her in the face. In her younger years she was a fearless fighter, and now she is letting fear get the best of her. She wouldn't let someone else call her a coward, yet here she is letting doubt stop her from doing what must be done. It's now or never.

"I knew your mother," Sif says. "I realized it last night."

Najah seems unbothered. "Yeah?"

"Yeah. She and I fought. I'm the one who took her hand."

"Ah," Najah responds, continuing her march.

"Got anything you want to say about that?" Sif is determined to have the conversation now. She expects tears or threats or violence. But not *Ah.*

"Not really. Mom wasn't the kind of person to hold a grudge." A flash of anger burns in Sif's heart at that, and she forces herself to quench it. "For the most part I don't think she missed her hand, anyways. People made accommodations if she needed them. It's funny, she always seemed kind of confused to me, like she was dealing with a lot that I couldn't see and didn't know how to sort it out. I thought it was just because we were always running, but now I think maybe it was mostly the stuff Aseli said. Like she was so ashamed of what she did that, instead of trying to figure it out, she swore off violence completely."

"Maybe so," Sif responds with a sigh.

"What did you fight about?"

Sif doesn't know what to say to that. Even after everything, it feels wrong to slander a dead woman to her child. Even after Buri. Not that it wasn't *very* tempting. "We were in Agartha, when she met the Wretched King. Before you were born, I'd bet. She wanted Him to teach her, and I was paid to kill her before it could happen."

"I'm glad you didn't." Najah laughs like she told a joke, but it dies out with a nervous quickness.

"I *thought* I did," Sif admits. "I was surprised to learn she was alive."

"Are. . . uh. . ." For the first time during their conversation, Najah hesitates. "Are we still friends?"

All at once, the noise in Sif's head becomes quiet. She exhales. "Yeah, we're friends. As long as you're okay with it."

"Sure. Mom didn't hold a grudge, like I said. Well, not about the hand. She was complicated. And I guess she wanted us to go to Ummun for a reason, so maybe we would have met and been friends anyways. Besides, you're both nice. Maybe she didn't think the fight was that bad."

Sif fights the urge to say that it *was* that bad. Though maybe if Benedicta was here, and Sif could keep herself from avenging Buri, she'd learn Benedicta had become a different person. How much change is enough to let the grudge die, though? Would Buri hold his death against Benedicta? She never learned what happened to the person Buri lost his eye to. He didn't seem to hold a grudge there, same as Benedicta might not have. Sif's situation seems more absurd than ever, to be traveling with the daughter of the woman who took away Buri. Even more that Sif would be fond of her. Obviously, none of that is Najah's fault, but that doesn't make it any less odd. Or painful.

Najah exhales loudly. "Fuck. I'm glad we're still friends. I was really worried."

Sif snorts, surprised to hear Najah swearing. "Yeah, me too."

Chapter 45

Old Sif, the Hermit

The outskirts of Ravinser

Najah looks up at the night sky. The air is alive with the buzzing of small insects and flutter of nocturnal wings.

"Tell me about Buri."

Sif's response is quicker than expected. "What do you want to know?"

"Anything."

Sif sits up. Shadows swim across her wrinkled face beyond the flickering campfire. "He was my best and oldest friend. He was thoughtful, brave, caring, and strong. Had about a hundred bad tattoos and couldn't cook for shit. Shockingly sober. He liked big men and boring music. Didn't speak much, but when he did it felt like he said a lot all at once. He trusted me, even though I was aways rushing into things without thinking. I once saw him punch a man so hard he actually lifted up in the air."

"Huh," Najah responds. "Was he really a giant?"

"Giants aren't real. He was pretty tall though." Sif laughs, revisiting a memory. "Had to duck under a lot of door frames."

"Cool." Najah rolls over on her side, looking directly at Sif through the campfire. "Did he teach you to fight?"

"A little bit. Most of that came from one of my skill-fathers, Pak. And my little sister Kanae used to spar with me. And some of the teachers in Ummun, once I was old enough to take trials. What about you? Tell me about your mom."

Najah sits up to better judge Sif's expression. "Are you sure you want to know?"

Sif nods, but doesn't speak.

"I miss her a lot. She used to tell me about different plants and what they could do. She kept dried flowers to make this gross tea out of when we camped. She told me to stand up for myself and other kids. She hated to see anyone in pain, even people she didn't like. She used to get sick and confused and cried a lot. I guess some of that was the part of the Wretched King inside her that's with me now." Najah lifted her fox pendant necklace into the light. "She made this herself. It had a better string at first, though."

A melancholy sigh escapes her lips. "I hope she's not mad at me for fighting."

"I think she'd be proud of you, either way."

"Really?"

"Sure. Who wouldn't?"

-

Around the ruins of the town proper, the Church of Druga has set up another camp, an inexplicable dead spot in the otherwise prosperous forest. Burnt out homes have been fortified, and a trench dug around the perimeter. Paladins work with soldiers and a handful of mercenaries to keep regular watch, with keen eyes, glinting metal, and thick leather. The encampment is small, which would make things more difficult. But they must not know the well is important, because the camp does not center it. The well is off-center to the southwest, near what may have been a fenced-in area for raising goats or cattle. It makes a kind of sense. Who is to say what Druga and the Wretched King know about each other? Maybe the well is a secret from the Wretched King and Mother Fog.

"Any idea what you need to do at the well?" Sif asks.

Najah sighs. "I wish I did. Maybe I just get close. Or kind of peek in. This is stupid. Aseli should've told us more."

"Tonight, I'll head down and start a fight. I'll pretend I got caught sneaking in. While I've got them distracted, you do what you need to."

"What if I never figure out what to do? Or what if you get hurt? We should just sneak in and kill them in their sleep."

Sif raises an eyebrow. It's a surprising suggestion coming from Najah. Sif isn't against some light murder when it comes to imperialists, but still. "Not a good plan with this many people. If we get caught, you won't be able to get near the well. All it would take is kicking over a bucket by accident to wake up the wrong person."

Najah furrows her brow. Over Ravinser, the lull of morning sunlight washes on old stone and broken wooden boards. The new hustle of soldiers on long-abandoned walking paths. Near the well is a big open spot where she used to play with other young kids. Along a wall nearby used to be her friend Ni'daa's home, and next door was where Najah lived with her mother, in a house that has since been completely destroyed. Her memories of that life are so dim and distant, but the shape of them wrenches at her heart. Back then, everything seemed much bigger. Now the town is a husk of itself and the mix of faint but pleasant memories with the reality of the encampment causes mist to gather at the corners of her brown eyes. When she had a stable home, this had been it.

"Shit," Sif hisses. Najah follows her gaze to Kisha, limping down the dirt road in the middle of town. She is accompanied by a pretty young man with curling blond hair and a zweihander. When she squints, Najah recognizes him as Salko, the man who noticed her and Ivon hiding in the prison and let them go.

Salko's eyes are half-closed, mouth set in a neutral pose, gait loose. He seems bored, like the reality of hunting down a fugitive for the presumed will of his deity isn't stimulating enough for his tastes. Despite that, Sif sees him paying unusually close attention to Kisha's movements. He's too young to have been in the Church's wars of expansion, but is definitely someone used to battle. That probably means strong-arming villages and hunting down worshippers of Siduri, Aneir, and Asthia. Sif grinds her teeth unconsciously.

Najah's face twists into fear and sadness at the sight of Kisha. "What if we left and came back in a few weeks? I bet some of the soldiers would leave to look for us somewhere else."

Sif shakes her head. "We should be brave. Even if we retreat, they can still track us down. They know this is where we want to be. Could be that we come back and they've fortified the area instead."

"You can't fight Kisha alone, though," Najah says. Her voice is grim, too grim for a young girl. Sif flashes a cocky smile.

"Don't worry, Kisha will have that young man to help her. Maybe with the two of them it'll be a fair fight."

Najah narrows her eyes, "You're not funny, Auntie."

"Yeah, I am."

-

That night they climb a tall tree to get a better look over Ravinser. Even with Sif's worsening eyesight and Najah's lack of training, they can tell something is off. Winding between the remaining homes is a figure in a dark gray cloak. The figure enters a building and, after a few moments, floats along to the next one. After several stops, the figure meets with Salko. The man maintains his disinterested posture, but his eyes are alert. Maybe the stranger is someone important. The figure directs him to a fire where a cauldron of stew cooks, and continues on their way.

"Who are they?" Najah whispers.

"Who knows. They aren't dressed like a soldier, unless there's armor under that cloak."

"So, what are they doing then?"

"Let's go find out," Sif says, swinging down from her perch.

Chapter 46

Young Sif, the Destroyer

Lost in the northern mountains

"Keno, you need to wake up now. Please wake up."

Sif stirs painfully at the sound of Sunna's pleading sobs. Her head feels like it's been crushed. The rain has turned to snow and the cold is soaked through to her bones. Something warm and wet presses against her.

"Sunna? Where are we?" Sif groans. Then, remembering what happened, "Where is Buri?"

"I don't know, Keno. He st—"

"We need to go back and find him!" Sif tries to sit up, but Sunnhilde grabs her by the wrist. Sif yanks her hand back angrily. When Sunna winces, Sif catches sight of the arrow jutting out from her side. Fresh blood is still pouring from the wound. Despite her injuries, Sunna has dragged them both to this small corner of the mountain, hidden between a cliffside and a small copse of evergreens.

"I need you to focus, Keno. Buri is gone. He wanted to buy us time to escape."

Sif clenches her fists and tightens her jaw, already blinking back tears.

"I don't know what happened to Ivon, but I can't find my way in this storm. Someone hit me with this arrow and I can't walk. I'm not sure why they haven't found us already, but they're closing in. If we turn back now, then Buri's death will have been for nothing."

Air condenses as it leaves Sif's nostrils. Her chest heaves with frenzied breaths.

"How could you let him do that?" she hisses.

Sunna meets Sif's eyes unapologetically and says, "I didn't want you to die.

Get over it."

Sif draws her sword and helps Sunna to her feet. Sunna stifles a cry of pain.

"We're not done talking about this," Sif assures her. Sunna doesn't respond. There wouldn't have been time to, anyways, before a mercenary stumbles on them, carrying an axe and a lantern in either hand.

"She's over here!" he yells. Sif drops Sunna and leaps forward. Sunna cries out in pain as she lands. The mercenary tries to redirect Sif's thrusting attack with the handle of his axe, but she changes the direction of her attack, instead sliding the blade down the axe handle and through his fingers. The axe and three of his fingers fall into the snow with a splatter of blood. The mercenary has just enough time to yell for help before Sif cuts his throat. She grabs his lantern from the snow and tosses it, hoping to throw off anyone who heard his cry. Where it lands, she can make out the lower halves of others coming after her. Bad decision. There are more people coming than she can fight in this condition. Their only hope is to run. Sif sheaths her weapon and grabs Sunna in both of her arms.

Sif travels north, up the mountain, still woozy from being unconscious, injured from the hike before and slowed down by the woman bleeding out in her arms. The path is dark and cut through with dense flora that snags on her as she tries to push through. The freezing air burns her lungs. Waiting in the shadow ahead is a sudden drop in the ground. Sif doesn't even feel her leg in the air until moments later when she tumbles into the snow, cracking a tooth and busting her head.

"Sunna. . ." she mumbles, frantically scraping for purchase as the mob catches up with them. She is only vaguely aware of someone pulling her sword from its sheath and tossing it away. Blows from gauntleted hands and thick-soled boots rain down on her. Someone ties her legs and arms and drags her through the bramble, bush, and snow. In the dim lantern light, she can see flickers of Sunna being dragged along nearby. In the horror of the moment, Sif has barely fought back, but seeing Sunna rage and kick and bite against their captors reminds her to have courage. Not for the first time, Sif reminds herself that nobody will be able to say Keno Sif died without a fight, without inflicting pain on the people who killed her. She will take as many people with her as she can, and make the survivors question whether their victory was worth it.

She kicks herself in range to bite a chunk from a soldier's exposed forearm. She swears and curses, thrashes, kicks, sends men to their knees. Her enemies are numberless, though, and in time they throw her against a tree and slide a noose around her neck. Her heart beats faster with fear. Not at her own death, but at Sunna's. In another tree to her right, Sunnhilde is being strung up ahead of her.

"Sunna!" Sif yells. "I'm sorry!"

"I know, my love."

Sif headbutts a man in front of her, gaining enough room to try and run for Sunnhilde. At the top of her lungs she screams, "Don't give up!"

A man grabs the end of the rope, already over a branch, and pulls Sif back. Sif coughs as she is yanked back by the noose around her neck.

"We'll see each other soon," Sunna swears through her bloodied, swollen face, before she is raised up and can no longer speak.

Sif kicks her feet as she is raised into the air, trying to find purchase against the trunk with her heels. In seconds, her vision starts to dim as the rope cuts off the supply of blood coursing through her arteries.

Everything goes black, and the cold of the mountain fades into nothing.

-

Sif coughs violently as blinding light propels her back into consciousness. She is lying flat on the ground, desperately gasping for air, hands and feet numb, and stars bursting in front of her eyes. Ivon flips her over, checking her pulse.

"Oh, fuck, you're alive."

"Sunna. . ." Sif croaks.

"Stay here," Ivon stammers, running to where Sunna presumably still is, but in her weakened state Sif cannot even muster the strength to turn her head and see. Tears run down her face in grief that is both a continuation of Buri's loss, and the knowledge of what further losses are to come. As she lays on the ground, Sif wonders if it was a mistake to stop the Wretched King, knowing that, in saving Atlas, Benedicta and her kingdom have been spared as well. From this day forward the whole continent could burn, for all she cares. If she never sees a single person again it will be too late.

Chapter 47

Najah Yden
The burned town of Ravinser

Najah waits at the edge of Ravinser for some sign that Sif's distraction has begun. The buzzing of insects playing their own secret melodies drifts from the branches above. Najah is focused. She is prepared. She is watching a small green frog hop through the grass, because the wait is soul-crushingly boring. She shakes out of it, redirecting her attention back to the village. Only, not much happens. In time, she finds herself mindlessly tossing sticks and stones, or following an army of ants as they march to and from a swallow's carcass. Gross. Laying eyes on the poor bird adds a small measure of grief to her boredom and Najah decides she is done waiting. Sif said it was time to be courageous, or something close enough to that. Surely Sif has started what she needs to. The time for action is now.

She slides down a hill, towards a trench and small fence circling the encampment. The trench is new, but the fence was there when Najah lived here. She gets dirt all up the side of her trousers and scrapes her palms, but the burst of exhilaration that comes with doing *something* is worth it. She reaches up to the top of the trench, fingers closing around dark green grass, and pulls herself up. The silk edges of a spider's web glisten like silver among the fence posts in front of her.

The cloaked figure enters her line of sight. Najah ducks down, and luckily the figure doesn't react. An acrid stench wafts by on the breeze from their direction. Najah wrinkles her nose. From where she lays, half-in and half-out of the trench, she can nearly make out their face. Curls of gray hair spring under her hood as she walks. She is definitely a woman. From around a building walks that pretty boy, Salko. Najah drags herself fully out of the trench and crawls on her stomach next to the ramshackle fence. The lure of mystery easily defeats the concern for safety in her heart.

"Is everyone asleep?" Salko asks. His voice is relaxed, his lids are slightly lowered. But his shoulders are too high up, and he is tapping his fingers anxiously on his thigh.

"Everyone who can be." The woman's voice is deep and melodious. Matriarchal. The voice of someone with confidence. A little like Sif's, but with a less northern accent.

"Can you still see my fortune?" The mask of disinterest slips just a little as he speaks.

The woman flashes a very mild smile. "Don't worry, young man. Everything is working out for you as predicted. Just continue to follow my instructions."

"Very well, my lady. Be safe, then." He nods and walks back the way he came.

The woman waits for him to leave and then, as though an eye in the back of her head has been trained on Najah this whole time, turns around and says, "You're safe, Najah. Please come out."

Najah draws her dagger, but keeps it hidden behind her back. She steps over a low part where fence has collapsed, but keeps her distance from the cloaked woman. "Good eyes, old lady."

"Oh, thank you. No, my sight is awful. I'm just used to watching my back." From this close a small scar on the woman's forehead is visible, along with a hint of dull red in her gray hair.

"More than that paladin?"

The cloaked woman chuckles. "Yes, much more. That boy has the entitlement and short-sightedness of an aristocrat. I'm sure he'll do well in politics. But I'm not here for him, I'm here for you and Keno."

"Oh yeah? Well, I'm good, thanks. I don't know you."

The woman lowers her hood and bends slowly to one knee. "You don't have to be afraid. I know what you're going through, and I'm not going to hurt you. You carry half of the nature deity, Druga, and an emissary of Mother Fog inside of you. It must be uncomfortable. I had a djinn inside of me once. It made my skin crawl, and I developed an odd craving for plums."

"Sounds scary," Najah offers, still clutching her dagger. "Except the plum part, I mean."

The woman shakes her head. "Not really. They weren't trying to hurt me. It's a long story. I'd like to help you, if you'll let me. Not to pressure you, but I had to pretend to make friends with some unpleasant people in order to be here."

"How can I trust you?" Najah asks.

The woman spreads her arms out for emphasis and says, "Well, you have that dagger and I'm unarmed. If you decide you don't trust me, there isn't much I can do to protect myself."

Slowly, Najah lets her hand fall from behind her back, revealing the dagger in her grasp. She wonders what Sif would do, imagines the old woman telling her to be brave. Najah has been practicing with her dagger for a long time now, and the strange woman in front of her is right. Najah has the upper hand here. Probably.

Najah agrees to be led to the well, but she puts her knife out as a reminder of how serious she is. The cloaked woman smiles. Not in a cruel way, but in a way like she thinks Najah is doing something cute. It makes Najah scowl. So much for having an advantage. Whoever this is, she's clearly used to talking people into things.

The walk is short. They arrive at the well in under two minutes with no resistance. "Why isn't anyone coming out?" Najah asks.

"I put them to sleep," the woman responds cooly.

"How? Magic?"

"No. It's harmless."

"Says you," Najah responds.

"You shouldn't knock over a gift as it's being handed to you. We're here."

Najah goes to sheath her dagger, but then rethinks it. "If this works, I'll thank you after. What do I do now?"

"Look into the water, of course," the woman says.

Najah begins to bend over the edge, then realizes she can't keep her eyes on the woman in the cloak. "Hey, stand over there. On the other side and back a bit."

"Sure, if that's what you want." The woman complies politely, moving back until Najah seems satisfied.

Najah peers into the water, but nothing happens. She groans loudly and raises her head back up to meet the woman's eyes. "It's not working."

"You have to move past the water, and into the dream. Into the kingdom of sleep."

"You want me to fall asleep standing here? On purpose?"

"It's not what *I* want. It's simply how it works."

Najah jaw slackens with disbelief at the woman, now standing across from her, clasping her hands patiently. "Who are you, anyways? How do you know this?"

"Focus less on me and more on your task, dear. Everyone won't be asleep forever. You'll need time to wake up as well."

"Great, thanks for the help," Najah says bluntly. The woman screws up her face and crosses her arms. Najah looks back down into the water and tries to focus. She hopes Sif is okay, wherever she is. Her mind wanders to Ivon, Jinta, to her mother, to her old home that stood not far from here. The night sky waves behind a rush of leaves rippling in the water below. Najah narrows her eyes. There is something gold flashing in the depths. Then maybe not. Najah curses under her breath.

"Why can't I ever fall asleep when I wan—"

A rush of darkness overtakes her.

Chapter 48

Young Sif, the Destroyer
The northern mountains

Despite the pain, the moment that Sunna gasps for air, Sif drags herself over without hesitation. Grunting with pain and exhaustion, she sits up and brings Sunna into her arms, weeping loudly. Sunna wraps her arms around Sif's torso and squeezes as much as she can muster. A few paces away, Ivon lets their dagger, dulled from the fight and cutting both women free, fall into the snow. They follow it, dropping to their knees and shaking. It has been a long night, and the night still isn't over.

"I know you're tired, dears, but we need to keep moving. They left you here to die because they're going to try and get a. . ." Ivon swallows their grief and disgust, ". . .trophy from Buri. They'll be back soon."

Sif's eyes flash at the mention of Buri's name. "Fuck you, Ivon. Keep his name out of your mouth. If you hadn't led us to Agartha, none of this would have happened. All of this is on you."

Ivon is stunned. "Are you kidding me? You wanted to go. You had dreams. I just saved your fucking life!"

"You wouldn't have had to if it wasn't for lying to us!" Sif roars back before her voice cracks and is overtaken by harsh, rasping coughs. Sunna tries to speak, but can only cough painfully in between gasps for air.

"I didn't force you to do anything. . ." Ivon stumbles over their own words, knowing that while the body of their words might be true, the soul is false.

"Buri is dead," Sif coughs pathetically, blood and phlegm mixing with the snow underneath her.

"I only wanted to protect you!" Ivon shouts. "If I had said we were being blackmailed, you would have rushed to Heron-Muse. Then what, Sif? The mages kill us all? Burn away our souls and use our bodies for labor? Force us to test riskier spells to see if the blowback will kill us, or just flay us alive instead? What do you fucking expect?!"

Sif clenches her jaw at Ivon, an inferno raging in her dark eyes, and wheezes out, "I would've trusted you."

Ivon stares at her disbelievingly for a time, then slowly rises to their feet. A trickle of tears streams down their cheeks and into their blonde mustache. "I'm sorry," they sob, stumbling towards Sif and Sunnhilde. "I swear to you both, I didn't know this would happen. It was supposed to be a quick job, grab some trea—"

"Shut up," Sif mutters, shaking her head. "You think I can't remember all the talk about treasure? You were just manipulating us to get what you really wanted."

"Sif, it wasn't about th—"

". . .and now you need us to help you get off this mountain alive." Sif meets Ivon's gaze. "But I don't care if you live or not."

Ivon steps backwards, bloodshot eyes wide and flooding with heartache. "Sif. . ."

"Wait. . ." Sunna manages to rasp out.

"I don't want to hear it," Sif growls. "Ivon, you better hope I never see you again."

Ivon's lips open and close uselessly, before they finally settle on what to say. Their voice shakes under the weight of their words. "If you really feel that way, then I'll go."

"Then go," Sif huffs, refusing to set eyes on them. Her words cut through Ivon's heart. Somewhere inside, they know Sif is acting out of grief and shock. But then, Ivon loved Buri too, and it is only natural to feel some guilt. Even guilt that isn't owed. Especially the part that is. Sunna tries to speak again but cannot.

"Fine," Ivon says. They turn and pause, thinking to tell the two women to leave soon so that Buri's death is not in vain. But instead, they walk off into the night, head and heart sunken in an ocean of loss.

-

In a sick sort of luck, Sif and Sunna were not far from Buri's home village, Feigrvoller. The funeral was less than a week later. A small group of locals helps bring Buri back to his old home. There, they hang dried flowers from the rafters, set up a shrine, bring food, keep vigil, and enlist a priest of Aneir to bless and prepare the body. Buri had no siblings and no living parents, but roughly thirty adults and all their children came to pay respects. Even a few warriors from other northern villages came. Sif recognized some people from Ummun she hadn't seen since she left, now all grown up.

As the day drags on, Sif's numbness and grief give way, a little bit, to the need to stretch her legs, so she and Sunna leave the funeral to walk outside. It's a bright, cloudless afternoon. The blue sky is interrupted only by smoke billowing out from the cabin where Buri's funeral is held.

Sif lights her pipe and takes a deep, deep, deep inhale. "How long will you be around this time?" she asks Sunna.

"I'm not sure. My network has been in overtime since we learned Queen Benedicta is alive. I'd like to solve that problem, but it's probably best if I lay low. Besides, I missed you. And you need me."

Normally, Sif would argue that she doesn't need anyone and everyone can do whatever the hell they want, but she doesn't have the heart for it and suspects the truth of the situation is obvious.

"I'd like to go home to Ummun and see my sister," Sif muses aloud.

"I'd like to meet your sister. She's a priestess, right? We'd probably have a lot to talk about."

Sif laughs. "I don't think you would like her."

Sunna's eyebrows shoot up in surprise. "You don't like your sister?"

"I love my sister. I think you would find her annoying."

"Huh," Sunna responds, temporarily speechless. "Well, I guess we'll see."

"Hey!" yells a tiny voice from the cabin. Behind them, a pale-skinned, dark-haired little girl stares at Sif from a few yards away.

"What?" Sif calls back. Before the girl can respond though, an older man, presumably her father, ushers her back inside and chides her for being disruptive during the day of mourning.

"Kids," Sunna comments off-handedly.

"Wouldn't know. Not a kid person," Sif says, taking another hit from her pipe.

"You can join me if you want." Sunna turns from her view of the mountains and forests to clasp Sif's hands. "When I leave. It'd be nice to travel together. Hurt some of the people responsible for this. It might be a while before we can kill the queen."

"Eh, I. . . maybe. I don't know." Sif sniffles gently and silently hopes she isn't about to start crying again.

"Do you think you'll be staying in Ummun, then?"

Sif shakes her head. "I don't know. I don't know if I can set eyes on the world again. I might kill the first of them I see. I. . . I just need time."

Sunna takes Sif's head in her hands, gazes into her brown eyes, and kisses her gently on the forehead. "You can take time. I'll come back to you."

Chapter 49

Old Sif, the Hermit
The burned town of Ravinser

Down in the camp, Sif leaps over the trenches, wincing as she lands. Her joints aren't as reliable as they once were. She finds a gap in the fence and passes through, then slits the throat of a careless mercenary who is relieving himself against a wall. If she's lucky, every fighter in Ravinser will be this short-sighted.

Dew has settled on the ground and as Sif stalks through the night she can feel the wet grass under her boots. The smells of fire, smoke, and cooking stew fill her nose. So do the scents of sweat, metal, and oil. The combination is uniquely repulsive. Sif plans to stay in the shadows until she can get a sense of where Kisha is. Kisha needs to be close enough so that when Najah comes down to the well there is no chance they'll interact, but also far enough that Sif can kill a few men and run before Kisha engages with her. Despite joking earlier in the morning, Sif knows she can't defeat her. Maybe with her limp, one on one, but not with all the backup Kisha has in Ravinser. Sif tries not to think of the man who accompanies her, Salko, and what complications he might bring.

The problem now, though, is that there seems to be no motion in the camp at all. Nothing from Kisha, nor any of the mercenaries, soldiers, or paladins. It's an insane way to try and keep an area secure. It must be a trap. Still, Sif grabs a rock and tosses it in the doorway of a building. It knocks around inside before settling back into quiet, but none of those inside react. Sif waits a beat, but still nothing happens. She's certain there were people resting in this building when they scouted the camp earlier.

She kicks at the ground, sending dirt and pebbles flying against the wall nearby. She tries to put on her best impression of someone who slipped trying to sneak, and hisses "Ah, shit!"

Still nothing. What in Siduri's name is happening here?

"Alright you fuckers, wake up!" She storms the building with her sword drawn, ready to cut someone down, but they're all in their beds, still as the dead. She nudges one with the tip of her sword. Nothing. She checks their pulse, and it's still there. It reminds her of Najah's curse. The thought does not sit well with her.

"They're asleep. . ." Sif murmurs to herself.

She remembers the cloaked figure who entered this room before she and Najah came down into the encampment. After the figure left this room, they stopped by a tent. Sif skulks to it, careful to stay out of firelight. Inside is a woman, sleeping. Her tent is full of an acrid smell that makes Sif's eyes water. Sif nudges the sleeping woman with the tip of her sword. Nothing.

"Hey!" A man's voice.

Sif spins around towards Salko, but the sleeping woman is still. This must be magic. Sif immediately worries it may be the Wretched King at work.

"Why are you doing that?" Salko asks in a tone that is disarmingly nonhostile. His arms are crossed. He looks down his nose at her as if she's a child he is disciplining, despite her being old enough to be his mother. She raises her sword to him.

"Don't do that," he sighs.

"Why shouldn't I? You're Kisha's. . . lacky or something, right? We spoke in Behno?"

Salko's lips curl in disgust. "Ugh. Yes, but that's a very rude way to say it. None of these soldiers will wake up. If you want to cause a distraction, you'll need to find Kisha herself."

He speaks like her plan is absurd and he finds the idea of it exhausting.

"Why don't you just yell for her?" Sif suggests. She isn't lowering her sword. "I can kill you both here."

He cocks an expertly shaped eyebrow. "I guess I could. Is that what it will take? I really don't want to drag this out. You must realize I'm the reason you got out of that prison."

"*Najah* got me out."

"Najah and the other one would've walked right into a group of soldiers heading out on patrol if I hadn't intervened. Honestly, even if I'm lying, what do you have to lose at this point? Show some civility."

"Alright, kid. Lead the way." Whatever this is, Sif is already in the middle of it. And a part of her does want to fight Kisha again. "You're Salko, right? Got a title or a family name? Figure I should know who to get revenge on if this turns out to be a trap."

"There's no need for any of that, Keno Sif," he responds casually, eyeing his fingernails. Salko is bewildering. At first, Sif can't tell whether he is being absurdly honest or playing his cards close to his chest. But within a few minutes, Salko brings her directly to Kisha, who is sitting alone at a fire. As they approach, the sound of footsteps catches her attention, and Kisha turns to face them.

"Sif, I'm glad Salko found you. It felt like things were getting too quiet. How did you get this far without alerting the guards? Stabbed them in the back, I bet. Maybe got your girl to do it for you. That was a cowardly move, last fight. There are rules to this, you know? You could at least try to act with a little honor."

Sif is surprised by Kisha. Stabbed them in the back? Does that mean Kisha doesn't know?

"They're asleep," Sif responds. "You really didn't notice?"

Kisha stands up and draws her sword. "Of course they are. Can't count on anyone these days. You should've killed them while you had the chance. Salko, hold her."

Salko grabs her arm lightly. Sif swings her fist backwards and narrowly misses his face. He dodges the blow and pulls his sword off his back, gripping it in both hands. Sif pivots to try and keep both of them in her eyeline, backing up against the side of an old barn. Nothing ends a perfectly good fight like a knife in the back. Surprisingly, Salko moves closer to Kisha instead of trying to flank Sif, who uses the extra room to get her back off the wall.

Kisha wastes no time. She bellows into the black sky and rushes Sif, throwing all of her weight into every attack. Kisha is finally, unfortunately, taking Sif seriously. Sif had been insulted by being treated as weak before, but she wouldn't mind being insulted one more time. At this point, knowing Najah is okay has more weight than her own ego.

"Let off!" Salko yells. Kisha backs up, but Salko steps forward, keeping Sif on the defensive. Is this their plan? To tire her out? If so, it isn't working well. Salko has such a heavy weapon that he is forced to put a lot of art in how he wields it. He puts an extreme amount of focus on the momentum of his attacks, always trying to plan two steps ahead. He isn't bad, but he doesn't have the decades of experience Sif does. Sif counters each move until Kisha screams at him to move and jumps back in.

Sif blocks Kisha's downward slice with her own weapon, but it's a feint. Kisha lets her sword clang off Sif's blade, then delivers a hook with her left fist meant to smash Sif's head into the wall. The older woman dodges back and then steps forward to lunge with her sword. Kisha knocks Sif's blade out of the way with her gauntlet and returns with a heavy overhead slash. Kisha isn't attacking the same as when the fight started. For one, her moves have become more predictable. Besides that, she has always used their brawls as an opportunity to speak and now she is eerily quiet, outside of the grunts of exertion and winces of pain.

With every strike, Sif sacrifices a little bit of ground, hoping Kisha will get sloppy if she thinks she is winning. Kisha is hoping to keep Sif on the defensive, tire her out and back her into a corner. But when it doesn't work, Kisha resumes attacking with more of her strength. It's an astoundingly bad decision. Kisha is young, but she is also limping on her injured leg; she's burning up.

Even though Sif is loath to admit it, she sees a little bit of herself in Kisha. Cocky, hard-headed, and a prodigy with a blade. They're even from the same region. Kisha is what Buri was worried Sif would become—someone who enacts violence for the sake of violence. Power for the sake of power. She is too fixated on her own mythology. She expected to have Sif in a casket by now, and the fact that the job isn't done is shattering the illusion. Maybe Sif shouldn't give her the impression her plan is working. Maybe she should put some more weight on that cracking glass.

Sif sets Kisha up for another heavy swing and, when she takes the bait, Sif ducks under the attack and cracks Kisha's nose with her forehead. The younger woman stumbles backwards, spurting blood.

"Let me in!" Salko yells.

"Fuck you!" Kisha yells back. She swings wildly at Sif, and the older woman doesn't even block it. She just leans back and lets Kisha's attacks slice pointlessly through the air.

"You're not better than me, old woman." Kisha spits.

"Didn't say I was."

"I don't fucking get it. You just want to waste your life, living like an animal? Why? Just stop fighting me!"

"I'm not arguing with you anymore, Kisha."

Kisha renews her attack with a roar. Somewhere in the oblivion of her anger, she has gained back some of the recklessness that made her hard to predict. It's an energy of movement that Buri gained through meditation and Sif gained through skill, drugs, or adrenaline in her youth. Kisha feints and ripostes. She kicks and claws. Sif acts in kind and before she knows it, their fight is as much a head game as it is physical. Adrenaline races through Sif's veins. Her movements are so effortless and fluid that she makes them without a conscious thought. It is pure skill and instinct. And Kisha is the same. A cruel grin starts to tug on the younger woman's lips. A bit of amusement.

Each step has the methodical, practiced air of a dance. Both women are goading each other into attacks, even into feints, hoping to trick the other rather than overpower her. Sif ducks under a horizontal slice and twists to thrust her sword up towards Kisha's face. Kisha leans back and kicks her in the hip. Sif falls to one knee and drags her sword down, leaning forward to gain some reach. The blade catches Kisha's armor but not her flesh. Kisha steps forward to stomp Sif's blade, but Sif swings it back into a reverse grip and punches the younger woman across her jaw. Sif doesn't realize her mistake until the sight goes out in her left eye and a devastating wave of pain replaces it.

Kisha wanted Sif to get close. When she did, Kisha grabbed Sif's sword hand and cut her across the face with her own blade. It was meant to be a killing blow, but some corner of Sif's mind was able to react in time to save herself. Blood pours down her face, but she's alive. Kisha grins down at her triumphantly. If she were more cautious, less self-assured, she would kill Sif now. But she is glorying in her moment of victory. Sif swings her sword, half-blind. Kisha takes a nimble step back, laughing at how little effort it now takes to defend herself.

"I knew it! I knew someone as weak as you could never beat me in a fair fight. You should've come with me when you had a chance, instead of trying to protect that kid."

Sif spits blood and offers Kisha a smile washed with red. "Come on, then. Prove it." She knows it won't take much to prove. This fight is over. But at least she can buy Najah some time. Kisha raises her sword.

She gasps as Salko's zweihander runs through her, gleaming tip sliding out of her stomach.

Sif stumbles back in surprise. Salko pulls his sword out with the calm of somebody cutting vegetables for dinner. Emotionless and utilitarian.

"What the fuck?!" Kisha gurgles, hands folded over her wound in disbelief. Salko kicks her sword away.

Sif stares at the young man with wild eyes. What is happening? Why now?

"What?" Salko asks, calmly setting his blade against the barn wall. "Do you want her to live? She's just a rabid dog. Someone was always going to have to put her down."

"Fuck you, Salko. . . You can't do this to me," Kisha murmurs. "They'll hang you for this."

Salko spits on Kisha's prone form. "Of course I can. I've always hated that about you, Kisha. You assume that because you're good at the game that you don't have to learn the rules. But the truth is, you're not even good at it. You were only allowed to have power because you're skilled at what you do. But when the fighting is over, nobody will want a barbarian in charge. We're creating a civilized world. There is no room for you in it."

Kisha wheezes and gurgles from her spot on the ground. Whatever she says is inaudible. Her fingers claw in the dirt as she drags herself away with agonizing slowness, like a wounded animal finding a place to die. Her strength gives out with a shudder only a few feet away. Sif holds one hand over the wound on her face, chest heaving as she gasps for breath, and watches Kisha bleed out. It's a pathetic end. Kisha doesn't deserve any better, but Salko's reasoning still makes Sif feel a little sick. Unarmed, but in reach of his sword, Salko waits with his arms crossed.

"What now?" Sif asks. "Think you can take me on your own?"

"Oh, I can absolutely take you like this," Salko responds. A note of uncharacteristic joy barely breaches his placid exterior, a leftover from his long-awaited victory. "But I'm going to let you live, for the same reason I helped you in the prison. A very well-regarded sage told me if I killed Kisha and saved you, I could finally earn my father's respect. You really don't know how humiliating it is for your own blood to put a *barbarian* above you. So, yes, I think I can kill you. But I'd rather not."

Sif tenses. Maybe. It wouldn't be much of a fight. But she swears to herself that she won't go down easy. Never go down easy. Always make them work for it.

Salko smirks. "Go on, then. Sunnhilde said not to hurt you, so I won't. Hurry back to the northern wastes. If I were you, I'd leave before the paladins wake u—"

Salko collapses like a puppet with its strings cut. Sif feels a warm breeze rush over her but hears no wind. Before she can react to Sunnhilde's name, she joins him unconscious in the dirt.

Chapter 50

Old Sif, the Hermit

An unknown land

Under a boiling sky, Sif stands before a ragged, iron tower. The sky reflects a strange color on the tower's walls, an ephemeral shade that flickers and bends around attempts to comprehend it. The red clay ground crawls and snakes beneath her in a motion that is sickening to behold. Flashes of lightning reveal monstrosities in the atmosphere. Far off, the sound of unfathomably huge footsteps echoes from the sky. All at once, hundreds of eyes roll around to face her from the storm clouds above. A whisper in her heart reveals the truth to her. This is the Wretched King's tower, from Najah's dreams. But this doesn't feel like a dream. Even Agartha had a faint otherness to it that this does not, a haziness that revealed its nature. This is painfully real.

Is this why Aseli sent them to the well? She had said it would release Druga, and Sif assumed Druga would then excise the Wretched King from Najah's soul. As usual, nothing is what it should be.

"Sif?!" Salko gasps from behind her. Behind her, Salko is on his knees, mouth gaping in terror at the nightmarish landscape around them. "What is this? Did Sunnhilde do this? That fucking witch, I knew it!"

"What did you say?" Sif asks, certain she didn't hear that correctly. Suddenly, faint stringed music reverberates from the tower. It has an allure to it, but not one Sif trusts. Still, there is nothing to do but press forward. Salko grabs her arm as she starts to walk away from him.

"Wait! You can't go in there."

Sif swats him back. "If you're afraid, then stay here."

"No. Nobody will say a barbarian has more courage than I do." He pushes himself to his feet and stumbles forward with a mad glint in his eyes. Sif finds herself wondering if he'll really be any help, or if the Wretched King will break him. As they continue their march, Sif can make out a figure standing in the doorway to the tower.

"Witch!" Salko cries out, rushing towards her.

"Sunna?" Sif whispers. Her heart skips a beat at the sight of those familiar gray-red locks of hair framing the face of her love. She picks up her pace, hoping to beat the young paladin to her. She doesn't, but neither does Salko treat Sunnhilde violently. He loses steam as he approaches her, withered by her stature.

"Sunnhilde," Salko says. "What is this Druga-forsaken place? Did you bring us here?"

Sunna drops her hood as Sif approaches. Her smile is broad and dazzling, but dies at the sight of Sif's bloodied face as it's illuminated by the light in the tower.

"Are you alright, my love?" Sunna asks.

Sif wraps Sunna in her arms, and lays her forehead on Sunna's shoulder. "I am now. I didn't expect to see you for a long while."

Sunna rests her head on Sif's, "I know. I was on the other side of the continent when I heard about you and Najah. Then. . . all this." She motions to the world around them. "It's taken a long time to find you. There's an embarrassing stack of letters waiting for you back home."

"What is this place?" Sif asks.

"We're on the back of Mother Fog, in the abyss." Her words say she finds it interesting, but her tone is weighed down by worry. All over Atlas, parents tell their kids stories about being taken to live on the backs of the Three Mothers as a warning against dangers both magical and mundane. Even Sif heard that story from her father as a child.

"How? Why not Agartha?"

Sunna shakes her head. "I haven't a clue. The mechanisms of deities and demons are far beyond what a human mind was built to comprehend. It might be better that we don't know."

"Sunna, what do we do?" Sif whispers. "I can't let anything happen to Najah."

"The Wretched King will have something that tethers Him to Najah. We should address that. Here, I have this for you. For the pain." She passes Sif a pouch of ghost tongue leaves. Sif pops one of the pale, thick leaves in her mouth and swallows. In only moments, the come-up starts. Her stomach ties itself in knots as the plant works its way into her bloodstream.

Sunna meets Sif's dilating eyes and asks, "Do you want to wait here until it's in full effect?"

Sif shakes her head. "No. Can't let anything happen to Najah. We have to go now."

Sunna steps aside, letting her wife take the way, and says, "Just get me to whatever is tying the Wretched King to Benedicta and Najah. I will do my best to take care of the rest."

Salko grabs Sunnhilde by her arm, roughly. "Fortune teller! You said if I protected Sif that my fa—"

Sunnhilde yanks her arm away, eyes shining with the promise of a fire that could consume Salko if he steps out of line again. "What I saw was that if I fed your pathetic ego, it would save a young girl and a woman I love dearly."

Salko pulls back, as if burned. "What? What am I meant to do, then?"

"Come with us and undo some of the damage your true god has caused, or stay here and die. I don't care either way."

Salko lingers at the entrance to the tower, frozen with fear and shame. Then, just as the footsteps of the two women begin to fade, he follows.

Despite the tall, crooked, jagged architecture of the tower's outside, inside it is only a small room at the bottom attached to a long, winding staircase that takes them to the top. Dust cakes everything on the ascent, and abandoned spider webs block the path. Hopefully abandoned. Sif doesn't want to see the kind of spider that would survive on the back of Mother Fog's writhing, red clay back. As they climb the ancient steps, the sound of a stringed instrument grows louder. It's a haunting, beautiful melody and, hidden within it, a sinister edge. It's the song of someone whose soul has been waiting for a long time in this tower. Who has been impatiently preparing for their release.

As they reach the top, a red light pours out from a single, curved stone doorway. Inside is a table and alchemical supplies, but the brightness forbids deeper examination. The music stops abruptly as she reaches the threshold. Sif motions for her companions to wait a moment, then steps through.

Inside is the Wretched King, sitting in a creaking wooden chair and holding a very fine violin. Red light pours from a small, round creature tethered to the ceiling by a chain, and flickers off of the violin's polished wood surface. This close, she can hear the creature clicking painfully. It sways over the Wretched King's head, making it difficult to look directly at Him. Piles of books have been scattered haphazardly across the room. Limbs of strange beasts twitch and thrash in glass jars, and behind the rusty bars of bird cages. The room is strikingly humid, and the smell of old books and unclean animals permeates it.

"Keno Sif. Hello again." This time, He is not speaking in the voice of His human self. It's a deep, croaking drawl. The sound of a drowned corpse, speaking back from beneath the sea of sleep. "Forgive me, it's been a long time since I've had to speak. Physically."

"I saw your play." Sif doesn't know why she is engaging Him. There is something hypnotic about this place. "You spoke then."

He shakes His head. "That was just a form I borrowed. It burned up, so here I am again. No, I need Najah now. It has to be her. She can take my place here in the dream, and I can take hers above. It's only fair; a deal was made."

The Wretched King motions to a hand in a jar nearby. Benedicta's hand, left behind at his throne in Agartha. The weight of Sif's decision all those years ago crashes down on her head. She lunges for the jar, only for it to float just out of reach and into the squirming limbs of the creature emitting red light above. The Wretched King steps forward, revealing His sunken face and crooked bones, wreathed in gold.

"Uh-uh," He chides her. "No, I'm afraid I cannot let you have that. But if you want, *we* can make a deal."

"I'll make a deal," Salko says, stepping into the room. He gestures at Sunnhilde. "This con artist promised me I could inherit my father's estate, which I see now was a falsehood."

The Wretched King smiles a wide and unnatural grin. Sunna dashes at Salko and drives a dagger underneath his armor before he can speak further. Seizing on the opportunity, Sif swings her blade at the light-creature, shattering the jar containing Benedicta's hand. Glass, flesh, and clear liquid spill downwards and scatter on the floor. The Wretched King grabs Sif by her neck and lifts her with a single emaciated arm, imbued with unnatural power. She drives her sword up through his neck and out the back of his head, to no effect.

Behind her, Salko and Sunnhilde are fighting for control. From behind Sif come the sounds of scuffling, of books and glass being knocked from their resting places. Sif lets go of her sword, lifts her arms, and swings them downward into the crook of the Wretched King's arm. His strength fails and she drops back to her feet, ripping her sword from His skull as soon as she lands. In the back of the room, Salko begins to scream in terror. The light-creature swings wildly above, screeching fearfully.

The Wretched King lurches forward to take Sif back in His grasp. He has power, but not skill. She dodges to the side and swings her sword through His legs. One of them is sliced clean from His body, and as He falls Sif whispers a thanks to the deity of luck, whoever that might be.

The Wretched King crawls frantically towards Benedicta's hand, His body jerking and twitching like a dying insect. Sif drives her sword through His back, pinning Him to the floor. She turns, heart in her throat, hoping to save Sunna from her opponent, when Sunna leaps over the Wretched King, taking Benedicta's hand in her own.

"What now?" Sif growls, desperately trying to keep her sword in her grasp as the Wretched King pulls Himself up from the ground, still impaled on her blade. There's nothing she can do to hurt Him, just like in Agartha.

Sunna produces a large, hollow gourd from her cloak. It has a rope at the top to tie to her belt, and a cork to keep in water or alcohol. Sunnhilde pops the cork from the top of the gourd and the strong scent of grain alcohol floats across the room, practically singeing Sif's nose hairs. Sunna takes a large gulp in between her cheeks, flings a puff of some alchemical powder from a pouch, and then winks at Sif. When she spits the alcohol down through the powder and at Benedicta's severed hand, it creates a trail of burning fire through the air and sets the hand alight.

The light-creature dims above them, and for the first time since they arrived, Sif can see her wife's full, beautiful glory. Her hood rests on her shoulders and the flame casts a triumphant light over her features, like the burning sun reflecting in water. Sunna says a short prayer, spoken in a melodic, foreign tongue and, even before it's finished, Sif begins to wake up, as if from a restful sleep.

Chapter 51

Keno Sif
Nowhere

Everything has gone white, stretching into an eternity of pale nothing. A warm wind, bordering on being uncomfortable, runs along Sif's skin. Before her floats a giant figure, feminine in appearance, with long, dark hair that waves and shimmers to the small of their back as if it has a life of its own. A rough-spun tunic covers their lithe form, and in their arms rests a small fox, eyes closed as they stroke its back. Near their knees, their form fades into translucence, but is gradually gaining color and shape. Sif gazes at them in awe and fear, wondering if she has died. Looking down on herself, she sees hands much younger than she expects.

The figure's voice is genial and curious, though it booms and echoes through the vast nothingness. "Who are you?"

Sif cranes her neck to meet their face. Her throat and mouth are unbearably dry. "Keno Sif of Ummun."

The figure's eyes widen in shock, before a disarmingly sincere laugh escapes their lips. They cover their mouth with dainty, ringed fingers. "That's so strange. I never would have guessed."

"I, uh. . . I don't understand."

The figure is almost completely whole now. They bend down to better see Sif, regarding her like a parent might a child. "We're almost out of time here, but thanks for your help, Keno Sif. I hope we meet again. I'd like to hear your version of how you came to Ravinser."

"Oh," Sif gasps, eyes sparking with recognition.

Before she can think of anything important to ask, the light goes out.

Chapter 52

Najah Yden
The burned town of Ravinser

Najah wakes on a bed of fresh grass, staring up towards the sky. Obscuring her view are dozens of tall longleaf pines. As she rolls over, pale pink wildflowers brush her cheek. Her dark hair shines under the touch of cold moonlight as she lifts herself up and leans against a well she had forgotten was there. She feels strange, in a way she has not felt since before her mother died. There is a lightness, but also an absence, inside of her. As she scans her surroundings, she almost doesn't recognize Ravinser. Plant life has completely overtaken the village. Trees that were young a moment ago have grown to an abnormal height, in an abnormally short time. Dozens of different wildflowers carpet the forest floor, petals swaying in the breeze like waves in the ocean. Weeds rustle against each other. Vines have climbed the tents and ruined buildings being used to shelter soldiers, and pulled them back down to rejoin the elements from which they were born.

Najah puts a hand on her sheath and finds it empty. Her dagger is missing. She searches under the flowers and pats herself down before realizing she's dropped it into the well. She's ready to beat herself up over it when a familiar voice says, "Hey, Najah. How you feeling?"

Sif stands behind her, a long gash across her brow and cheek narrowly missing her blackened eye. Sunna is nearby, marveling at the changing village. Najah nods but is on the verge of tears. "Yeah, I'm fine."

Sif doesn't buy it. "What's going on? You hurt?"

What is there to say? She's been running for years now. Hurt doesn't begin to explain it. She's tired and bruised and mourning and overjoyed and relieved and somehow a little guilty. But what comes out is, "I lost my dagger."

"Eh? Don't worry about it. I said I'd get you a sword. We can grab one from a dead paladin. They're all plant food now."

Najah shakes her head and wipes her eyes, "No, I don't want that. I don't want anything *they* had their hands on."

Sif shrugs. "Well then, take mine. I kinda wanted Kisha's, anyways."

Najah is taken aback. "Are you sure?"

"Sure. It might be a little heavy for you, but you'll get used to it. My uncle gave it to me a long time ago."

"Thanks, Keno." Najah reaches out to take it. As she does, the blade dips down into the dirt. Sif was right about it being heavy. The older woman removes her scabbard and passes it over as well.

"We've got a couple of minutes if you want to put that on," Sif says.

"Keno. . . what happened?" Najah asks.

Sif lets out a dramatic exhale and shrugs. "Kid, I have no clue. I don't think Aseli was being honest with us about the plan, but it seems like we cut your connection to the Wretched King anyways."

"Aseli?" Sunnhilde asks. "Who is that?"

"Aseli of the Wood. Weird thing to call yourself, but she's a forest spirit."

"Aseli of the Wood is a forest spirit?" Sunna exclaims, disbelievingly. She takes a deep breath and sits down in a bed of flowers. Of the three of them, only Sunnhilde would know of Aseli's old tales.

"I'm cured though, right?" Najah asks.

"Probably," Sif says.

"Yes, of course you are, Najah. Don't listen to Keno," Sunna says, still grappling with the knowledge that the forest is inhabited by an ancient historian.

A broad, effortless smile spreads across Najah's face. She still has a life to live. She'll have to hide out somewhere else, but it'll be easier without the Wretched King connected to her and whispering in the ears of the Church of

Druga. And it sounds like she won't have to go alone. It's been so long since she had anything like a future, that at some point she had stopped planning for it. It seems too good to be true, and for a moment she is convinced that she is misunderstanding Sif.

"Hey, what did you mean when we said we have a couple of minutes?" Najah asks.

"Until the three of us get out of here. Or did you want to sleep in this creepy place until the Church gets here?" Sif grins, wide and obnoxiously self-assured, but appearing to Najah just like the Keno Sif out of myth. Destroyer of demons, savior of lost princesses. Surprisingly decent cook.

"Psh. No. Shut up. I meant, where are we going?"

Sif takes Sunna's hand and squeezes it. "Where to, my love?"

Sunna kisses Sif on the cheek and says, "I don't know where we *should* go, but I know where we can. At some point I'll need to leave. I'm going to visit some of the people behind the Church and make sure they aren't a problem in the future."

"We can do that," Najah says, doing her best impression of a confident, seasoned warrior.

Sif laughs at her and, turning back to Sunna, kisses her hand and says, "I'm at your service."

"Oh my," Sunna jests, fanning herself with her free hand.

"Anything for a beautiful woman." Sif gazes lovingly into her wife's eyes.

Najah makes a face. "Ugh. Can we go? I've got everything together and you two are honestly making me nauseous."

"You should be taking notes, you brat! One day you'll meet someone you'll want to seduce, and nobody is as good as me."

"Gross. No, I won't." Najah makes a disgusted face and starts walking off. And on like that it continues for several hours, until the silence and peace of the darkness nudges them into rest, and lulls them into sleep, far away from Ravinser and any danger.

Chapter 53

Keno Sif of Ummun
A jail cell, decades earlier

Keno Sif laughs out loud as the old man she had robbed earlier, and who has chased her through half of the district, is thrown into the cell next to her. "That's what you get for reporting me to the guard!"

The older man regards her casually from the dirt floor. He has a close-shaven head, a black beard, and is missing one eye. The other is bright and green, like an emerald in the sun. "Didn't go to the guard."

He sits up, snorts, then spits blood onto the floor. "Fair's fair. You beat me that time. No reason to involve anyone else, far as I care."

"I'm unbeatable," Sif brags, leaning back with her hands behind her head. It's a pose she imagines makes her look untouchable. Being at least half a decade from adulthood, the old man isn't inclined to take her seriously.

"Usually am, too."

"Yeah?" she says. "Then how'd you get put in here, old man?"

He chuckles and asks, "How did you? And my name is Buri. I'm not old, yet."

Sif huffs. "It's different, alright? I got tricked. A dozen adults, all armed to the teeth, and they snuck up on me while I was distracted."

"Hmmm. If you say so." Buri's tone makes it obvious he doesn't take much stock in her excuse.

"I'll prove it!"

"I'm listening, little girl. What will you prove?"

"I'll prove I'm unbeatable. And *my name* is Keno Sif. I'm not little."

Buri realizes with a shock that she's serious. She is barely more than skin and bones, unarmed, and is more than willing to plan a jailbreak with or without him. It occurs to him that if he doesn't watch her, she might hurt herself trying something more ambitious than her skill can account for. Despite his lingering annoyance at having his pocket picked by her earlier in the day, her sheer audacity is hard not to respect.

"Fine. How do we break out?" He stands up and brushes the dirt from his trousers.

"Not now." She waves her hand for him to sit down and begins whispering. "At some point there is going to be a shift change, where new guards come in and the old ones leave." She produces a small lockpick from her tangled hair, then puts it back just as fast.

"You're hoping they'll leave us alone during the switch? Seems unlikely."

"No. I'm not new here, *Buri*. I heard the guards talking, and there's only going to be one keeping watch tonight. The other died in a bar brawl and there isn't anyone to replace her yet. Two of us, one of them."

"Hmmmm." Buri pretends to muse over her plan for a bit. "I'm curious what you would do if I weren't here, unbeatable Keno."

"It's just Sif. In Ummun it's rude to call someone by their personal name."

"Ah, I'm from Feigrvoller, to the east. Met a few Sifs from Ummun before. And one Vol. I'm in, Sif."

"Fine. Once we're out of here, I'll prove that getting thrown in here is a fluke, then we split ways."

Buri nods, trying to hide how amusing he finds her bluster. "Very well."

Chapter 54

Old Sif, the Destroyer
Kirokh, the kingdom by the sea

Kirokh is a small but wealthy kingdom on the east coast of Atlas, with a capital that juts out into the sea in a style of architecture that is *deeply* precarious but was, at the time of the kingdom's founding, ingenious. Now the struts and beams have withered, and the most dangerous sections have been abandoned under King Vide's order, until the royal architectural guild can repair or deconstruct it. For Sif and Najah, now aged several years, it is a blessing and a curse. A blessing because the royal guard behind them, and Mother Fog's remaining paladins after that, aren't as familiar with this section of the city as with the ones closer to the palace. It gives the two women a much-needed edge as they make their escape, swinging a pack of gold and jewels stolen from the royal vault.

Sif has a head of mostly gray hair, and a new scar from where Kisha struck her in their last battle. She wears light armor, mostly leather, and from a quick look it would appear—incorrectly—like she has learned to take better care of her armor and weapons. Najah is taller and has adopted an easy smile, with the posture and mannerisms of a swashbuckling hero from the stories she likes to read. She wears bits of steel armor to protect herself, immaculately polished and repaired with the same care as she treats Sif's, at least whenever the older woman will agree to let her repair it. She spends much of her coin on new armor and clothes; the only old thing she keeps around is the sword Buri gave to Sif, and which Sif passed to her years ago.

Behind them, the trampling feet of dozens of Kirokh soldiers run in pursuit. The wooden floor creaks and groans below them, and through the slats in the boards the sea is visible far, far below. A series of ropes, set up to run messages and small items down the corridors, vibrate with the movement. A board breaks under the weight of a soldier near the rear, and they're saved from certain death only by the quick reaction speed of their comrades. Rotten boards spiral slowly downwards into the crashing waves below.

"You hear that?" Sif asks Najah as they run further out into the abandoned district. Her breathing is heavy, while Najah keeps pace with ease. Golden sunlight and saltwater wind both flood in through gaps in the old corridors. "We better watch our step."

"Do you need to take a rest, Auntie?" Najah jokes. "I can hold them off for a while."

"Oh, you're back on this, huh? Win a few dozen duels and all the sudden you're untouchable. Give me a break, kid," Sif complains, but behind her words are only pride. Najah is her first and only student. Seeing her do so well is not just an honor, but a joy. She's grown so much from the angry, fearful, grief-stricken, and borderline-helpless child Sif met long ago.

Najah skids to a sudden stop as one of the Church's paladins turns a corner ahead of her. The paladin is a muscular woman with long brown hair, who made the foolish mistake of taking most of her armor off in order to reduce her weight and gain the speed necessary to cut off Najah and Sif. The smart move would've been to stay home.

The paladin raises her mace. Before she can swing it, Najah connects a downward kick to her knee. The bones and ligaments in the woman's leg *crunch*. The paladin falls to her knees and swings her weapon desperately, and sloppily, at Najah's feet. Najah simply hops over the attack and brings her own sword down in a fatal slash. The paladin collapses quietly.

Najah turns to Sif and imitates the sound of a crowd at the Hvek fighting arena. "Najah! Najah!"

It is then that the rest of the royal guard and paladins catch up.

"Fuck!" Najah yells, breaking off in a sprint. It is only as they begin to lose their pursuers that the part of the old district that is still standing ends. The rickety wooden hallway goes on for less than a dozen feet before abruptly leading into a long drop over the sea. A seagull roosting on a beam flies off as they approach.

Sif turns to Najah and nods. "Time to see how much of those lessons really sunk in."

"You shouldn't blame our untimely deaths on your teaching, Keno," Najah says with a grin.

Sif guffaws and, upon the arrival of their enemies, draws her sword. Their opponents outnumber them so heavily that the whole narrow corridor is filled with bodies. They stand shoulder to shoulder, bristling with weapons and confidence.

Then the ground beneath them begins to creak. Loudly. The combatants get only a brief moment to consider what that means before the ground beneath them drops several inches.

The soldiers begin to panic and push each other in a desperate bid to escape the collapse.

"Shit," Najah swears, fear in her voice for the first time since the chase began.

The corridor roars with the sound of splintering wood and bending metal. The break happens underneath the soldiers, turning the horizon to the north and south several degrees on its side from Sif and Najah's view. They begin to slide back out towards open air when Sif grabs the rope set up for transporting small goods, and uses her free hand to grab Najah's wrist. "Take the rope!"

The floor, walls, and ceiling around them separate just as Najah grabs hold. Soldiers fly past them and out into midair. One grabs Sif's leg in a stroke of luck before Najah strikes him in the throat and, under the weight of unexpected pain, he lets go of her and tumbles after his comrades. Sif and Najah swing downwards, spinning uncontrollably as the section of the district above them that still contains soldiers begins to give as well. A half dozen choose to leap into the sea on their own, hoping they'll survive the drop. Najah watches them fall with an odd satisfaction. She imagines the woods around Ravinser growing just a little taller, a little further out, Druga flexing their divinity as the weight of colonialism is lifted off of them.

The next section of the district collapses. Najah shuts her eyes tight as the corridor passes around her, and their length of rope increases. In the distance, a small boat with a red sail approaches the sea below. Above Najah, Sif smiles.

"Great, just in time to see us die," Najah says.

"Have a little confidence," Sif responds.

Najah shuts her eyes, trying not to get nauseated by the swinging and spinning of the rope. "You just told me not to be cocky!"

"Sunna!" Sif yells, ignoring her protégé. The next section above, after some resistance, collapses as well, swinging the duo closer to both the ocean and the cliffside that most of Kirokh's capital rests on. The momentum finally sends the sack of gold out from Sif's grip and tumbling into the water below.

Sif curses nearly every deity she can recall as the pack opens and glittering jewelry becomes lost in the waves.

"Cheer up, Auntie. There may be some left when Sunna arrives below."

"How about I help you find out, ladies?" calls out a masculine voice some thirty feet above. A soldier looks down at them, then chops their rope with a swing of his curved sword.

The two women yell with awe built equally on fear and exhilaration as they're released into the open air.

They plummet towards the glistening blue water with wide eyes and adrenaline pumping through their veins. Faster than they expected, they crash painfully into the sea. Under the water, Najah opens her eyes to see beams of light illuminating the blue-green sea, and jewelry slowly descending like shimmering rain. She checks to see if her mentor is okay, then grabs as much gold as she can before surfacing. Sunna pulls them both over the side.

"Are you two okay?" She wears a sly smile that says she knew they would make it. Or at least *believed* they would.

Najah looks up at the blue sky and laughs, even though it hurts. "I'm fine. I think I sprained something, but that was fun. And I got some of the gold."

Sif sits up with a groan. Her leg stretches out, causing the gold and jewelry on the boat's floor to clatter against each other. "Nothing you can't fix for me," Sif says to her wife, crow's feet wrinkling as she winks.

Najah groans. "Ugh. Honestly, you two."

Together the three of them sail towards the horizon, flush with enough wealth to live well for a few weeks in whatever kingdom hasn't received a bounty notice yet. The ghost of the past hasn't been exorcised from their hearts, the present is fraught, and the future is dangerous and uncertain. But they have each other, and they know that their hearts, minds, and dreams are their own.

About the Author

Jay lives in Florda with his wife and two cats. When he's not writing, he enjoys weightlifting, going on walks, listening to any music he can get his hands on, and x-men comics.

www.ingramcontent.com/pod-product-compliance
Ingram Content Group UK Ltd.
Pitfield, Milton Keynes, MK11 3LW, UK
UKHW020501120325
455992UK00020B/721